HOW TO KILL YOUR GYNAECOLOGIST

SHARON DOBBS-RICHARDS

SHAZ&JEN
PUBLISHING

It can be hard to take the time out to ask ourselves who we truly want to be – not what we think other people will approve of or accept, but who we really are. When you listen to yourself, you can make the choice to step forward and learn and change […] There is nothing more attractive – you might even say enchanting – than a woman with an independent will and her own opinions.

— ANGELINA JOLIE, ELLE MAGAZINE

DISCLAIMER

Although the inspiration for this book was drawn from my own lived experience of a delayed diagnosis of ovarian cancer this is a literary work of fiction. Names, characters, businesses, places, events, conversations and incidents are products of the author's imagination and are fictionalised. Any resemblance to any persons living or dead is purely coincidental.

This book contains discussions around the anger women feel when they are diagnosed with late-stage ovarian cancer. The aim of the book is to raise awareness of the signs and symptoms of ovarian cancer, to empower women to challenge the medical profession when they feel they are not being listened to, and to start a conversation around women's gynaecological health. It also intends to bring some light and humour to a difficult subject thereby raising important issues in an entertaining way. The actions taken by the characters in pursuit of their medical advisors are not endorsed by the author and the novel is in no way intended to comprise medical or personal advice.

For any unfamiliar medical terminology please refer to the glossary at the end of the book.

1

LIZ

MID-AUGUST 2019

*L*iz sighed as she clutched her phone in her hand. She stared at the screen and then pressed dial.

'Hello Kurt,' she said. 'Are you ready?'

'As ready as I'll ever be, love. How's my boy?'

'Oh, he's fine. He's right here.' Liz placed her arm around Alfie. 'Alfie, your dad's on the phone.'

Alfie grabbed the phone from Liz.

'Hiya, Dad.'

'You alright, son?' Kurt asked. 'I hope you're behaving for Aunty Liz.'

'Of course, Dad.'

'Now you be a brave lad today and make your mother proud.'

'I will.'

'Alfie, Alfie,' shouted his sisters as they came into view on the screen waving at him and giggling. 'Hiya, Liz,' they shouted.

Liz peered at the phone, smiled and waved back at them. 'Are you ready, girls?'

The girls stopped smiling and stared at Liz with sombre looks on their faces. 'Yes, we are.'

Liz nodded and smiled nervously. 'Take care, girls. We

have to go now. It's nearly time. Good luck. We're thinking of you.'

Kurt appeared back in view peering at the screen. 'Right luv. Ready when you are.' He nodded his head and winked at Liz. With that Kurt rang off.

Liz squeezed Alfie's hand and turned to Olivia.

Olivia placed a hand gently on Liz's shoulder. 'You alright, babes?'

'I'm fine.'

'Of course you are darlin'. You're going to make those fuckers stand up and listen.'

'That's the plan,' said Liz as she straightened her shoulders and looked down at her phone again. 4.57 p.m. She tapped the phone screen several times and flicked right until she arrived at the contact group she had been looking for. She pressed send then turned to the small group of people behind her. 'It's time, guys,' she shouted, as she waved an arm in the air.

Olivia and Alfie stood either side of Liz. They both grabbed her hand and stepped out onto the road. Sarah, Jusu, Jordan and Dwayne came and stood beside them. 'Here comes our Joan of Arc,' said Olivia.

2

LIZ

*L*iz sat for some time staring absently at the wall in front of her. She couldn't quite make sense of what had just happened. All she knew was that the bottom had fallen out of her world.

She had tried several times to run through the sequence of events in her mind. It was no use. There was nothing but utter chaos in her head. Liz felt slightly wired as if she had consumed several doses of caffeine. She tried to calm her mind. She needed to think logically. She attempted to slow her breathing… in through the nose, out through the mouth… but it could not prevent the pit of nausea rising in her stomach. The room started to feel as if it was spinning, the floor buckling beneath her made her grab onto the sides of the bed to steady herself. Her head hurt and her mouth was dry. Liz needed some water but was too paralysed with fear to reach out for the glass resting on her bedside table. 'It will pass; it will pass,' she whispered, attempting to reassure herself. Her breathing was becoming more rapid. Liz could feel a full-blown panic attack coming on.

The floor did not open up. After a while her breathing slowed down and the room began to settle. She collapsed back into the pillows, shaking and sobbing. No one had noticed the seismic shift in her universe. She could hear the familiar sounds of people talking, walking up and down the corridor outside, going about their normal routine oblivious to what she was going through.

Liz wanted to scream and throw something at the wall. She wanted to demand everyone stop and feel her pain as she did. She wanted to get off this crazy roundabout. Did anybody care?

So here she was, instantly written off from society within minutes. Her life changed forever. There would be no going back now.

Liz turned to her left and looked out of the window above her. Stretched out in front was a perfect warm sunny October afternoon. There was hardly a cloud in the sky. A plane came into view circling overhead. Where was it heading in to land? Gatwick? Heathrow? London City? It was a Friday afternoon. Who might be on that plane? People visiting London for a weekend away, or husbands and wives at the end of an exhausting working week racing home to their families and loved ones? Liz suddenly realised that she'd been in blissful ignorance of how cruel life can be. She promised herself that if she could have another chance she would never again take life for granted.

Liz rested her head back on the bed again and felt the comfort of the pillows supporting her aching head. It was too much to take in. How did this happen? What would Gareth do without her? Why had she been told she was fine by every doctor she had seen over the past ten months? Was it a practical joke? Maybe that was it. Everyone was in on it and soon they would come bursting through the doors saying, 'Surprise, the joke's on you!' But they didn't…

———

Liz wanted to kill him as soon as it dawned on her that he was covering up her real story.

He had written to her lawyer saying her disease had proven to be extremely aggressive and that she was struggling significantly with this, believing that she had received sub-standard care. He also led the lawyer to believe that he had discussed this with her and had offered to discuss it further at any stage if it would be helpful.

That was bollocks. She had never been allowed the opportunity to discuss it with him and hadn't seen or heard from him since the surgery. He was cocky in his reply; he knew he would get away with it. Because he didn't cause the cancer, the lawyer said, it was difficult to prove negligence, despite Mr Kuntz-Finger refusing to perform the blood tests and scans she requested.

Liz got great pleasure out of pondering over what it would be like to stare into Iain Kuntz-Finger's eyes as he lay dying and say, 'Now tell me you're sorry.' She wanted to see the look on his face when he realised that the world was going to continue spinning without him.

I just need a way to kill him and get away with it, she thought. The ultimate crime and the ultimate revenge. She wanted to be the nightmare in his bad dream. He was an arrogant man so she didn't care about his feelings, and the way Liz saw it, a world without arseholes is always preferable to a world full of them.

That was the moment Liz decided to kill her gynaecologist.

3

ALICE

*A*lice looked around the living room of her Knightsbridge flat and realised she was oh so very bored. She was bored with her dull and dreary husband, her dull and dreary and rather pretentious friends. God, she wanted to have some fun, damn it. Four o'clock was gin time. It was only three thirty.

'Well, sometimes one just has to break the rules,' said Alice as she headed for the drinks cabinet.

Hugh turned up at six. By this time Alice was ever so tipsy. She had forgotten she was supposed to be going to dinner at seven with Hugh and his rather boring work colleague Harry and his wife Fi. She couldn't face the thought of having to make small talk when her head was doing a little dance all of its own. She sighed deeply, lifted herself wearily off the couch and went into the bathroom to ready herself for what could only be yet another tedious evening.

———

The evening went as planned… well… up to a point. Harry, or Jaba the Hut as Alice referred to him, droned on and on about his new merger. Hugh attempted to keep pace, both trying to outdo each other with their prestigious clientele and colleagues, name dropping every five seconds. Fi wore a permanently frozen expression, the result of years of relentless cosmetic procedures. She attempted to pull a smile from her heavily injected lips, with what appeared to Alice to require a similar effort to that of moving set concrete. She resembled a Barbie doll that had been partially melted.

Fi thought that beauty was on the outside and had spent years trying to keep her husband despite the eleven affairs he had had. 'Flaunting it in my face,' she had said. To make up for his infidelities he would flash the cash and tell her how she could do with just a little bit more work. So Fi would dutifully make an appointment in Harley Street and then 'disappear' for several weeks, returning looking a little tighter and 'refreshed'. She had suggested Alice come with her on one of her 'retreats' but Alice really did not think she could cope with the pain. Alice had had a phobia about needles ever since she was a child.

'So, Alice darling, I was thinking about another retreat. You know, one of those health spa weekends. No surgery needed if you don't want to, darling. It would be good for a giggle, don't you think? Victoria and Diana are keen. If we all checked our diaries and came up with a date… Alice.'

Alice was miles away. God, how long was this evening going to last? She forced a thin-lipped smile in Fi's direction. 'Sorry. What was that?'

'The retreat, darling.'

'Oh yes, let me know and I'll check the diary.' Alice leant forward resting her elbow on the table and screwing up her nose as she stared at Fi's face intently. She ran her index finger over the outline of her lips with a continued look of intense concentration.

'Alice, are you okay?'

'Yes, darling. Just checking my lipstick.'

'What?'

Hugh and Harry had stopped mid-conversation and were now staring at Alice. Hugh was silently praying that Alice was not about to cause another scene.

Alice continued to stare intently at Fi's face for several moments. Then she spoke. 'Darling, your skin's so tight my reflection is practically bouncing off of you. It is really a wonder that there's any skin left to stretch.'

She lifted her hand up and brushed it lightly against Fi's face with a look of wonderment.

Fi recoiled in horror at Alice's touch, not quite believing what had just happened.

Hugh took a sharp intake of breath beside her. 'Alice, enough!'

Alice sighed and thumped her fist down on the table in frustration, while continuing to stare at Fi. 'Listen, you're wasting your time, Fi dear, if you think you're still in with a chance with that,' Alice jabbed her finger towards Harry, 'after eleven affairs, then you are more of a fool than I imagined.'

'I beg your pardon,' stuttered Harry. 'You apologise right now.'

Fi's expression remained unchanged, but Alice knew from the look in her eyes that behind the permanently frozen facial expression and the ensuing few seconds of complete silence, that Fi was mortified.

Wearing a painted smile, Alice looked across the table at Hugh and Harry and then pushed her chair back. She could sense that she also had the attention of the other diners as she caught the veiled whispering from the nearby tables. She turned to Hugh with an icy glare.

'I'm going home. Are you coming?' There was silence as she met Hugh's stony gaze. 'No? Well, I'll see you at home.' Alice turned on her heels and walked outside to hail a cab, leaving Hugh, Harry and Fi staring after her, open mouthed.

Alice smiled to herself as she thought of the hours of

arse licking Hugh would have to endure to repair that damage.

———

'Why do you have to be so bloody petulant all the time?' Hugh raged. 'You never put yourself out for my friends. Harry is good for business you know. Fi's such a lovely woman. How could you do that to her?'

'I didn't do that to her. She did it to herself with that pathetic husband of hers pushing her into it. God knows what I'd look like if I'd injected myself every time you shagged one of your floosies,' sneered Alice. 'Which one is it at the moment, by the way? Penelope? Isn't that the name of the new secretary?'

'My God, woman, you're impossible. What's got into you lately?' Hugh tried to change the subject, hoping Alice didn't see him flinch. She had warned him if she ever caught him in the act again she would leave him and clean him out. He shuddered at the thought of losing all her family money and access to Middlemoor Manor, her family estate.

'If you'd make a bit of an effort to socialise it would help our situation tremendously.'

'Which situation is that?' Alice asked.

'Our social situation, for God's sake.' Hugh exclaimed. 'We've had to employ a great deal of damage control in the past with that godforsaken son of ours.'

'Oh, here we go. I wondered how long it would take before Tarquin came into the equation.'

'Thank goodness for Sophie. She's certainly played her cards right, that girl. We could have a future Royal there with her children.'

'Do you think I give a shit, Hugh?' barked Alice. 'I'm sick of your constant whining about Tarquin and his "little problem". I go to your bloody dinners and I sit and smile

9

when I'm meant to, but I draw the line at going away for a weekend with those creatures.'

'Creatures,' shrieked Hugh. 'God, Alice you're impossible.'

Alice burst into tears.

She was crying a lot lately. She always felt so tired. The GP told her it was her age. The abdominal pain and bloating were the worst. Annabelle had made her go for a colonic when the GP informed her she didn't have IBS. Sex was painful physically, but for Alice it had been painful mentally for some time. She despised Hugh and had done so ever since she'd caught him and one of his secretaries on the office desk late one night. She had an inkling about his affairs, but to actually catch him in the act... Alice had never forgiven him.

4

LIZ

FEBRUARY 2017

*L*iz was working in the office. It was so busy; there was never any peace.

The pain was sharp. Her chest was so tight it prevented her from breathing in too deeply. Liz held onto her side. It was the same pain she'd felt several times over the last few days and here it was again. She had just eaten lunch. Maybe the satsuma was too acidic. Liz made a mental note to try and not eat on the run all the time.

She tried to carry on with her paperwork, but the pain was increasing in intensity and it was becoming hard to breathe. As she tried to focus on the report she was meant to be completing, a sharp pain exploded from her lower right abdomen up into her diaphragm. Liz groaned and immediately crawled off the chair onto the floor, cradling her abdomen. She tried to straighten up and continue typing while kneeling, but the pain was so intense that she gave up and curled up into a ball on the floor. She was starting to sweat and her pulse was racing. 'My God,' said Liz out loud.

Perhaps I should call for an ambulance but... surely it's just a passing pain. It could be wind. I mean, people suffer from dreadful wind pain sometimes. She'd read about people experiencing terrible abdominal pain. They'd been given intravenous analgesia and fluids only to then let out the most explosive fart and feel like a new person. No. No good, Liz thought she was going to pass out.

The door to the office opened and Rebecca was standing there. She stared down at Liz curled up on the floor.

'Have you lost something?'

'Do I look like I've lost something?'

'No, not really.' Rebecca stepped into the office glancing down at Liz. 'So what are you doing on the floor?'

'Dying,' replied Liz.

'Well, could you die on the chair?'

'I felt it might be preferable to die on the floor, seeing as there's less distance to fall.'

Rebecca shrugged. 'Suits me, but you're making the place look a mess.' She then edged closer, her eyes narrowing as she leant forward, taking in Liz's pallor and the fact she was sweating profusely. 'What is going on?' she asked with a hint of suspicion in her voice.

'I'm not feeling too good.'

'I can see that. How long have you been like this?'

'About an hour or so. I'm sure it'll pass.'

'We're getting an ambulance,' Rebecca said, as her voice took on an air of concern.

Liz gasped as she held the edge of the chair and struggled up onto her knees. 'No, I should be okay soon.'

'What kind of pain is it?'

'It's a sharp knife-like pain, bursting up into my diaphragm on my right side. It's hard to breathe properly. It's so bloody painful.'

'What about some Buscopan?' Rebecca started fishing around in her bag and a few seconds later produced a flat foil sheet of tablets. 'Here, take this. It'll help with the spasms.'

'No. Honestly, I'm fine.' Liz waved the pills away with her hand.

'You don't look fine. Now take this,' Rebecca insisted, pushing the pills into Liz's hands.

She took the pills and obediently swallowed them down with some water.

Rebecca moved towards the door. 'I'm getting an ambulance,' she announced.

'Okay, I'll see someone,' Liz replied as she sighed in resignation and picked up the phone.

Liz managed to get a private GP appointment later that day.

———

'Hi, how are you feeling?' Mark asked.

'Oh, not too good actually. I think it's something I ate. You know, I was rushing and then sat straight down and ate my lunch. I need to slow down. It's probably just trapped wind or something.' Liz tried to laugh but a spasm caught her off guard and she winced as she clutched her right side.

'I think we need to examine you,' Mark said. 'It looks painful to me.' He indicated for Liz to follow him over to the examination couch.

'Does this hurt?' he asked, prodding her abdomen a few minutes later.

'No.'

'Here?'

'No.'

'Here?'

'Ouch. Yes, there,' said Liz as Mark felt the base of her right rib cage.

'What painkillers have you taken?'

'Buscopan and paracetamol.'

'I think you need to be seen by one of our gastroenterologists,' Mark announced.

———

Mark referred her to a gastroenterologist, who fortunately had just had a cancellation half an hour beforehand. He examined her abdomen. Numerous scans and bloods were ordered, and Liz was told to book in for an ultrasound scan of her abdomen with a gastroscopy to follow in the next week or so.

The results came back a week later – nothing wrong.

The following two months of chest infections, abdominal bloating and urinary tract infections with recurring episodes of the right sided pain certainly didn't feel like nothing wrong.

Liz's life suddenly revolved around visits to A&E and her GP.

5

VICKY

MARCH 2016

*V*icky was pretty pissed off. Life had been tough. A real school of hard knocks. Growing up she had been made to feel she was always just a little bit too ugly, too slow, too plain. When she met Kurt, she thought she was finally going to be happy. That all changed the day he went to the bookies to collect his winnings after the football match and never came back. She received a phone call from the local police station asking her if she could come down as her husband had been arrested for shoplifting and assaulting a shop owner with the remnants of a whiskey bottle.

'It was just an altercation, luv,' he'd said. 'I only wanted to buy some fags an' a bottle of whiskey. I forgot I'd spent all me dosh down the pub so I was a few bob short, that's all.'

Kurt proceeded to tell Vicky how the shop assistant had told him he would have to put the whiskey back, but Kurt didn't like the way the shopkeeper was addressing him, so he decided to teach him a lesson. If he couldn't have the whiskey then the shopkeeper couldn't have it either.

'I didn't mean to hurt him or nothin'. It's just he started getting on me wick. Ya know what I mean? I was off me nut, I 'ave to be honest. I could see meself smashing the bottle over the counter. The next thing I knew I was jumping over the counter and threatening the geezer with a large piece of what was left of the whiskey bottle. I dunno what got into me, luv. Honest. Then he started crying and pleading with me. A grown man crying and pleading. I couldn't handle it no more. I tried to apologise and calm the geezer down, but I forgot I still had a large piece of glass in me hand. Didn't realise the old bill had been called. I said to the geezer, "Come on, mate. No hard feelings. Shake on it." I went to shake his hand… I didn't even manage to get out of the shop. It was propa nasty. There was blood everywhere.'

It probably didn't help Kurt's case that he was high at the time.

———

About three months after Kurt was sentenced, Vicky collapsed with abdominal pain. She was taken to hospital and told she might be having an ectopic pregnancy. When that was ruled out she was sent home. The abdominal pain continued for weeks and was accompanied by irregular bleeding, so Vicky made multiple visits to her GP in search of relief and an explanation for the cause of her discomfort.

Jagpal Dhillon was a middle-aged, short, slightly rotund man who was a partner in the estate GP practice. She felt that, to them, she was a single mother of children to multiple fathers and therefore considered a nobody. She was a time waster, a drain on society. They didn't see the young girl born on a council estate who had hopes and dreams. Dreams which were quashed from a young age by a father who drank too much and didn't love her enough, who pointed out her plain looks and all her flaws. A father who told her she would be lucky to find a steady job or a man.

Vicky still had dreams. She had never let go of them.

She was fed up with the GP appointments. It was bad enough that she had to wait for an hour or so to be seen but then they never even looked at her. They were so busy staring at the computer screen and typing up the prescription. The end of the conversation was always signalled by silence. She knew that was the cue that her time was up. But now she was having chest and urinary tract infections as well. It was like she was peeing razor blades. As soon as the antibiotics cleared things up, the symptoms came back.

'Hormones? Maybe the early menopause,' her GP said.

'Drink more water and less wine,' he said.

Easy for him to say when you had a house full of screaming teenagers and a pile of laundry facing you at the end of a hard day's work.

Vicky held down two jobs to make ends meet. She had her cleaning job in the evenings and then her care home job during the day. Her mum, Janice, looked after the children after school which helped somewhat, but Vicky felt so exhausted lately that she could barely get out of bed in the mornings. Kurt kept phoning, telling her how much he missed her. She couldn't bear the prison visits. He was always expecting her and telling her how life would be different when he got out. Sure... where had she heard that before.

6

SARAH

*S*arah was sitting at home in the Home Counties enjoying her morning coffee and thinking about life in general. She looked out of the conservatory window. The early morning sun was starting to thaw the large expanse of perfectly manicured lawn. Sarah put the coffee down on the glass top wicker table in front of her, savouring the warmth of the liquid on her tongue as she twisted the diamond pendant necklace she was wearing in her fingers. She closed her eyes and thought back to the day her husband gave it to her… The day her twin boys were born.

She couldn't believe Arthur and Charlie were twenty-one already and at university. Where had the years gone? They both looked like their father. The look on George's face when they were born. Sarah's labour had been long, and when the twins finally arrived she was exhausted. Sarah and George had both sat on her bed, each holding a tiny bundle. Life for them was complete. They had their family unit right there. Four-year-old Jess sitting on the bed pleading to hold one of her baby brothers. 'Just for one minute, Mummy. Please?' They had let her hold each one in turn.

The midwife soon arrived and settled the boys down and

attempted to usher Jess and George out. 'She needs some rest, poor girl,' she exclaimed.

George kissed Sarah on the forehead and held her hand as he looked into her eyes and said, 'I love you my darling. You've made me the happiest man in the world today.'

'I love you too,' Sarah had said. Then George presented her with the pendant.

'Oh, George, it's beautiful,' sighed Sarah.

George placed it round her neck. She kissed him. 'I'll wear it always. I promise.'

'I'll see you tomorrow,' said George.

That night Sarah slept the most peaceful sleep she'd ever remembered. It only seemed like yesterday.

She had read about empty nest syndrome but thought she would be okay. There was plenty to occupy her. She had a large group of friends who lived locally and her parents lived only two villages away. Her mother and father visited every second weekend. Sarah was close to her sisters Trish and Laura, and they would regularly meet up for coffee and shopping in the local high street and organise shopping trips and theatre excursions into London. Trish was a year older, so all her children had flown the nest as well. Laura was a 'mistake' according to her parents. She was ten years younger than Sarah. Laura had Alex who was seven and Ellie who was eight whom Sarah adored.

Every morning, Sarah loved to walk in the local woods with her dog Patrice, a salt and pepper miniature schnauzer. He was five years old and a very loving little boy. She thought she might get another dog now the boys had gone. Company for Patrice. Betsie and Boris her two cats might not be so keen. Betsie was a long-haired Burmese. Boris was a Tonkinese. They thought they ruled the roost and did they make sure Patrice knew it.

Patrice loved going out with Sarah. He loved having her to himself. She would dress him up in a red tartan bow tie or neckerchief which always guaranteed admiring comments from fellow walkers. He loved the attention.

———

It was a beautiful morning. Sarah had just returned from her daily walk in the woods with Patrice. She'd had to shorten the walks lately much to Patrice's consternation. She had been feeling so tired. Poor Patrice felt rather let down. It was the urinary urgency that was so bothersome. Sarah would ensure she didn't drink much before the walk, but then it still happened. She would need to pee all of a sudden. She just could not hold on. What ensued was a mad dash behind the bushes with Patrice standing guard. Sarah had been feeling uncomfortable in her abdomen for quite some time. Her GP had referred her to a gynaecologist in London who had been treating her for urinary tract infections. The infections didn't seem to be resolving, though. She had given up champagne and reduced her alcohol intake but nothing seemed to help. She was beginning to feel full very quickly soon after eating but the consultant said it was probably the menopause. Sarah had started buying bulk supplies of chocolate bars and Kit Kats, which she hid at the back of the pantry so George wouldn't see. He'd mentioned she'd put a bit of weight on last week and she had resorted to wearing loose clothing as she felt so uncomfortable with anything around her waist. She lived in jersey leggings and tunic tops now. Her sisters both commented on her appearance saying she looked drawn in the face and her legs were still as thin as ever. Odd, she thought. God, she wasn't going to end up fat and lonely, was she? Maybe George might find a younger model. Doesn't bear thinking about thought Sarah, as she stood in the pantry trying to reach her Kit Kat stash.

———

Mid-February 2017

Sarah can't remember how she felt when the GP told her she was referring her to the local gynaecology team for further tests. The GP had looked concerned when she arrived and had arranged for her to have an ultrasound scan and a blood test. The GP questioned how long Sarah had been treated for the urinary tract infections by Mr Ashren.

'Oh, ever since I first saw him,' she said. 'He doesn't seem concerned, though. Is there something wrong, doctor?'

———

Late February 2017

Sarah opened her wardrobe doors, pushing aside the array of clothes on display, and reaching for her staple 'going out' attire. She pulled on a floral corduroy three quarter length sleeve tunic dress with deep front pockets, a pair of black woollen Marks and Spencer tights and her knee length tan winter boots. She hurriedly pulled her long blonde hair into a pony tail and rushed out of the door.

Patrice watched forlornly from the window as Sarah drove away. Why had she not taken him with her, he wondered.

'Meoww!' Hissssss. Betsie raised a clawed paw, not wanting to miss an opportunity to taunt Patrice, free from any reprimand. She took a swipe at Patrice from behind and then sauntered off with her tail in the air.

Sarah drove herself to the local hospital. No need to worry anyone unnecessarily; it was just a routine check-up. It was a gorgeous day. She had the radio on and was listening to Eric Carmen's *Make Me Lose Control*, singing along to it hoping to calm her nerves a bit.

When she arrived at the hospital she parked the car and went to reception and asked for directions to the imaging department. A very nice young man came out and collected her from the imaging waiting room. She chuckled to herself. He could have been mid-thirties, but according to Sarah everyone looked so young since she'd turned fifty.

She was watching the ultrasound screen, as the young man explained what he was doing. He pointed at the screen describing what he was seeing. Suddenly he stopped speaking and just stared fixedly at the screen. 'Umm,' he said as he paused the screen. He put the probe down.

'We may need to do a further scan. I can see some fluid and something on your ovary.'

'Is that good or bad?' asked Sarah.

'I'm sure it's nothing, but we just need to check. I'll have a word with my manager,' he said as he turned and left the room.

He did not return for some time.

Sarah sat and waited.

When he eventually returned he was with an older woman. She checked the image and advised Sarah that they would need to arrange a CT scan. She was seen rather too quickly for her comfort. After the scan she was told to take a seat.

Several phone calls later she was informed she would be staying overnight. It was explained that she needed a drain inserted to drain a large amount of fluid collecting in her abdomen. Sarah was unsure what that meant. No one seemed to want to answer any further questions and she got the distinct feeling that people were avoiding direct eye contact with her.

Was that why she was so breathless? She thought it was another of those chest infections she had been getting recently…

She explained that she needed to get home as Patrice was waiting for his evening walk and the cats needed feeding. A lovely young nurse said, 'I think this is slightly more important. Can we phone your husband?'

That was when Sarah knew something was wrong.

She would play that moment in her head, tirelessly, over and over again, like a broken record Why hadn't she known? Maybe she'd be able to change the course of events if she replayed it over and over just enough times…

7

IF ONLY

If only they had been listened to...
If only their concerns had been taken seriously...
If only they had trusted their instincts, their bodies,
*   and had had the courage and support to be able to*
*   challenge their consultants...*
If only their anger and frustration at their delayed
*   diagnoses had been acknowledged as*
*   understandable by the medical profession...*
If only they had been given more than five minutes to
*   hear, and discuss, their diagnoses with their*
*   respective consultants...*
If only they had not been shut down by the medical
*   profession every time they tried to seek answers...*
...then maybe, just maybe, things might have turned
*   out so differently.*

Liz, May 2017

*L*iz sat nervously in the waiting room of the four-storey listed building. The room was peppered with several women.

She had raced from work, anxious not to be late. This was the guy, or so she had been told, and Liz had managed to get a cancellation slot. His secretary had made it very clear when she phoned that his diary was extremely full.

'Well now, let's see… he has a full clinic on the sixteenth, and then let's see. Oh dear.' There was a long pause at the other end of the phone and then the sound of tut tutting as the secretary checked the diary again.

'Oh, here we go. The eleventh of July! All booked.'

Oh great. Months away.

Liz had bumped into Georgia, one of her work colleagues, the next day. Georgia had been the one who had given Mr Kuntz-Finger's details to Liz after stopping her and saying she was concerned about her collapse and subsequent chest infections. Liz asked her if she had any other recommendations as she didn't know if she could wait months to be seen.

'Oh no, no. You can't wait that long,' said Georgia. 'I have some contacts; I'll speak to them.'

After a brief phone call Liz was moved forward to the 25th May.

'We can't afford to wait,' she said. 'Now, I've told his secretary I'm concerned about you.'

'Why? Do you think it sounds like something serious?'

'No, but you want to get to the bottom of things, don't you?' questioned Georgia.

Liz wished her old gynaecologist hadn't retired, she'd been such a lovely, caring and empathetic doctor.

She remembered back to the day of her laparoscope nearly nineteen years prior. The gynaecologist had sat next to her on the bed and held her hand. 'I owe you an apology, my dear. You have endometriosis and I'm afraid that it's to such an extent you might never have children. I suggest you find a nice chap and settle down ASAP if you have any intentions of trying for a family.'

Liz was relieved more than anything as she'd needed an

answer to why she'd been experiencing such dreadful periods every month. By the time she met Gareth, though, it was too late for children.

————

Liz shuffled in her seat and glanced down anxiously at her phone, checking the time displayed on the screen. This man's taking his time. Probably letting me know how busy he is. Liz shivered. Maybe it was the nerves, but she was glad she had worn her corduroy coat. May could be such changeable weather.

Liz thought back to the look on the ultrasongrapher's face when her image came up on the screen two weeks prior. She'd noticed a shadow of concern pass over his face as he studied the screen in front of him. 'Have you ever had any gynae issues before?' he politely asked, turning to look at her.

'I have endometriosis, so there have always been issues. Why? Is there something wrong?'

Liz glanced over at the ultrasound screen. She could make out an ovary with a dark shadow on it.

A slight look of relief passed over the ultrasonographer's face. 'I'm not sure if you can see here, but there are what appear to be cysts on both of your ovaries,' he said as he pointed to the screen.

'I can see that. Yes,' replied Liz nodding at the screen. 'Is this okay?'

'Probably nothing to worry about,' he said. 'We'll do a trans vaginal ultrasound just to check, seeing as you're here already. There's no point sending you back to the GP for another referral for that. If you're happy to go ahead we can do this today. It'll save time to do it now.'

'Okay,' she said closing her eyes.

Liz was at the GP surgery two days later asking for a

private referral. She didn't want to wait around in the NHS system. Her GP agreed and referred her immediately.

So now with a little help from Georgia, here she was waiting to be seen.

———

Liz glanced back down at her phone again. Ten minutes had passed since the last time she had checked the time.

'Mrs Fitzpatrick, you can go up now,' said the receptionist.

Liz leant down and collected her bag. She smiled at the receptionist as she went past.

'Thank you.'

The receptionist smiled back at her. 'Up the stairs on the first floor,' she instructed as she waved her arm in an upward flourish, 'the secretary will meet you at the top of the stairs.'

Liz followed the receptionist's directions up an elegantly carved dark wooden staircase. She looked upwards as she ascended the stairs. A slim middle-aged bespectacled woman was smiling down at her from the first-floor landing.

'This way please,' she said as she waved her arm in front of her. 'He's ready for you.'

On reaching the landing Liz saw a large open door to her left, and at that moment, a rather tall middle-aged man of medium muscular build appeared and began ushering Liz into the room with a wide sweep of his arm. As she went to enter he held out his hand. 'Iain Kuntz-Finger.' She shook the rather large limp hand that was offered to her. He was what Liz guessed some women might call distinguished. He had a full head of dark red wavy hair. This was complemented with a pair of slightly arched eyebrows that stared back at the recipient from behind a pair of dark blue horn-rimmed glasses. He wore a dark suit and a white shirt with a rather colourful bow tie. Mr Kuntz-Finger waved to an empty short-backed leather chair in front of his desk as he said, 'Take a seat.'

He walked around to his side of the large antique mahogany desk and sat down, pulling the chair in behind him.

'Well now, so let's see what's going on.'

He slowly and deliberately read the scan report. Liz sat in the chair nervously waiting for him to look up. It seemed like an interminably long time.

There was a mantelpiece directly behind Mr Kuntz-Finger. An old antique clock was sitting in the centre directly in Liz's line of sight. The clock ticked slowly in the background. There were two floor length sash windows to Liz's right which opened out onto a balcony over the street below. The faint noise of traffic drifted upwards past the windows, on the afternoon breeze. The clock chimed on the quarter hour.

Mr Kuntz-Finger was shuffling the pages of the ultrasound report. Liz could feel her anxiety rising. She hated doctors' rooms. Ever since both her parents had died of cancer she felt they were only places to be given bad news. Iain Kuntz-Finger began to scribble a few notes on a piece of paper to his right then looked up at Liz as if surprised to see she was still there.

'Tell me about your symptoms, then.'

Liz explained that her GP had been concerned about her recent scan results in addition to her history of feeling bloated and full very soon after eating.

'It started in December. I started feeling very tired. Then I had a chest infection and a urinary tract infection, one after the other. I was given antibiotics… things would settle for a while but then it would flare up again.'

Mr Kuntz-Finger looked up and stared at her waiting for her to continue.

'Ummh, ahh, I forgot to give you the GP referral letter,'

Liz said as she leant over and fished it nervously out of her handbag. She handed the envelope over to him.

'It explains that I have been having lower abdominal pain, bloating and urinary urgency.'

Mr Kuntz-Finger took the envelope from Liz. He read it and then put it to one side. He leant back in his chair staring down at Liz's letter.

'So you have endometriosis.'

Liz nodded. 'Yes, since 1998. It was diagnosed under laparoscope.' He scribbled a few further notes.

She explained to Iain Kuntz-Finger the collapse she'd experienced at work in the February. 'I was referred to a gastroenterologist... Dr Jacobs... one of your colleagues... who ruled out any IBS or gastric problems. I was then tested for asthma last month, but this was also negative.'

Mr Kuntz-Finger barely looked up from his desk. Liz noticed he had abandoned his pen and was now staring down at his hands clasped in front of him on the desk.

Liz cleared her throat nervously and continued. 'My mum died of lymphatic cancer but there was a gynae history which we are unsure of. She had a hysterectomy which we think may have been cancer related. She was young when she died. Only forty-seven. Then there's my dad. He died of prostate cancer and then my cousin on my mum's side, well, she had breast cancer.' Liz was starting to feel anxious. She could feel the words tumbling out of her.

He peered up at her through his arched brows. 'Right well then, we'll order an MRI of your pelvis and see what that shows.' Mr Kuntz-Finger leant forward placing a form on the desk in front of Liz and tapping it with his pen. She thought he'd been writing notes, but it must have been the MRI form, as he handed the form to her already completed.

'Let's get this done and we'll see you in a couple of weeks with the results. It should tell us if there's anything to be concerned about.'

Liz took the form and stared at it blankly. Had he listened to a word she said?

It dawned on her that he had not asked her many questions.

'Uh, okay.'

Mr Kuntz-Finger stood up pushing his chair back. He began to walk around the side of the desk and across to the door. 'You can make an appointment with my secretary for two weeks' time.' He opened the door, indicating that the consultation was now over.

Liz stood up from the chair and hesitated for a second. She glanced around the room taking in the examination couch. Maybe times had changed. Maybe the examination couch was only for appearances sake. She thought she would at least get her pulse checked and possibly be examined. No bloods? Was he not going to check her lymph nodes? Liz frowned. Not even a check of her abdomen? She was complaining of abdominal bloating and abdominal pain. Was he not going to feel where the pain is? She'd made an effort to put her best underwear on and he wasn't even going to examine her abdomen.

'Umm, okay,' she said again. Liz walked towards the door, took the limp hand that was offered to her and shook it. The door closed behind her. She turned and stared at the closed door for a second, with a slightly puzzled expression.

'This way, my dear,' said the secretary who was waiting for her ready with the diary open.

'Two weeks then, dear. Let's see…'

———

What an odd woman, thought Iain. She seemed to be waiting for something else. Not sure what but he was used to it now. Some of these women were rather odd.

Iain sat back at his desk and phoned his wife Louise.

'Hello, dear. Did you manage to arrange to get Lulu to drop my suit to the dry cleaners? Yes. Mmmm. I'll need it for the summer party next week.'

8

LIZ

JUNE 2017

'How did you get on?' asked Georgia. 'What did he find?'

'Nothing. He's ordered a scan.'

'What about when he examined you?'

'He didn't examine me. He only ordered a scan.'

Georgia frowned as best she could through her botoxed forehead. 'He didn't examine you? Hmm, that's a bit odd.'

'Very odd. I wondered that. I thought all gynae patients would be examined.'

'Well, he knows what he's doing. You should be in safe hands. He's ordered an MRI so that should show anything up.'

I bloody well hope so, Liz thought.

───

'The MRI is clear. It shows nothing.'

Liz was feeling rather ill at ease. This can't be right.

'Are they sure they have the right one?'

'Well Ms Fitzpatrick, it is Ms Fitzpatrick isn't it?' Iain Kuntz-Finger chuckled. He leaned over her paperwork and read from the top of the MRI report. 'Ms Elizabeth

Fitzpatrick.' He read out her date of birth. 'Is that you?' He then took her clinic notes to compare and read again from the top. 'Ms Elizabeth Fitzpatrick.' Once again he read out her date of birth.

Liz was in no mood to find it particularly funny. He was making her feel like a fraud.

'Yes, that's me, the last time I checked,' she said rather sarcastically.

He chuckled again. 'Well, unless these scans have been mislabelled, there's nothing wrong with you. In fact, if I compare these two scans I would think they were two entirely different people! From your history I was expecting to find all manner of things, but there's nothing. You have a fibroid so if that continues to bother you then you can come back in six months or so.'

Liz was confused. Was he insinuating something sinister had gone on?

If Mr Kuntz-Finger was confused then there is no hope in hell for me, she thought. Liz's heart started to pound and her lips began to feel dry. She suddenly felt very queasy. She held onto the arms of the chair and took a slow deep breath and cleared her throat.

'Perhaps we need to investigate this further. This doesn't make sense. None of it. Could we order another scan? How about a CT scan of my abdomen? This pain in my diaphragm won't have been captured in the pelvic MRI, and that's still there. Shouldn't we check this pain out?'

'That's completely unnecessary,' Mr Kuntz-Finger replied.

'Or what about a laparoscopy? If you took me for a laparoscope you could see inside and check everything. That was how my endometriosis was discovered all those years ago, and they found out I might never be able to conceive. Endometriosis doesn't just disappear. None of this makes sense.'

'You're asking for needless tests,' he replied matter-of-factly. 'Unless of course you want to undergo unnecessary procedures which could put you at unnecessary risk? You could have your bowel perforated, which seems a bit of a risk to take when the scan is clear.'

'Well, ummm, no, not if you really think that it's unnecessary. You're the specialist. It just doesn't make any sense. I definitely have pain that won't go away and I don't feel right. What about a blood test? You don't think it's anything sinister?'

'No. Definitely not,' Mr Kuntz-Finger firmly replied.

'I would like the CT scan, though,' suggested Liz. 'Surely it'll be more specific than the MRI, and it would pick up the pain in my diaphragm.'

'No, absolutely not,' replied Mr Kuntz-Finger again. 'I will order you a pelvic ultrasound. If that's clear then there's no need for you to come back and see me.'

'But.'

'An ultrasound it is then.'

'So, you trust the person who reported the MRI?'

'Yes, with my life. He's worked with me for many years.'

Liz shifted herself nervously and then leant forward in her chair. 'So just to make clear then… you're wanting me to go for a pelvic ultrasound only. You're not going to scan my abdomen or diaphragm. No bloods. If the ultrasonographer says it's clear, you'll write to me to tell me this… but you don't wish to see me again?'

'Correct.'

'And you're not concerned about the fact I had endometriosis confirmed all those years ago and now it appears to have somehow disappeared?'

'No,' he replied.

Liz was not sure why he refused to do any further tests. It was private healthcare so there was no tight cost restriction. He obviously thought she was a hypochondriac.

Liz stood up. Iain Kuntz-Finger remained at his desk and without looking up continued scribbling some notes.

Iain Kuntz-Finger sat at his desk. What a woman! How demanding. Who did she think she was coming in here and demanding all manner of tests? Another perimenopausal woman. He certainly had his fair share of them. So anxious about 'the change' and losing their sexual appeal. Not that this one had much to lose anyway. There was nothing wrong with her.

Her poor husband, Iain thought. Wouldn't fancy being him.

———

The letter from Mr Kuntz-Finger arrived in early July. Liz opened it to find a couple of sentences confirming her recent pelvic ultrasound was normal. Iain informed Liz this was very reassuring and that he had written to her GP expressing his concern at the original ultrasound.

———

Dr Phillips opened his post to find a letter from Mr Kuntz-Finger regarding his patient, Liz Fitzpatrick. It confirmed Liz had no endometriomas on her ovaries and he questioned the original ultrasound which Dr Phillips had ordered. The letter ended with Mr Kuntz-Finger saying that 'either way Liz would not be undergoing any treatment at this point in time.'

'Oh well, I guess that's that, then,' said Dr Phillips, feeling very confused.

———

Liz was upset. She knew there was something wrong with her. Why had he not taken any bloods? Why had he not examined her lymph nodes or her abdomen? She'd described the pain coming from the right side of her diaphragm and yet he didn't seem interested in this at all.

She had googled her symptoms and ovarian cancer and a ruptured ovarian cyst were possibilities, yet he was telling her there was nothing wrong with her. Everyone now thought she was a hypochondriac, including her husband.

Liz was fighting back the tears as she stood next to Gareth in the kitchen while he cooked supper.

'Hun, he's the guy. He's told you there's nothing wrong,' said Gareth, in an attempt to placate her.

'Why didn't he scan my diaphragm, though?'

'I don't know, hun. Perhaps you're over thinking things. Maybe it's your job. Maybe you need to take a break.'

Liz could feel her anger rising. Even her husband now thought she was overreacting. She scowled at Gareth.

'So, you're just going to agree with everyone else. It's all in my head, is it? Perhaps I should see someone else.'

'What good's that going to do?' Gareth threw his arms in the air in exasperation. 'He's an expert. They're hardly going to find anything else, are they?'

'I'm tired. I'm fed up of everyone telling me I'm okay, when I am not okay. He wouldn't let me have any further scans or a laparoscope.'

Liz was now sobbing. She raised her hand and pointed at Gareth.

'If I die because of him I want you to sue the arse off of him.'

'I doubt it'll come to that, hun.'

'Let's just see about that. I know my body better than anyone and something's not right.' Liz turned and ran up the stairs, sobbing.

Gareth sighed and turned back to cooking supper. Hormonal women. There's nothing worse.

October 2017

As Liz lay in her hospital bed waiting for Mr Kuntz-Finger to return from his weekend away, this scenario came flooding back to her. Should I have trusted him? How had he missed this? Maybe he was having a life crisis himself? There had to be a reasonable explanation.

As the evening wore on and the lights dimmed in her room, Liz managed to turn on the lamp above the bed, and amid her tears and frantic phone calls to and from friends and family, she suddenly realised she might be going to die.

9

IAIN

EARLY OCTOBER 2017

*T*he late afternoon sun was warm on Iain's face as he rested poolside on a lounger at the Kuntz family villa in the south of France. He closed his eyes and sighed as he looked forward to his last weekend of sun before returning to London and a long winter of bitter cold English weather. He could taste the salt air and smell the scent of lavender from the large terracotta pots surrounding the pool. Sebastian, Amelia and Oscar were laughing and playing on the beach below with Louise. Stretching his arms above his head, he took a deep breath, opening his eyes to admire the clear blue cloudless sky above.

The phone began to buzz and dance across the low wrought iron table beside him. He sighed, then picked it up and stared at the screen. Dr Lewis's name was flashing. He answered the call holding the phone to his ear.

'Hello, Iain Kuntz-Finger?' asked the voice at the other end.

'Yes.'

'This is Dr Lewis. We have a patient of yours here. By the name of Elizabeth Fitzpatrick? You saw her in May and June. She's just been admitted with abdominal pain. We've done a scan and taken tumour markers and done both an ultrasound and CT scan. It appears she has ovarian cancer which has spread to her abdomen.'

'Hmm. She saw me in June, you say?'

'Yes.'

'I think I remember her.'

'Well, she's wanting to speak to you as soon as possible. She doesn't understand why it was missed in June.'

'I'll be in on Monday. I'm away for the weekend. The earliest I can see her will be Monday evening.'

There was silence on the other end.

'Anything else?' asked Iain.

'Umm. She's rather upset.'

'Right, well tell her she can see someone else if she wants, otherwise she'll have to wait until Monday. I wouldn't advise that, though. She's best waiting for me. Send all her details to my secretary.'

'Okay.'

Dr Lewis hung up the phone. What a rude man. Right, I'd better tell her she has to wait until Monday.

When the call finished, Iain shut the phone off and placed it on the table again. His mouth felt rather dry and he lifted the glass of water from the table, taking several sips. His hand was shaking. Sitting on the side of the sun lounger with his feet on the warm stone slabs, he held his head in his hands. His mind was working overtime trying to remember everything about the woman… then it all came back to him. Suddenly he felt rather unwell. At least he'd stalled for time and would now have all day Monday to get Prashant to recheck the scans.

'Well, that's the weekend ruined,' he muttered to himself.

10

ALICE

FEBRUARY 2016

'*H*ello Alice,' said Dr Pinkham.

Alice was sitting in the consulting room of her private GP, Dr Pinkham. He had been her family GP ever since she moved to London. She was very fond of him. He was the sort of person everyone wanted for a family GP. He probably should have retired years ago.

'I wouldn't know what to do with myself, would I dear?' he would exclaim to Alice. 'My wife likes me out from under her feet.'

'Would you like a cup of tea, dear?' asked Dr Pinkham as he ushered Alice into the consulting room.

'No, I'm fine, Percival.'

He glanced through Alice's notes and then peered over his glasses at her. 'So, things are no better?'

'No, not really, I'm afraid.'

'Let's examine this tummy of yours.'

Dr Pinkham shuffled over to the examination couch waving at Alice to follow him. She got onto the couch and he proceeded to prod her abdomen. After a great deal of 'tutting' and 'oohing' and 'ahhhing' Dr Pinkham asked Alice to hop down off the examination table. As she sat back down in the chair, he began making some notes, then looked up and peered through his glasses at her.

'I'll refer you to a gynaecologist.'

'Nothing serious, is it?'

'Hopefully not, my dear, but we can't be too careful, can we? We need to find out the cause of all this discomfort you're having. I'll refer you to a chap I know. He's a fine chap and very well connected. Only the best for you, Alice,' said Dr Pinkham, as he winked at her. 'Now how's the family?'

Dr Pinkham looked back down at his notes as Alice began to update him on Hugh and Sophie's lives. After a few minutes she stopped and stared at Percival. There was silence for several minutes.

Alice cleared her throat. Dr Pinkham didn't move. She cleared her throat again. Still nothing.

'Dr Pinkham?'

No reply.

Alice got up from her chair and moved around the side of the consulting desk. He didn't move. She put her hand on his shoulder as he let out a rather loud snore causing his glasses to shudder on the bridge of his nose. Alice smiled fondly, breathing a sigh of relief. She leant over to an armchair behind Dr Pinkham and placed the light blue angora blanket around his shoulders, giving him an affectionate pat on the arm. She turned and smiled, quietly closing the door behind her, shaking her head as she left. He really should start to slow down, she thought, but being the loving kind man that he was he just kept on going out of loyalty to his patients. What would they all do when he was gone?

Alice walked up to the reception desk.

'Mary?'

'Yes, Mrs Ellis Bledisloe.'

'Dr Pinkham's rather tired and resting for a bit. Could you check on him in a little while?'

'Oh, of course. He didn't fall asleep again mid-consultation, did he?'

———

Alice waited for what seemed like an interminably long time. The receptionist was rather full of herself. Alice didn't like people like that. The reception area was very busy as it accommodated several different floors of consultants. Eventually she was directed to the lift which took her up to the second floor. It resembled a hotel rather than clinical premises. She was shown to a high-ceilinged room with elaborately carved corniche work and a rather large, elegant chandelier hanging from the central ceiling rose. The room was painted in a pale blue tone with plush cream carpet. The furnishings consisted of a large elaborately carved walnut consulting desk positioned in the middle of the room, with a large black leather chair on one side, and two antique chairs on the other. An examination table was just visible from behind a Japanese hand painted screen to the far left-hand side of the room. To the right of the room were two sets of French doors opening out onto the balcony.

'Ah, Mrs Ellis Bledisloe I presume,' said the short fat little man who was appearing around the corner of the consulting desk, offering Alice a chubby hand. 'I'm Reginald Fuker Howard.'

Reginald appeared quite comical. He was wearing dark blue trousers and a bright pink shirt which was stretched quite tightly over his bulging abdomen. He had a brightly coloured red silk tie and a bright red complexion to match. He had a full head of wavy greying hair and a pair of very bushy eyebrows which Alice thought rather resembled a pair of furry caterpillars.

'Call me Alice.' She smiled and shook his hand.

He ushered her to one of the two antique chairs and

then waddled back round to the other side of the desk and sat down.

'Now tell me what's been happening, my dear.'

'Well,' started Alice. 'I've been having these tummy pains which seem to be getting worse, and I've been feeling extremely tired lately. I appear to keep having urinary tract issues which Dr Pinkham feels are going on for a little bit too long. My stomach feels so incredibly bloated all the time and I start to feel full so quickly after eating. For example, we were out the other night at the theatre and then went to dinner afterwards—'

'Where did you go to dinner?' he interrupted.

'Umm, Nobu,' replied Alice.

'Ooh Nobu, very nice. I had their Chilean sea bass umami, and it was delicious. Do you go there often? Now, the theatre, well, I love the theatre. What did you see?'

Alice frowned. 'I thought we were discussing my abdominal pains?'

Reginald waved one of his fat little chubby hands dismissively in the air. 'Oh, yes. Sorry, my dear, continue.'

'So, the abdominal pains…' Alice stopped mid-sentence as her gaze followed Reginald, who was up out of his chair waving his arms towards the examination couch.

'Right well then let's get you up on the table and examine you,' he said as he patted the examination couch invitingly.

'But I haven't finished.' Alice sighed.

A few minutes later Reggie was padding his chubby little gloved hands across Alice's abdomen.

'Oh yes, a little bloated. We'll give you some antibiotics for your urinary tract infection and we can do an ultrasound of your bladder and pelvis. Have you thought about taking up some cycling to help with your weight, dear?'

'What?'

'Cycling. For the weight on your tummy, my dear.' Reggie patted her tummy lightly. 'It's great all-round exercise and, well, to be honest it would do you the world of good. You have lovely slim legs, but I think you're carrying just a little bit of extra weight around the middle. Hormonal probably. You girls all get like that at this stage in life. Nothing a healthy diet and exercise wouldn't fix.' He smiled at her as he extricated his gloves from his chubby hands with an elasticated pinging sound and discarded them into the bin.

Alice didn't like his tone. 'And what about you?' she enquired.

'Excuse me?'

Alice turned to face Reginald, pointing a finger at him as she sat on the edge of the examination couch. 'You. What about you? What do you do about your excess weight? Whatever it is it's clearly not working.'

––––––

Alice was furious. She went back to Dr Pinkham and voiced her disapproval about the pretentious rude little man he had sent her to see.

'Oh dear, dear,' Percival muttered. 'I'm dreadfully sorry. He's a fine chap and I'm sure he didn't mean any offence. Anyway, the ultrasound is clear so let's just wait and see, shall we?'

––––––

Alice returned to the pretentious little man again two months later in the April.

'Now, see here,' she said. 'I do think you ought to examine me again. I don't think your scan is right, old chap. I'm still in a lot of discomfort.'

'Right, well let's get you up on the examination couch again, then.' Reginald Fuker Howard 'ummed' and 'ahhed' for several minutes as he palpated Alice's abdomen.

'What is it? Just spit it out for goodness' sake, my dear fellow,' said Alice as she peered up at Reginald.

'Nothing.'

'What?'

'Nothing wrong, my dear.'

'Are you sure?' questioned Alice as she sat up and began to get dressed, feeling rather annoyed.

'Yes. I'm afraid it's just your age, my dear.'

'My age? What has my age got to do with it?' Alice pointed a finger at Reginald and waved it under his nose. 'And before you say anything don't even think about mentioning my weight again.'

'You girls all have to go through it at some stage,' said Reginald. 'If it continues then perhaps we could get an MRI, but there's no need for that just yet.'

'And what about my vaginal dryness?'

'Umm.' Reginald appeared slightly flustered at Alice's question.

'For goodness' sake,' Alice exclaimed. 'I thought you were a gynaecologist.'

'Well, yes. You could use some lubricant for that,' said Reginald, holding up his index finger and twirling it round in a circular motion.

'What sort?'

'Excuse me?'

Alice sighed with exasperation. 'What SORT of lubricant?'

'KY jelly is fine. Just slap a bit up there if you want to, you know.' Reginald pointed to Alice's crotch.

'You know what? If by "you know", you mean sex, then no I don't want to "you know". The reason being that my husband currently repulses me.'

'Oh, dear, dear,' Reginald tutted.

Alice pointed to her crotch. 'Do you need to have a *look* down there?'

'Well now, only if you think it's necessary.'

'*Necessary!*' shrieked Alice. 'Of course I think it's *necessary*. If I didn't think it was necessary, I wouldn't have mentioned it.'

'It's just that we don't tend to do too many internal examinations as women complain that they find them rather degrading. We tend to scan more nowadays.'

Really, this man is the limit. Alice's patience was wearing thin.

'My dear fellow, I can assure you it is nothing to do with my age. I think you're a rather rude and condescending little man and perhaps I might be best served by another specialist.'

Alice began to gather her things.

'Now look here, old girl,' said Reginald.

Alice froze in her tracks, then turned to Reginald locking him with an icy stare. 'Don't you *ever* call me that!'

'Well, umm, I was only meaning to say—'

'I really don't give a rats arse what you were trying to say, you shoddy little man,' Alice growled. 'I have never been so insulted in my life. Now get out!' Alice threw her arm towards the door indicating for Reginald to leave.

'Umm.'

'What?' shouted Alice.

'Err, it's just that this is my office.'

'Well then,' said Alice, realising her mistake, as she raised her chin upwards with steely determination, 'I guess I will be the one to leave.' She turned and walked towards the door.

Reginald shuffled over attempting to intercept her at the threshold. He held out his hand.

Alice threw a look that froze him in his stride. 'I really think we're beyond that, don't you?'

Reginald winced, dropping his hand to his side, as if in reaction to being bitten by some venomous creature.

Alice turned and left the room, leaving the door wide open.

'Dear, dear,' muttered Reginald. What a fiery woman. Hormones. They all seemed so hormonal. No wonder men dominated medicine. He began to imagine a medical world full of female hormones. 'We'd never get anything done,' he muttered to himself. He turned and waddled back to his desk as he whistled a rather catchy tune he'd heard on the radio earlier then sat back down at his desk and began to wonder what his wife might be preparing for dinner that evening.

11

LIZ

EARLY OCTOBER 2017

*I*t was late in the evening. Iain was hovering at the foot of Liz's bed.

'I don't think it's ovarian cancer,' he announced. 'When we looked at your scans we saw that the mass is behind the ovaries, not on them, so we need to find the source. It may be breast or pancreatic cancer.'

Liz was confused. 'But they did the blood test for breast and pancreatic cancer and these were normal. Dr Lewis confirmed that the ovarian cancer markers were elevated. He said they were over 400 and the normal is less than 36.'

'Well, we need to make certain of what we're dealing with. I'm organising a breast ultrasound and for you to see our breast specialist.'

With that he was gone. Liz was beginning to feel something was not right. It just didn't make sense. Dr Lewis had told her that she had ovarian cancer. Now she was being told by Mr Kuntz-Finger that he thought she had ovarian secondaries with another cancer as the primary. She was reeling; her gut instinct was that she had ovarian cancer. It made sense.

The scans couldn't lie… Or could they actually be

wrong? Had they been read correctly? She couldn't think straight. Trust your instinct, Liz, she thought.

If there's one thing she could smell it was fear and bullshit from a thousand paces and she was beginning to get a distinct whiff.

―――――

Iain went out to the nurses' station and leant over the desk.

'Pass me Ms Fitzpatrick's notes,' he said to the receptionist.

The receptionist obediently collected the notes and passed them to Iain.

He began to scribble in an entry.

He ordered a biopsy and insertion of a drain for the fluid in her abdomen, questioning ovarian cancer as the cause. He noted down disseminated disease in the abdomen but the speed of presentation and some symptoms as not entirely typical of ovarian cancer.

Unfortunately for Iain, Liz would eventually read this entry.

Two days later he made another entry confirming the biopsy results as showing high grade ovarian cancer and the need for Liz to undergo radical surgery to save her life.

―――――

'We've got the biopsy report back from the lab and we are 99 per cent sure that your cancer is of ovarian origin. We're going to plan for surgery next week.'

'You have all the results back, then?'

'No, not all.'

'But I thought you wanted to wait for all the results?'

'Well, we're pretty sure now.'

They were sure? Liz was confused.

Liz knew she would have to tell Olivia. She couldn't face speaking to her on the phone. The emotion was all too raw, so she decided to message her.

Olivia,

I don't know how to tell you this but I've just found out that I have ovarian cancer. It's spread to my abdomen. They're going to operate next week. I've been sent home for a few days to rest and build my strength up.

Liz

Liz was resting on her bed at home. The phone buzzed beside her. Olivia's name appeared on the screen.

'Babes,' shrieked Olivia down the phone in her south London twang. 'What the fuck? You can't be serious! I can't believe it. I just read your message. What? Hang on.'

Liz could hear muffled voices in the background.

'Sorry. I've just rear ended some poor bastard. I got your text and was so upset I didn't see him. Rammed him right up the arse.'

Liz could hear a raised voice coming closer in the background.

'Yeah, alright, mate,' Olivia shouted. 'Keep your hair on. Can't you see I'm on the phone?'

'What is his problem? Some people.' Olivia growled down the phone. 'Anyway, babes, how come that guy you saw never picked it up? This isn't right.'

Liz couldn't get a word in. She decided to wait until Olivia had calmed down.

12

LIZ

LATE OCTOBER 2017

*L*iz was lying in the intensive care unit the morning after her surgery. She stared straight ahead trying to absorb the news Iain was relaying to her. He was standing at the foot of the bed again.

'We couldn't get everything, I'm afraid. There was too much. We tried but the area on your diaphragm was too tricky to get at without causing complications. There are also two small areas on your bowel. We didn't do a colostomy. I spoke to Tristan, the oncologist, during the surgery and he advised to leave this. He recommended we get your incision line healed so we can start you on chemotherapy as soon as possible. This option gives you the best possible chance of survival.'

How could this have happened? How could it have been left to get this bad? Liz just couldn't take it all in.

'Have you told my husband?'

'Yes. I'll leave you for now and check on you tomorrow.'

With that Iain Kuntz-Finger was gone.

When Gareth came in, he looked tired and his manner was strained. Liz knew he was trying to be brave for her.

'Hi, darling.' Liz wanted to sound upbeat in front of

him. She didn't want any negativity at the moment. 'Mr Kuntz-Finger's been in. He told me the news.'

'What did he tell you?'

Liz repeated what Mr Kuntz-Finger had said.

'That's what he told me.' Gareth sat down in the chair beside Liz and held her hand. They just sat in silence for some time.

———

Liz had been out in the chair for a few hours in the morning. It took three nurses to move her. She was allowed back to bed in the afternoon but had to promise she would sit out in the chair again in the late afternoon.

Iain Kuntz-Finger had told the nurses she could eat, so they were trying to feed her some salmon and mashed potato. Liz wasn't sure she should be eating so soon after major abdominal surgery. They'd just pulled the length of her colon outside of her body, washed her abdomen out and then proceeded to squeeze her colon back into position, like a length of sausages, being tucked into a very small bag at the butchers.

'Oh, babes, you look like shit. God love you. Give me a hug.'

Liz was too tired to talk so Olivia just sat and held her hand until Joanna arrived.

Liz's breathing had deteriorated. She felt very breathless.

Joanna had flown in from New Zealand. It had been a devastating blow for Liz's family as they'd lost both Liz's mother and father to cancer. The siblings were all very close and Joanna assumed the place of her mother in times of need. When Liz had been diagnosed she instructed Joanna to stay where she was, but Joanna would not hear of it. Liz phoned her when it was confirmed with the lab that she definitely had ovarian cancer.

'I know I asked you not to come, Jo, but I need you more than ever. I'm so sorry to ask but could you come over?'

'I've already got a flight booked,' replied Jo. 'I land in four days' time.'

'Thanks Jo. That means so much to me.'

———

Joanna was sitting in a chair next to Liz busy phoning all the family to update them on her progress. She held the phone up to Liz's ear. Her sister-in-law Ella wanted to speak to her.

'I don't have any energy,' Liz gasped. 'I don't think I'm going to make it, Ella. This is too hard.'

There was a moment's silence on the other end of the phone before Ella began. 'You will not give up, do you hear?' came the shrill voice down the phone.

Liz sighed. She was exhausted beyond words. Exhausted from the months of fatigue and discomfort. Emotionally scarred from the constant dismissals as her symptoms all being 'hormonal'. And now she was facing the biggest fight of her life. She felt like a marathon runner facing 'the wall' with the crowds cheering her on, fading in and out as her senses heightened and then dulled, her body awash with pain at every movement as she tried to push herself gathering every last inch of energy she could muster. The problem was the only finish line she could see in front of her was death.

'You have three nephews who are relying on you to get through this, Liz. You *WILL* be there watching each of them walk down the aisle one day, because they need their aunt, and are relying on you to be there for them. You will *NOT* give up. Do you hear me?'

Liz wondered how she was going to get through the next hour let alone another ten or so years. Her eldest nephew was only eighteen, so unless he was intending on marrying young, Liz had a long way to go.

'Okay,' sighed Liz in resignation. She didn't have the energy to argue.

'Right, so you can stop feeling sorry for yourself, grab whatever energy and reserves you can muster and get yourself ready to crawl out of that deep black hole you're in,' Ella commanded. 'You can and will do this, Liz. We need you here with us. I don't want to hear any more of this negative talk. We are not losing you. You hear me?'

'Uh huh,' said Liz, as she began to feel a flame of annoyance and determination flicker inside of her.

Ella was sharp as a tack and knew exactly which buttons to push. She threw down the gauntlet knowing Liz would not be able to refuse the challenge.

13

LATE OCTOBER 2017

*I*ain was in his multi-million-pound home enjoying his Saturday morning. He had woken up, showered and dressed and then walked downstairs to the familiar sound of the children playing in the lounge with the Saturday morning children's tv on in the background. When he peered into the lounge, he saw Sebastian and Amelia playing with their toys. Oscar was sitting on his knees in front of the television set with his favourite soft toy Stick Man on his lap. He was so attached to his toy. Iain had spent countless hours reading Stick Man stories to Oscar. Smiling to himself, he went into the breakfast room and sat at the table by the bay window overlooking the perfectly manicured garden. He placed his mobile phone down beside him. The warm October sunlight was streaming in through the window bathing the room in a warm glow. Iain picked up the copy of the weekend edition of *The Times* and started to open it out on the table.

'Scrambled eggs?' Louise asked, from across the kitchen counter.

'Hmmm?'

Louise sighed. 'Eggs. On toast. For breakfast.' She held up two eggs.

'Yes, thank you.'

Iain had only got through about ten minutes of the paper when the phone beside him buzzed and started to dance across the table.

He tried to ignore it but as soon as the phone rang off it began buzzing again. He sighed, put the paper down and answered it.

'Hello, Mr Kuntz-Finger, this is Violet. From the hospital. It's Ms Fitzpatrick, I'm afraid. She's really unhappy and is demanding to see you. She insisted I phone you and ask you to come in and speak to her.'

'Yes, well, tell her I'm busy at the moment.'

Louise set a plate of scrambled eggs on toast down in front of him and mouthed 'coffee?' Iain nodded at Louise.

Violet had either chosen to ignore Iain, or just simply had not heard him, as she continued, 'She came back from intensive care last night. She's been vomiting and complaining of uncontrolled pain. She also thinks something's not right with regards to her diagnosis and wants to discuss it with you.'

Iain's ears pricked up. He sat up in his chair and leaned in to the phone, lowering his voice. 'What exactly did she say?'

'She said she thought you were hiding something from her. She also said that every time she said anything to the doctors, they didn't listen and they missed the exact cause.'

Iain suddenly had a sinking feeling in his stomach. He felt rather hot and beads of sweat started to form on his forehead.

'Okay, tell her I'll be in shortly.' He ended the call and placed the phone back down on the table.

Louise had just placed a freshly brewed cup of coffee in front of him. He pushed the plate of scrambled eggs aside, folded the newspaper, placing it on the breakfast table beside him slowly and methodically.

'Shit!' he muttered under his breath.

'Sorry,' said Louise. 'Is something wrong?'

'Just work. A rather difficult patient, I'm afraid. I have to go in.'

'Oh no, but what about your breakfast? You haven't finished it.'

'I'm not that hungry.'

Iain hurriedly drank the fresh coffee and went upstairs to change.

Louise stared after him, sighed and shrugged. Iain was so short tempered lately. Another Saturday morning on her own with the children again. Not that that meant anything. All her friends were in the same boat. 'The price you had to pay for the lifestyle you want,' they all said. So they all put up with the late nights, left the children with the nannies and would meet up for dinner and drinks. She had recently joined a running group. They would meet up in the mornings on Hampstead Heath after the school run. Once they'd completed their morning run they would go for coffee in Hampstead High Street. It wasn't a bad life and all in all Louise felt the sacrifices were worth it… apart from Iain's moodiness.

———

'I want to discuss with you the sequence of events leading up to my diagnosis.'

'I'm not prepared to discuss this with you at the moment. It wouldn't be helpful. You're a very ill woman and you need to concentrate on getting better to give yourself the best possible chance of survival. Now I understand you are in pain—'

'Of course I'm in pain. Look at my abdomen.' Liz pulled the blankets down to reveal her distended abdomen. 'You can see it's completely distended. I've thrown up during the night and still have vomit in my hair.'

Liz picked up her left hand, grabbed a strand of vomit-dried hair and shook it at him.

Iain Kuntz-Finger shrank back, recoiling, attempting to avoid any stray bits of vomit which might come his way.

'Don't you want to examine me?'

He remained standing at the foot of the bed. He did not relish the thought of going near someone with vomit-streaked hair. 'No, I don't want you to have to move. You're comfortable in that position so that's fine. I don't need to come any closer.'

Liz sighed with exasperation and pulled the covers back over her abdomen.

Iain took the drug chart from Violet and scribbled on it.

'Right, we'll add some extra analgesia to make you comfortable.'

Liz rolled her eyes. She decided not to tell Iain that his fly was down.

Silently fuming, she ran over the conversation she'd just had with Iain Kuntz-Finger in her head.

'I'm not prepared to discuss this with you.' That's what he had said. Those exact words. 'Hah.' Liz spat the words out. 'I know what that means. He knows he's fucked up. He can't fix it so he is going to try and cover his tracks. Just one of those things is what he said. He knows he can get away with saying that as there's no screening tool.'

Liz knew what was coming. She knew now, that if she acted unreasonably, he would document her as struggling psychologically and refer her for counselling for her anger. People would be queuing up to pat her hand, telling her she was having a life shock and, with time, she would get over it. She felt as if she was up against a wall in a dead-end alley and he was standing there holding a gun to her head about to pull the trigger. Unless, of course, she agreed to play nice.

'Bastard,' screamed Liz at the wall.

———

Iain made an entry in the notes documenting Liz as 'appearing very distressed' at her diagnosis and that she felt the medical team were 'hiding things' from her. He also documented her earlier statement to Violet that 'every time she complained of something that doctors were missing the underlying cause.'

24th October 2017

'What is my prognosis?' asked Liz. She was sitting up in bed clutching a soft toy Stick Man her nephews had sent her. She found it very comforting to hold and it helped with her anxiety for some reason.

Iain stood in his usual position, at the edge of the room, ready to make a quick exit.

'As I've said before, it wouldn't be helpful to discuss things at this point in time. You're a very sick woman.' He stared at the Stick Man and thought of his son Oscar. What on earth was a grown woman doing with a child's toy?

'Why did you cancel the oncologist appointment today? I thought he was coming this morning. My husband was waiting but he's going to have to go to work now. My sister had arranged to come in especially early, but I had to phone her to tell her not to come in.'

'He was. I didn't think you were in the right frame of mind to deal with it, so I cancelled it. Now that you seem to be in a more positive frame of mind, I'll flick him an email and see if he's okay to come in tomorrow.' Iain made a swiping motion with his right index finger as if sending an imaginary email.

Liz stared at him, shrugged and sighed. So this was the game she had to play...

Iain went out to the nursing station.

Gareth arrived back on the floor. As he approached the nurses' station, he saw Iain Kuntz-Finger coming out of Liz's room.

'Hello. How is she?' asked Gareth.

'She seems a bit down. I think it's important that she has things to motivate her.'

'I brought in some photos. Pictures of her travels… and she wants to go skiing again.'

'Yes, those things are all good.'

Iain beckoned to the nurse. 'Ms Fitzpatrick's notes please.' He turned back to Gareth. 'Can I ask, are you medical?'

He frowned wondering what the significance of that question was. 'No, I'm not.'

'Oh okay.'

Gareth thought he saw a look of relief pass over Iain's face.

Iain took the set of notes which had just been handed to him by the nurse, opened up the file and began to write an entry.

Gareth waited for a minute in silence, then realised that had been the signal that the conversation had come to an end. He shrugged and walked towards Liz's room. As he reached the door he turned and looked back towards the nurses' station. Iain was standing there with his head bent forwards over the set of notes. Not exactly personality of the year, thought Gareth.

———

Iain scribbled a brief note that he was 'having the discussion again'. He noted the need to continue to support Liz psychologically and that he would discuss her psychological support needs with Tristan. He stood for a few minutes chewing on his pen and then, feeling suddenly inspired, documented that he had discussed psychological help with her husband.

Unfortunately, once again for Iain, both Liz and Gareth would read this entry at a later date.

———

BASTARD. I will hang you by your balls you arrogant man.

Liz sat in her hospital bed and threw her pen at the wall. It crashed to the floor. She wanted to kill him but first she had to get out of here. They all said she was so ill and needed surgery as soon as possible. She'd been advised to see him again to clarify if anything had been missed. He told her that he had checked and that nothing had been missed. She was so weakened from the cancer that they'd told her she couldn't be operated on for a week after the diagnosis was confirmed, so she'd been sent home to build herself up for the surgery. During that time Liz had phoned the gynae nurse and said her husband was concerned that this man had missed something and had asked if he was the best person for the job. She was reassured that this was the guy who could sort everything out, so why now did she think she had made a dreadful error of judgement?

Up until a fortnight ago she was crawling around trying to convince everyone she was unwell. No one would listen. Her work colleagues thought she'd become a hypochondriac as she'd moved from one doctor to the next, trying to convince someone there was something actually wrong with her. The fact that Iain Kuntz-Finger had told her there was nothing wrong with her ovaries, was probably the reason that the emergency department sent her home with several litres of fluid in her abdomen, informing her she possibly had IBS.

Liz practised her deep breathing and gradually began to think more rationally. What was that saying? 'Don't get mad. Get even.' That was it. Right, she had to play the game. 'Play the game, play the game.' That is what Danny De Vito had said in *One Flew Over the Cuckoo's Nest* and she was trapped in one hell of a cuckoo's nest at the moment. She would play the game. She would apologise for being rude and tell him she realised she needed to focus on getting better. She would smile appropriately, and once she was ready… she would make him pay.

14

VICKY

I'm so sorry, Carol. I can't come in. I'm sure it's nothing... Yes... Maybe just a virus. I'll be back next week... I will. I promise.' Vicky ended the call and prepared to get out of bed.

She managed to get a GP appointment for two days later and received yet another dose of antibiotics.

'Are you sure you know what you're doing?' Vicky frowned across the consulting desk at her GP. Dr Dhillon looked up from the computer screen at her with a look of annoyance. He studied her carefully then returned to typing up the prescription, waited silently for it to print and then held it out to her without uttering a word.

'My chest's sore again. My abdomen's sore and swollen again. Aren't you going to examine me?' She waved her hands, pointing in the direction of her abdomen. Vicky had had enough of being fobbed off. She was sick and tired of the derogatory looks being thrown at her and being made to feel as if she should apologise for inconveniencing everyone every time she presented at the surgery. 'I'm not well and all you do is sit there writing prescriptions. You're useless,' she shouted as she snatched the prescription Dr Dhillon was holding out to her. She stormed out into the waiting room when she realised she'd forgotten to slam the door, so she circled back, grabbed the door handle and slammed the door *really* hard.

————

Jagpal shuddered at the sound. He rolled his eyes and sighed. He was tired. He was fed up with dealing with the clientele from the nearby estate. He dreamed of a private GP practice in Harley Street. How did he end up here?

His family was so proud of him. He was born in Delhi but sent to England to medical school. They'd had such high hopes for him. He drove a BMW and he lived in a large modern detached home in Kent just outside of Eynsford village. He had been able to send his three children to private school. His two boys Sunny and Tej had gone on to study medicine in London. His daughter Jashan had finally been married off to the son of a grocer who owned several stores across the south east of England.

Preeti, his wife, well, she was another story. She was a fierce woman. She had been beautiful once, but the ravages of time had hardened both her appearance and her soul. Small in stature and after the damage of three pregnancies, her once svelte figure had contorted out of shape. Jagpal thought she was holding a little bit too much weight. Her face was permanently covered in several layers of make-up, but nothing could disguise the disappointment on her face which he saw every time she looked at him. She was a very demanding wife and nothing Jagpal did ever seemed quite enough. He had to work hard to get Preeti the things she wanted. Sometimes he felt she was holding his head just below the surface of the water trying to slowly drown him…

And now this woman thought she had the right to shout at him. This English single mother. He tutted disapprovingly. Her children have come from three different men and her latest husband is doing time. These English women were a different breed. He found it hard to understand them. In Delhi her kind would be outcasts for such disrespectful behaviour. He was a doctor. A respected GP. He would assess his patients and prescribe. It was not his fault she lived an unhealthy lifestyle. Day after day, week after week it was the same complaints, the same people. He was sick of it. He was now on blood pressure tablets which he was sure was due to patients like Vicky Wallis. Perhaps he should plan a trip home to India to see his family. They were so proud of him there. They would treat him like a god.

———

Vicky was screaming in pain lying on the trolley in the corridor. Alfie was crying and holding onto her hand. 'Mum, Mum, it's okay, Mum. I'm here.'

'I know you are, darling. Where's your nan?' Vicky asked, as she gasped through the pain.

'She's coming. Bronagh's on her way too.'

———

The painkillers were starting to weave their magic. Vicky opened her eyes. The pain had been unbearable. A tube was attached to her abdomen with a large amount of fluid draining from it, collecting into a plastic bag. Vicky picked up the bag to examine the fluid. The bag felt warm. She felt so much better once the tube had been inserted, as if a valve had been released and all the pressure in her abdomen began to lift.

Had she passed out during the procedure? Yes, she must have. Alfie was holding her hand, looking up at her with tear-stained cheeks. Those big dark eyes... God, how she loved those eyes. He leant over to kiss her hand. She smiled as she felt his head of soft red curls against her arm. He looked up and smiled back at her wrinkling up his cute freckle spattered nose.

Vicky could not keep her eyes open any longer…

———

'Vicky, darling.' It was Janice.

'Hiya, Mum.'

'How're you feeling, love?'

'I'm okay. Much better.'

Vicky glanced around her and tried to sit up. 'Where are the children?'

'I've sent them home, love. The doctor's here to see you. He's asked me to stay for a while.'

A young man approached the bed and held out his hand.

'Hello, Mrs Wallis. I'm John. We've scanned your abdomen and there was a large amount of fluid inside, so we attached a drain to your abdomen to drain it off. This should make you feel more comfortable. We've performed a CT scan as well and I have the results here...'

John hesitated. 'I'm afraid it's not good news. You're in the advanced stages of ovarian cancer. It's in your abdomen, your lungs, bowel and liver. The good news is it has not yet reached your brain or bones. We can start some chemotherapy to try and shrink the cancer and then possibly some surgery. The surgery would involve removing your ovaries, uterus, cervix and the omentum. We would also need to take some of your bowel away which would mean having a waste bag attached permanently to your abdomen. That's something we can discuss once we see how you respond to the initial chemotherapy.'

Vicky blinked. She was trying to put the words together.

She was struggling to process what she had just been told. That couldn't be right. It didn't make sense. The hole opening up in front of her was very black and appeared to be widening, sucking her towards it as if trapped in a vacuum. She tried to scream but no sound came. She blinked, and then looked from the doctor to her mother, and back again. She could see Janice's tears and all she could think about was 'what about my beautiful children? Who will take care of my children?'

'Mrs Wallis? Did you hear everything I said?'

Vicky just stared blankly back at him.

John turned and looked questioningly at Janice.

Janice nodded and then in a voice that sounded hoarse and broken said, 'I think she heard. She just needs to take it all in and process it.'

John smiled a knowing sad smile, sighed and then touched Vicky's hand. 'I am really sorry. If there's anything you need, please, just ask.'

Vicky just continued staring blankly ahead.

'Thank you, doctor,' said Janice.

John nodded, patted Janice's hand, then got up and left the room.

Vicky continued to stare blankly ahead.

'Oh, my poor girl. My poor, poor girl.' Janice stood up from her chair and sat on the bed hugging Vicky so tightly. Vicky could feel her mother's body shaking uncontrollably as her mother began to cry. She didn't have the energy to return her mother's embrace. Vicky just continued to stare vacantly at the far wall over her mother's crying shoulder.

Vicky frowned. How long had that paint on the opposite wall been peeling for, she wondered.

———

Jagpal went through the pile of letters on his desk before starting his clinic. One stuck out from the rest of the pile. It was from the local hospital and had the large practice stamp on it with the words 'new cancer patient' scrawled across the top.

He picked it up and read it. 'Oh shit.'

TRISTAN

LATE OCTOBER 2017

'Tristan D'eath, Ms Fitzpatricks's oncologist,' announced Tristan to the nurse at the desk, as she smiled up at him in welcome.

'Take a seat. We're waiting for him.'

'I'm sorry?'

'If you take a seat over there.' Linda pointed to a rather oversized arm chair opposite the lift. 'He hasn't arrived yet.'

'No, I am the oncologist. I'm Tristan D'eath.'

'Oh, I'm sorry.' Linda blushed a light shade of pink. 'Let me gather everyone together and I'll let Ms Fitzpatrick know you're here.'

Linda laughed to herself as she walked away in the opposite direction. 'My, my,' she said to herself, 'what a name for an oncologist.'

—————

Joanna brushed Liz's hair. Liz didn't have time to have a wash. She straightened up her crumpled hospital gown, brushed her teeth and put some lip gloss on.

Gareth arrived. Liz went through her list of questions

once again with him and Joanna as if planning a military attack. Then they all sat and waited in silence. Where was he? Liz's life was now dependent on someone she had never met before.

After about fifteen minutes there was a knock at the door. Linda's head appeared around the edge of the door.

'He's here,' she announced. 'Are you ready?'

Liz took a deep breath. 'Yes, we are.'

The door opened and in walked a young dark-haired man with a trail of nurses behind him.

Liz looked behind the young man, searching for someone more senior to be following him in. This must be the registrar, she thought.

No one else came in.

'Hi,' he said as he smiled and came over to Liz and shook her hand. 'I'm Tristan D'eath, your oncologist.'

She smiled back at him. 'I'm Liz.' She indicated to her right and then to her left. 'This is my husband Gareth, and this is my sister Joanna.'

Liz studied the man in front of her. So this was Mr Kuntz-Finger's right-hand man, Tristan the oncologist who's been sent in to salvage my remains. Liz wondered how someone so young looking could have the knowledge to get her out of this predicament and his surname definitely did nothing to reassure her.

Tristan sat there in his black suit with his crisp white open neck shirt and rather smart cuff links. His short dark hair was gelled to within minutes of its life. He seemed to know what he was talking about, though. He answered all Liz's questions and strangely she felt she could trust him. Well, maybe not completely… maybe just a little bit?

He reassured Liz that ovarian cancer was hard to pick up in the early stages and said he didn't think a laparoscope would have picked anything up any earlier.

What a strange thing to say, thought Liz. Had Mr Kuntz-Finger mentioned that Liz had asked for a laparoscope when she initially saw him in the May and June? Was he asking Tristan to back up his story? Liz frowned. She would have to be on her guard.

———

The daily ritual of blood taking had resulted in Liz's body resembling a virtual pin cushion. Her arms were black and blue. She had no veins left. Chemo would require regular venous access so Tristan informed her she would need a portacath inserted into her chest for them to administer the chemo.

Liz had the portacath inserted a week later. Three weeks after surgery the chemotherapy began.

———

Tristan, November 2017

Tristan sat behind his mahogany desk gripping the edges to steady himself. He'd had a very busy day. Starting work early that morning, he'd completed his NHS rounds and then made his way for coffee in the high street. His clinic had started at eleven and patients had been back-to-back all day. The oncology nurse specialist Anna was with him for the afternoon.

Anna was having friends round that evening. She still hadn't decided what to prepare for dinner. She would have plenty of time to go to Marks and Spencer on the way home, though.

Tristan had been preoccupied on and off throughout the day. He was hoping he could get away on time for his boxing class that evening. He'd just bought some new rather smart black patent leather shoes and was wearing them for the first time. He couldn't help but keep looking down to admire them, although they were starting to pinch a bit. He would have to limit the time he wore them for. He would try to remember tomorrow to bring his comfortable pair of loafers to change into. He needed to buy some more hair gel tonight. If he finished on time, he could get across to the nearby department store and then be at his boxing class in good time.

These distractions all went out of the window when Liz Fitzpatrick arrived, as this woman was really losing it.

'You can sit in that chair all day long and talk until you're blue in the face. It won't make any difference... I don't believe a word you're saying and I never will.'

She was half sitting, half leaning over the desk pointing at Tristan as if she was about to leap across and hit him. She appeared half mad. Her hair was thinning from the first round of chemo and she was possibly high on the steroids he'd prescribed, so he guessed it might be best to just let her run with it. She would tire herself out eventually, he hoped. Anna, bless her, did try to interject but was swiftly cut down as Liz snarled and began to shout at her also.

Liz had seemed so placid and sweet when Tristan first met her. Iain had warned him she might be angry and that he thought she might be starting to investigate her care.

Tristan explained it was just one of those things and that it was common for the signs and symptoms to not appear immediately; the scans were not great at picking up the early stages of disease. He avoided the question of why no tumour marker had been taken by Iain. 'Best not to draw attention to these things,' Iain had said.

When Liz questioned how it had not been there one minute and then an aggressive raging tumour the next, despite her presenting for over nine months, he explained she had a very aggressive form of ovarian cancer. Unfortunately she wasn't buying into any of it. He should never have asked about her recent counselling session. That was what had set her off. She said it wasn't helpful in respect of the fact that she'd been misdiagnosed and nothing would ever help her come to terms with that. Tristan stupidly tried to explain yet again how the disease was aggressive and the scans had not seen anything.

This was going to be a problem. He would have to warn Iain.

16

LIZ
NOVEMBER 2017

*L*iz was raging. How dare Tristan try and make excuses for that man! Mr Kuntz-Finger was an idiot and she proceeded to tell Tristan that if Mr Kuntz-Finger ever came near her again she would kill him. She demanded all her notes and asked to be taken out of his care. She proceeded to tell Tristan how Mr Kuntz-Finger had even omitted to perform a physical assessment and therefore could never have come to a differential diagnosis. She quoted section 2.2 of the national guidelines on the ovarian cancer diagnosis pathway, with regards to physical examination being integral to the clinical examination process.

'If it was so integral, why had it not happened?' she demanded.

Tristan couldn't answer all her questions. He looked frightened and slightly shocked as he shrank back in his chair.

Liz could barely see through the tears. 'That man never even examined me,' she screamed. 'Don't you think you've heard the last of this. I'm going to get to the bottom of this if it takes all but my last breath. How can a scan show something one minute, be clear the next and then three months later have cancer spreading like wildfire? You must think I'm thick. Everyone's looking at the scans and not at the bloody patient sitting in front of them. And another thing,' Liz jabbed her finger repeatedly at Tristan, 'you would think if you are going to rip open someone's abdomen and tear their ovaries out that they would look at the suture line at least once in the post-operative period.'

Where was Gareth? He should have been here by now. It was typical that he was late. Just when Liz really needed him. He would probably turn up as they were attempting to put the straight jacket on and whisk her away to the Nightingale psychiatric hospital a few blocks away.

As if right on cue there was a gentle knock on the door, and in walked Gareth.

'Hi, hun.' Gareth leant over planting a kiss on Liz's cheek and sat down. 'Did I miss anything?'

Gareth was met with a deathly silence.

Liz slowly turned back in her chair to face Tristan and Anna with the sweetest of smiles painted across her face. 'We've just been discussing my lack of care, haven't we?'

'Oh right,' said Gareth beginning to feel slightly on edge as he settled down into the armchair. He glanced from Liz to a rather shocked looking Tristan and the nurse. He knew well enough not to ask anything further. He was certain he would get a blow-by-blow account from Liz afterwards.

'So, how long have I got then?' Liz demanded, directing her question at Tristan.

Tristan looked down at his desk and started to nervously shuffle some papers in front of him.

Liz leant forward in her chair and said in a low growl, 'Come on then, give it to me. Or do you want to withhold that information from me as well?'

'Umm, you have been told your prognosis, haven't you?' Tristan prayed that at the very least Iain had done that for him. But no… it appeared not.

Liz frowned looking upwards, cocking her head to her

left, as she sucked on her lower lip, trying to create an image of intense concentration. 'Ohh yes, let me see now... In a letter from you... Yes that's it.' Liz pointed a finger at Tristan. 'I received a letter from *you* saying it was obviously a difficult and anxious time for me with a diagnosis of an advanced malignancy. So if that's what you mean by being told about my disease, then yes, I guess so.'

Tristan started frantically reshuffling his papers, attempting to look through them, but not actually being able to focus on anything. He was beginning to feel quite terrified of this woman.

'Umm,' he stuttered. 'but you were told before that.'

'No. No, I was not,' she bellowed. 'You asked me what I understood about my diagnosis when I was in hospital. I *told* you I had *not* been told anything, but that I thought that it was possibly stage three or four cancer. I asked Mr Kuntz-Finger several times to discuss this with me. He told me that he didn't think it would be helpful to discuss my prognosis as I was a very sick woman, and needed to concentrate on getting better to give myself the best possible chance of survival. Would you care to expand on that because here's your chance?'

————

Tristan didn't get his hair gel that evening and he was late for his boxing class.

Anna had to get takeaways for her dinner guests. They were not impressed.

————

A less than 50 per cent chance of living past the next three to five years. That's what he said. What the fuck? How did this happen? Gareth just sat staring at the wall, dumbfounded. He'd told his wife to believe in Mr Kuntz-Finger and now look what had happened.

———

Tristan phoned Iain.

'Hi Iain. Sorry to bother you but I thought you should know. Elizabeth Fitzpatrick is not very happy.'

'I guessed she wouldn't be,' replied Iain, sighing.

'Well, I've just had her in my rooms for a follow up and she was rather irate.'

'Oh?' Iain sat upright in his chair like an animal sensing danger.

'Yes,' continued Tristan. 'She's refused to continue under your care. She has requested that no further correspondence about her be given to you, and she said she's going to leave no stone unturned as she thinks she was misdiagnosed.'

'Oh dear,' said Iain, realising this was not going to go away any time soon.

'She's asked for another gynae oncologist to see her. She also mentioned contacting a lawyer.'

17

IAIN

*I*ain had a sick feeling in his stomach all evening.

'Would you please keep quiet?' growled Iain to Sebastian, Amelia and Oscar. They were arguing again about which car was better… a Porsche or a Lamborghini.

Oscar had Stick Man on his lap and started poking Sebastian with its arms. 'Lamborghini, Lamborghini, Lamborghini.' Amelia hit Oscar with her doll so Oscar retaliated by poking Amelia with Stick Man.

'Go away, Oscar. Stop annoying me,' whined Amelia.

'For goodness' sake,' shouted Iain, as he grabbed Stick Man and threw him. The children's eyes followed Stick Man's flight path as he flew across the room and hit the far wall. As he landed on the floor the children's wide-eyed stares moved from the toy's lifeless form up to their father. Oscar's eyes were the size of saucers. A few seconds later came the tears. And a blood curdling howl.

'Why did you do that?' demanded Louise, as she raced to grab Stick Man from the floor and then embraced Oscar in her arms, trying to soothe the sobbing child.

'Daddy tried to kill Stick Man,' giggled Sebastian.

'Poor Stick Man,' said Amelia crossing her arms across her chest in consternation. 'Daddy is *mean.*'

Oscar let out another wail as Iain sighed in exasperation and stormed off.

That night Stick Man went missing. He was nowhere to be found. Louise searched everywhere. Oscar was hysterical. He could not sleep without him. He was inconsolable for days.

———

Stick Man sat in the window of the charity shop staring vacantly out onto Hampstead High Street. He'd had a rough few days.

Louise was about to meet a friend for coffee. She popped into the shoe shop to pick up her new running shoes then walked back out on to the high street, lost in thought. She was worried about Oscar. He was struggling to sleep. He was such a sensitive young boy. Louise couldn't fathom what could have become of Stick Man. She had questioned Sebastian and Amelia. They genuinely appeared to not know. She would have to buy another one and embroider Oscar's initials into its head, hoping he wouldn't notice.

Louise found herself outside the charity shop next door to the coffee shop. She quickly glanced at her reflection in the window and flicked her hair behind her ear and straightened her jacket. She did a double take as the image she saw in the corner of her eye registered in her brain. She recognised that vacant stare. There was Stick Man staring straight back at her out of the window.

'Hmmm,' Louise said. She moved closer and her eyes narrowed. All Stick Men looked the same, but there was something about this one. This was no ordinary Stick Man. She entered the shop.

Louise walked up to the counter and pointed to the window display. 'Could I have a look at that Stick Man please,' she said to the shop assistant.

'Of course.' The assistant retrieved the toy from the

window display and handed him to Louise. She checked the top of his head to see OKF embroidered in black thread.

'How much?' asked Louise.

———

'I have a bone to pick with you,' said Louise that evening, as she sat down for supper with Iain.

'Hmmm,' said Iain.

'Yes. I found this in the local charity shop.' She produced Stick Man and shook it at Iain.

Iain looked slowly up from his meal. 'Really? Well buying another one of those ridiculous looking toys is not going to help, is it? I mean, the boy should be playing with dinosaurs not soft toys.'

'It is not another one. It's Oscar's Stick Man.' Louise was shaking the toy at Iain and pointing to its head. 'See… I embroidered his initials on the top of his head to avoid losing him. So, my question to you is, how did it get to the local charity shop? I'm guessing you had something to do with it?'

Iain looked back down at his meal, attempting to appear disinterested. He decided it might be best to concentrate intently on cutting his carrots which were lying on the dinner plate in front of him. Without looking up he replied, 'I really don't know what you're talking about.'

Louise leaned over the table and growled though her teeth. 'What the hell is the matter with you? What kind of sick person takes a child's toy and gives it away to a charity shop? Oscar has been inconsolable for weeks. I don't know what's going on with you lately but you need to take a long hard look at yourself.'

She pushed the chair back, intentionally scraping the legs of the chair on the floor as loud as possible, stood up, turned and strode across the room. 'Oh, and you can sleep in the spare room for the foreseeable future,' she called over her shoulder. With that she disappeared into the hallway slamming the door behind her.

Iain threw his fork across the room. It hit the far wall and clattered to the floor.

'Fuck! Damn that Fitzpatrick woman.'

18

SARAH

LATE FEBRUARY 2017

*S*arah was admitted to the gynaecology ward after the drain was inserted. She thought she was going to pass out when they did it. The doctor explained she needed to be awake but when he forced the tube through her abdominal wall she screamed. Thank God that was over. Now, hopefully, she could rest.

George arrived with a grave look on his face. He had managed to get Trisha to take Patrice for a walk and feed the cats. Laura was settling her children but had already left ten voice messages.

'Laura, I'm okay. Please don't worry the children,' she pleaded.

'Of course not, darling, but I had to tell Mum and Dad, they would have killed me if they'd found out afterwards. They're on their way. Mum will drive your car home for you.'

'I'm so sorry to have worried everyone so needlessly,' said Sarah. 'I'm sure it's just a routine scan and the fluid's probably nothing. You know us women once we hit the menopause. Everything starts going south!'

———

'Hello Mr and Mrs Postlewaite,' said a rather distinguished young man. 'I'm Charles, the gynae registrar.'

Sarah smiled at the young doctor. 'One of my twins is called Charlie.'

'How old are they?' asked the registrar.

'Twenty-one, both at university now. All my babies have flown the nest. It's just the two of us. Oh, and Patrice our dog, and our two cats Betsie and Boris.'

'That still sounds a handful,' said the lovely Charles.

Sarah was not sure if it was the name, but she decided she was fond of Charles.

He dragged a chair up to the side of the bed. It was only then that Sarah noticed that he had a nurse accompanying him. He introduced Lisa, who stood at the end of the bed. This was starting to look ominous, Sarah thought.

George anxiously looked from Lisa to Charles. 'Do you have any news from the scans?' he asked.

'Yes, we do,' replied Charles. 'Mrs Postlewaite, can I ask you how long you've been feeling unwell?'

'Ooh, I've been feeling unwell for some time.'

'And can you describe what you mean by unwell?'

'I've been complaining of feeling bloated, feeling full very quickly after eating, urinary frequency and urgency, lower abdominal pain… but my GP knows this and referred me to a gynae consultant in Harley Street. He's been treating me for urinary tract infections for over six months now.'

'Mrs Postlewaite…'

'No, please call me Sarah.'

'Sarah, your scans show a large amount of fluid in your abdomen. A sample of that fluid has been sent to the lab.

We've put a drain in which should help make you feel a bit more comfortable for now. The CT scan gives us a much clearer picture of what's going on. We have taken some blood and are running some tumour markers and waiting for these results to confirm our suspicions.'

The lovely Charles paused for a moment. 'Sarah, I'm afraid this is not good news. You have cancer which has spread to your abdomen. We suspect this is ovarian in origin… Could you give us the name of the consultant you saw in Harley Street? Sarah…'

———

Sarah felt like she was having a bad dream. She remembered the countless visits to her Harley Street gynaecologist. She had asked him if he needed to take a blood test but he had reassured her these were not necessary. So why were the doctors taking tumour markers for ovarian cancer? A Ca 125 test, they said. Hers came back elevated at 1986. They told her the normal was thirty-six. So why didn't her gynaecologist take a simple blood test? She'd googled her symptoms and asked Mr Ashren if it could be ovarian cancer. He'd chuckled and said, 'No, you have a urinary tract infection.'

———

'We have the results of your blood tests and biopsy results. We can confirm you do have ovarian cancer. It has spread into the abdomen. We'll need to operate and try and remove what we can. Depending on what we find, we can then make a plan. You'll require chemotherapy following surgery. We normally plan to do this fairly quickly, usually within three weeks. I am so sorry. We will do everything we can.'

19

LIZ

*T*he chemo was relentless. Liz was petrified when she'd gone for the first infusion. It was the sense that as soon as the first infusion started she would have to accept she was a cancer patient. Up to that point she could convince herself she was still 'normal'.

Liz had lain on the couch in the chemo suite, with Gareth holding her hand, willing the chemo to go and do its job. Twenty-four hours after the chemo she required an injection to boost her white blood cells. The following day she couldn't move. To lift her head from the pillow required every ounce of strength she could muster. It was a sense of being slowly poisoned… drip… drip… drip. It felt as if the life force was gradually being sucked from her body. Every movement made her body ache. Her thighs felt like lead weights and she had to live with a constant background nausea. She was given strong antiemetics, but these had their own set of unpleasant side effects… Liz had never given birth, but she likened the experience of her first post chemo poo to this. At one point she was convinced she was pulling Lego bricks from her rear end.

Twenty-one days after the first chemo her hair started to fall out. That was the worst bit. Losing her hair. Liz had resorted to wearing headscarves. She had spent over eight hundred pounds on a wig, but it was too itchy and uncomfortable so ended up in a drawer. She'd managed to master different headscarf styles and had a few 1920's style bamboo hats which she quite liked. Olivia offered to shave Liz's head in an attempt to get rid of the last long wispy remnants of hair that remained attached to her scalp. As Liz stared into the bathroom mirror waiting for her hair to be shaved off, she saw an emaciated balding woman staring back at her.

'Are you ready?' asked Olivia, as she squeezed Liz's shoulder gently.

'Yes,' whispered Liz. She took a deep breath. The tears began to fall down her cheeks as she could not contain her emotions any longer.

It actually was not that bad once she had it shaved off.

Gareth said she suited having a bald head. They say love is blind and Liz definitely felt this was true in Gareth's case. Every time she would put a new outfit on, buy a new pair of shoes or just get ready to go out, she would ask him, 'How do I look?'

He would always reply, 'You look a picture, hun,' and kiss her. Liz didn't know what she had done to deserve him.

Liz would say to Gareth, 'But you'd say I looked beautiful even if I had two heads.'

'I'd prefer it if you had two heads then you could talk to yourself,' he replied.

Gareth sometimes dreamed of that scenario... most often when she was on her soap box about something.

When Gareth said, 'In sickness and in health,' she never thought those words would mean so much. Gareth bathed Liz when she was too weak to wash herself. He would cook meals and bring them upstairs to her when she was too weak to walk. He was there when she was crying from the pain or vomiting from the chemo. He stayed up all night when she was on a high from the steroids... just sitting, talking to her.

He was there at every appointment. Liz could see the fear etched on his face. He couldn't stop worrying about what was happening to his wife and what the future might hold. One moment they had their whole lives ahead of them and now it was a future so bleak... How could this have happened? Liz had always said, 'At least we have our health and we have each other. That's all we need.' She knew that a future alone was not one Gareth was looking forward to; he was trying to stay brave for her sake.

———

Liz decided to ignore the information given to her. They had said 'don't google anything.' To Liz this therefore meant google everything. She had a Master's degree and could read a research paper. She was not an idiot.

How to kill your gynaecologist unfortunately came up with no results. There were some interesting results on gynaecologists killing their wives, though, which didn't surprise her. She googled Tristan to find out how well qualified he was. He seemed to know what he was doing so she guessed he couldn't be completely thick. She googled the chemo regime she was given. It was not that she didn't trust Tristan... she now questioned everything.

———

Unfortunately for Iain, Liz decided to gain access to all her medical notes. He had changed the date of her collapse in his notes to his colleagues from February to several months later and documented Liz as never having had endometriosis. She engaged a lawyer to investigate, but he informed her that they would need an expert opinion for the case to be considered. It was no surprise that there were few gynae medical experts in the country.

20

ALICE

MAY 2016

*A*lice woke with dreadful right shoulder and chest pain. Her abdomen also felt very bloated. She had tried laxatives but they didn't relieve the distension. They only gave her diarrhoea. It had been three months since the pelvic ultrasound. The results had been clear but she'd felt increasingly worse. Dr Pinkham had completed another referral, to another gynaecologist at Alice's request. This appointment was scheduled for next week. She definitely wasn't going back to that dreadful little Fuker Howard chap.

Alice couldn't deal with the discomfort any longer. She rose from her bed and phoned a cab, then she went to her dressing room and started opening drawers, grabbing a grey cashmere turtleneck sweater, some yoga pants and a mid-thigh length cashmere shawl collar cardigan from her wardrobe. She placed a pair of flat black pumps on her feet before scribbling Hugh a note for when he woke.

A message flashed across Alice's phone screen telling her the cab was waiting. She quietly made her way downstairs, closing the front door softly behind her. Alice stopped for a few seconds to look behind her at the door. For some reason she felt nothing would ever be the same when she returned. A slight shiver went down her spine. She shuddered, pulled her cardigan around her shoulders and walked down the steps onto the pavement, out into the cool night air.

The journey didn't take long in the early hours of the morning. The cab dropped her at the entrance to Chelsea and Westminster emergency department. As soon as Alice entered she could tell she was going to be in for a long wait. The waiting room was very busy. She went up to the desk and gave her details and was given a number and told to take a seat. She managed to find a seat on the far wall between a young man with a rather large gash on his forehead and what appeared to be a very confused elderly man.

After an hour and a half, the triage nurse came to find her. Alice was taken to a curtained off area where the nurse took a brief history, bloods and asked for a urine sample. She was then sent back into the waiting area.

About another two hours passed before Alice was seen. The young man in the waiting area had long gone. The confused gentleman had managed to flood the men's toilets after stuffing his socks in the sink.

Alice was finally shown into a cubicle. A young female doctor came in and examined her chest.

'It's my chest and shoulder pain, on the right-hand side, that's so bad,' said Alice. 'I'm not having a heart attack, am I? I mean it's the wrong arm.'

'I think you may have some fluid in your chest,' said the young doctor. 'We'll send you for an ultrasound.'

Alice went for the ultrasound and then returned to the waiting area and once again sat and waited.

———

'Mrs Ellis Bledisloe?'

Where was that voice coming from? Alice opened her eyes. Oh no, how did I get here?

'Mrs Ellis Bledisloe, you're in hospital. How are you

feeling?' said a young girl hovering over her. 'My name's Lucy,' she continued. 'I'm the gynaecology registrar. You came in last night to A&E and collapsed after your ultrasound scan.'

'Oh my goodness, I'm so sorry. I hope I didn't make a fool of myself,' Alice replied apologetically.

'Not at all,' said Lucy as she sat down in the chair next to Alice and held her hand.

'Are you okay, dear?'

'Yes, I am.' replied Lucy. 'Mrs Ellis—'

'No, call me Alice, dear.'

'Alice,' repeated Lucy. 'Alice, we have reviewed your ultrasound results and you have a large amount of fluid in your abdomen, as well as your lungs. We're going to need to drain the fluid in your abdomen and send a sample of this and the fluid in your lungs to the lab. Draining the fluid from your abdomen should make you more comfortable. Your husband is on his way.'

Alice found the drain insertion into her chest excruciating despite the sedation, but she got through it and only passed out once. She couldn't get rid of a sense of impending doom and thought everyone looked rather too concerned to be performing routine tests. A sample was sent off to the lab. She also had a CT scan and was transferred back to her room. When she arrived back on the ward Hugh was there causing chaos at the reception desk, demanding Alice be taken to a private room immediately. She could hear him before she even reached the ward.

Hugh rushed towards her. 'Oh, darling, there you are. I've been worried sick.'

'I'm fine. Stop fussing and please stop trying to move me to a private ward. I'm sure I'll be going home soon.'

———

'I am afraid you have stage four ovarian cancer… incurable… spread to the lymph, brain and lungs. The fluid in your lungs is from your abdomen… We will refer you to the oncology team as we are unable to operate. They will discuss the treatment plan with you. It may be a combination of chemotherapy and some brain radiotherapy to try and shrink the tumours and make you more comfortable. I'm so sorry…'

Alice thought she was dreaming. A nightmare, yes that was it. It had to be. If she had cancer the doctors would have found it before this. She thought of Reginald Fuker Howard and suddenly felt rather ill. You wait until I get my hands on that fat little bastard.

'Where's Tarquin?' Alice asked. 'I want to see Tarquin.'

'Do you think she's okay, Daddy?' asked Sophie. 'How on earth are we ever going to find Tarquin?'

———

Tarquin was on a cloud. It was blue and purple, and the ants were dancing to *Staying Alive* on an old man's head. The old man had one eye and three legs. A rainbow appeared and then exploded into a thousand stars. Tarquin's hands started to grow. Sprouts were coming from beneath his nails… wait no… snails… God, they were snails not nails. He had to get moving. Where are my legs? They're here somewhere. I know I put them here somewhere.

'Hello,' said the man in the balloon. 'Where are you going? Would you like to come along in my balloon?'

Tarquin said, 'Yes please,' without even saying a word.

The man in the balloon smiled and beckoned him. Tarquin hopped in. Of course, there were his legs. He still had them.

'Oh God, I've pissed myself again,' moaned Tarquin as he rolled over in a pile of wet bedclothes. His head hurt and his body shook. He was hungry. Helen was coming down as well and she was ravenous.

'Let's look for some food,' he said.

They left the flat and realised they had no cards or money on them. They were so hungry. They passed a cookie shop and Tarquin's stomach grumbled. He found an old chair in the alley at the back of the shop. He picked it up and ran round the front, throwing the chair through the window. Glass shattered over the pavement and the alarm went off.

Helen and Tarquin jumped through the broken window and started filling up bags full of cookies. They were stuffing them in their mouths as they filled up the bags when the police arrived. They were so full they couldn't move from the middle of the shop floor. 'Whoah man, careful. Watch the cookies, man.'

Tarquin was in the cells waiting for his mother to come and get him out. Where was she? She always came and bailed him out. He wasn't sure if she was going to bail Helen out again, though. He'd phoned her on her mobile but it had gone to voice mail. How long would she leave him here?

———

'Reggie? This is Percival. Uhh huh. Yes. Oh yes, dinner was lovely, thank you. Umm, listen old chap, just a heads up. Alice Ellis Bledisloe. Yes, that's right. Well, umm, the thing is, old chap, she's been admitted to hospital and they've confirmed she has stage four ovarian cancer. Reggie? Reggie? Are you there?'

Reginald had put the phone down on the desk, staring at the wall opposite. He took a deep breath and picked the phone up again. 'Yes, yes Percival. I'm still here. Well now, that's dreadful news. I should go and see her. She'll need surgery, I assume.'

'No, too far gone for that, I'm afraid. It's everywhere.'

'Dear, dear,' muttered Reginald. 'She was a fine woman. Oh well, can't be helped. Still I should pop in and see her.'

'I wouldn't do that, old chap,' warned Percival.

'Why not?'

'Well, she has said she doesn't want you anywhere near her.'

'Oh dear, dear,' muttered Reginald again.

He suddenly didn't feel too well.

21

LIZ

JANUARY 2018

*B*y chance, Liz found a forum online for ovarian cancer survivors. Maybe talking to others who have been through the same thing might help me, she thought. She created an account under the name of Fitzypat21 and decided to introduce herself. She might have said a bit too much for her introduction but she actually felt better once she had got things off her chest. She received several replies. Mostly sympathy from fellow sufferers who extolled the virtues of being found earlier than her but then slowly more replies came in from people in exactly the same situation, and some were in a much worse state.

Fit bit:

My mother was admitted last night to A&E. Please can we have some advice? We don't know what to do. She's been complaining of abdominal pain for over a year now and has been to so many doctors. Today, she collapsed at home with abdominal pain and we rushed her into hospital. They scanned her and now she's having fluid drained from her abdomen but they think her stomach has been perforated. The on-call doctor doesn't seem to know what to do. We've been told we have to wait until Monday for the surgeon to review her. We're so worried.

Fitzypat21:

Oh God, that's terrible. Are you all okay? How are you coping?

Fit bit:

Too late. Mum passed away an hour ago.

Susy75:

I was diagnosed with stage four ovarian cancer. I went to A&E and they told me I had irritable bowel syndrome. They sent me home. Two weeks later I was back there and collapsed. That was when they found it.

Mary Lou 26:

I have stage four ovarian cancer. I was turned away by the GP for nine months with 'indigestion' and saying I was a hypochondriac. If only I'd been taken seriously…

Sallymae may:

My GP missed it and a gynae specialist diagnosed me with a uterus infection without a physical examination. Finally, another GP sat down and went through the symptoms with me. I was at the end of my tether just sobbing. I was stage four when it was found.

Vicks71:

I was diagnosed with stage four ovarian cancer. I went to the GP and he told me I was worrying unnecessarily. He treated me for urinary tract infections for six months.

Lucinda x:

I was diagnosed with stage 3c ovarian cancer. I went to doctors for over nine months and they kept sending me away. It was only when I collapsed and had to be blue-lighted to A&E that it was found.

PatriceP:

Hi. Welcome to the party, Fitzypat21. I was under my gynaecologist for over six months and he said I had a urinary tract infection. When I went back to tell him I had been diagnosed with ovarian cancer stage 3c, he seemed genuinely surprised.

AliCe65:

I had been under a gynaecologist for several months after presenting with urinary issues. I had an ultrasound which I was told was clear. I continued to have pelvic discomfort. I was told it was my age. When I saw him again I had a physical exam and complained of continuing pain. A month later I was suffering from shoulder and chest pain which eventually led me to being diagnosed with a pleural effusion and 1.5 litres of fluid drained and analysed after presenting to A&E. They did a CAT scan and I was diagnosed as stage four high grade serous.

I don't know what else I personally could have done. It's incredibly frustrating and I go over it sometimes but I can't change my diagnosis.

Day in and day out the same messages kept arriving in Liz's account.

Daisy56:

You need to concentrate on getting yourself better Fitzypat21 and learn to bag your anger. You have to let it go and forgive. I like to go for walks with my family to ground me.

We'll be under the fucking ground and long forgotten if Daisy56 keeps bleating on about forgiveness, thought Liz. And who's she to tell me how to deal with my anger anyway?

22

MR DINESH ASHREN

LATE FEBRUARY 2017

*W*hen Sarah phoned Dinesh Ashren's secretary and asked to speak to him urgently, he didn't reply for twenty-four hours. When Sarah told him the news, he seemed genuinely surprised and told her he would contact her GP to find out the details. He said he was sorry to hear the news and that the disease must be very aggressive seeing as there were no signs of it during the time she had been under his care.

Sarah explained that there would be a wait for surgery at her local hospital and she was being transferred to a private facility. Dinesh immediately offered to perform her surgery.

He put the phone down. He was shaking. Beads of sweat were starting to appear on his brow. His mind was racing. He leant forward and buzzed Gloria.

'Gloria?'

'Yes, Mr Ashren?'

'Could you bring me Sarah Postlewaite's notes,' he demanded.

'Yes certainly, Mr Ashren.'

Gloria sighed. He sounded like he was in another of his bad moods. This was going to be a fun day. She opened the filing cabinet drawer and flicked through until she located Sarah Postlewaite's set of notes. She lifted them out of the filing cabinet and took them into Mr Ashren.

'Are you okay?'

'Yes, I'm fine.'

'You look pale.'

'Must be something I ate. Could you leave me please, Gloria? I have quite a bit of work to get on with.'

Gloria shrugged, turned on her heels and slammed the door behind her.

Dinesh gritted his teeth as the sound of the door slamming resonated around the room. 'That damn woman,' he muttered under his breath, 'she really gets on my wick.'

He opened the file lying on the desk in front of him and looked at his handwritten notes. They were rather brief. The dates she visited and not much medical history. It only mentioned her two pregnancies and her menstrual history. Then he had mentioned her bladder scan as being clear and the antibiotic courses she had been put on.

Bugger! Why hadn't he written any more? Everyone expected too much of him these days. He was a busy man. At least in the NHS they gave him junior doctors who he could blame for poor note taking. That was their job.

He felt rather ill. He poured himself a glass of scotch. That made him feel a bit better. No, he was being silly. No one would question him. He had ordered a scan and it was clear. So what if he hadn't done a tumour marker or recognised her signs and symptoms as ovarian cancer? They all banked on people referring to it as the 'silent killer'. Some of the ovarian cancer charities were making noises and trying to stop people referring to it as this, but it wouldn't stick. The medical profession would leave themselves wide open if they allowed this to happen. At least he could monitor things if she was still under his care. He smiled, as he poured himself another scotch, put his feet up on the desk and relaxed back in his chair.

23

LIZ
MAY 2018

*L*iz did not get very far with her legal campaign. She went back on the forum to vent her frustration and anger at the injustice within the system.

Fitzypat21:

I cannot believe it. My lawyer says that unfortunately the expert's report supported my consultant in saying that he hadn't caused any neglect, as I would've had cancer even if he had detected it at an earlier stage, and the treatment would possibly have been the same. If I wish to continue to pursue him down the legal route I'll probably lose, and as he's barely documented anything in his medical notes, it would be my word against his. How is that right? I feel like they're trying to shut me up.

Apparently it doesn't seem to matter that if I'd been diagnosed earlier I would have had a greater chance of surviving.

AliCe65:

My dear girl, I sympathise with your concerns. You're having such a dreadful time, as are we all. I do hope you get some response from your dreadful consultant. I do hope you're looking for another one! I would give you some advice but mine was a complete idiot as well which is why I have stage four. PM me anytime if you need to chat.

Vicks71:

What a pack of bastards, Fitzypat21. It's unbelievable that we have to accept such poor bloody standards of care. I'm with you on this. We need to campaign for better care. My GP was useless. He completely ignored me.

Admin@supportdesk:

Could I please remind everyone that foul language is not appropriate for this forum. We need to be mindful of other users in the group. While we understand that some members are having a difficult time dealing with their diagnoses and treatment regimes, we cannot ignore bad language or inappropriate content in conversation threads.

Vicks71:

Are you fucking kidding me?

Admin@supportdesk:

Vicks71. If you would like to contact us directly we can discuss our online policy regarding content for posting. As previously mentioned, we cannot condone foul language or inappropriate content.

Vicks71:

I apologise if I have offended anyone with my foul language. Unfortunately I've just spent the last two years dealing with a terminal disease. A disease which could have been diagnosed at a much earlier stage if I hadn't had the misfortune of having a wanker of a GP. So if I do sound rather angry then I think I'm justified in sounding off somewhere. Would you prefer I 'bag my anger' as Daisy56 suggested to poor Fitzypat21? I mean, I could do that, but then I might have to just kill myself, as what's the point?

Admin@supportdesk:

Vicks71. I have referred your post to one of our nurse advisors. She can phone you to discuss. It might be a good idea to set up some counselling to help you process your anger. We are here for you.

Vicks71:

What the fuck?!! Seriously? Why does everyone think anger is a bad thing? I have every right to feel anger. If I don't express it, it could eat me up.

AliCe65:

My goodness, Vicks71, you are on fire! I think you and I might get along very well! PM me please. Let's swap details.

PatriceP:

Ohh, could I please swap numbers as well? I'd love to stay in touch with you both.

Admin@supportdesk:

Vicks71. We have reminded you about foul language…

Vicks71:

Yes I know you have. Unfortunately I am and therefore I have to you wouldn't read about it. I cannot believe so unfortunate.

PatriceP:

Vicks, I think your feed has just been edited!

Liz chuckled. How funny. These women sounded hilarious. But maybe she did need to bag her anger. Maybe she did need to see a therapist again. She'd attended an initial therapy session and decided it was not for her. The therapist sat there and listened to Liz sounding off. Every so often (usually after a long silent pause) the therapist would look at Liz and say, 'So how does that make you feel, Elizabeth?'

Maybe talking to the wall would be more helpful. At least she could throw something at the wall. She kept imagining ripping the clipboard out of the therapist's hands and throwing that at the wall. Now that would be satisfying…

24

JUNE 2018

'Those bastards would love me to get a brain tumour,' said Liz.

The headaches were blinding. She could hardly sit up and the room was spinning. Tristan had warned her about the side effects of Avastin. It was to stop the blood supply to her cancer cells and she needed eighteen infusions in total on top of her chemo. Liz was back at work a few days a week and didn't want to take any more time off. She phoned the resident doctor at the chemo clinic. He told her to take a paracetamol and go home and rest. Two days later she still had headaches. She phoned Tristan's secretary to say the headaches were not going away. Tristan organised a brain MRI.

'We've found something on your brain stem. It's tiny but we need to investigate further,' said Tristan. 'The report said it is indicative of metastatic burden… leptomeningeal disease. You may need whole brain radiotherapy.'

Leptomeningeal disease, cancer of the central nervous system. A slow and painful death.

Liz sat in front of Tristan an emaciated bald version of her former self. She patted her headscarf gently with her hand, checking it was still in position on her head, and then attempted to wipe the tears running down her cheeks. She didn't know how much more she could take. Every time she rallied and picked herself up she would be dealt another blow. It was like being a novice boxer in the rink with a pro. Iain Kuntz-Finger would be ecstatic.

She was rushed into hospital. A biopsy of her central spinal fluid was arranged. Several days later she was informed it may have been a false alarm as the tests were clear. They would monitor her every three months with a MRI of her brain and take bloods.

Hmm, funny how everyone panics now at the slightest symptom, she thought. A complete change to this time last year.

July 2018

AliCe64:

You poor thing! What a ghastly time you are having! I too have got nowhere with my consultant complaint and feel there are many more of us girls out there who are too sick to do anything about the poor care they've received. If you're in London perhaps we could meet and make a plan for action?

Fitzypat21:

I would love to meet up. Perhaps we could have coffee?

AliCe64:

Wonderful, my dear. I will PM you.

AliCe64:

Hi Vicks71 and PatriceP. I've just spoken with a new girl on the forum and she's based in London. She appears to be having a tough time, as are we all. Her gynae consultant sounds about as switched on as our idiots. She is very upset and angry and having trouble getting answers about her care. It might be nice for us all to meet up. How about lunch at my flat in Knightsbridge?

Vicks71:

Alice,

How about two weeks' time on the 27th? That would be great. I can text you my details.

PatriceP:

I'm free on the 27th but nothing after that for some time. Unfortunately my cancer has come back so I'll be starting chemo again the following week. Let me know the time and I'll be there. Who is the girl you are talking about?

AliCe64:

Twenty-seventh it is. For lunch around midday? The newbie is Fitzypat21. Gosh darling, we are all in the wars, aren't we? Take care of yourself.

PatriceP:

Hi Fitzypat21. I'm Sarah. I'm a stage 3c ovarian cancer patient and I have been in touch with AliCe64 and Vicks71.

You sound like you could do with some support from other OC girls. We're meeting up on the 27th, if you're free, at Alice's place in London. It would be wonderful to meet you.

Vicks71:

Hi Fitzypat21. Can't wait to meet you. Just to let you know we're all going to use our own personal emails from now on. We've PM'ed you all our contact details. I'm not allowed to swear on here so considering every second word is a swear word we thought it best I limit my presence.

Fitzypat21:

Understood. I saw the previous posts from admin.

Can't wait to meet you all.

———

Alice was excited about hosting a coffee session with people who sounded rather interesting! They might actually be people she could consider real friends at last. Now that would be fun. Maybe they could even go away somewhere for a weekend together.

25

LONDON

27TH JULY 2018

*A*t last, Liz thought, some like-minded people.

'What are you going to do?' asked Gareth.

'We're just meeting up for coffee at the moment. We'll see where it heads from there.'

'Right well remember, hun… don't get mad, get even.' Gareth planted three kisses on Liz's cheek. It was always three kisses.

'I'll see you tonight. Love you. Oh, and feed the cats before you go.'

'I love you too.'

With that he was gone.

Liz looked down at the two large hungry pairs of eyes staring up at her imploringly. Blossom, her long-haired brindle tortoiseshell cat sat alongside her son Peregrine, a rather large and affectionate black shorthaired creature. 'Hmmh let me guess. Hungry?'

'Meowww,' came the reply as Peregrine wrapped himself around Liz's legs. 'Right, let's feed you guys and get this show on the road.'

An hour later Liz was making her way into London and across to Knightsbridge. She walked from the depths of the busy underground Piccadilly line out into the warm sunlight and turned left onto the bustling Brompton Road past Harrods, continuing for several blocks eventually turning left into Egerton Gardens. Liz crossed to the right-hand side, gazing above her to admire the lovely set of old red brick apartments in front of her. The street was a sanctuary from the busy Brompton Road which was only metres away. Each apartment had a balcony overlooking the street below. Liz walked up the steps and peered at the door with the brass name plate. She read through the list of occupants as she wondered what it would be like to be able to afford to live in a street like this. Alice was obviously well off.

She checked her appearance in her phone camera. Her hair was starting to grow back, to the point where she'd had her first haircut since the chemo. Everyone thought she suited a pixie style. Were they just being polite? Liz had applied a light dusting of make-up and was wearing jeans, red ballet pumps and a blue and white patterned cotton sleeveless high neck top. She pressed the buzzer for flat number two and waited. A moment later the front door clicked as she was buzzed in. She walked up the narrow stairway and saw the front door to the flat was ajar.

'Hello,' she called out as she knocked on the door.

'Come in, my dear,' said a tall slim lady with short dark grey hair. 'You must be Elizabeth. Welcome. I'm Alice.'

Alice looked rather elegant in an Audrey Hepburn kind of way, with a wide welcoming smile. She was wearing a pair of black tailored wide leg linen trousers, a pair of black satin mules with a satin cream sleeveless high neck top.

'Sarah and Vicky are here already,' Alice said as she waved her hand behind her in the direction of the lounge. 'Come through, my dear.'

She ushered Liz through to a bright high-ceilinged lounge with two floor length doors opening onto a balcony.

The furnishings had the appearance of old money. There were several extremely large Georgian period oil paintings of not particularly attractive aristocrats with gilt edge frames adorning each wall. The room was furnished with two large comfortable old sofas facing each other, adorned with throws and large embroidered cushions. Issues of *Horse and Hound* and *The Lady* were piled on top of a large old mahogany coffee table which was positioned between the two sofas.

'Vicky, Sarah. This is Elizabeth,' said Alice as she fluttered her arms across towards Liz.

Two women seated on one of the sofas turned to greet Liz.

One was slightly overweight and of average height with shoulder length blonde hair (which looked very wig-like) pulled back into a pony tail. She had no make-up and was wearing trainers and faded blue jeans with a white T-shirt covered by a navy hoodie.

The other woman was average build with platinum blonde hair worn in a short bob. Wig? wondered Liz. She was wearing an oversized white linen blouse and navy blue linen trousers with navy blue pumps.

The two women stood up.

'Hello, how are you. I'm Sarah. It's lovely to meet you at last,' said the blonde woman in the linen blouse, offering her hand to Liz.

'Yeah, can't believe we all made it,' said the other woman. 'Hi, I'm Vicky.'

'I'm Liz,' said Liz shaking their hands in turn.

'Right girls,' said Alice, clapping her hands together. 'Now the formalities are over we can all sit down and relax. Is everyone for coffee? Now, if any of you are vegan, don't worry. I have oat milk and Maria does a wicked oat milk latte.'

'Oh, yes please,' said Liz. 'That would be wonderful.'

'Urgh,' said Vicky. 'Not for me. I'll have a normal latte with full fat cream.'

'Vicky, you should cut down on dairy, you know,' said Sarah.

'It's so difficult when you have five kids and it's very expensive to buy these milk alternatives.'

'I guess it must be,' Liz agreed.

Alice disappeared into the corridor.

'Who's Maria?' asked Liz.

'The maid and cook,' said Vicky. 'I think our hostess is rather well off.'

Alice reappeared and a few moments later a small Filipino woman with a crisp white apron over a grey dress with white piping scuttled in carrying a tray of coffees and pastries. Once the women had all settled down they began sharing their stories.

'It's very clear that we have all been through the mill,' said Alice.

'So, the question is, what do we do about it?' asked Vicky. 'No one seems to want to know. I'm just told it's the silent killer and it's hard to detect.'

'Yes,' said Sarah. 'I get told that all the time. They tell me that if I'd been diagnosed earlier, I'd still have had the same outcome. I don't understand. If I'd been diagnosed earlier then I would have an increased chance of surviving. When you say that, they change the subject. I feel that people are just hoping you'll listen to their ridiculous explanation and then either get tired, or ill, and go away. No one seems to want to put a value on our increased chances of surviving if we had been diagnosed earlier.'

'Too right,' said Vicky. 'My GP ignored my symptoms for months. When my husband got out of the nick and went to complain, they banned him from the surgery. If I could get my hands on that man, I'd kill him.'

'I'm certain my doctors hate me,' said Liz. 'I remember everything they say and repeat it back to them when they contradict themselves. I sometimes do it just for fun as it gives me great pleasure to see them sit and squirm. They deserve it if they aren't prepared to do anything about it.'

'Well, I'm not sure what the best course of action is,' said Alice. 'The fact we have made the effort to meet up is a start. Have any of you joined any of the campaigning with the support group?'

'Yes,' said Liz. 'I've enquired and will do some campaigning but I don't feel that will be enough. I mean most of the campaigning is around getting women to recognise their signs and symptoms and then going to their GP. That doesn't address the issue of what happens if you do go to your GP and the GP fobs you off or ignores your symptoms. Most women might not ask for a second opinion. And then there's my scenario which I was shocked to find is more common than I thought. What do you do if your GP refers you to specialists who ignore your symptoms or refuse to order specific tests and don't even look at the patient in front of them?'

'I don't know if anyone will support you in challenging the medical profession and the way they practise, my dear,' said Alice. 'It's one of the last male dominated bastions and they do not look kindly on anyone challenging them.'

'They have to change,' said Liz. 'Survival rates for ovarian cancer have only had a slight improvement since the 1970s. I mean look at breast cancer and how good the survival rates are.'

'Well,' said Alice, 'that's because men like breasts. They can't see your ovaries and they seem to think it's a disease of the menopause. Women have served their use to society once they reach that stage. We've given birth to, and nurtured, the next generation. We're only going to retire and drain the system in our pension years. What politician would back a campaign to improve statistics on a disease that only claims 4,000-plus women a year in the UK? There's no more money in the pot so you would be encouraging the government to take funds from cancer funds such as prostate, lung and breast cancer where there are much higher numbers of people afflicted, with a greater survival rate. It has so much more of a positive spin on it, and politicians *do* love a positive spin.'

Liz sat and stared at Alice aghast. 'So you think we're wasting our time, then? Just like everyone else has consistently told me since I began questioning my poor care. You think we should just go home to our husbands, curl up and prepare to die? We should just not worry that unless we do something to change the system other innocent women will follow us heading for the same fate?'

Liz was visibly shaking with rage.

Vicky and Sarah exchanged concerned glances.

'Well girls,' Alice said with a grin, as she turned to Sarah and Vicky. 'I told you. Here is our Joan of Arc.'

'Your what?' Liz was struggling to contain her anger.

'Joan of Arc,' repeated Alice. 'She was used to rally troops into battle in the Hundred Years' War. We have our own Hundred Years' War, and you sound like the ideal person to help us win it.'

'I know who Joan of Arc is,' said Liz impatiently. 'I just don't get what that has to do with me.'

Liz shook her head in astonishment.

'Alice, me shouting from the rooftops about the unfairness and injustices of the world does not win battles. I've learnt very quickly that my concerns are legitimate purely from the fact that my concerns are not being addressed by the medical profession. They're trying to contain me. And I don't like fire, so being burnt at the stake is not really my idea of fun.'

'I think if we pool our resources maybe we can come up with something,' suggested Sarah.

'Yeah,' said Vicky. 'Some mouthy women wouldn't go amiss. Nothing like girl power, I say.'

They were still chatting at three p.m.

'Oh my goodness, I need to be heading home,' said Sarah as she glanced at her phone checking the time. 'This has been so good to sit and chat.'

'Yeah,' said Vicky. 'We'll never get a plan in place unless we meet regularly or for a weekend, maybe. It's a shame we all live in different corners of London.'

'I suggest we all meet up again soon, health willing,' said Alice. 'How about we all have an integrative weekend retreat?'

'Wonderful,' said Sarah. 'Could we work it round my chemo? I start again next week and I'm not sure how I'll be feeling.'

'As long as it's not too expensive,' said Vicky.

'Don't worry about that,' said Alice, 'it will be on me.'

'Count me in, then,' said Vicky, smiling.

'Great,' said Liz.

Alice smiled as she slapped her hands on her thighs in delight. 'Right, that's settled then.'

———

After Liz, Vicky and Sarah had left, Alice poured herself a gin and tonic and sat down on the sofa. She smiled. For the first time in ages she had actually enjoyed herself. Sarah and Vicky were interesting, but that Liz… now she was a fascinating creature. A very angry woman. Just what they needed for their campaign. I'm going to be busy, Alice thought, as she tried to recall the name of the retreat Fi had recommended. Now what was it called again? Spring something? Springfield Hall, that was it.

'This is all going to be rather fun,' said Alice.

'Madam, why you talk to nobody?' Maria came bustling in to the room dressed in a bright yellow T-shirt and jeans. 'I go home now. You be okay? I don't like when you talk to nobody. So sad.'

Maria wagged her finger at Alice. 'I tell Mr Hugh if you keep chatting to nobody.'

'God forbid.' Alice raised her eyes skyward. Maria walked around the edge of the sofa and sat next to Alice. 'Madam, I cook your supper. It is in the microwave. I left instructions on bench for heating up. And madam, please, not too much.' Maria wagged her finger at Alice's gin and tonic.

'Oh good God, Maria. What are you? The police?'

Maria giggled and bent forwards to kiss Alice on the forehead.

'Yes, yes, alright.' Alice smiled and waved Maria away. 'Now off with you. See you tomorrow, my dear.'

Several moments later Alice had managed to find the number for Springfield Hall. She picked up the phone and dialled.

———

Alice set about organising the retreat. There were regular communications back and forth between the women.

'Sam Sherlock is meant to be amazing. They have a shaman and a herbalist and they do yoga and hot stone massages,' said Sarah, as she read from the website.

'They also do reflexology,' said Liz. 'It does sound lovely. Will we have time to discuss our campaign to raise awareness?'

'Of course, my dear,' said Alice.

'What about alcohol?' asked Vicky. 'I ain't going nowhere that bans alcohol.'

'Oh my dear, they always ban alcohol at these places. All you need to know is that when you've been to these retreats as many times as I have, one soon learns how to get round these things,' said Alice.

'Alright then,' said Vicky, 'you're on.'

26

INTEGRATIVE RETREAT
SEPTEMBER 2018

The women spent the morning packing before making their way to Ullswater in the Lake District. Liz, Alice, Vicky and Sarah all met at Euston Station for lunch and then made the three-hour journey by train to Penrith. At Penrith they hopped into a taxi and were driven for the final half hour of the journey. Springfield Hall was a secluded retreat set amongst woodland about ten minutes' drive from the nearest village, Glenridding. The taxi turned into a large stone gated entrance and continued along a long tree lined drive. This eventually opened up to a wider sweeping gravel driveway. As the taxi rounded the last bend of the drive the sixteenth century grade one listed stone facade of Springfield Hall lay before them. It was nestled amidst twenty-four acres of rolling lawns and veteran crab apple and oak trees. The group of weary women crawled out of the taxi and stood admiring the impressive facade of the Hall alongside the pyramids, cones and tapering spirals of the expansive topiary clad formal lawn which several people were ambling across.

'This place is amazing,' exclaimed Vicky running into Liz's room as soon as they arrived. 'Look at the bathrobes.' She came rushing back out of the bathroom with a bathrobe in her arms stroking it like a cat. 'And look at the garden.' She gasped as she peered through the heavily cross mullioned window taking in the view of the sweeping lawn and perfectly manicured flower beds below. With that she was gone, banging the door behind her.

Liz sat down on her bed and absorbed the silence. She wasn't sure how much progress they were going to make. She'd had conversations with women on the forum before and they were enthusiastic to start but then due to illness or treatment nothing ever happened. These girls seemed nice enough, but she didn't want to be a vehicle for their anger. Liz had had that experience many times growing up, where she was the one willing to make the noise only to find when the chips were down, her so-called supporters had gone and left her to face the lions on her own.

Well, at the very least she could enjoy the weekend, she thought. The weekend agenda was on her bedside table. Dinner was at seven p.m. There would be pre-dinner juices and introductions, followed by a personal health needs assessment. Saturday morning started with yoga before breakfast. Then there was a shamanic healing followed by mindful meditation.

———

Vicky looked at the brochure and groaned. 'What the hell did I agree to this for?'

Pre-dinner juices. Were they having a laugh? She needed a pre-dinner drink.

She pulled out the scotch from her bag, grabbed a glass from the table and filled it. It was going to be a long evening.

There was a knock at her door. She quickly ran and hid the bottle and glass in the bathroom.

'Just a minute,' she yelled, hurriedly wiping her mouth with the back of her hand.

Alice was standing on the threshold with a knowing grin. 'Hello, my dear. I think I know what you were just doing.'

She pushed past Vicky and glanced around the room as if looking for someone. 'So now, be a dear and pour me one too,' she instructed.

Vicky smiled as she went into the bathroom to retrieve the bottle and the glass.

Alice took a glass from her pocket and held it out. They sat on the end of the bed and polished off a glass of scotch each.

———

The women all met and went downstairs into the bar for seven p.m. There was a small crowd already gathering.

Vicky took one look at her green juice and passed it to Sarah.

'Here you go. Have one on me.'

Sarah pushed it back to Vicky. 'No Vicky, you have to drink it.'

'There's no way I'm drinking that! It looks like puréed grass and smells like weed. Hmmmh if I could dry it out maybe I could smoke it?'

Sarah sighed. 'Honestly Vicks, you're something else. Have you been drinking?'

'Maybe just a little bit.' Vicky giggled as she glanced knowingly across at Alice.

Sarah followed Vicky's gaze and had her mouth open about to speak.

'Now, dear,' said Alice, halting Sarah in her tracks, 'we are here to have fun.'

'You might have told us it was a wellbeing retreat,' said Vicky.

'What's wrong with that, my dear?' asked Alice.

'They'll all be over the top about health for a start,' said

Vicky. 'Before you know it, they'll be telling us to talk about our emotions. *That's* the problem.'

'Oh come on,' said Sarah. 'Let's just wait and see what happens.'

———

The women were seated at a table in the corner of the dining hall. The main was red pepper and courgette filo pastry on a bed of tomato herb sauce and new potatoes, with a side of steamed broccoli with almond flakes and a butternut squash.

'This is really nice,' said Liz sizing up the plate of food in front of her.

'There's no meat,' said Vicky. 'I always have meat. I hate to think what they're going to serve for dessert.'

'It's a vegan Eton mess,' said Alice.

'A what?' questioned Vicky.

'You know I'm not looking forward to tomorrow. I hope they don't split us up,' said Sarah trying to change the subject from food. She wasn't sure how Vicky was going to survive the weekend without any meat or sugar. 'The whole point of this weekend was to spend time together getting to know each other.'

'We'll all be together for the late afternoon fire-talk session. I hope they have some marshmallows to toast,' said Vicky, closing her eyes for a moment as she conjured up an image of marshmallows being toasted over a fire. All slightly gooey and so soft and sweet, pink and white sugary softness melting as it touched her lips.

———

At six the next morning there was a soft knock. Vicky rolled over and attempted to go back to sleep again. There was another knock at the door.

'I'm asleep,' she yelled.

Another knock.

'What the actual fuck?' she muttered, as she dragged herself out of bed and opened the door wearing her 'what time do you call this' look.

A young blonde woman in a black mandarin collar top and plain black trousers was standing at the door. 'You're going to be late for the morning yoga session,' she announced with a disapproving look on her face. 'You need to get a move on.'

'I don't believe this,' Vicky muttered. She sighed, kicked the door closed in the woman's face, went back into the room and pulled on her yoga pants. About five minutes later she joined the others on the lawn. Mats were laid out ready for them.

The instructor Sam Sherlock was a renowned yoga teacher. Vicky had only ever tried yoga once before and hadn't been back. She'd thought it was gentle exercise but found it difficult to get into, let alone stay in, the poses. The instructor had tried to get her into a down dog position, but she had ended up feeling so completely contorted and then had difficulty controlling her wind. Her friend Chantelle refused to take her back to another class.

Vicky took a mat at the back of the class with Sarah, Alice and Liz. There was a man sitting next to her who seemed to be quite adept at getting into the poses. At one point they were instructed to go into a down dog position when he suddenly farted extremely loudly. Vicky jumped with fright and screamed. Everyone turned to look and study her for a moment then turned back to the front and quietly continued. Vicky started giggling, falling into a heap on her mat.

Sam Sherlock walked over to her. 'Is there a problem?' she enquired politely.

'No, not here. But you might want to check on him over

there,' Vicky said, thumbing in the direction of the man next to her.

'Sorry?' questioned Sam.

'He farted. I thought I was going to end up in China.'

'We all need to expel the toxins from our bodies,' Sam said, looking very serious.

'Yeah, not at that volume, though,' said Vicky. 'Nice one, mate.' Vicky gave the man the thumbs up. 'It's normally me who does that. Although I have a bag now… see.'

The man quickly went back in to a pose not wanting to see or hear about the intricacies of her colostomy bag.

By the time breakfast came round, Vicky was ravenous. As they walked into the dining room Sylvia, the supervisor for the retreat, clapped grabbing their attention. She was a tall thin pasty bespectacled woman with angular features and wavy brown hair. 'Now ladies and gentlemen, we have put your names on the seating plan here.' Sylvia tapped a large display board mounted on an equally large easel. 'So we expect you to move around and get to know each other.' Sylvia smiled as she glanced around the room peering over her glasses in a headmistress-like manner.

'Oh no,' moaned Sarah and Vicky.

Vicky went up to the servery, got her breakfast and sat down at the nearest table.

'What are you doing?' asked Sarah, coming up behind Vicky. 'This isn't your table.'

'Yeah, and this is not my normal breakfast either. What *is* this shit?' Vicky exclaimed as she held up a rice cracker and shook it at Sarah.

Sarah rolled her eyes skyward in exasperation.

'My dear,' said Alice, addressing Sarah, as she slid in to the seat next to Vicky. 'We will sit where we want. I certainly did not pay someone to tell me where to sit.'

'Excuse me,' said Sylvia politely as she approached their table and pointed towards the display board. 'Would you mind sticking to the seating plan?'

'The answer is no, my dear,' replied Alice.

'We would like you to all get to know one another,' suggested Sylvia with a thin-lipped smile, trying to hide her irritation.

Alice smiled back up at Sylvia. 'Well now, I'm sure there will be plenty of time for that later. At the moment I would like to get to know these lovely women better. Now be a darling and excuse us. We have a great deal to catch up on,' said Alice as she waved Sylvia away.

———

The morning class was a shamanic healing session.

The women all laid on their mats and were told to imagine a portal into the underworld. The sound of shamanic drums indicated they were to start their journey.

Vicky thought she saw a rabbit and a frog.

Liz found a kangaroo hopping along a path, and then she came to an oasis where she met a rather large tiger. He patted her head, then proceeded to slice the top of her head off and filled it with sand. The tiger replaced the top of her head back and she climbed on its back and went for a walk along a ridge.

Alice saw an owl which started pecking at her head. She kept trying to smack it away. It turned out she was smacking the shaman in the head.

'I saw nothing,' said Sarah. 'I couldn't do it. I just kept laughing. It's so silly.'

By the end of the day the women were feeling rather tired. Liz was looking forward to a long hot bath. Vicky had been asked to leave the mindful meditation class for eating a Twix which had promptly been confiscated from her and this had left her in a rather foul mood. Alice had a dreadful headache and Sarah was missing Patrice. They looked a mournful bunch trudging to the late afternoon fire-talk session.

'So now,' said Owain as he stood in the middle of the circle next to the fire, holding out a polished stick adorned with Celtic symbols. 'This is the talking stick. When the stick is passed around, the person holding it will be the person to talk. I want you to introduce yourself and tell us your story.'

'This should be fun,' whispered Liz to the others.

The stick went round the circle and each person told their story of why they had come to the retreat. There were two men with burnout, two women with anxiety, two with depression, one woman with IBS and a man with a dreadful skin condition, triggered by stress, which gave the appearance of his skin peeling off in sheets. As he spoke the skin was gradually forming a dusting around his feet. Vicky's turn was next. She took the stick gingerly, shaking it to ensure there were no more loose particles of skin. 'Sorry mate,' she said.

He shrugged dejectedly. 'I'm used to it.'

Vicky stood up and introduced herself.

'Hi, I'm Vicky and I have ovarian cancer. I've been told I may only have a year or so left.'

The rest of the group sighed and shook their heads.

'What?' asked Vicky.

'I think they're empathising with you,' Owain said. 'It must be difficult.'

'Yeah, it is considering the bastard GP didn't pick it up for over nine months.'

'It is called the silent killer, so it's hard to detect. Most unfortunate for you. You're obviously very angry. I think Zahara may be able to help you with some chakra realignment,' offered Owain.

'I think what might be helpful is if I realigned my fucking GP,' said Vicky.

Owain raised an eyebrow and coughed nervously. 'Right. Well, we can also concentrate on your anger issues tomorrow with Morag.'

'But I haven't finished yet.'

'Next please.' Owain pointed at the stick in Vicky's hand indicating that it be passed to Sarah.

Vicky rolled her eyes and passed the stick over.

Sarah took the stick and stood up. 'Hi, I'm Sarah and I have ovarian cancer too. I've been told I'll be lucky to survive past five years.' The other members of the group looked at each other, sighed again, and shook their heads.

Sarah continued talking. 'I feel the same as Vicky, so I guess I'll get my chakras realigned as well.'

Owain scribbled notes on his clipboard while Sarah passed the stick to Alice.

Alice stood up. 'Hello everyone. I'm Alice. I have ovarian cancer and have also been told I have maybe a year or so left. I was ignored by my consultant for several months and I'm beyond angry.'

Owain could be heard once again scribbling furiously on his clipboard. Goodness Morag and Zahara were going to be busy tomorrow.

'Actually, I'm completely pissed off,' continued Alice.

'Alice, I think this is good that you have expressed your emotions, as did the others, and we can work more on this anger in our anger workshop tomorrow. We have one more person left.' Owain waved towards Liz.

Alice sighed and passed the stick to Liz.

Liz took the stick and stood up. She looked around at the group. 'Hi, I'm Liz and I also have ovarian cancer. I've been told I have a less than 50 per cent chance of surviving the next three to five years. I was also misdiagnosed after presenting for over nine months to specialists. If I'd been caught in the earlier stages when I first started presenting, I would've had a 90 per cent chance of surviving the next three to five years. I am angry too but… could I please ask what the point of this cosy little club is?'

'Excuse me?' Owain looked up from his clipboard seeing Liz for what seemed to be the first time.

'*This*,' said Liz as she waved her hands around to

encompass the group. '*This* is not helping anyone. We're all sitting round a fire and given only a few seconds to tell our story. When we want to tell you we're angry no one lets us talk. No one listens. You want us to only get angry in the confines of a safe place for you. What about us? Does anyone give a real shit about how we're feeling?'

'Uhh,' Owain said nervously. 'Now, we can't have negativity and anger. It will only feed your cancer. You need to contain this anger for now. We'll enable you to develop the skills to process this anger tomorrow in the anger management class. Right, now everyone let's move on.'

'*Sit down!*' Liz shouted as she waved the stick at Owain.

'Excuse me?' Owain was about to tell the woman to sit down when he realised it might be in his best interests not to challenge her. It may have been the anger he thought he saw in her eyes…

Liz moved towards him as if to challenge him. She pointed to herself with her free hand while she raised the stick as if she was about to hit him. 'I still have the stick and I have not finished speaking… *so sit down!*'

Owain looked helplessly around at the group for support. They were all looking at Liz expectantly. Realising he had lost control of the group, he sat down.

'I am angry, and I bet all of you are angry. If you've been to your GP or specialist and they have picked up your diagnosis, then great. You were lucky. Some of us (Liz waved to Alice, Sarah and Vicky) have not been so lucky. We've been let down by a system that would lead us to believe that ovarian cancer is a silent killer. That is bullshit. They want us to believe it's a silent killer because then they think we'll shut up and take our medicine. Well let me tell you, we will not sit down and shut up any longer. So when you look around this fire take a long hard look at these three women next to me and remember our names as we are not taking anything lying down. The bastards who misdiagnosed us will never forget us. Oh and Owain, you said that negativity feeds cancer, yet you ask us to process our feelings. How does that work? I'm sick and tired of having to behave a certain way because of how society tells me I should behave. It's never got me anywhere.'

Liz turned to leave, hesitated, before turning back and throwing the stick into the fire. She looked around at the group. 'None of this is okay. It will never be okay.'

She turned and walked away.

Vicky brushed off her trousers and shrugged. 'It was a pretty crap fire-talk anyway. Next time organise some marshmallows, Owain.'

Vicky, Sarah and Alice all raced off trying to keep pace with a rather enraged Liz.

'I think this calls for a drink,' said Alice to Vicky and Sarah as they raced after Liz.

The circle sat silently waiting for instructions. Owain was still staring after the women as they continued to walk off into the distance. He completely forgot his talking stick that was now being used as kindling for the fire.

'Umm, right people, now let's hold hands and start some breathing exercises to rid ourselves of any negative emotions.'

———

Alice was in her room, laughing. 'You certainly told them, my dear.'

'It was such a waste of time,' fumed Liz.

Vicky was sitting on the edge of the bed concentrating on eating a Twix.

Liz frowned at her. 'What are you doing? Can't you stop eating all that bloody rubbish?'

'It's not rubbish to me,' said Vicky.

'Oh, leave her be,' said Sarah. 'Everyone has a choice in how they deal with their illness.'

'Yeah,' said Vicky. 'I'll eat what I like as long as I like.'

'You'll be pushing up daisies before you know it, then,' growled Liz.

'Mmm,' said Vicky. 'Whatever. Someone's rattled your cage today.'

'They're so pretentious. I'm fed up with people's attitudes and the way they look at you when you say you have ovarian cancer.' Liz tilted her head to one side mimicking the pitiful look and shrugging her shoulders while mouthing 'Oh dear'. 'Even most of the doctors look at you like you're already dead.'

'Right girls. I think what's needed is a howl at the moon session tonight,' suggested Alice. 'Something to vent the frustrations and cheer us all up.'

'A what?' asked Vicky.

'After dinner we'll sneak out to the woods and light a fire and have a howl at the moon session. We can swear and kick and scream and laugh and cry. The four of us together. I have a rather large bottle of red wine and some scotch. We have music on our phones, don't we? It'll be fun.

'Deal?'

'Yes deal,' said Vicky and Sarah.

'Liz?'

'Oh alright. Deal.'

27

*A*fter dinner they snuck out to the woods at the back of the Hall. Alice had discovered an old fire pit in the woods that afternoon. They were armed with mobile phones, alcohol, glasses, pillows and blankets. Vicky made sure she had filled her pockets with snacks. There was a full moon hanging in the sky, bathing the grounds in a pale white glow. The group raced across the lawn towards the trees, attempting to avoid being seen. Once in the woods they picked their way along the path for a short distance using the dappled moonlight to illuminate their way. When they were a safe distance from the Hall they used the light of their phones to navigate to a large clearing. There were several large logs around the fire pit. The women gathered up a pile of twigs and built a fire. Alice reached into her jacket pocket, withdrawing a lighter. As the fire began to crackle and bathe the clearing in a warm orange glow the women set about laying down their collection of pillows and blankets on and around the logs. Once they had made themselves comfortable, Alice took charge of pouring the drinks. They raised their glasses to each other.

The women sat there for several hours talking about their lives and how cancer had changed them forever.

Sarah spoke of her fears of not seeing her daughter walk down the aisle or not seeing her sons graduate from university. She worried about her dog Patrice and if anyone would look after him and love him like she did. She worried that her husband had worked so hard to provide them with the life they had, and now he was facing a future retirement alone.

Alice told the others how she regretted never standing up for herself more. She described the heartbreak of Tarquin's downward spiral into a world of drug abuse.

'When Tarquin was found doing drugs it was too late. His septum had eroded away from all the cocaine use and he was hooked on heroin. We tried him in rehab several times and eventually gave up. Hugh blamed me of course. Sophie on the other hand is like her father. A real little socialite. She was reading *Who's Who* at five. She can't get through a sentence without name dropping. She's an irritating little madam.'

'What's happened to Tarquin?' asked Liz.

'He's in a squat in London somewhere. Hugh doesn't know but I deposit money into Tarquin's bank account. He was in prison recently, waiting for me to post bail but I was unwell. He left me a message and Sophie picked it up. She didn't tell me until weeks later. She left him there and told him to rot.'

'Oh dear,' they all said in unison.

Alice could feel herself tearing up. Time to change the subject before one gets too emotional, she thought to herself. 'But this is nice,' she said, smiling into the fire and pulling her blanket around her shoulders. 'What about you, Vicky? Tell us a bit more about yourself.'

Vicky began to tell them about her children and the struggles she had faced bringing them up on her own.

Bronagh and Stacey were Vicky's eldest two girls. Their dad Phillip had hung around for two years, enough to get Vicky pregnant twice, and then did a runner.

Hayley and Briana's dad was no better. At first Joe doted on her and even took on her two girls like they were his own. Within a year Briana was born. Two years later came Hayley, but Joe was already looking elsewhere. Vicky was a bit upset the first time he called her a fat pig, but she quickly dismissed it and resolved to stop eating so many ginger nuts and chocolate fruit and nut bars in one sitting. Not much later he hit her. She thought she must have imagined it to start with. He came home one night so drunk that she tried to convince herself he didn't know what he was doing. He leant over and kissed her. She told him he reeked of booze. The next thing Vicky knew, Joe had her pinned up against the wall with his hands wrapped around her throat telling her what a fucking ugly bitch she was. She was gasping for breath and pleading for him to put her down. He shouted at her to stop whimpering, telling her how pathetic she looked.

All Vicky could think about was the children in the room next door, praying they were fast asleep, and couldn't hear what was going on. Then everything went black.

She woke up to find herself in a hospital bed with facial cuts and bruising. Joe had gone to town on her, Janice had said. Joe was brought in under police escort. He was demanding to see her. He pleaded with her not to press charges and promised never to do it again. Vicky believed him. Janice was always there to pick up the pieces and take care of the children for her. After Vicky's fifth hospitalisation, he just disappeared.

A friend said she thought someone had said he'd been seen in York but they couldn't be sure.

Vicky then told them about Kurt's prison stays and how this time he had promised that when he got out he would go down the straight and narrow. She said she knew he wouldn't, but she loved him, and that was all that mattered. 'It's like some sort of holiday park to him, the amount of time he spends in there.' Vicky laughed.

'Don't you worry that if something happens to you, and

he's inside, there'll be no one to look after the children?' asked Sarah.

'No, my mum will get custody of them. My eldest is nearly ready to leave home. I worry about them all the time, though. They know I'm ill but they don't realise how ill.'

'We'd love to meet them someday,' said Liz, placing her hand over Vicky's, a gesture of comfort.

'You never had children, Liz?' asked Alice.

'No. I was told in my twenties that my endometriosis was so severe that I might never have children. I learnt to come to terms with it quite early on. When I met Gareth he already had a son from his first marriage so I had an instant family.

'I lost my mum and my dad to cancer, and I always worried that if I had children and something happened to me I couldn't bear them having to go through the pain that I experienced losing my parents so young. So I guess that's how I came to accept not having kids.'

Alice patted Liz's hand. 'Well, it's a shame, as you would have made a wonderful mother. A fiercely protective one, but a wonderful one.'

'Thanks,' said Liz.

'So,' Alice said, 'have we decided what we are going to do to these men who have ruined our lives?'

Vicky stood up to stoke the fire. 'I guess we need to rough them up a bit. That'll be the enjoyable part.'

'The medical profession tends to close ranks,' said Liz. 'They have a culture of denial and shame which keeps doctors from ever talking about their mistakes. They should be reflecting on their mistakes to learn and improve their practise. You all know about the brick wall I met when I complained about the idiot I had looking after me. When I questioned my oncologist about the care I received he couldn't really say much. Which I guess is understandable. The poor sod's left to clean up the mess he's inherited.'

'Well,' said Alice, as she took another gulp of her scotch,

'the government aren't going to do much, are they? There's that debate in the House of Commons next month but I'm not holding out. I wrote to my MP asking him to attend but he hasn't even bothered to reply to me as one of his constituents.'

Sarah sighed and nodded in agreement. 'Same here with mine.'

'It'll probably be an empty room,' said Liz.

'No one seems to care about ovarian cancer,' said Alice. 'Seven out of every ten women diagnosed in the later stages have been presenting to doctors for over six to nine months. It's considered the deadliest of all the gynaecological cancers. The fact that better care and screening could help save those lives doesn't seem to factor into the equation.'

'We need more females in the gynaecology sector,' said Vicky. 'I mean who are these men, thinking they know all about gynaecology when they don't even have a pair of ovaries themselves? You go to them and tell them you're unwell, and all they do is sit there and tell you you're possibly starting to go through "the change" and it must be "due to your hormones".' Vicky put up both her index fingers to make emphatic speech marks around the words.

'If gynaecologists are missing the signs and symptoms then the GPs don't have a hope in hell of picking it up. There are so many stories I've heard of women going through the same experience or far worse,' said Liz. 'We have to do something to try and change things.'

'But what exactly?' asked Sarah. 'You've approached your lawyer; we've approached our GPs. I've volunteered to talk to medical students telling my story, but that's only one little step. How do we make the general public more aware of the signs and symptoms and empower them to challenge the medical profession and put pressure on them and the policy makers to change practice?'

'It will take a lot,' said Liz. 'Modern medicine is in danger of losing their greatest tool – human touch. I've spoken to a number of women who were never physically examined. They were scanned and yet we're told the scans might not pick up the disease in the early stages. I mean, I had endometriosis, so clearly when my second scan showed no endometriomas and apparently no sign of me ever having it, this should have been discussed with me. A physical examination would have shown my uterus in a fixed position due to scar tissue if the scan was wrong. Was this done? No. I should never have been dismissed from the consultant's care without investigating what happened. Endometriosis doesn't just vanish, so why weren't any alarm bells ringing at that point? I don't blame my GP. I put full responsibility with my consultant.'

'Dreadful,' said Alice. 'Mine was an absolute imbecile. He was more concerned about where my husband and I went to dinner and tried to put me on a diet. He was an absolutely rude little man.'

'Mine was always shooing me out of the room, saying he could only give me ten minutes,' said Vicky. 'If you have more than one problem you have to come back for another appointment. So he expected me to go back out and book another appointment. Horrible little man.'

Sarah nodded in agreement. 'Mine was so pretentious. When I asked him why my cancer had not been picked up earlier, he said he was shocked and surprised to hear it was ovarian cancer, as there had been no signs, but I don't understand that. I'd been referred by my GP with urinary urgency and frequency, abdominal bloating and abdominal discomfort as well as feeling full quickly. These are all classic signs and symptoms of ovarian cancer so that doesn't make sense. These are gynaecologists and this is their bread and butter, isn't it? I asked him about the menopause after my surgery. He said if I was having any trouble, that I could contact him and he would prescribe me some HRT. But my cancer was hormone linked. Quite high in fact, so I can't have any HRT.'

'This is the problem,' said Liz. 'If we let them get away with this then we're leaving them to let loose on other poor innocent women. They can't even perform the most basic of tasks.

'Did any of your surgeons talk to you about what the implications of surgery, including the menopause, would be on your lifestyle and sexual health?'

The other women all looked at each other blankly and shook their heads.

Alice leant forward, pausing for a moment as she took another sip of her scotch. 'Is there something specific you are referring to, Liz?'

'Well, for one, there's the shortened vagina.'

The women looked at each other again blankly, then back at Liz. 'The what?' they all said in unison.

'The *shortened* vagina,' repeated Liz. 'If you've had a radical hysterectomy then you have a shortened vagina. They have to sew it up when they remove the cervix. That means sex is painful as there's not so much room as before. And when you think about the vaginal dryness which you also get from the menopause, you're in for a double whammy. Kind of important don't you think?'

'Ohh,' said Vicky. 'I wondered what they did with it. No wonder sex has been painful.'

'I don't know of any other medical specialty where they could get away with not discussing the side effects of surgery in this way,' continued Liz. 'I mean, would men find it acceptable to have surgery and not be told that their penis had been shortened? Could you imagine? They'd be up in arms. It's time the gynaecology sector was overhauled. This second-rate treatment has to stop. We have to empower women to challenge the medical profession over women's health issues. Look at the pelvic mesh scandal for example. It's gone on for far too long. What about this KY jelly nonsense as well?'

'What KY jelly nonsense?' asked Vicky.

Liz let go of a long, annoyed breath before replying. 'It's so drying and damaging to the vaginal tissues. Yet doctors continually use it. Women should be using organic vaginal moisturisers without all this crap in it. We need moisturisers which are pH balanced, which will restore moisture, rather than exacerbating the problem. It's unbelievable how we are treated. And then there are the speculums. Don't get me started on the speculums.'

The others all looked at each other confused, shrugged, then looked back at Liz expectantly.

Liz threw her arms in the air in exasperation. 'This is what I mean! This is how we let them get away with this. Come on guys. Get with the programme.'

The others continued to stare blankly at Liz, not quite sure what was coming next.

'Oh jeez.' Liz slapped her forehead lightly. She shifted forward on the log using her hands to reposition herself into a more comfortable seated position then continued. 'Why are we still being subjected to internal examinations with an instrument which has barely changed since the original design in the 1840s? The man who designed it, a James Sims, is considered the father of modern gynaecology. The medical profession looks up to him. What they don't tell you is that they pulled his statue down in Central Park in April this year following a number of protests. Why?' Liz paused for added effect.

'Because he spent years using enslaved black women as guinea pigs to test medical procedures without using any anaesthetic. *That* is why.'

'The bastard,' muttered Alice, as she took yet another sip of her scotch.

Vicky and Sarah exchanged horrified glances and shuddered.

'Those poor women,' said Sarah.

'He also developed a procedure called the Battey procedure,' Liz continued. 'Guess what that was?'

The women leaned in. 'What?' they all whispered, wide eyed.

'It was a procedure to treat female hysteria or delirium. Husbands would hand their wives over to this Dr Sims when they felt they were behaving irrationally and he would remove the women's ovaries.'

'You are kidding me,' said Vicky with a look of horror clouding her face.

'No, I'm not. He also called three of his children Fanny, Florence Nightingale and… wait for it… Merry Christmas.'

The women laughed. Vicky nearly choked on her mouthful of wine.

'He sounds absolutely dreadful,' said Alice. 'I'm sick and tired of the medical profession telling everyone that a smear is painless, simple and over in minutes. I doubt there are many women given the time needed to perform the examination in comfort or to have their needs addressed. They wonder why women miss cervical smear appointments. The other thing is they don't explain that smear tests do not screen for ovarian cancer. I wish I'd known that.'

The others nodded in agreement.

Liz stood up and stoked the fire with a stick lying on the ground. She then started pacing and waving the stick in the air.

'Oh here we go,' whispered Vicky to Sarah. 'That must have been the intro. The main show is about to begin. It's like having one of those windup toys… wind it up and then watch it go.'

Sarah tried to suppress a giggle.

'Women are human beings with complex feelings around bodily autonomy,' said Liz continuing with her oratory. 'We all have different vaginal and cervical anatomies which means we can all have different experiences of the same procedure. We should be accommodated with regards to different sized speculums dependent on the length of our vaginas, our childbearing status, our age and whether we are sexually active or not.' She stopped and turned and pointed the stick at Alice. 'Have you been for an internal examination or a smear and been offered a different size of speculum? How would we know if they were considering these aspects as they don't discuss it with you, do they?'

'No, I only thought there was one size,' said Alice.

Then Liz pointed the stick at Sarah. 'You?'

'No,' said Sarah, 'but...'

Liz's eyes narrowed suspiciously at Sarah. 'But what?'

'Ummh, don't they use plastic ones nowadays that you can ratchet down?' Sarah offered tentatively. She didn't know how Liz would react to being challenged and somehow was not keen on finding out.

'Yes, yes, they do Sarah, but who told you that?'

'I think I read about it after I was diagnosed.'

'Exactly,' replied Liz. '*After* you were diagnosed.' Liz swung round pointing the stick at Vicky. 'And you?'

'No, never.'

'There *are* different sizes! If they can change the size of the speculum, don't you think they could discuss it with us? Wouldn't that be inconvenient if we all started asking what sized speculum they were going to be using on us? It would make the examination more comfortable but why would they accommodate us? We're only women, after all, and we're just meant to suck it up and take it. All those poor women with retroverted uteruses are left to endure painful examinations. They probably don't even know they have a retroverted uterus as no one thinks it important to tell them. Shut up and put up, isn't that what they say? If we say anything, we're seen as being difficult.'

'One thing is clear,' said Alice, 'these bastards are first in the firing line. One thing that facing my mortality has done is made me realise who gives a fuck about the rules. They don't give a fuck about us, dears.'

'Alice, Alice, Who the fuck is Alice,' chanted Vicky.

'Ohh, I love that song,' giggled Alice.

'Rules are made to be broken so let's beat them at their own game,' said Vicky.

Sarah's eyes widened. 'That sounds serious. What are we planning to do then, guys?'

'I guess we could have a bit of fun. You have to break a few eggs in order to make an omelette,' said Alice.

'But what happens if something goes wrong?' queried Sarah.

'I know I haven't got much time on the old clock, so I'm quite happy to take the wrap if anything untoward happens,' offered Alice.

'Me too,' said Vicky. 'I mean what could be worse than what we're already facing?'

'You know what? You guys are right,' said Liz. 'Let's do this. It's about time these men got a taste of their own medicine.'

'Okay,' said Sarah. 'But can we do this on our own? I mean what if one of us is sick? Look at me with my chemo.'

'Hmmm,' said Alice. 'Good point. We could hire a hit man.'

'Hit man,' gasped Sarah. 'What are we planning on doing?'

'Having a bit of fun,' purred Alice.

'I am so going to enjoy this,' said Vicky.

'Hang on,' said Liz. 'I know someone who might be able to help. She's a good friend and would be very discreet. We'd have to plan ahead and see if she can be available when we need her. She runs her own business. She's a hairdresser.'

'What's she going to do? Give them a haircut?' suggested Vicky.

'No. She can look after us,' sighed Liz, exasperated with Vicky's banter.

Vicky took a sip of her drink. 'I hope she's a good laugh.'

'She is more than a laugh,' said Liz. 'I'll have a chat with her and see if she'll help us.'

'Sounds good,' said Alice as she stood up and moved towards her jacket.

'Now my lovely ladies, it's time to howl at the moon.' She pulled her phone from her jacket pocket and tapped at her phone screen. The tune of Smokie's *Who the F**k is Alice* started filtering through the night air. The women started swaying and dancing around the fire holding hands as they started to sing.

28

$\mathcal{T}$he early morning knock on the door was not heard. The retreat workers reported in to reception that they were unable to raise the four women. Sylvia went up with the keys and opened their rooms to find them empty, with pillows and blankets missing and none of the beds slept in. A search of the grounds was undertaken and the women were found sound asleep in the clearing with the empty wine bottle and scotch bottle beside them. The retreat's security staff walked across the floor of the clearing. Vicky was the first person they reached. One of the security staff shook her gently to try and wake her, but she started swatting him away with her hands.

'Shoo go away.' She rolled over, opening her eyes, squinting up in the morning light at the blurred figure towering over her.

'Ummm, guys. Hey guys, wake up,' she said, as she scrambled to her feet and started shaking the others.

Within fifteen minutes they were all escorted back to reception and then herded into the retreat manager's office.

'Hhhhmmmhh,' Sylvia said, as she cleared her throat. She slowly looked down at the desk, rearranged some papers and then slowly looked back up at the four women seated in front of her.

'The management reserve the right to cancel your booking at any point if we feel that your behaviour will jeopardise or impact on the stay of the other guests. Your behaviour last night—'

'Now just one damned minute,' interrupted Alice.

Sylvia shrank back in her chair. 'Excuse me. I was speaking.'

'Yes, my dear, but I really don't care. Now you, young madam, can keep quiet for once and listen to me. I paid good money to come here with my friends. I was informed this was a reputable retreat but from what I've seen so far I sincerely doubt it is. A load of namby pamby from what I gather. I'm sure that would not go down well in London when I get back. So here is what's going to happen. You are going to forget what happened last night, as it is frankly none of your damned business, my dear girl. We will continue to enjoy the treatments the spa and beauty room has to offer for the duration of our stay and tonight we will be dining out at the local steak house.'

'What?' shouted Liz.

'The steakhouse, my dear… in Penrith,' continued Alice shooting a deathly glare at Liz, getting up to leave. The others jumped up to follow her.

Alice stopped at the door, turning around to face Sylvia. 'And be a dear and order in a bottle of Bollinger. Have it sent up to my room this evening at seven p.m. sharp with four chilled champagne glasses, and we would like the taxi booked for seven thirty.'

Vicky looked at Sarah, rolling her eyes, and giggled.

With that Alice left the room. The three women followed her leaving an affronted Sylvia to order champagne and a taxi or face the prospect of having her retreat badmouthed across London society.

'Seriously. A steak house? What do you expect me to eat

at a steakhouse?' said Liz, throwing up her hands in frustration as they walked off down the corridor. 'What about the local pub? That might do vegan food…'

─────

October 2018

Gareth was sitting at his desk working on a set of accounts. His colleague was sitting at the desk across from him.

'So how is Liz?' asked Anne.

'She's doing really well. She's met a few women from her support group and they've become quite friendly.'

'Oh, that is nice,' said David, who was sitting next to Gareth.

'She appears a lot happier and loves the company. They went on a retreat last month. Nearly got kicked out for bad behaviour.'

'Ohh,' said Anne. 'Sounds like they're having fun.'

'They have a lot in common and are actually planning a ski trip together in January. I think it's doing her the world of good. It keeps her from thinking about getting back at her consultant. To be honest, I was getting quite worried about her at one point. She was so fixated on getting him back that I was worried she was going to make herself ill again.'

'Perhaps she just needed to work things out in her own time,' suggested Anne.

'You're right. I was beginning to worry that she might try and kill him or something. It wouldn't have been much fun spending my time between work and visiting her in prison,' joked Gareth.

Anne and David laughed and shared a nervous glance.

Gareth shuddered as he felt a cold shiver travel down his spine. Doesn't bear thinking about, he thought, as he returned to his set of accounts.

29

_____

LATE OCTOBER 2018

*A*lice and Liz were seated in the waiting room of Alice's MP's surgery.

'Mr Fillerup-Standing will see you now,' said the officious sounding receptionist. They followed her into his office.

Jeremy Fillerup-Standing stood up from behind his large desk. He was a tall slim man, dressed in a pink shirt and a navy blue pinstriped suit with a bright red tie, he looked about sixty, with a head of receding white hair and beady eyes set behind a pair of horn-rimmed spectacles.

Liz noted that he had an air of smugness about him. No surprises there she thought as she took the limp handshake that was offered.

'Good morning, ladies. Please take a seat,' he said indicating the two empty chairs on the other side of his desk.

Liz and Alice sat down.

'Now how can I help you?'

'We would like to speak with you regarding ovarian cancer,' said Alice.

'Ovarian cancer?'

'Yes, ovarian cancer,' replied Alice.

'Right. I'm not sure how qualified I am to discuss it with you but fire ahead, ladies.'

Jeremy Fillerup-Standing shifted in his seat uncomfortably and gave a nervous cough.

'You do know where the ovaries are located, don't you?' asked Alice leaning forward and tapping her hand on the desk.

'Well, umm, yes I think I do. What is it you would like to discuss?'

'You do recall me writing to you to ask you to raise awareness of this disease?' questioned Alice. 'And you never turned up to the House of Commons debate, did you?'

Jeremy shifted in his seat again. 'I am rather busy. Maybe my secretary still has the letter?'

'So you didn't read my letter?'

'I'm not sure. What is it I can do for you exactly?'

'Could you tell us what you are going to do to raise awareness?'

'Awareness? Well now, I'm not sure that's really what my role as an MP is,' he replied perfunctorily.

Alice continued to interrogate him.

'But you represent the people in your constituency?'

'Yes.'

'You represent them in parliament and voice their concerns?'

'Yes but…'

'So, you don't think ovarian cancer is important?'

'No… I mean yes.'

'No or yes?' interrupted Liz.

'Now listen, ladies.' Jeremy waved his hands about. 'I'm a very busy person. I can't go round asking for more funding for a disease that only kills a few thousand women a year.'

'Ahhh, now we're getting somewhere,' said Alice. 'You *do* know something about it.'

'Well, a bit,' replied Jeremy. He didn't want to admit

he'd googled ovarian cancer only a few minutes before the women had entered the room.

'It kills just over 4,000 women a year in the UK,' corrected Alice, 'So you know that there has only been a slight improvement in survival rates since the 1970s and yet other cancers which have dramatically increased their survival rates such as breast, bowel and prostate get more attention and funding.'

'You might need to talk to the health secretary about that. I think that's more his domain than mine, so to speak.'

'We've tried. We have written letters to all our MPs and the health secretary but we were referred back to you. We were told that unless we were one of their constituents we couldn't correspond with them directly. So here I am as one of your constituents,' said Alice.

'Oh, right.'

Alice folded her arms across her chest and sat back in her chair. 'We have all the statistics here and we'd like to know what is being done about a national audit on ovarian cancer.'

'I didn't know there was one,' replied Jeremy.

'Exactly, my dear fellow, so what are you doing about it?'

'Now ladies, I understand your concerns but I really cannot help you.'

'Can't or won't?' said Liz.

It took Jeremy another fifteen minutes to wrap the conversation up. He promised to look into it for them. He'd noticed the other woman seemed to be constantly fiddling with her phone.

As Liz and Alice left, Jeremy phoned his PA.

'Don't ever let those two mad women back in here again.'

Hormonal, menopausal women was all he needed right now. He laughed to himself as he threw their paperwork into the filing tray. They didn't realise that they were asking him to move money from one pot to another. If the health secretary increased the funding for ovarian cancer it would have to be taken from the prostate, lung, breast or bowel fund and these cancers were doing so well. They were producing the figures the health secretary needed to see. An increase in survival rates and far more people afflicted. That's what the public need to hear.

―――――

Liz was once again ropeable. 'What an arrogant twat,' she said.

'I'm sorry my dear,' said Alice. 'I really did think he might be more receptive than your dreadful MP. Did you manage to video it all? Perhaps you should ask yours why he never replied to your letter and why he never attended the House of Commons debate?'

'Because that would be an absolute waste of my time,' said Liz, as she stormed off along the street attempting to hail a cab.

'At least I tried,' Alice muttered.

'What did you say?' Liz turned back and snarled at Alice.

'Nothing.' Alice shrugged, shaking her head and throwing her hands up in the air.

―――――

'I'm writing to the prime minister,' announced Liz.

'Oh dear,' said Gareth.

'Sit down and listen to my letter.'

'Do I have a choice?' asked Gareth pouring himself a Guinness to watch the football. He sat down on the couch with the television on in the background which was now positioned directly behind Liz.

'Dear prime minister,' began Liz, '…and I was in agony… my GP… abdominal pain.'

'Hmmmh.' Liz frowned, tapped her index finger against her lip and then scribbled some notes while mouthing silently to herself.

'Okay… so let me read that bit again.'

'Dear prime minister,' began Liz again, '…and I was in agony… my GP… abdominal pain.'

Gareth rolled his eyes and attempted to peer around Liz to try and get a glimpse of the screen.

'Then I thought if I put in a sentence here about the statistics and then added that Mr Kuntz-Finger had completely ignored my symptoms, that would make it sound punchier, don't you think?'

'Mmmmm,' said Gareth.

'So what did I say?' Liz challenged Gareth.

'You were talking about ovarian cancer.'

'What about ovarian cancer?'

'How you were misdiagnosed.' He suddenly jumped, with his fists clenched, moving to the left of the sofa, urging his team towards their goal without lifting his gaze from the screen.

Liz adjusted her position to ensure she was back in front of the screen blocking his view of the match.

Gareth threw his arms up. 'What are you doing?'

'Repeat the last sentence back to me.'

'I'm trying to watch the match, hun. Can't it wait?'

'No, it cannot. I have an advanced stage of cancer because some idiot couldn't be bothered to take a simple blood test. What's more important… football or your wife?'

'I'll let you know after the match,' muttered Gareth.

'What did you say?'

'My wife,' said Gareth resignedly, 'I said my wife.'

'So, what did I say?'

'I can't remember it exactly,' said Gareth still trying to look around Liz to see the screen.

'Typical man,' raged Liz. 'An absolute arsehole. That's

why we are all dying because of men like you.' Liz stormed off up the stairs.

'Well, maybe if you ask me when the football's not on,' Gareth called after her.

He would apologise later. For now, he could relax and enjoy the match. Liz would be occupied on the computer tapping away for hours. She'd have forgotten all about it by the time she came back down. Gareth did love her but she could be hard work. He'd heard the story so many times. A dog with a bone is how he would describe her.

------

1 November 2018

Liz opened the envelope. She pulled the letter out which had the parliamentary coat of arms at the top with the 10 Downing Street address written underneath. What followed was a brief acknowledgement of her recent letter.

Dear Ms Fitzpatrick,

Thank you for contacting the prime minister. We are terribly sorry to hear of your health difficulties.

The Department of Health and Social Care has responsibility for the matters you raise. I am therefore forwarding your email to them.

Thank you, once again, for writing.

Yours Sincerely (followed by an indecipherable signature that resembled a spider's vomit).

Correspondence Officer

30

OXLEAS WOOD, GREENWICH

NOVEMBER 2018

'*I*'ve written a letter to the prime minister,' said Liz. 'I heard back and basically they just passed my letter onto the Department for Health and Social Care.'

'Oh dear,' said Sarah.

'I'm not surprised. You could be waiting a long time to hear anything else,' said Vicky.

'I'm not surprised either,' said Alice, as she closed her eyes and turned her face up to the sun, soaking up the warmth of its rays.

The women were all sitting on a park bench, drinking tea outside the café at the top of the meadow. Patrice was sitting at Sarah's feet looking rather smart, all wrapped up against the chill of the crisp November morning, in his red tartan dog coat and red tartan neckerchief.

'Alice and I also went to her MP,' said Liz. 'Do you know what he said to us?'

'No, but I bet you're about to tell us,' said Vicky. Sarah and Vicky started giggling.

'It's not that funny,' said Liz with a hint of annoyance. 'Come on, guys, we need to get serious. We need to become more aggressive in our approach.'

'Okay, sorry Liz,' said Vicky. 'What exactly do you have

in mind? If you've written to the prime minister, with no luck, after everything else we've done then what's left?'

'Vicky's right,' said Sarah. 'You mentioned at the retreat we were going to do something to get these men to sit up and take notice. Without the support of the politicians and the law we cannot force the medical profession to change practice. A practice that has been operating in a specific way for many years.'

'If we can't change the system then perhaps we need to change the way we interact with it,' suggested Alice. 'Don't get mad get even. Isn't that the phrase?'

Liz smiled.

'This sounds interesting,' said Vicky rubbing her gloved hands with glee. 'I could do with some excitement. Are we going to murder someone?'

Patrice whimpered and jumped up onto Sarah's lap. 'Oh no, Patrice. Not you my dear. You are just too gorgeous to do away with,' said Sarah as she cuddled him.

'I'd better phone Olivia. She should be here by now.'

Liz tapped at the screen on her phone, placed her ear phones in her ears and squinted in concentration.

'Hiya Olivia. Where are you?... Oh okay. We've had a cup of tea. Let us know when you pull up in the car park.'

Liz tapped at the screen and turned to the others.

'Right. Olivia will be here in ten minutes. She's coming from Bexleyheath and is in Welling now.'

'Patrice darling,' whispered Sarah. Patrice put his two front paws on Sarah's chest, his bearded little face looking up at her panting expectantly. Was it a walk? He was desperate for a walk. He was ready to go.

'Now you must be on your best behaviour, Patrice my dear, as we've got visitors arriving any minute.' Patrice raised his bushy eyebrows at Sarah and let out a bark.

148

Olivia parked up her blue BMW soft top convertible in the Oxleas Wood car park. Liz walked over to greet her. Alice, Vicky and Sarah stood slightly behind Liz with their mouths open. A slim woman about forty stood before them. Olivia's long black hair was brushed to a glossy perfection beneath her brown fake fur hat. She was wearing a pair of dark blue denim skin tight jeans with a camel coloured cashmere roll neck jumper visible beneath a black padded gilet, brown leather gloves and a pair of brown sheepskin lined boots.

'Hiya. It's fuckin' freezing. What a right bloody mare coming through Welling, babes. It's such a bottleneck down there. Sorry to keep you.' Olivia peered behind Liz, smiling at the others and waved. 'Hiya. I've got me babies here.' She indicated to the back door of the car. There was an instant sound of yapping from the back seat.

'Yap yap yap yap.' Mocha the Yorkshire terrier and Snowy the Bichon Frise were sitting in the back in their car seats. Olivia adored them and hardly went anywhere without them. They were the children she never had.

She went round to the boot and pulled out a small pram.

'What's that for?' asked Vicky.

'It's me pram for Mocha. She's such a princess. Her legs are so short and dainty so we have to push her.' Olivia attached a bum bag to the pram which contained her dog poop bags.

Alice peered at the pram disbelievingly as Olivia placed the long-haired Yorkshire terrier, complete with a pink bow in its hair, inside the pram and then proceeded to wrap her up in a miniature patchwork quilt.

'Oh I see you have the quilt I made her,' said Liz fondly.

'Of course,' replied Olivia. 'It goes everywhere with her.'

Alice grabbed Liz by the elbow and whispered, 'You are asking someone who pushes her dog around in a pram to help us? She seems completely mad.'

'Mad in a good way,' said Liz with a smile.

Olivia then lifted Snowy out of the back seat and lowered him to the ground on his lead. He yapped at their heels with his white coat and pink candy floss ears and bright yellow paws displayed in full glory as he jumped about in the nippy autumn air.

'What the fuck is that?' asked Vicky. 'A dog with pink ears and yellow paws.'

Snowy looked up at Vicky. 'Grrrr.'

'Yap yap,' said Mocha as Olivia placed a soft green, grey, orange and white toy duck in the pram.

'Is that it's toy?' asked Vicky pointing to the duck.

'No babes, this is Snowy's. He loves ducks. 'Don't you my boy?' cooed Olivia.

'Yap, yap,' said Snowy in agreement.

'Olivia,' said Liz, 'meet Vicky, Alice and Sarah.'

They all gave her a hug and then followed Olivia and Liz back to the café.

Sarah whispered to Vicky and Alice. 'This is going to be interesting.'

'Yes very,' said Alice.

'They're *dogs* not babies,' said Vicky.

Patrice was sniffing the air. He was rather interested in his new playmates.

'I'll just get a coffee, babes,' said Olivia to Liz. 'Can you mind the babies for me?'

Olivia ordered a take away coffee while the others stood waiting outside the fenced off area.

A few minutes later the door to the café opened and Olivia appeared, shouting to Liz. 'Liz, they've got scrambled eggs. Are we okay to get some breakfast for my babies?'

Olivia disappeared back inside as quickly as she had appeared, without giving Liz any time to reply.

Vicky glanced at Sarah and Alice with a hint of annoyance. 'I guess that's a yes then.'

'Oh come on guys, she's hilarious,' said Liz as she struggled to disentangle herself from Snowy's lead which he had managed to encircle around Mocha's pram several times without Liz noticing.

'Is she seriously going to feed them scrambled eggs?' Vicky asked Liz.

Right at that point Olivia came striding over to the gate. 'Give me their bowls, would you?'

Liz handed Snowy's lead to Alice and fished out two stainless steel dog bowls from the holdall bag Olivia had hanging on the pram. Olivia exchanged her coffee for the dog bowls Liz handed her.

'Ta, babes.'

Olivia disappeared again and then returned a few minutes later with the dog bowls full of scrambled eggs. She placed the bowls on the ground, lifted Mocha out of the pram and took Snowy's lead from Liz sitting him next to Mocha. Mocha and Snowy devoured their scrambled eggs while the others all watched in awe of what they were witnessing. Patrice stood stock still with his head to one side, ear cocked and his tail twitching. Sarah was holding his lead rather tightly. The scrambled eggs smelt delicious to Patrice. He went to sneak just a taste of them from Mocha's bowl but Sarah had his lead too tight and pulled him back. Patrice whimpered.

'No Patrice,' she said firmly.

He gave up and lay dejectedly on the grass on his belly with his head resting on his paws and daydreamed about scrambled eggs. 'Oh, come on then,' said Sarah. 'Walkies.'

Patrice jumped up wagging his tail in anticipation. Sarah and Patrice made their way down the main meadow.

When Mocha and Snowy had finished their meal, Olivia washed the bowls under the tap at the dog watering point and they all sat for several minutes on one of the park benches overlooking the meadow.

'You know there's a reservoir under here,' said Liz, as she waved her hand in front of her at the meadow laid out in front of them.

'Really?' said Alice.

'Yes, it holds London's water supply. See that building down there at the bottom of the meadow?' Liz pointed down the left-hand side of the meadow to a small building at the edge of the path.

'Yeah,' said Olivia.

'That's the pump house.'

'Shut the front door,' exclaimed Olivia. 'Are you serious? You mean to say we've been walking here all this time and never knew that? Where did you find that out?'

'I read about it last week. It is funny how we just walk around going about our daily lives completely oblivious to things right under our very noses.'

'Huh,' said Vicky.

'Hmmm,' said Alice in agreement.

'I love walking here. You can walk for about three hours and only need to cross two main roads. It's kept me sane when I have my low days. You can walk the Green Chain Walk all the way to Crystal Palace, you know.'

When Sarah and Patrice returned they all headed back to the car park. They jumped in their cars and headed down to Greenwich for lunch, parking in Maze Hill Road along the western side of Greenwich Park. Liz was still receiving her maintenance Avastin infusions every three weeks which meant she had terribly sore feet. Sarah had not finished her chemo so was still very fatigued. Alice and Vicky were on their third series of chemo. They were still suffering with aching joints and fatigue so the day had been planned around short bursts of energy with frequent toilet and refreshment stops along the way.

———

The group of women entered Greenwich Park via Vanbrugh Park Gate. They walked along the path following the left-hand fork with the flower garden to their left. They continued along past the bandstand, and then turned to their right at the Pavilion Café following the main drive towards the observatory. It was a beautiful sunny day and the view from the observatory down onto Greenwich and the City looked glorious. They stood in front of the statue of General Wolfe admiring the panoramic view of the Queens House below, with the majestic twin domes of the Royal Naval College jutting skywards, and the Thames winding lazily past in the background.

'This is one of those moments when you appreciate being alive,' said Alice.

'It is glorious, isn't it,' agreed Sarah as she inhaled a deep breath of the midday air. Facing skyward she closed her eyes feeling the warmth of the sun on her face.

'Yeah fuckin' amazing, babes,' said Olivia. 'Your wedding venue still looks amazing, Liz.'

Liz looked down at the Old Royal Naval College and smiled. 'It does, doesn't it.'

'Wow,' said Sarah. 'Is *THAT* where you got married?'

'Yes, in the Painted Hall. The dome to the left.'

'My goodness. That must have been rather wonderful,' said Alice.

'Best day of my life.'

'Gosh, me feet are killing me,' said Olivia. 'How much further?'

'Down the hill and then along the river,' said Liz casting her arm across the landscape to the right.

'What are you moaning about? You want to have chemo and then try and walk with your feet raw and bleeding,' Vicky said facetiously.

'She has a fuckin' attitude,' muttered Olivia to Liz. 'What is her problem?'

'It's called cancer, I guess,' said Liz.

Olivia grimaced and rolled her eyes.

———

They were all seated around a table in the cosy warmth of the Cutty Sark Pub. The Georgian bay window their table was located next to overlooked the Thames, providing the women with an excellent view of the comings and goings of the river traffic.

'So, if these politicians won't listen to you why don't you go to the press?' said Olivia.

'I tried that,' said Liz as she sipped her glass of red wine. 'I told my story of my A&E visit. It didn't do much. Nothing came of it.'

'Fuckers,' said Olivia.

'I guess at least they apologised,' said Liz.

'We must be able to do something about the other guys, though,' said Olivia.

'Yes, we just have to decide what,' said Alice as she leant in towards Olivia who was sitting next to her. 'My dear, I have to ask... how much Botox have you had?'

'Ohh loads, babes. Everything about me is fake, even these,' she said, as she pointed to her chest.

'I don't think this is though,' Alice said pointing to Olivia's heart.

'No, that's the only genuine bit of me left.'

'Hmmmh,' Alice thought she was going to really like this interesting creature.

'I'm pleased that the Every Woman study has been published, it confirms everything we've all experienced,' said Sarah. 'At least we know there's something to back up our poor experiences.'

'It's one thing to collect the information but what are they going to do now they have it?' asked Alice.

'Considering the poor response we got from the attendance at the House of Commons debate, I guess not much,' said Vicky.

'Alice, what did you mean earlier when you said don't get mad, get even and to change the way we interacted with the medical system?' asked Sarah.

'Well, Liz and I have decided the best approach is to shake the individuals up a bit... maybe turn the tables. I wonder how they would feel to know they had a 50 per cent chance of surviving the next three to five years.'

'Sounds like Russian roulette,' said Vicky.

Alice smiled and shook her head. 'No, not that dire, but we have a plan to shake them up a bit. First things first, though. We need a little break. I thought we'd start with a ski trip to my chalet in Meribel in January. That's why we wanted you to have your passports ready. My chemo regime will have finished by then. Vicky, you'll have completed yours by then, won't you? So, that will make things a little bit more relaxing for us.'

'My treatment will finish next week so as long as I take my calcium I should be fine,' said Vicky.

'The trip is on me,' said Alice.

'Olivia's a brilliant snowboarder and has agreed to accompany us and look after us in case any of us fall ill,' said Liz.

Olivia beamed at the others and raised her glass to them. They all clapped and toasted her. Then they all toasted their holiday host Alice.

This is going to be so much fun, thought Alice.

'Yap, yap, yap,' said Mocha and Snowy at Olivia's feet.

'Woof,' agreed Patrice.

After lunch the group, satiated by their meal, walked slowly back up the hill towards the observatory with the backdrop of Greenwich behind them.

Alice, Liz and Olivia were a few paces behind Vicky and Sarah.

'Are we going to tell the other two what we have planned,' asked Liz?

'Oh no, not just yet. Let's wait until we're in the resort. It'll make things so much more fun,' said Alice.

'Oh Alice. I love it. You are wicked,' laughed Olivia.

Liz had found out Mr Kuntz-Finger was going to Meribel for a conference. Quite by chance she had found out via a friend, who was a friend of Mr Kuntz-Finger's secretary. They had been chatting about their bosses being away and Virginia had let it slip to Liz. Liz mentioned it in passing to Alice and Alice helped with the detective work. It didn't take the two of them long to find out the location and dates of the conference. When they found out it was Meribel, Alice offered up her chalet.

'Are you sure?' Liz had asked.

'My dear, the place is empty. We used to rent it out but it became such a bore. We tend to only use it for Christmas and family vacations. Sophie uses it more than we do nowadays. It's no problem. It'll make a great break for us all in that fresh mountain air. There's plenty of room. It'll be such fun.

'You can catch up with Mr Kuntz-Finger and confront him or do whatever you want to do to him. You said you wanted to shake him up a bit so now is your chance.'

'Well, okay,' Liz had replied rather hesitantly.

Alice had shot a look of annoyance as she started shaking her finger at Liz. 'What? A touch of cold feet now the opportunity is in front of you, my dear. You said you felt that the experience of cancer had woken you up to the world and that after that nasty brain scare you promised yourself you would never let life pass you by. You said you wanted to grab life by the balls. Well, here's your chance to put a finger up to that Kuntz-Finger chappy and show him who's in charge here.'

It didn't take long for Alice to convince Liz of the path they were to take.

'I don't want to show him who is in charge… I want to do much more than that.'

31

CHALET CLOUSEAU, MERIBEL MOTTARET

JANUARY 2019

The chalet was tucked right into the hillside and faced out onto a blue run which ran straight down into Meribel Mottaret's main chair. The view from the main balcony was a panoramic view of the valley below, and of the steep red run on the opposite side of the valley, which also led down to the main chair.

The chalet had been bought by Alice and Hugh twenty years prior. Alice learnt to ski when she was very young and had always been an avid skier. It only took a few telephone calls for her to arrange chalet staff. Sophie's friends knew someone who knew someone out in the Alps. The sad story of Alice's disease and imminent demise had completed the social circuit, and over drinks and canapés, deals were made. People who existed to bemoan the trials and tribulations of doing charity for 'one's own' shook hands and went to bed that night feeling rather smug and pleased with themselves. Of course they'd never laid eyes on Alice but the story was just 'oh so sad, darling, that I couldn't possibly not do anything to help.'

The chalet could sleep up to ten people so everyone could have their own room if they chose to do so.

Olivia and Liz caught an early morning Uber from Liz's place.

Olivia was laden with gear. Liz had never seen so many bags.

'Babes, can I take some of your weight allowance? I'm sure I'm going to be so far over. You know me, I like to look me best at all times.'

The Uber driver and Gareth looked at each other and sighed as they struggled to load the bags into the boot.

'Right, is that everything?' asked Liz glancing around the pavement.

'Yes, everything's in the cab. You enjoy yourself, babe,' said Gareth, as he kissed her goodbye. 'I'll miss you. Promise to take care of yourself and try not to speed down those slopes,' he joked.

As if! Liz thought to herself. She was a safe skier. She liked to ski at a gentle pace taking in the alpine scenery, listening to the gentle swish swishing of her skis in the snow as she traversed the piste.

Liz had never been skiing without Gareth. She wondered if she'd find it strange not having him next to her on the slopes. She hadn't dared to tell him about Mr Kuntz-Finger being in the resort at the same time. Gareth and Liz shared everything but this was something she felt would be best kept from him.

She waved out of the rear window of the cab at Gareth until he disappeared from view.

Olivia was brushing her hair down with her hand and pouting into her phone. 'Just doing a selfie for Facebook. Hopefully we're going to teach this guy a lesson. Ohh I can't wait. What do you think the chalet will be like? This Alice bird sounds absolutely minted. Where did she get all her money from?'

'She's from a very wealthy family, and then married well.

Money's not everything, though, Olivia,' Liz said, as she wagged a finger at her. 'Alice might have money but she says she's been unhappy for many years. The sad thing is that she says she now has more real friends in us than she ever had.'

'Oh no. That's so sad. We'll keep her entertained. I can't wait to get on me board and throw some moves. Then at the end of the day we can hit the bars.'

'Olivia, you're going away with four women with late-stage cancer. This is not some Club Med holiday. You won't forget what we're there for, will you?'

'Course not, babes. You know me always focused on the job, but I can multi-task. Multi-tasking is me middle name.' Olivia patted Liz's thigh reassuringly. 'Don't worry, I'll make you a nice cup of cocoa and tuck you all in at nine before I hit the clubs.'

'Olivia!' Liz scolded, as she playfully slapped Olivia's arm.

———

The Uber driver offloaded the two women at Gatwick airport. They trundled in to the check in area to find Alice, Sarah and Vicky were already there holding their place in the queue.

'Over here,' called Alice.

Liz and Olivia made their apologies as they navigated their luggage around people already positioned in the queue. Once they were all checked in and had their boarding passes they went through passport control. The security clearance was a lengthy process. Alice had metalwork from previous foot surgery which triggered the scanner. She was also carrying a large quantity of medication which she had to produce paperwork for.

The flight left on time and was uneventful. Alice had arranged a mini bus taxi to collect them from Grenoble and take them on the two-and-a-half-hour journey up to the resort.

Olivia kept everyone entertained en route telling them stories about her babies Mocha and Snowy. She'd left them with her ex-mother-in-law, Brenda, who lived nearby. Olivia and Brenda had remained close after Pete left for Dubai. She felt closer to Brenda than she did her own parents. They did everything together, went to the gym, went shopping, stayed home and drank wine…

They stopped for a toilet break in Moutiere and then made their way up the mountainside to the resort. The last part of the journey was about half an hour up a winding road following a slow stream of vehicles all sleepwalking their way to the same destination. There was a light dusting of snow on the ground as they started their ascent up the mountain. By the time they reached the halfway point the snow was already lying heavy on the ground and the tree branches were laden with snow. Tiny snowflakes were swirling past the window rising and falling gracefully as if in tempo to an invisible conductor. As the snowfall intensified the minibus driver's windscreen wipers struggled back and forth attempting to keep the windscreen clear.

As they drove through the village, Vicky was mesmerised. She'd never been to a ski resort before and was like a child in a sweet shop.

'This is so amazing. Look at the snow on the ground and the buildings look like gingerbread houses. It's just like in the movies.' She peered up the mountainside at the majestic snow-covered rocky peaks rising and falling in tune to their own silent rhythm.

When the minibus finally arrived the staff were on hand ready to greet the women and offload their luggage.

The chalet was a warm and welcoming lamp-lit haven from the snowstorm that was gathering pace outside. They removed their outdoor shoes and moved into the huge pine clad lounge with its cosy sofas facing a large roaring fire in the open stone fireplace. Rooms were allocated. Alice had the master bedroom on the second floor. The entry floor had the main lounge and kitchen and dining area with two bedrooms. Vicky and Sarah took these as they said they would not be able to make it up any stairs once they started skiing. Olivia and Liz were on the first floor.

Vicky sat on her bed watching the snow fall onto the balcony outside. She couldn't contain her excitement. She was in a ski resort in the French Alps. Since when would this have happened if she hadn't got cancer? Maybe some good can come of something bad she thought as she wiped a tear from her eye.

There was a knock on her door. Sarah poked her head in. 'Tea and lemon drizzle cake is ready in the lounge.'

'Coming,' said Vicky.

———

Alice smiled as she sipped her tea. Now this was nice. All her friends together having fun. Liz sat next to her and touched her lightly on her arm. 'Are you okay?' she asked gently.

'I'm fine. Just a little tired. This last round of chemo has really done me in. I can't seem to get my energy back. The fresh mountain air will do me the world of good.'

'It's predicted to be a fine sunny day tomorrow,' replied Liz. 'We can go and get Vicky her skis and try her out on the nursery slopes. Are you sure it's safe to have her chasing after other skiers, though?'

'Oh, she'll be fine,' said Alice. 'That girl has balls. She'll probably be the one who catches him.'

———

Olivia was busy chatting up the chalet boy. He must have been all of fifteen but he was not bad looking.

'Right, so come on then, where's all the action happening at night?'

Olivia was leaning on her elbows across the kitchen counter. She flicked her long black shiny hair over her left shoulder as she sat precariously on the kitchen bar stool ensuring her rather expensive breast implants were displayed beneath her rather tight and low-cut vest.

'I'm thinking I might need to check out some clubs.'

The young chalet boy flushed bright red as he began relaying names of clubs in the resort.

'Olivia,' shouted Liz. 'Please stop distracting the poor boy. He's in charge of our dinner. If it's ruined, we'll blame you.'

Olivia apologised to the boy and sighed as she plopped down on the sofa next to Liz. 'Sorry, babes.'

The snow continued to fall all afternoon and into the night, cloaking the resort in a heavy blanket of snow.

Dinner was amazing. Canapés of black olive tapenade with crostini toasts and pear and blue cheese wrapped in jambon cru were served by the fire along with glasses of champagne. They then moved to the dining table for a starter of halloumi wrapped in jambon cru with melon and mint salad, followed by a haunch of venison with peppercorn sauce, pomme purée, pan fried carrots and parsnips. Liz was served mint and melon salad followed by a winter chestnut stew. When the raspberry chocolate fondant turned up for dessert Sarah could not fit another morsel in. Vicky eagerly volunteered to finish Sarah's dessert off for her.

'No sense letting it go to waste is there,' she said as she tucked in.

After the meal the women all rolled over to the sofas in front of the fire to finish off with a cheese board and port. When the chalet staff left, Sarah, Vicky and Alice decided that they were suitably plastered.

'What the heck, one more won't hurt,' said Alice.

'I think that's enough,' said Liz.

'Oh no, I'll be fine,' said Alice.

'Perhaps some water, then,' suggested Liz, as she got up and walked back over to the dining table. 'Just for a while. We need to discuss our plans for tomorrow.'

'Just chill. Come and sit down and have a drink, Liz.' Olivia patted the sofa invitingly next to her.

Liz frowned as she began to spread the piste map out on the dining room table. 'I'm afraid that we're all here to do some work. Fun's not the only reason we're here.'

'What do you mean?' asked Sarah, clutching a cushion protectively to her chest.

'Well, Alice and I have found out that Mr Kuntz-Finger is going to be in the resort next week,' Liz announced.

All eyes turned to Alice.

'How did you find that out?' asked Vicky.

'Quite simple really,' said Alice soaking up the attention. 'It was quite clear from Liz's friend that Mr Kuntz-Finger's secretary seemed to revel in telling people how popular he was, including the details of his social calendar. All it took was a phone call to book an appointment as a potential client. She asked me when I was thinking of booking and warned me he was very busy. So I asked which weeks he would be away. She gave me next week which matched what Liz's friend had said and I said "ooh I bet he is skiing. I love skiing". She said he was off skiing at a doctors' conference in Meribel and that he needed to get away as he had been so busy lately. I couldn't believe our luck that it was Meribel.'

'My goodness you are clever,' said Sarah. 'I never would have thought of doing that.'

Alice sighed. She really did find Sarah rather dim at times.

'Very smart,' Vicky said tapping the side of her head with her index finger.

'Anyway,' continued Alice. 'I googled the conference and found out which hotel it was being held at. We now know when he'll be arriving and can watch the hotel and the lifts. As luck would have it, Hugh and I are friends with the hotel management so I have a copy of the meeting programme.'

'We have five days to get ready and get Vicky up to speed on those skis,' said Liz.

Vicky and Sarah absorbed the information they had just been given.

Liz waved at them gesturing for them to come over to the table.

'No time to lose. Come on. We need to plan our attack.'

Sarah looked nervously at Vicky, but Vicky was up and already at the table.

Liz began pointing out the hotel Mr Kuntz-Finger would be staying at and then the chairlifts he would possibly be using.

Olivia looked at Liz. 'So, have we decided? Are we going to just give him a scare, or what?'

'Just a bit of a nudge,' said Alice.

32

*O*livia hadn't had the courage to tell anyone yet that she had invited Dwayne and a couple of his friends. They were due to arrive tomorrow, so she was sure they could all relax and enjoy the day together, and she would break the news later. Dwayne and his friends were very easy to get along with, so it was going to be fine. 'Well, I bloody well hope so otherwise it'll be a disaster,' muttered Olivia to herself.

'Right, let's get down to the ski hire shop and collect Vicky's gear and hit the snow,' called Olivia as she walked out of the dining room. She was wearing a bright green and white snowboard jacket and black snowboard pants. She had black snowboarding boots and a pair of green and black gloves and a pair of ski goggles in her hand. On her head she had her favourite mint green, chocolate brown, and grey striped woolly hat.

Liz laughed when she saw her walk past. 'Olivia, you look like a mint chocolate ice cream!'

'A what?'

'A mint… oh never mind.' Liz waved her hand dismissively 'The moment has gone.'

'Come on, let's go, I've got me Box Scratcher,' said

Olivia as she picked up her snowboard, giving it a friendly tap.

'Your what?' Vicky laughed.

'Me board.' She lifted the board up to show Vicky. It was a green, black and white patterned snow board, with white bindings.

Vicky rolled her eyes, chuckling to herself as she followed Olivia out the door. Vicky was wearing an old fleece and salopettes of Liz's. Alice had lent her an old ski jacket.

'We'll meet you at the ski hire shop,' Olivia called to the others over her shoulder as the door closed behind them.

Vicky opened the chalet door and stepped outside into the deep soft snow. The chalet staff had been up early digging a path, but she couldn't help jumping into the large mound of snow next to the front steps and lying on her back performing snow angels.

'Get up, you mad woman.' Olivia laughed.

Vicky smiled and looked skywards at the morning sun. She struggled back up onto her feet, dusted the snow from her trousers and inhaled a large breath of crisp mountain air, before following Olivia to the ski hire shop.

'Why's she in such a hurry?' demanded Alice, turning to Liz. 'This is a holiday, you know. Well, a holiday with a mission. I haven't finished my croissant and porridge yet.'

Liz smiled at Alice as she took out her piste map and unfolded it on the dining room table. 'We need to sort Vicky out and see how well she can ski this morning, then I suggest some of us go and check out the runs. It's going to be soft and porridgy after that heavy snowfall last night.'

Sarah was lying on the couch, still in her pyjamas, and had not put down her phone all morning.

Alice turned in her chair to look at Sarah. 'What are you doing?' demanded Alice. 'You've been on that phone texting all morning.'

'I'm just checking that my sister's walked Patrice and fed the cats.'

'Right, well, put that down now and enjoy your holiday,' Alice said, pushing out the chair beside her indicating for Sarah to sit next to her.

'Are we really going to do this?' asked Sarah hesitantly, as she dragged herself up off the couch and walked over to the chair. 'I mean, we can change our minds, you know. We haven't done anything yet so it's not too late to back out.'

'We are not backing out,' barked Alice. 'I'm afraid we've exhausted all avenues and these men will have to pay the price. They should not be allowed to go on practising. Think of all the women who have been misdiagnosed, and then how many more will be, unless we do something about it.'

Sarah sighed as she bit her lower lip and nodded reluctantly. 'Okay,' she said. 'We won't be out too long though, will we? I wouldn't mind coming back for a coffee. I doubt they'll have oat milk on the slopes and I'm used to having my oat milk latte at half eleven.'

'You can have as many oat milk lattes as you want, Sarah,' said Liz. 'Now go and get your ski gear on. Olivia's already out the door. We'll have to catch them up.'

They went to the local ski shop and collected Vicky and Sarah's ski boots, poles and a helmet.

Liz had brought all her own gear and Alice had hers at the chalet so they were soon kitted out. They eventually headed to the main chairlift in Mottaret with Vicky struggling to adjust to walking in heavy ski boots and staying upright while attempting to carry a pair of skis over her shoulder. The morning was spent teaching Vicky how to get her skis on and off. Once she had mastered that and was able to stand unaided, Alice and Liz taught her how to snow plough.

Olivia sat on the side of the piste listening to some music on her phone. After a while she got up.

She'd become slightly bored and had had enough of

sitting on cold snow. 'I am off for a bit of a recce,' she announced.

'Don't go too far,' Liz shouted after her. 'We'll stop for coffee soon.'

'Laters, babes,' waved Olivia as she hopped on the chairlift and disappeared up the mountain.

———

Liz sensed Olivia was a bit on edge. Maybe she was imagining it. Was it the fact she'd dragged her friend into a plot to teach these men a lesson? It was nothing to do with Olivia, after all. That in itself was the problem. They needed someone to assist who the men wouldn't recognise. And if you were looking for a woman with balls, it was Olivia.

Half an hour later Olivia was back. By this stage Vicky had managed to master a snow plough. She had fallen over about thirty times but was actually loving it. The schnapps that Alice had in her hip flask also helped. They went back to the chalet for coffee and then Vicky attempted the button lift. Vicky managed to fall off only seven times. The first time she forgot to let go and was dragged several metres screaming blue murder. They shouted at her to let go but she didn't hear them.

After lunch they were back on the slopes. The afternoon was spent going up the button lift again and mastering the snow plough further. By the end of the day Vicky was able to traverse a section of an easy blue. Fortunately for Vicky she didn't have a fear of falling.

'I think tomorrow we can go on the chairlift and take you right to the top of the blue and bring you down it,' said Alice.

Vicky smiled triumphantly. 'My legs are killing me, but I don't think I've ever had so much fun in my life.'

Olivia found Liz in the lounge, reading.

'So, babes, I need to ask you something,' said Olivia cautiously.

Oh God, here it comes, thought Liz. 'What?'

'Well, it's like this. You know Dwayne, my fitness instructor?'

'The one you were shagging as soon as Pete was out the door?'

'Yeah. Well, the thing is, I kinda invited him and his two mates to come skiing with us.'

'You what?'

'It was a spur of the moment thing, you know. They got so excited about it. I mean we have a whole fucking chalet to ourselves. These guys love boarding and skiing. We go to the snow dome normally. To actually get free board in a ski resort is an amazing opportunity for them, babes. They're lovely guys.'

'Stop, Olivia,' said Liz holding up her hand. 'Where are they?'

'Oh, they're not here yet. They're flying in tomorrow. They can help us with our mission to get your guy back. I told them your story and they think it's well bad.'

'Wait, hold on a minute. You told them what we are going to do?'

'Not really, I mean, well, kind of. But they were fine with it. Anyway, they're arriving tomorrow. Do you think Alice will be okay?'

———

Liz waited until after supper when everyone had a glass of wine (or two). She stood up. 'Guys, Olivia has something to say.'

Olivia shot her an imploring glance. 'Oh, you tell them. Please?'

Liz gave Olivia a long hard stare. The room was silent as the others waited expectantly for Liz to speak.

She took a long deep breath. 'I think we may have to call the mission off as Olivia has invited some friends who are arriving tomorrow.'

Alice raised an eyebrow. 'And who might these friends be? I don't think it's anyone I know; I haven't invited anyone else.'

'I am so sorry, Alice,' said Olivia leaning over and patting Alice's arm. 'I wasn't thinking. They're lovely guys and close friends of mine.'

'Guys?' questioned Alice. 'You invited guys on our holiday? The last thing we need right now is more men in the picture.'

'They're good looking, if that helps.'

'Humph,' said Alice. The room went quiet. Alice appeared deep in thought. She tapped her fingers on the dining room table for several minutes then turned to Olivia. 'How good looking?'

'Babes, they're fucking gorgeous. Here, I'll show you.' Olivia reached for her phone and tapped it several times before handing it to Alice.

Alice stared at the screen then pointed. 'This one here, what's his name? I quite like the look of him.'

'That's Dwayne… and he is kinda spoken for.'

Alice raised an eyebrow at Olivia.

'I think I can gather what that means. Well, I don't blame you, dear. He is a bit of a dish.'

Vicky was up standing behind Alice. 'Looks pretty good to me too,' said Vicky with a twinkle in her eye. This was going to be a brilliant holiday she thought as she sat back in her chair. She wasn't sure how she was going to be able to move in the morning. Her bottom was aching and she had noticed earlier when in the shower that she had several bruises appearing on her legs. Fortunately she had no stairs to walk up to get to bed.

'My legs are killing me. I might need some deep heat rubbing into them. Do you know if these guys are any good at massage?'

33

$\mathcal{T}$he next morning rooms were rearranged to accommodate the new sleeping arrangements. Alice had the chalet staff running around changing bed linen. Olivia moved into Liz's room. Sarah and Vicky agreed to share a room which left two rooms available for the guys. Alice sent the chalet staff back down the mountain for extra supplies from the hypermarket.

'We're going to have quite a little party here, aren't we?' said Alice.

I wonder what Hugh and Sophie would think if they knew I was hosting three good looking young black men from Brixton, she thought gleefully.

Alice pulled Olivia aside and whispered, 'Olivia, these young chaps… are they bringing anything with them?'

'Ski gear you mean?'

'No. You know,' said Alice, as she put her middle finger and index finger up to her lips and dragged on an invisible spliff.

'What fags?'

'No. Marijuana, cannabis.'

Olivia's eyes widened. 'Ohh, Alice you minx, you! My boys are always getting high and rolling a bit of weed.'

'Well, I wouldn't mind some. Just as a favour for my hospitality, say.'

'They'll only be too happy to share. Their shit's good stuff, I'm telling you.'

'Really? Do you think when we get back to the UK that they might know a supplier?'

'Of course, babes.'

Alice was suddenly feeling quite pleased with herself. 'And, Olivia,' Alice leant in towards Olivia, tapping the side of her nose, 'don't tell Elizabeth. She's such a party pooper.'

———

Liz pulled Olivia aside.

'Olivia, promise me you're not shagging Dwayne again. I don't think it'd be a good idea to be having any of that going on in the chalet. The walls are pine. They're not that thick.'

'No, babes, no hanky panky, I promise.'

'Okay,' Liz said with doubt in her face and shaking her head. 'I think Alice has taken the arrival of extra guests quite well.'

'No need to worry about her. I get the feeling she's quite looking forward to this visit.'

Liz frowned at Olivia. 'Olivia, what have you done?'

'Nothing, babes. Honestly.'

'You have. I can tell. I know that look,' Liz said shaking her finger at Olivia.

'No, babes. Nothing. She just said she thinks the company might be nice for us. Don't worry, they won't tell anyone about our plan. They're solid. I promise.'

———

Sarah had decided to take it easy and enjoy the sun on the balcony of the chalet.

Liz and Alice took Vicky to the top of the blue run. Vicky was still a bit rusty on the chairlift but with Alice and Liz either side of her she managed to get on and off, albeit with some timely instructions. 'Sit. Head back. Bar coming down.'

The first time they ascended the mountain, Alice pulled the bar up as the chair approached the lift station. She had forgotten to warn Vicky. The bar went up. Vicky wasn't prepared to find herself hanging precariously on the edge of a small narrow ledge, with a howling biting cold wind lashing into her, and the view of a sheer drop beneath her. It only took a second for this to register. She screamed, throwing herself back into the seat which only caused her to slide her bottom forward and throw herself off balance, she thought she was going to fall out. Involuntarily, she grabbed onto Alice's arm. The chair started to sway in response to Vicky's panic. Liz quickly grabbed the bar and pulled it back down. She managed to calm Vicky by getting her to focus directly ahead for a few seconds, until the chair shuddered into the station, when Vicky could see the safety of the ground fast approaching below her dangling skis. Then the bar was raised again. Liz and Alice managed to get Vicky off in one piece, but she was visibly shaken, and it took several minutes before she could contemplate the short gentle blue run back down the mountain.

They decided to teach Vicky without poles for the time being. Neither Liz nor Alice favoured the idea of becoming impaled on the end of a ski pole.

Alice was a competent skier. She could turn and ski backwards if needed, so it was decided she would lead the group, with Liz bringing up the rear. Olivia boarded alongside them. Halfway down the run into Mottaret, the group came across a children's snow park. Alice decided it would be good practise for Vicky to attempt going through the short tunnels. Vicky hadn't managed to progress any further than a snow plough. She had managed to fall over a few times, but when she was upright she kept pace with Alice's lead. With some added help of schnapps from Liz's hip flask she could even notch the speed up a bit further.

Vicky was snow ploughing through the tunnels. She smiled to herself as she snaked her way down the piste with the sun shining on her face and a gentle breeze tickling her cheeks. A swish swishing sound behind her made her look to her right. A group of about twenty children were snaking their way down the slope past her. Vicky turned to get a closer look at them. What she didn't realise was that whichever way her body turned her skis would steer her that way. By the time Vicky realised this it was too late. What ensued could only be described as panic. The children sped past. Her pace gathered as she followed the children into a fenced off area. Ahead of her the children and their instructor all came to a sudden halt in front of a wooden hut with a rather colourful giraffe standing outside.

Vicky's knees were locked. She tried to bend them, but it was no good. She had no control over her legs. Her mind was a jumble of instructions. She was frantically trying to pluck some useful information from her brain about controlling her skis, but it was no use. The children were now directly in front of her. She tried to steer away from them as she envisaged multiple tiny brightly coloured fatalities spread across the piste like an exploded pack of Smarties. Vicky used all the strength she had left to throw her body to the left. Just in time. She sped straight past the children and closed her eyes for a split second and breathed a sigh of relief. When she opened her eyes a line of inflatable penguins were waiting to greet her. Vicky threw her arms out in surprise and shock. She went to scream. Bam! The first penguin impacted with Vicky's body. The force of the impact threw the penguin backwards flying into the penguin behind it, then the next and then the next falling like a set of dominoes. A few seconds later Vicky had come to a complete stop. She was lying prone with her arms and legs splayed out on top of the first penguin. Her skis had released and were lying in the snow. There was complete silence.

She slowly lifted her head not quite believing she was still alive. There was a loud squeal of laughter. Vicky turned to look behind her to her right. The group of children were pointing and laughing at her. Some had fallen over in hysterics. Olivia was lying on her back in the snow beside them, convulsing with laughter.

Liz and Alice skied over to help Vicky up.

'Are you okay?' Liz was trying hard to suppress her laughter.

'No. I'm not okay,' she replied. 'I think I've burst my colostomy bag.'

———

'I've never been so embarrassed,' said Vicky once they were back at the chalet. 'I don't know if this skiing's for me.'

'Oh, come on,' said Alice. 'It's all part of the fun.'

'It all sounds rather horrific,' said Sarah. Sarah turned to address Alice and Liz. 'I think you're pushing her too hard.'

'She's enjoying herself,' said Alice.

Vicky went for a shower while Liz soaked her clothes and put them in the wash. Once she'd had a hot shower she felt much better.

Liz placed a bowl of hot soup on the table and pulled out a chair indicating for Vicky to sit down. 'Right, sit down and have some butternut soup. Then we'll leave you to rest for the afternoon.'

'No, I'm fine. I want to go out again.'

'Are you mad?' asked Sarah.

'Yeah. I guess I am.'

Olivia was sitting opposite Vicky. She peered over at the

176

soup. 'None for me Liz. It reminds me of Vicks' burst colostomy bag.'

Vicky had just spooned a mouthful of soup into her mouth. She threw an icy stare at Olivia and then burst out laughing, spraying the mouthful of soup across the table. Both Olivia and Vicky were in fits of laughter for several minutes.

Liz shot a 'what have they taken?' look at Alice and Sarah as they sat on the couch watching Olivia and Vicky.

'Oh God,' said Vicky, once she had gained her breath back. 'My stomach hurts from laughing and the rest of me just… well, it just aches all over. At least I can laugh at me own misfortune.'

'Seriously, babes. You are prime time viewing,' laughed Olivia. 'It was so funny when you fell on those penguins! I nearly pissed myself laughing.'

Alice hoped that Vicky wouldn't give up. They needed the extra pair of hands and Alice was getting great satisfaction out of teaching someone to ski. It gave her a sense of purpose for once in her life.

34

*J*usu, Dwayne and Jordan arrived at about four p.m. Alice had arranged for the taxi to pick them up from the local train station at the bottom of the mountain.

The girls were all back in the chalet by the time the boys arrived. The chalet hosts had left fresh baguettes, jam and Nutella and the afternoon tea menu was written carefully in white chalk on a small piece of black board. The cake was a coffee and banana walnut loaf. Once again there was a vegan option. Liz made hot chocolate for the girls, but not without warning them about the perils of dairy produce.

'I keep telling you it's filled with hormones, guys. You need a plant-based diet. You can't just rely on medicine to help you. You have to look at your lifestyles and try and help yourselves a bit.'

'That's all well and good for you, miss stage 3c,' said Alice. 'But I'm stage 4b and taking dairy out of my life is not going to make much difference to my lifespan. I want to die happy so bring on the chocolate and wine.'

Liz held up her hands in defence. 'I know, I know, but I'm just saying.'

'You can keep on saying it, but it's falling on deaf ears,' said Alice.

'Hear, hear,' said Vicky, as she clicked her fingers in Liz's direction. 'Now hurry up with that hot chocolate.'

Liz turned and stared out of the kitchen window surveying the hillside covered in clusters of pine trees and cosy chalets with smoke swirls rising from their chimneys. She had thought she was in charge but she was starting to feel there might be anarchy in the ranks.

There was a sound of the front door banging and heavy footsteps, followed by the customary clunk of boots stamping off snow. Then followed the creaking sound of the long stool in the porch straining to take the weight of three very tall muscular young men as they sat down to remove their outdoor shoes. Liz turned in the direction of the noise, waving at the women and said in a hushed tone. 'Guys, I think the boys are here.'

Several minutes later in walked three tall handsome athletic looking young black men.

'Hiya,' they all said in unison as they stooped to enter the lounge.

Olivia jumped up and squealed. 'My boys! Come here and give me a hug.'

'This is going to be fun,' Vicky said with a wide smile on her face. 'They're way more gorgeous in person.' It was then that Vicky realised she had dropped her cake all over the floor.

The tall man with shoulder length dreadlocks threw Vicky a wide rather cheeky grin which revealed a gold tooth on the top right-hand corner. She blushed and busied herself with retrieving the remains of the cake from the floor.

'Hi. I'm Dwayne,' he said as he addressed the women, wrapping his arm tightly around Olivia's waist.

'Jordan,' waved the slightly shorter man standing next to Dwayne as he smiled revealing a perfect set of white teeth.

He had neck length corn rows and the most beautiful wide dark eyes.

'And I'm Jusu,' said the third young man. He appeared to be the youngest of the group. He removed his back to front baseball cap to reveal a head of short, cropped hair and yet again was wearing a gorgeous smile which revealed a perfect set of pearly white teeth.

'My dears,' said Alice, waving a hand dismissively at the boys' trousers, 'what's the thing with the trousers?'

The boys exchanged glances nervously and looked at each other's track pants.

'What do you mean, babes?' asked Olivia.

Alice pointed back to the boys. Jordan and Jusu were both wearing baggy track pant bottoms which were slung quite low below their hips exposing a large section of their boxer shorts.

'That. The boxer thing on display. I've never understood why young men wear their trousers so low. Are they not concerned they might fall down completely? Fashion is so odd, dear.'

The boys glanced at each other again and smiled.

'That's the fashion trend. Besides, they never know when they might need to get them off in a hurry,' Olivia said, trying to suppress a giggle.

———

Dinner that night was a rather raucous affair. The boys had found the nearest Spar and bought some beer.

After dinner the chalet hosts left the wine and cheeseboard and said their goodbyes. Everyone moved over to the comfortable sofas by the roaring log fire. The women wanted to hear the boys' stories so they all settled down to listen. Alice was fascinated by how they had struggled on a day-to-day basis growing up. It was a completely different world to the one she had known.

Dwayne told the women how his dad was a security store guard and his mother was a hard working market stall owner. He was one of five children and he relayed how growing up in a two-bedroom flat at bedtime was a first in first served situation with regards to beds. If you didn't get to bed in time it was a mattress on the living room floor. He had been dragged into gang life at a young age due to the state school post code lottery. A friend of his dad's dragged him out of the gang culture when his son was stabbed to death. He didn't want to see Dwayne ending up dead like his son. Eventually he got into fitness and then set up his own personal training company running fitness boot camps which is how he met Olivia. His dad's friend convinced him to give something back to the community by volunteering to help other young gang members in a gang rehabilitation scheme.

Jordan told them how his mum had died very young of cancer while he and his younger sister where still toddlers. His dad was a postman and had to raise them on his own with the help of their aunt. He ended up embroiled in the gang culture which was rife on his estate. If you didn't join, you wouldn't survive, he said. He loved music and was now a DJ doing the club circuit.

Jusu relayed how his dad was a chef and his mum was a seamstress. They had immigrated from Sierra Leone when he was seven. He had four brothers and sisters. His eldest brother was killed in a gang stabbing and it was Jusu's dad that rescued Dwayne from gang life. It was a natural progression on the estate to drift into gang life. He tried to keep it from his family but he knew he couldn't hide it forever. He had a strict Muslim upbringing which was in conflict with the western culture he was exposed to in everyday life growing up in London. He'd been a promising footballer and had been recruited to start in a local football youth academy. He couldn't believe his luck and saw it as a way out of life on the estate. Just before he was about to start at the academy, he was approached by one of the gang leaders and asked to help steal some mopeds from a shop in Clapham. They managed to get the mopeds and make a getaway, edging round the northern edge of Clapham Common at speed. A car had stopped next to the middle white line in the road and due to the speed he was travelling at, Jusu hadn't seen the car indicating to turn right into the side road opposite. He went straight over the bonnet, flying through the air across the road, and hit a high brick wall. The bike flew across and hit the wall behind him, shattering into pieces. When he came to, and realised what had happened, this woman was standing over him asking him if he was okay. He couldn't talk as he was in shock. One of the other gang members saw what happened and came running back to him, grabbing and pulling him up, shouting at him to run as the cops were in close pursuit. Jusu then described how the woman somehow grabbed both him and his mate and had them pinned by the scruff of their necks up against the wall.

'It was like she was mental, man,' he said. 'She told the guy who was in the car to call the police then she was shouting at me an' all. I couldn't work out what she was sayin'. Then I realised she was pointing at my leg saying it was broken and it was then I saw that my bone was stickin' right out of my leg.'

'Oh my God,' said Sarah, cringing at the thought.

"Yeah,' continued Jusu, 'there was blood and bone. It was awful. Then she started shouting at my mate saying, "If you want to be a coward and run, you run, but you're not taking him with you." She started telling me how I needed to go to hospital or I'd lose my leg.'

He paused for effect and looked at the women. They were all silent hanging on to Jusu's every word. He continued, 'So my so-called mate runs off, gets on his moped and legs it, leaving me behind. Can you believe it?'

'Oh no,' said Vicky.

'But then, right, this crazy chick starts telling the police where the bikes have gone. She was screaming at them instructions saying the bikes was stolen and they had gone that way as she pointed down the road.' Jusu pointed for effect. 'The police asked her if she wanted a job. She was fierce, man. Anyways, I went to hospital and had my leg fixed. They say I would've died of an infection if I'd done a runner so in a way the crazy chick saved my life. It still aches now and then. I can ski okay with it. But then I couldn't play football no more so I just drifted back into the gang life. I had a criminal record so I didn't see any other life. Then Dwayne helped me get out and I met Jordan in the rehab centre. I eventually got a job as a bus driver and Jordan got me a part time job as a bouncer in the club he DJ'd at.'

'Wow, that's far from boring,' said Vicky.

'So how are you enjoying the skiing, ladeez?' asked Jusu.

Amid shrieks of laughter the women began to share the story of Vicky's skiing attempts from that morning.

Liz was worried that they hadn't discussed any more of their plans. She hoped things were not going to fall behind. These boys might be quite a distraction. They would only have one chance at this and it needed to be right.

'So gurls,' said Dwayne. 'Olivia tells me you want to teach some of these mother fuckers a lesson.'

'Yes, we do,' said Alice. 'Are you going to help us?'

Liz choked on her drink.

———

'I don't know why we have to bring other people into this,' complained Liz, as she was getting ready for bed. 'It's going to get messy and complicated. I mean what if they tell someone?'

Liz was plumping her pillows rather a little too energetically. 'This could jeopardise everything, Olivia.'

Olivia was lying on her bed staring up at the ceiling

while stroking her hair gently with her hand. She sat up on one elbow and faced Liz. 'Listen, babes, do you want my help or not? Those fuckers have ruined your lives. They don't care about any of you. They don't have a conscience. I can't see them checking up on you and apologising for not listening to you. I mean that wanker of yours even covered up his tracks in his medical notes. He deserves his balls cutting off, babes.'

'But what has that got to do with you telling these guys?' said Liz throwing her arms up in the air.

'You know me. I've always got a plan,' said Olivia soothingly. 'I told you, these guys are solid. They can act as scouts and decoys. Once we locate your guy, we can take a photo and share it. They can be the ones to get up close and knock into him pretending to have a friendly jostle at the chairlift queue and then the tracker goes in. Simple, babes.'

Liz sighed. 'Alright, but we're going to have to be careful,' she said shaking a finger at Olivia.

'What?' asked Liz.

Olivia was studying Liz. 'Nothing,' she paused for a moment, 'it's just that the story Jusu told is kinda familiar. That was you, wasn't it? The woman who pinned him up against the wall. I mean what are the chances of that exact same situation happening twice in the same place?'

'Yeah well, don't advertise the fact,' replied Liz, 'I'm hoping he won't put two and two together as my hair was longer then. The police asked me to testify but I didn't want to for, you know, health and safety issues.'

35

*A*lice felt rather tired the next day. Everyone had finished breakfast. There had been another large snowfall in the night and it was predicted to continue to fall all day. Outside, the mountain was still covered in a blanket of white with an accompanying shawl of silence. Visibility would be low so Vicky's lessons would be limited to the nursery slopes. Several chairs were closed higher up the mountain and were likely to remain that way for the rest of the day. As they were all preparing to leave Alice announced, 'I have a blinding headache. I think I'll stay behind today if you don't mind.'

'Of course, that's fine,' said Liz as she turned to address Sarah. 'Come on, get your gear on. That means you have to step up and help with Vicky's ski lesson.'

'What?' Sarah sighed and dragged herself up off the sofa. 'I was thinking about staying in too,' she said, with a hopeful tone.

'No. Not today,' said Liz firmly.

'Right, I'm off with the guys to check out the runs, babes,' said Olivia. 'Not sure how high we can get with the upper chairs being closed but we'll have a look.'

'You know what you're looking for?' questioned Liz. 'We

want a nice quiet run with some trees and a few concealed lips. Something we can manage to scare him with.'

'I know, babes,' she said, waving dismissively at Liz as she walked out the door.

Olivia and the boys arrived back at the chalet at lunch time. They'd decided to call it a day due to the bad weather. Olivia went to check on Alice who was upstairs in bed.

'This view is amazing,' she exclaimed as she entered Alice's bedroom. A king size pine bed adorned with a multicoloured patchwork quilt was positioned up against the wall, facing floor to ceiling windows which stretched the breadth of the room. The windows opened out onto a large balcony which, in clear weather, provided a panoramic view of the snow-covered valley below.

'The perks of aristocracy I guess, my dear,' Alice said patting the bed, indicating for Olivia to sit on the edge. 'Now come and tell me all about your fascinating life.'

Olivia sat down and chatted. She was not a bad old stick thought Alice. Very feisty. She wished her Sophie had some of that spirit in her, but sadly she took after her father… dull and boring, a social climber married to a dull and boring City executive.

Olivia brushed her hand against Alice's forehead. 'How's your headache?'

'Oooh, much better since you came along and cheered me up.'

She chuckled. 'Shall I get you a cup of tea?'

'That would be nice. A biscuit would be lovely as well. A nice malt biscuit, I think. They're in the kitchen.'

Olivia returned several minutes later with a mug of steaming hot tea and a plate of malt biscuits. 'The boys are all asleep, the lazy buggers,' she exclaimed, as she settled back on the bed next to Alice.

'On a holiday one can do as one pleases,' said Alice. 'I must say I do enjoy everyone's company. This is the most fun I've had in sometime.' Alice sipped her tea. 'Could you pass me my medication box over there?' She pointed towards a chest of drawers with a red plastic case on top.

'Of course.' Olivia placed it on the bed and opened it up to find an array of pill packets.

'Alice, what the hell is this? You're taking more drugs than Ozzy Osbourne!'

'You always make me smile, Olivia dear.' Alice foraged around in the box and then opened up a blister pack and popped a couple of pills.

'What are these steroids for?' asked Olivia, waving a packet at Alice.

'The brain, my dear. My cancer's everywhere, I'm afraid.' She placed a finger to her lips and said, 'Shhhhh. Don't tell the others. They don't know about my brain. I don't want them to know. It'll only upset them.' Alice then tapped a finger to her head. 'You know, make them think they might be next.'

'Oh Alice, give me a hug, you poor lady,' cooed Olivia, as she grabbed Alice and hugged her tightly to her chest. 'You can count on me, darlin'. I won't tell a soul.'

36

THE FIRST MOVE

IF AT FIRST YOU DON'T SUCCEED, THEN TRY AGAIN.

*T*he tracker was in Iain's back pack. The boys had managed to make the friendly jostle at the chairlift queue look friendly enough.

'Yo bro, don't fuckin' push me, man,' Dwayne had said to Jordan.

'I ain't pushin' you, bro.'

'Whoah sorry, man,' said Dwayne as he bumped into Iain Kuntz-Finger. 'Didn't mean to do that. It's just my friends here being stupid.' Dwayne glared at Jordan and Jusu, who laughed playfully back at him.

Iain turned and shot a look of annoyance at the young black man with the dreadlocks who had just pushed into him and was now patting his back in an apologetic manner. He shrugged the man off and moved forward in the queue, managing to edge in front of the three men. The group next to him wanted to sit together so Iain was fortunate enough to get a chair on his own.

As Iain sat on the chairlift, he adjusted his back pack behind him and then admired the view. It was a glorious day with not a cloud in the sky. The sun was shining above trees still heavily laden with snow from last night's snowfall. Iain closed his eyes and held his face up to the warm rays of the sun, feeling the cool mountain breeze on his cheeks. He smiled and thought how wonderful it was to get away and relax. A nice break on his own until the summer family holiday. That wouldn't exactly be a break, though. Two weeks with three children in tow… Work had been tough going lately. That damned Fitzpatrick woman kept cropping up. Just when he thought she was gone she would reappear. She had pursued legal proceedings against him. Thank God that had failed. I should never have seen her, it's always the ones you fit in that cause the trouble. Iain wasn't used to people questioning him. He was too busy for that nonsense, what with his family commitments and a busy social calendar which went hand in hand with being a successful consultant. Why couldn't she just accept what everyone said and deal with it? He didn't give her the cancer so why should he get the blame?

She had argued that he never physically examined her. Iain had to admit to himself that he didn't really like touching patients unless it was absolutely necessary. Such a messy business. Scans were so much more clinical. And these feminists banging on nowadays about gynaecological examinations being degrading… you just couldn't win. Patients could be rather tiresome at times.

Iain had told her, when she was diagnosed, that she was a very sick woman and needed to concentrate on getting better in order to give herself the best possible chance of survival. Unfortunately, in this instance it hadn't shut her up. He'd spoken to Tristan and warned him she was feisty and asking a great deal of questions. He limited the details of her presenting signs and symptoms to Tristan. When Iain checked his original notes he realised they were quite basic. Fortunately, he hadn't written in the date she'd collapsed, so he was able to change this to the summer in his correspondence to colleagues. No one had been any the wiser. Iain scribbled on her inpatient notes that she did not present with symptoms typical of ovarian cancer so hopefully he had that side covered. Who would take her side if it came down to who said what? He was a reputable surgeon, and she was only an infuriating woman with cancer who was bound to be hormonal, bitter and angry and looking for someone to blame. Iain sighed.

He got off the chairlift and started to ski down the slope, completely oblivious to the fact that the three young men who had been behind him in the lift were following him.

———

Olivia was standing on the side of the piste halfway down the mountain on sentry duty. She spotted Iain heading towards the chairlift where Alice was stationed. Olivia phoned Alice. 'He's going for the chairlift now. Can you see him?'

'Yes.' Alice was at the entrance and had been looking for Iain's bright yellow ski jacket. She spotted him straight away.

'Liz and I will head up on the chair here and ski down to the top of your chair.' Olivia whistled to Liz and they both moved over to the chairlift.

'Right let's get ready,' said Alice. 'Sarah, I want you to try and get one side of him, and I will get the other.'

Sarah wasn't feeling very confident, but found Alice rather fierce, so didn't argue. 'Okay,' she said as she clipped her boots into her skis and moved into the queue beside Alice who was already angling her way towards the front of the queue.

Iain Kuntz-Finger came to a halt at the back of the queue. Alice was positioned at the front to the left and made to look as if she was waiting for someone behind. Sarah held back behind Iain, to his right. The queue was short so it didn't take very long for him to make it to the front with Alice and Sarah sliding in either side of him. They went through the barrier and hopped on the chair together with Iain in the middle.

The chair groaned and shuddered as it swept away. The valley floor opened up beneath them, revealing a large wide treeless piste stretched out below. The sun was shining as its rays reflected on the snow, causing the snow crystals to dance and shimmer like thousands of tiny diamonds reflecting in the light.

'What a beautiful day,' exclaimed Alice as she breathed in deeply, inhaling the fresh crisp mountain air.

'Yes, it's lovely,' said Sarah, smiling to herself.

Alice leant forward across the bar to speak to Sarah. She smiled apologetically at Iain who was now stuck between the two women.

'Kate darling, have you got my snacks? Kate?'

'What? Oh sorry, Lucinda. No, I don't think so, but I thought I gave you my energy bars this morning. Why don't you check your jacket pocket?'

Alice rummaged in her jacket pocket. 'Oh yes, you're right. I can feel them in there. I'm a bit peckish.'

Alice turned to Iain. 'This skiing makes one so hungry don't you think?'

'Oh yes very,' he said politely.

'What have you got there?' asked Sarah, leaning forward to speak to Alice.

Alice took a bite of the bar and then studied the wrapper. 'An oat and apricot bar. Rather yummy actually. Would you like one?' She waved it at Sarah.

'Yes please,' said Sarah.

'Would you like one too?' Alice waved the oat bar at Iain.

Iain smiled and shook his head. 'No thank you, I'm fine.'

'I'm sorry. So rude of us passing things across you,' said Alice. 'I'll pass it behind.'

'Here, Kate dear,' said Alice as she passed a bar to Sarah behind Iain. 'Oh no, I nearly dropped it.'

Iain leant forward to give the women more space to make the oat bar exchange. The woman called Lucinda who had been offering the oat bar was fiddling with something behind him.

'Oh dear… Sorry, I won't be a moment. I've got myself caught,' said Alice.

It was too tight for him to turn in the seat and with his helmet his sideways view was restricted, so he didn't see Alice with the carabiner clip she had slipped from the sleeve of her jacket, attempting to clip one end to the chair and one to his back pack.

'Not to worry. All fine now,' she said as she turned back in her seat. 'Sorry about that.'

Alice and Sarah sat munching their oat bars for the remainder of the chair ride. After about ten minutes they saw the lift station ahead. Iain looked from left to right and nodded at both women.

'Are you ready?' he asked, as he went to raise the bar.

Sarah squealed. 'Oh no, please, not too soon. I'm scared of falling.'

Alice looked at Iain and grinned. She put her finger to her head as if to indicate Sarah was mad.

'Alright, Kate. We'll only lift it once we get past the sign to raise the bar. Don't panic, my dear.'

A few seconds later they passed the sign to release the bar. There was a clattering as they all readied their skis and poles into position. Iain lifted the bar. As the chair came into the station Alice and Sarah went to ski off waving to the lift man to attempt to distract him. Iain moved forward and placed his skis down in contact with the snow. Something clipped the back of his skis as he took off. He overbalanced as he felt an impact from his right-hand side. He fell to the ground, clipping the back of the skis of the older woman to his left who had offered him an oat bar. She fell down in a heap in front of him.

———

The lift man shouted and the chair came to a grinding halt. Iain gathered himself and looked up, trying to work out what had just happened. The chair had rotated around to the left behind him and was about to descend back down the mountain again. The woman to his right had somehow managed to get her backpack caught in the chair and was being dragged along hanging precariously on the edge of the chairlift. She was screaming hysterically. Iain's skis had come off in the fall. He managed to leap to his feet and rush over to the woman. He went to release her to find that she had a carabiner climber's double clip which had somehow become clipped on one end to her back pack and on the other to the iron rail at the back of the chair. He unscrewed the clip releasing her from the chair. The woman fell to the ground in a heap, sobbing hysterically.

———

Sarah had prepared herself to ski off rapidly so as not to get caught by Iain's skis. When she went to stand up she immediately realised something was wrong. She was pulled back onto the chair and attempted to push herself up onto her skis again quickly, but she was still being held back as if she was caught on something. She gave another almighty push… it was no good. She was still caught. Sarah's skis went from under her and she found herself hanging half out of the chair. Her poles were flailing in her hands and her skis collided with Iain's. Alice had fallen as well, but Sarah hadn't noticed, she was now only focusing on staying alive. She was being dragged along with the chairlift and could see the abyss which was about to open up in front of her, as the chair contemplated its descent back down the mountainside. With only millimetres to spare the chair shuddered to a stop. Sarah looked up to see a figure hovering over her and then felt herself fall, her cheek pressed hard into the cold packed snow.

The voice said, 'Are you okay? Hello? I'm a doctor.'

Sarah's eyes opened. There was Iain hovering over her.

'Are you okay?' he repeated, as he knelt down in the snow beside her. 'I think you've given us all a bit of a fright.'

'I'm sure she's perfectly fine,' said Alice, dismissively. 'The silly woman has somehow managed to get her backpack caught. She *really* is impossible!'

Sarah moved to sit up, glaring at Alice.

Alice managed to convince the lift operator that all was okay and that she would take Sarah to the medical centre. He frowned and studied the two women.

'I'm fine. So sorry for the fuss. It really was rather silly of me,' said Sarah, as she dusted the snow from her salopettes. 'I forgot to unclip myself. Silly me.'

'Unclip yourself?' questioned Iain.

Sarah looked up at Iain, smiling. 'Oh yes. You see, I have a fear of falling so I normally clip my backpack on during the ride and then unclip myself just before the end. I guess I got distracted when the bar went up too early.'

Iain raised a quizzical eyebrow. 'Are you serious? You can't just unclip yourself with that.' He pointed to the carabiner which Sarah now had in her hand. 'Well, I suggest you do something to address your fear of falling if you wish to pursue skiing as a hobby.'

'I think I just might do that,' said Sarah, as she threw an icy stare over in Alice's direction.

———

Iain wasn't sure what had happened, but he knew it had been a close shave. As the two women sorted themselves out, another friend on a snowboard had come along fussing over them exclaiming to herself, 'My God, babes, what have you done?'

Iain sat on a mound of hard packed snow while he had a swig of whiskey from his hip flask to steady his nerves, watching the women from a distance. What an odd couple of women. How could anyone attach their own back pack to the chair rail? It was then that he recalled the oat bar exchange and the older woman claiming she had got herself caught behind him. He felt unsettled for the rest of the day, not sure if it was due to the chairlift scenario or the unsettling feeling he felt when the girls skied off with their boarder friend. They had skied over to a fourth member of the group, another woman, standing some distance away. Iain assumed she was skiing with the boarder originally. Her goggles were up on her helmet, and it may have been the shadow on her face, but he could have sworn she was staring directly at him. He felt there was something familiar about her but he wasn't sure what. He didn't like the way she was staring.

'Hmmm,' said Iain. What were their names? Was it Kate and someone?

———

'For God's sake! What happened?' said Olivia.

'I'll tell you what happened,' shouted Sarah. 'She,' Sarah stabbed a gloved finger in Alice's direction repeatedly, 'she tried to kill me!'

'Now, now dear,' said Alice, throwing her hands up in defence. 'It was a mistake pure and simple. One runs risks like this when trying to execute a master plan.'

'Are you kidding me?' screeched Sarah. 'I not only nearly got dragged down the mountainside hanging upside down in a chairlift, but I've made myself look a complete fool in front of everyone!'

'Guys,' said Liz as she held both her arms up as if about to conduct a concerto. 'Just calm down. We need to focus. We've missed our opportunity to scare him. We'll have to go to plan B. I hope he hasn't found the tracker.'

Sarah threw her arms up in the air. 'I cannot believe

that's all you're worried about! Thank goodness the lift man noticed what was happening and stopped the chair. If the clip had snapped any later I would have been dead. DEAD. You hear me! We only wanted to scare the shit out of him, and instead you nearly killed me.' Sarah was incandescent with rage.

'Guys, we need to be more careful,' said Liz. 'We can't have any mistakes. We don't want the police after us. Do you think he'll be able to recognise either of you again?'

Alice shook her head. 'No, we used the names you gave us. I wore Hugh's jacket and hat that were in the chalet and Sarah wore Tarquin's old jacket.'

Liz clicked her skis back on and grabbed her poles. 'Right, guys, let's go back to the chalet. The boys and Vicky are already there waiting for us. That's enough for one day. We need to get you out of this gear so he doesn't recognise you again.'

'Excuse me,' said Sarah, waving her arms in front of the others. 'What about the part about me nearly being killed? When are we going to address that issue?'

Liz sighed and leant forward on her ski poles as she stared intently at Sarah. 'Sarah, you seriously need to harden up. Put your big girl pants back on and get moving.'

Sarah stared back at Liz narrowing her gaze. 'I don't think we should pursue this,' she said stubbornly.

'What do you mean?' asked Liz.

'Despite me nearly being killed, are you sure he's a bad as you say he is?'

Liz sighed as she muttered under her breath, 'Here we go.' She looked up at Sarah, her voice taking on a sarcastic tone. 'No Sarah, I just made it all up.'

Sarah leant on her poles. 'I'm sorry, Liz, but he just seemed so lovely and concerned for my welfare.'

Liz put her hands on her helmet. 'I don't believe this. Are you serious? Sarah you are such a pushover. And besides you can't back out. We made a pact.'

Liz could not listen to any more nonsense. She turned and sped off down the run without even a backward glance.

The others all looked at Sarah. 'She's right you know, my dear,' said Alice. 'Too late to back out now I'm afraid.'

'What? She can't force me to do anything I don't want to do.'

'She can be very persuasive,' said Olivia.

'As can we all,' said Alice.

Sarah looked at them both. 'What do you mean?'

Olivia shrugged. 'We're all in this together. We made a pact. That fucker left her for dead as did yours. Never forget that.'

Olivia pushed off on her board with Alice alongside her.

Sarah sighed and shook her head. 'I can't believe I've got myself mixed up in this nonsense,' she said to herself, as she clicked her boots into her skis and followed them down the mountain.

———

That evening Olivia and the boys decided to take the girls for an après ski session at a bar halfway up the mountainside. It was positioned on the blue run back to the chalet. Handy in case they were too tipsy to ski back. They all sat outside on the deck in their ski gear, watching the last of the day's skiers slowly weaving their way down the slopes. The setting sun casting a warm glow over the slopes. The music from the bar was drifting down the valley as if chasing the skiers down the side of the mountain.

'This is glorious,' Alice said to Olivia. 'I don't think I've ever had so much fun! And these boys… these boys are just wonderful!'

'Yeah, babes, they're gorgeous aren't they,' replied Olivia.

Alice ordered champagne. Vicky was up on the deck attempting to dance in her ski boots with Jusu and Jordan.

She'd had an easy day so her aches and pains had eased off a bit. There was the clunk of approaching ski boots on the decking as Dwayne came over, took Alice's glass out of her hand, and placed it on the table. He held out his arm beckoning her up to the dance floor. Alice tried to shoo him away but Dwayne was having none of it.

'You go girl!' laughed Olivia, as she got up and helped pull Alice out of her chair and dragged her onto the deck.

Liz put her glass down, stood up and stretched, admiring the view. She turned to Sarah, who was still silently fuming, and held her hand out.

'What?' asked Sarah.

'Come on, Sarah. After all you've been through. Are you going to let a little thing like this ruin everything? It was a genuine mistake on Alice's part. She didn't do it intentionally. Now come on, we're on holiday. Live for the moment.' Liz smiled, spread her arms out and turned in a complete circle as if showcasing what lay before them. 'Look where we are! Let's enjoy it.'

Sarah smiled at Liz, then stood up. 'I guess you're right.'

Liz put her arm around Sarah as they walked towards the others. She squeezed Sarah's shoulders. 'I know I'm right.'

Vicky and Olivia were attempting to climb onto a long trestle table on the deck along with Jusu and Jordan. Alice and Dwayne were cheering them on. They started bumping and grinding to the music.

'This could be a long night,' said Sarah to Liz.

37

THE CHASE

'*R*ight,' said Jordan. 'I've just heard from Dwayne and he says your guy's on his way. He's coming down the run right now.'

Olivia checked the tracker app on her phone and saw a dot heading towards them on the screen. They all turned to their right and peered up into the distance. A few moments later they could see Iain's bright yellow jacket coming down the piste. Dwayne was following a short distance behind to Iain's left. Dwayne put up his hand to wave to the group. They all waited, expectantly, hoping Iain would turn onto the run directly below them. He came swiftly down the piste above them as if he was continuing forward down the red run, which traversed directly across the red run they were hoping he would turn down. They all held their breath, praying he would turn off to his right. Olivia was already up, with her goggles pulled down over her eyes. She was getting ready to push off on her board when suddenly, Iain slowed down, appearing to be considering his route. He stopped for a moment, looked up at the signposts a few feet away and then pushing off on his skis he turned right onto the run in front of them.

'Right guys, this is it,' said Olivia as she pushed off. 'I'm after him.' In a few seconds she was flying down the slope behind Iain.

Jusu was already positioned halfway down the run, waiting. Jordan phoned ahead and warned him to get ready. Alice was up on her skis and had taken off very quickly behind Olivia.

Sarah looked at Liz. 'I can't believe we're actually doing this,' she said as she leant forward on her poles clipping her boots into her skis.

'Someone has to teach the guy a lesson,' said Liz as they both pushed off on their skis. 'I just hope Vicky stays where she is.'

———

Vicky was sitting at the picnic area overlooking the run, under strict instructions from Liz and Alice to stay there until they came to get her. She was humming away to music on her phone, while watching skiers snaking their way past on the runs below and getting bored and rather annoyed that the others didn't want her there when they confronted Iain. Vicky loved a confrontation. She glanced at her phone screen to check the time. Only a minute had passed since she last checked. She sighed, staring skyward and drumming her fingers on the picnic table. Her phone buzzed. A text message, accompanied by a skier emoji, from Jusu lit up the screen.

They r on the run.

Vicky stood up from the seat and walked to the edge of the picnic area, leaning forward to peer down the slope. I can't really see anything from here. She looked to her right and made out what appeared to be a fairly wide trail. Hmmm, I might get a better view if I followed the trail. It appeared to run towards the run the others would be on. Right, that's it. She walked back to the picnic table, clipped her skis back on and shuffled to the edge of the picnic area.

As she leant forward she positioned her skis into a snow plough position and edged onto the trail.

———

Iain was soaking up the morning sun and enjoying the wind on his face. The run started on a gentle downward incline through some pine trees before opening out to a very steep slope hugging the mountain to his right, with a sheer drop into the valley below on his left. He navigated his way down the piste. The valley below stretched out before him. A chocolate box scene with a collection of snow-covered mountains spattered with clusters of tiny hamlets and trees. Iain was lost in thought. When the skier behind him tapped her poles to warn him she was about to overtake, he gave a start. She moved swiftly past. He didn't clock any details about her apart from thinking she had an excellent skiing technique.

A few seconds later he heard the slush of a board and the intermittent rasp as it hit patches of ice. Iain found boarders particularly annoying especially when they sat down in the middle of the piste. This was generally just over a lip, when you were least able to stop. He turned to glance at the boarder approaching behind him. Hmmm, thought Iain, she looks strangely familiar. It was the green and brown and grey striped hat. He must have seen her earlier. He faced back down the slope for a few seconds and then turned back again as he heard the boarder coming closer. It was then that he noticed there was another skier behind the boarder, who looked like one of the men who had jostled him at the lift two days ago. The young man glided effortlessly past. Iain's nostrils recoiled as he did a double take. The man was skiing without poles. He had his hands clasped behind his back, dreadlocks flying out behind him and appeared to be smoking a joint as he skied along.

'Yo bro, what's up? Lovely day init?' the man said in

greeting. And with that he was gone. Iain could sense the female boarder was now closing in on him. Why couldn't he shake off the feeling that she was following him? He slid sideways, bringing his skis to a stop. The woman boarder swept past, smiling at him and giving a quick wave as she went. Iain shrugged as he studied her disappearing into the distance. He couldn't be completely certain with all the gear she was wearing but he got the impression she was quite good looking. He smiled and shook his head as it dawned on him. She fancies me.

'You've still got it, Kuntzy boy,' he said out loud to himself as he pushed off on his skis again. Perhaps he could catch her up.

A few seconds later he turned a corner. The gradient of the slope started to increase dramatically. He began picking up speed. He flew over a lip, becoming airborne for a second before landing back on the piste, swaying left and right to maintain his balance. Iain was in the zone and enjoying the rhythm he had going. Another lip. Airborne. Back on the piste. Left then right. Another lip. Airborne again. Back on the piste. As he landed he swung out to the left-hand side of the piste and then back into the right… Fuck! Those bloody boarders were sitting down right on the right side of the piste. Iain instinctively swerved to the outside but had to immediately turn back inwards to avoid a sheer drop to his left. He managed to get round the boarders and safely back onto the piste just below them with inches to spare. As he landed and tried to correct his stance, he heard a scream to his right. There was a blur of colour and skis coming from the slope above. A skier was coming down through the trees and snow out of control. Iain only had a second to react and swerved again to his left, but the skier was already on the piste and millimetres from impacting with him. The skier fell onto their back with their gloved hands scrabbling to catch onto anything to slow them down. They clipped the front of Iain's skis, and due to the speed he was still travelling at he was propelled out of control back towards the left-hand side of the piste. He felt the inside edge of his right ski catch. He tried to bring it up clear of the snow but it was too late. There was nothing to stop him. Iain managed a cry of surprise as he fell over the edge of the slope. The snow was soft but the rocks and branches were sharp. Everything must have happened in seconds but to Iain it felt like slow motion. There was snow everywhere. Iain could hear the crack of bones breaking as he fell forwards. His head was going backward and forward and he felt his leg twist up behind his back, at which point he was sure his hip had dislocated. Suddenly an overhanging tree and a large snow drift brought Iain to a stop. There was silence. Then nothing.

38

'What the fuck, babes,' shrieked Olivia. 'I think you've killed him.'

Olivia stood at the side of the piste, bending forward with her hands resting on her knees, peering down the slope to see if she could see any sign of Iain Kuntz-Finger.

Vicky was lying in a heap on the piste. Jordan, Dwayne and Jusu were staring at the girls as if they couldn't quite take in what had just happened.

Jusu started laughing. 'Oh my dayz. Oh my dayz.'

'You were lucky you managed to fall on your back and slow yourself down or you'd be dead alongside him,' said Olivia to Vicky.

Dwayne and Alice walked over beside Olivia. They all peered over the side looking for any signs of life. Nothing. They turned back, looking at each other, shrugged in resignation and shook their heads.

Olivia went to check Vicky was okay.

'Oh guys, I was out of control. I was up at the picnic table waiting like you said and then I got so bored. I saw your texts and thought if I just came a bit closer then I could see what was going on. I wanted to take a look over the edge. There was this trail so I went over to it. When I looked over the edge my skis went forward and I couldn't control them,' wailed Vicky. 'The next thing I was gathering speed and coming down the slope. It was so bumpy and got really narrow. I thought I was going to die. I could see the run in front of me and tried to turn onto it but I couldn't stop in time. My legs couldn't take any more, so I just fell over.'

'Well, you've certainly done a number on that fucker, babes,' said Olivia.

Alice was still peering over the side of the mountain. 'I think we'd better go,' she said as she turned back to the others.

The swish swishing sound of approaching skiers made them all turn and look. Sarah and Liz came into view.

'What happened?' asked Liz, as they both skied to a stop. 'Vicky, we told you to stay at the picnic area. How did you get down here? Have we lost him?'

'We sure have, hun,' said Olivia. 'In fact, Vicky managed the whole thing single-handedly. I think you'll find the fucker at the bottom of this slope,' said Olivia, pointing off the side of the piste.

'What?' said Liz.

Sarah went completely white. 'Is he… is he?'

Olivia looked at her. 'Dead, babes? Not sure, but he went over the edge pretty bloody fast and there's no sign of life so far.'

'Nothing,' said Dwayne. 'No signs of life. I've just checked.'

'Oh hell,' said Liz. 'What do we do?'

'I suggest we all go home and have a nice glass of wine,' said Alice.

'But we can't leave him there. He could be injured,' said Liz.

'Hang on a minute,' said Alice, her voice taking on a hint of astonishment. She walked towards Liz. 'Is this the guy who left you with cancer raging through your body and didn't give a shit? He then tried to cover all his tracks and in doing so has dramatically reduced your chances of survival. The same guy you said you wanted dead. You think now is the time to pull the morality card on us? We're all here because of you, my dear. You had better remember that.'

Liz went quiet. Everyone turned to face her. She looked from one to the other and then down to the ground where Vicky was still lying on her back squinting up at her. 'Yeah because of you, I'm now a cold-blooded killer,' said Vicky.

'Listen guys, the intention was to shake him up a bit and possibly injure him, not to kill him. Could we at least report to the police that we saw a skier go off the edge and we think he was out of control? At least then we would know if he was alive or dead.'

'We could say he swerved to miss us. I could say my board was playing up and I stopped to adjust the straps,' said Olivia. 'But how do we explain Vicky?'

'She was in front of you, and when he swerved the boarders he went straight into her,' said Alice.

Olivia was sitting on the snow next to Vicky.

'You were out of control.' Vicky and Olivia started giggling.

Liz frowned at them. 'What's so funny?'

'This, babes,' said Olivia, sweeping her hand across the slope. 'This whole thing's funny. You organised for us to come out here to get revenge on this guy and now we've managed to kill him by accident.'

Vicky was rolling around with tears in her eyes. 'Oh, and I think I have burst my stoma bag again, guys.'

'Bloody hell,' said Olivia. 'Keep away from me. We had garlic last night, babes.'

'Guys, please focus. If we have to make any police statements, we're done,' said Liz.

Alice stepped towards Liz, brushing snow from her salopettes. 'Well then, my dear, you'll have to decide what you want to do rather quickly as we haven't got all day. If anyone else comes down this run they might wonder what all the fuss is about. You really are the most, Elizabeth.'

Sarah started crying.

Liz put an arm around Sarah. 'It's okay, Sarah. We'll think of something.'

'I can't go to prison,' sobbed Sarah. 'I thought we were just going to shake them all up a bit.'

'Well fuck me, babes, but that bastard's well and truly shaken up,' squealed Olivia.

'Come on, man,' said Jusu. 'It was an accident. Let's just chill and wait a bit to see if he starts shouting or something.'

They sat on the side of the piste for about five more minutes. Several skiers came past, slowing down. One couple stopped to check they were okay as they saw Vicky lying on the ground with Liz leaning over her. They quickly moved on when she smiled at them and pointed at her burst colostomy bag, which Liz was helping her to clean up.

Liz eventually reached for her phone. 'I'm going to have to phone the mountain rescue. I can't do this. I can't live with myself. He's an absolute idiot but if we don't do something we're as bad as him.'

'No need, darling,' purred Alice, as she dragged on a joint Dwayne had handed her. 'There's a chopper already on its way.' They looked skyward following Alice's extended gloved arm. A black dot in the distance against the clear blue sky. Then they heard the *chuff chuff chuff* of the blades of the approaching helicopter.

'Either someone's seen him fall or he's alive and well. I suggest we get the hell out of here,' said Alice.

———

The group began making their way back to the chalet by descending slowly along the red run which hugged the side of the mountain. Although Vicky was shaken and bruised she managed to get back on her skis. Alice instructed Vicky to stand directly behind her hugging her round the waist. By placing Vicky's skis on the outside of Alice's, they managed to get her to a point where a gentle blue run intersected with the red run they were on.

When the group reached the blue run, they sat for a moment on the side of the piste silently watching the helicopter hover above, giving Vicky time to rest. They could just make out the rescue workers in the distance attempting to retrieve Iain Kuntz-Finger's body.

After a short rest they began skiing down the blue run. Vicky managed to slowly snow plough her way back down the rest of the run with the air around her permeated with the aroma of her burst stoma bag.

––––––

Alice decided to head off ahead of the group and meet the rescue helicopter at the helicopter pad at the bottom of the valley. In her excellent French she managed to find out from the crew (by saying she was looking for her friend who was not answering their phone and she wanted to check who they had collected) that someone skiing off piste had heard a cry and looked up to see a man tumbling down the mountain. Alice peered over at Iain's ashen face. He was unconscious and looked to be in rather bad shape. He was attached to an oxygen mask and several bits of medical tubing, which were in turn attached to various devices.

'Oh, sorry,' said Alice. 'No, that is definitely not him. Sorry to have bothered you.'

Iain was flown out to Grenoble.

––––––

Back at the chalet everyone got out of their ski gear. There was not much conversation. They all appeared to be in a reflective mood absorbing the enormity of what had just happened. Jusu and Jordan went about lighting the fire.

'I'll get some coffee and teas on the go,' said Liz tapping Sarah lightly on the arm. 'Sarah, will you help me?' Sarah followed Liz into the kitchen. The chalet staff had laid out fresh bread with jams, a vegan sweet potato brownie for Liz and chocolate brownies for the others. The staff had been given the night off. This meant the group had the chalet to themselves to discuss the day in private without any watchful eyes and ears. Vicky came into the lounge and appeared to be limping.

Olivia jumped up to help her to the sofa. 'Vicks, are you okay?'

Vicky winced as she tried to sit down. 'I think I've hurt my foot. It's pretty sore.'

'Let me have a look.'

Olivia lifted Vicky's foot up onto a cushion and removed her slipper and sock.

'Ohh, it looks a little bit swollen. Did you twist it in your boot when you fell?'

Vicky rolled her eyes at Olivia.

'Twist it! I was all over the place. You saw me. I was out of control. I'd be surprised if I haven't broken anything!'

'But can you remember feeling anything pull?'

'What, aside from my whole body as I careered down the side of the mountain?'

'Right, let's get some ice on this and elevate it. If it's no better in the morning we'll have to go to the medical centre. Liz, can you bring some ice in here?'

Liz busied herself getting ice from the freezer while Olivia plumped pillows attempting to make Vicky more comfortable.

'Painkillers, Vicks?' asked Liz.

'Morphine would be nice.'

'I don't have any of that, I'm afraid.'

Dwayne got up and disappeared for a few moments. He

came back with a plastic bag and placed it on the coffee table.

'This might help.' He opened the bag and pulled out a lighter and some ready rolled spliffs.

'Now you're talking,' said Vicky.

'Where the hell did you get all this dope from?' demanded Liz.

Dwayne tapped the side of his nose and smiled at Liz. 'I could tell you but then I'd have to kill you.'

Olivia giggled.

Liz frowned back at them.

Alice smiled. 'I'd better cancel our restaurant booking for tonight. We can order take away instead. It's the best Indian you'll ever taste, my dears.'

'No, we can still go,' said Liz. 'Put those spliffs down.'

'I can't,' said Vicky. 'I doubt I'll be able to walk very far. Just out to the cab might be difficult. Is it far?'

'It's just outside Meribel Village on the other side of the valley,' said Alice. 'It depends if you can sit with your foot down for dinner.'

'I don't think I can, to be honest,' said Vicky as she stared down at her increasingly swollen ankle.'

'That's decided then.' Alice opened Tsaretta Spices menu on her phone. After several minutes of deciding what everyone wanted, she cancelled their booking and placed an order from the take away menu.

———

'Well, one down and three to go!'

'What? Do you think this is funny, Alice?' Sarah looked up at her, appearing slightly shocked. 'Do you have no moral compass?'

Alice's eyes narrowed as she settled back into her armchair with her elegant long arms draped over the arms of the chair. She placed her slippered feet on the edge of the coffee table, as she crossed her legs, and then took a long, drawn-out puff of the spliff in her right hand, inhaling slowly, as she rested her head back on the cushion behind her.

'Well now, that depends what you would describe a moral compass as. I prefer the definition of not bowing to social, economic or political pressure and being consistent in my beliefs regardless of the consequences, even if the consequences mean harm or even death. What about you, my dear?'

'I believe it's a set of values that guide a person with regards to ethical behaviour and decision making,' said Sarah. 'I think you might find that means drawing the line at murder.'

'Hmmm, interesting,' replied Alice. 'These men are the ones lacking a moral compass and the system is allowing them to get away with this. So, if society and the system continue to protect them and their behaviour then perhaps it's time for us to bend the rules and teach them a lesson.'

Olivia started clapping. 'You go, Alice darlin'.'

'You're right,' said Liz. Vicky nodded in agreement as she winced and attempted to reposition her swollen ankle on the cushion.

Sarah shifted nervously in her seat. She couldn't believe she had been talked into this hair-brained scheme. It suddenly dawned on her… the realisation they were now in too deep, and that she appeared greatly outnumbered.

'But what about the consequences? We could go to prison if they find out what we did.' She shuddered at the thought. She had images of the scenes from *Orange is the New Black* where Miss Rosa is taken for her chemo treatments handcuffed in the back of a prison van. That was not going to happen. They had a plan and Alice did say she was willing to take the wrap. Or was she? That was a while ago that she had promised that. She might have forgotten. What if someone else died first? Oh my God, the embarrassment for her family. Suddenly Sarah felt a bit edgy. She didn't want to say anything, though. She wasn't sure that she wanted to find out what it would be like to annoy Alice.

'You're obsessed with prison, my dear girl,' said Alice. 'They won't find out. We all need to keep our nerve and everything must stay within this group. Never mention it to anyone. Not your husbands or girlfriends or family. You hear me?' They all nodded silently. 'So stop worrying, Sarah. The four of us have all been given what could be seen as death sentences because of these men and no one even seems to bat an eyelid about that.'

'That's so true,' said Liz, as she rested back on the sofa between Sarah and Vicky. She squeezed both their hands. 'We're all in this together.'

Sarah glanced around the room looking at them all. The boys were lounging on the opposite sofa with Olivia lying across them on her back, completely stoned. Sarah smiled and squeezed Liz's hand. She had never felt so alive. What the heck. Perhaps it was time she let go and lived for once in her life.

———

'These gurls are fuckin' mental, man,' said Jusu, lying in bed that evening.

Jordan was lying on the bed opposite with his arms tucked behind his head. He turned his head on the pillow to face Jusu. 'Yeah man, I thought dying women would be all quiet an' boring, bro.'

39

The phone buzzed on the kitchen counter. Louise reached over and grabbed it. 'Sebastian,' she shouted, 'put your jacket on please. We need to leave. Hello?'

A gentleman with a thick French accent came onto the line.

'Hello. Madame Kuntz-Finger?'

'Yes?'

'This is Monsieur Marat from Grenoble hospital. We have your husband here. Monsieur Iain Kuntz-Finger?'

'Yes, that's my husband,' Louise gasped. 'What's happened?'

'I am afraid he was injured in a skiing accident today. He skied off the cliff. He is stable but he has a minor head injury. He also fractured his leg and, ahh, needs surgery for these tonight.'

'Oh my God,' exclaimed Louise.

Iain Kuntz-Finger came back to the ward that evening. He was in a great deal of pain when he woke and couldn't quite work out what had happened. His right eye was swollen shut and he had cuts and bruises all over his body. His left lower leg was in a below knee cast and elevated on several pillows. When he breathed, it hurt. He felt like he had cracked some ribs.

'Monsieur, you have been in an accident. You know. With the skis. You have broken the leg.

'Your wife… she is coming here… on the plane… to Grenoble. You understand?'

Iain closed his one good eye again and drifted off into a deep morphine filled sleep.

———

The girls decided that the rest of the week would be taken at a much slower pace. Vicky could hardly move with all her bumps and bruises. They took her to the local medical centre to get her foot and ankle checked. An x-ray and scan later, she was reassured it was only a strain. They bandaged the foot and ankle and instructed her to rest for a few days.

———

'Are you okay, hun?'

Liz sat at the table, on her phone to Gareth as she looked out over the valley below. It was a lovely sunny morning in Meribel. 'I'm fine. Why?'

'I read in the paper today there'd been a few serious accidents at Meribel and one death.'

'That's nothing out of the ordinary for a ski season, is it?' replied Liz, laughing.

'No, I guess not. Well take it easy. I miss you, babe.'

She loved it when he called her babe. 'I miss you too. Love you.'

'I love you too. See you in a few days.'

Liz put the phone down on the table and rested back in

the deck chair continuing to admire the view. She smiled to herself. For the first time in a very long while she felt happy, very happy indeed.

———

Iain spent the week in Grenoble hospital and was then medevacked back to the UK. Louise had flown out to be by his side and arrange for him to be repatriated. He had a displaced spiral fracture of both the tibia and fibula. The surgeon had to pin the bones back into position and place his leg into a cast. He was told he was very lucky not to have fallen any further down the mountain. Fortunately for him, there had been a young sapling growing out of the side of the mountain, which had a mound of compacted snow surrounding its base. Iain had landed in it and broken his fall. He'd been concussed and had no recollection of anything immediately leading up to the crash, or afterwards, until he woke up after the surgery.

He was off work for six months and then walked with a permanent limp. The strange thing was he couldn't stop thinking about the woman he had seen a few days before the crash, the one he saw staring at him after the chairlift incident. He couldn't think for long, though, as every time he tried to remember, he would get a dreadful pain behind his eyes.

40

LATE FEBRUARY 2019

$\mathcal{S}$arah was standing in the queue at the local post office. She'd been grocery shopping in Hitchin and the boot of the car was full of frozen food. Twice, she had forgotten to post the twins their new woollen hats and scarves she'd knitted for them, so she was determined this time to send them. She had driven past three post offices when she suddenly realised they were still in the car with her.

Her feet and legs were aching. How long was this going to take? She peered anxiously towards the front of the queue. Margaret was at the counter supervising a new assistant who appeared to be struggling with a basic grasp of what the role of post office counter assistant entailed.

Sarah sighed impatiently and shifted from one foot to the other, scratching the side of her head. Her wig was so itchy and her hair was only just starting to grow back. She'd been told the last course of chemo wouldn't result in complete hair loss but unfortunately for Sarah it had.

About ten minutes later she found herself at the front of the queue, so she walked over and placed her packages on the counter.

'I need to pay for the postal bags. Could I have first class to London for each package, please? Oh and I have a card here and postage for airmail to Canada.'

'If you could put the first package on the scales, dear,' said Margaret. 'Now Davina,' she said indicating to the assistant, 'you need to check the weight of the package. So check your list. See there. It tells you the weight and what postage is required.'

The young assistant nervously checked the postage following Margaret's instructions.

'Excuse me, dear,' came a deep voice from behind Sarah. 'I'm in rather a hurry. Now, I need to pay for some stamps.'

Sarah turned as she felt someone leaning over her shoulder. Humphrey Smythe St John was hurriedly pushing some money under the counter window.

Davina looked nervously towards Margaret for direction.

Margaret peered through the glass at Humphrey as she beckoned towards Sarah.

'I'm sorry, Humphrey, but we're dealing with this customer first.'

'Well, I am in rather a hurry. I have the right change and I don't need a receipt. I've been waiting in the queue for some time now. You won't mind will you, Sarah dear?' he continued as he patted Sarah's arm affectionately.

'As a matter of fact I do mind.' Sarah's reply came out as a whisper, which no one seemed to hear. If anyone had heard, they chose to ignore it. No one ever expected Sarah to complain.

'One book of first class and one book of second class stamps please,' said Humphrey.

Sarah sighed in resignation.

'We don't have any books left,' said Davina, looking towards Margaret for guidance.

'No, we're out of books, but we can tear some out of the stamp folder,' suggested Margaret as she tapped at the folder.

Davina flicked through several pages until she came to the page of first class stamps. 'How many stamps in a book?'

'Twelve, dear,' replied Margaret with exasperation.

'Oh Okay.' Davina began counting and tearing out stamps from the folder. 'One, two, three, four, five, six.'

Margaret sighed and rolled her eyes.

As Davina continued to count, Sarah felt her patience wearing thin. She took a deep breath but could not contain the anger any longer.

The words ground through Sarah's teeth but still only came out as an inaudible low growl. 'I said I do mind.'

'Hmmm? What's that, dear?' said Humphrey distractedly, as he tapped his fingers impatiently on the counter. 'Bless you. How are you anyway? You should be at home with your feet up.'

'Twelve,' said Davina triumphantly, waving the stamp, as if holding a prize.

Something inside Sarah suddenly snapped. It was as if someone had flicked a switch.

'I SAID I DO MIND,' she roared, as she felt the floodgates open.

Everyone stopped what they were doing and stared in shocked surprise in Sarah's direction.

Davina stood open mouthed. She let go of the stamp and it fluttered and came to rest on the counter in front of her.

'Who the hell do you think you are swanning in here, jumping the queue when everyone else has been waiting patiently? I've had it up to here with people like you.' Sarah raised her hand above her head, indicating her level of annoyance. 'Taking advantage of people's good nature, full of your own self-importance. Did it ever occur to you to consider how long I've been standing in this queue?'

'You asked me how I was, but you don't really care, do you? Well, let me tell you how I am. I feel dreadful. My feet hurt, my body aches, I can barely drag myself out of bed some mornings.' Sarah reached up to her head, grabbing her wig and ripping it from her head to the accompaniment of a symphony of gasps from her onlookers. 'And I am completely fucking bald and starting to grow a beard. How do you think I'm feeling?'

Humphrey paled. He appeared to be shaking. A drop of Sarah's spittle landed on his nose. He didn't dare to attempt to try and remove it for fear of drawing further attention.

'And then to top it all off, I get a tosser like you coming in here and pushing in front of me,' continued Sarah, as she prodded Humphrey's tweed covered chest with her index finger.

Humphrey began to turn a shade of red as he felt everyone's eyes bearing down on him. Then for a few seconds, there was complete silence as everyone in the room absorbed Sarah's outburst.

When Humphrey realised she had finished her assault he began to nervously gather his things up.

'Oh dear, dear,' he tutted, 'I have really upset you, haven't I? I am sorry, my dear.'

Humphrey turned to Davina. 'Please, serve Sarah. I'll come back another time.' He made a hasty retreat for the door but not without everyone in the shop forming a guard of honour for his walk of shame. When the door closed behind him all eyes travelled back to Sarah.

'Huh,' she said, as she shook her head in disdain at Humphrey's recently departed form.

For the first time in what seemed like forever, Sarah felt exhilarated. She felt a weight rise from her shoulders. With an air of renewed confidence, she turned back to the counter to be served. Davina was sitting at the counter with her mouth still wide open.

'Right, Davina,' commanded Margaret, as she pushed her gently, 'shift aside and let me attend to Sarah. We need to get this queue moving.'

As Margaret began to serve, Sarah could hear

whispering behind her in the queue and several muffled giggles. She busied herself with the impossible task of positioning her wig back on her head without the aid of a mirror. She didn't fancy the cold walk out to the car without any hair and she'd drawn enough attention to herself for one day.

Once Margaret had sorted Sarah's post out, she turned and left the shop, but not without an address to the small crowd behind her.

She jutted her chin out in a look of fierce determination. 'Good afternoon, ladies.' The small crowd stood silently taking in Sarah's appearance.

Sarah's wig was placed precariously on her head, in a somewhat lop-sided fashion, and it had begun to take on the form of a partially dismantled bird's nest. No one was brave enough to attempt to point this out to her.

'Well, well,' said Vera, the local busybody, 'that was rather entertaining, wasn't it? I was only queuing for my pension. That was better than an episode of *Coronation Street*.'

'The poor girl,' replied Edna. 'She's not well. I think she's under a lot of stress. Caroline says that she's struggling with her diagnosis. Blames the specialist, you know. One of them fancy Harley Street boys. Fat lot of good that did her.'

'No! Ohh, poor thing.'

'And apparently her George is having a rough time dealing with it as well.'

'So sad… and to think so young.' Vera tutted.

'Doesn't sound like she's got long left.'

'Oh dear.'

It took approximately twenty minutes for George's mother, Caroline, to have the finer details of her daughter-in-law's outburst relayed to her.

After supper, Caroline dialled George's number.

He sighed as the phone began to ring on the table beside him. It could only be Mother. No one else used the landline apart from:

A) cold callers

B) it was a life and death situation i.e the twins had run out of money

C) there was no mobile network connection

George picked the receiver up as he shouted, 'It'll be Mother. I've got it.'

Sarah was resting on her bed upstairs but jumped up, grabbing the receiver on the upstairs phone at the same time as George. I wonder what Caroline will have to say she thought, knowing full well that the village gossip exchange would have been in overdrive. She listened in to the conversation from the safety of her bed.

'St John has phoned me, darling... and half the village busybodies as well.'

'What about, Mother?'

'Your wife's outburst in the local post office today.'

There was a moment's silence on the line. Sarah took a deep breath as both she and Caroline waited for George's reply.

'Outburst? What outburst are you talking about?'

Sarah thought she could hear George's voice take on a cautious tone.

'I'm afraid she made quite a scene. Took poor old St John to task. He apparently jumped the queue as he was in rather a hurry... she practically ripped him to shreds. The poor fellow is beside himself. You know he's got a dicky heart.'

'Well, why did he jump the queue, the silly old chap? Sounds like he might've quite rightly deserved it.'

Sarah smiled silently on the other end of the receiver. Good old George, always jumping to her defence.

She could detect a rising hint of annoyance in Caroline's tone. 'Well, it's not just him, darling. What about me and my reputation? She can't go round behaving like that despite... you know.'

'You know what?'

'Oh darling. Don't make me say it. It's such a dreadful…'

'Cancer!' shouted Sarah down the phone. 'It is called cancer!'

Sarah slammed the receiver down. Typical. She threw herself back down on the bed, sobbing. Caroline was always only concerned about her reputation.

Caroline held the receiver at a distance away from her ear, staring at it as though she was examining something rather distasteful. She studied it for a few seconds, and then returned the receiver to her ear.

'You see, darling, she's not right. She's been acting rather odd. Ever since she hooked up with those other ladies from that group.'

'Okay, Mother. I'll have a word.'

Several moments later, George made his way up the stairs and hesitated outside the bedroom door. He thought he could make out a faint sobbing sound. 'Sarah,' he called cautiously.

There was no reply. He called again. No reply. George decided he would have to brave it. He opened the bedroom door. Fortunately for George, his years of rugby had not gone amiss. He always approached her crying fits as if executing a well-planned line pass. He waited for the ball. He saw the pair of slippers flying through the air as soon as they left Sarah's hands.

'Go away,' she screamed. 'Just leave me alone.'

George managed to catch one of the slippers as the other hit the door and landed with a thud on the rug. He made his retreat, pulling the door closed behind him, went downstairs and picked up the phone.

Half an hour later Sarah heard a soft tap on the bedroom door, followed by her sister's soothing voice.

'Sarah, darling. It's me, Trisha. Can I come in?'

41

EARLY MARCH 2019

*L*iz and Vicky drove through the quaint Hertfordshire village of St Ippolyts. They passed through the centre admiring the architecture of the sixteenth century timber framed homes and seventeenth century gabled houses.

Five minutes later they made a right turn down a country lane and then a right into the gravel driveway of Brinkley Lodge.

'Wow,' gasped Vicky. 'Sarah ain't short of a bob or two either, is she?'

'No, it doesn't look like it,' agreed Liz, as she studied the grade two listed Elizabethan timber framed home in front of her. She parked the car at the side of the front entrance and they walked up to the arched heavy oak front door framed by a gnarly garland of bare wisteria branches. Liz picked up the wrought iron lion's head door knocker and announced their arrival. They were greeted by Patrice's welcoming barks from the other side of the door.

'Hello,' said Sarah, as she opened the door. 'Get down, Patrice!'

Patrice loved visitors. He had seen Sarah preparing

lunch and couldn't contain his excitement when the guests finally arrived.

'Sorry,' said Sarah, as she pulled Patrice away.

'Don't worry,' said Liz, patting Patrice's head. 'He's just excited to see us, aren't you darling?'

'Wow wow wow woow,' said Patrice in agreement.

'Come through.' Sarah ushered Vicky and Liz through into a spacious oak beamed lounge with an inglenook fireplace at one end. The floor was of heavy warped oak and covered in Persian rugs.

There were large patio doors opening out onto a paved terrace which gave way to a wide pristine lawn bordered by shrubs and a view of a large open field beyond.

'Please sit down,' she said as she indicated to several cream fabric sofas covered in bright cushions and throws.

'Blimey,' said Vicky looking round the room as she sat down, 'these bankers certainly earn a load of treacle. I better not tell Kurt about this place. He'd be casing the joint.'

Sarah smiled and made a mental note to ask George to review their home security system and contents insurance.

'Alice is on her way. She's somehow managed to get herself lost. Her chauffeur just phoned me. For some reason she thought I lived in Cottered.'

'Where's that?' asked Vicky, making herself comfortable on the sofa.

'About twenty minutes away. She insists it was the chauffeur's fault, but I can't see how, as she gave him the wrong details. He ended up wrangling my number out of Alice and phoned me. They should be here shortly. Would anyone like a drink?'

Sarah busied herself laying out nibbles and pouring drinks while Patrice chose to curl up on Vicky's lap. It was an ordeal. Poor Patrice. He could smell the women and knew they were all unwell. He so wanted to comfort them all. He had spent several moments sniffing both of the guests and decided this one was the sickest, so he jumped up and spread himself on her lap.

Several moments later there was an impatient knocking at the front door. Patrice growled as he opened an eye and cocked his ear. He jumped up and ran to the front door.

'Her Majesty has arrived,' said Vicky, winking at Liz, as Sarah made to answer the door.

Alice's voice came floating down the hallway. 'Dreadful darling. Absolutely dreadful. What a mix up! Silly man.'

Alice then appeared and collapsed in a dramatic fashion on one of the sofas. 'Darlings! Here at long last.' She turned to Sarah adopting a commanding tone. 'Now where's that gin and tonic, my dear?'

'Isn't it a bit early for that?' questioned Liz.

Alice raised an eyebrow. 'Not after the journey from hell I've just had to endure, my dear. We've been driving in circles for ages. I really am quite positively dizzy.'

Vicky and Liz shrugged at each other.

Patrice was going to be busy. He sniffed at the new arrival. No, this one was dreadfully ill. He would have to minister to her first. He jumped up and sat in Alice's lap.

'There you go,' said Sarah, as she placed a gin and tonic in Alice's hand.

'So, Sarah, what was the outburst you were going to tell us about?' asked Vicky.

'Outburst?' Alice laughed, as she stroked Patrice's head. 'Sarah you're so placid. I can't imagine you having an outburst.'

Sarah sat down and sighed. 'Well, it was definitely an outburst. I was just so angry. I feel like I'm on such a short fuse lately.' She relayed the incident to the others.

'Good on you,' said Liz. 'I wouldn't apologise for that. It feels good to finally get things off your chest, doesn't it?'

'Yes, but I feel like I'm being such a bitch. Ever since Meribel, actually.'

'I hope you're not going to blame me for that, my dear,' said Alice.

Sarah shook her head. 'Of course not. I've played the dutiful wife, mother, daughter and daughter-in-law. Now with this diagnosis, I just feel I need some time for me. I don't feel like I've lived. I gave up my career in fashion when I had Jess. I want to sew again. I want to enjoy what life I have left. I don't want to play the dutiful banker's wife sitting around waiting for my husband to come home.'

'I don't know… I wouldn't mind living here and doing nothing all day,' said Vicky, admiring the surroundings.

'It's hard on George, though. He's struggling with it. You know men, they don't really talk about things.'

Liz nodded in agreement. 'Yeah, Gareth's the same. I tell you what, why don't Gareth and George meet up for a drink? They both work in the City.'

'Is that a good idea?' asked Sarah. 'I mean, have you told Gareth anything about Meribel?'

'God no.' Liz laughed. 'He'd have a heart attack.'

'I would introduce him to Hugh,' suggested Alice, 'but unfortunately Hugh is rather an arse.'

'Yeah, and my Kurt's inside yet again, doing time, so he ain't gonna be much company neither,' said Vicky.

'That's settled then,' said Liz. 'I'll arrange it with Gareth.'

42

*G*eorge pulled his scarf tightly around his neck, to protect himself from the biting cold wind, as he made his way down Fleet Street towards the Old Bank of England pub positioned between Sweeny Todd's barber shop and Mrs Lovett's pie shop. It was his work local, so he had suggested this as his and Gareth's meeting place.

As he opened the door he was greeted by a warm blast of air and a cacophony of noise from his fellow drinkers. He glanced down at his phone and then scanned the room. A man matching the image on his screen stood up and waved at him from one of the comfortable leather sofas. George walked across the hall beneath the high extravagantly decorated ceiling adorned with massive chandeliers, past the huge wooden bar, and made his way towards Gareth.

'Hiya,' said Gareth standing up and holding out his hand, 'Really nice to meet you, finally. I got your text so I got you a pint.'

'Thanks, cheers.' George shook Gareth's hand.

George took his coat and scarf off, sat down and took a sip of the cold beer and sighed. It had been a long day.

'So, how are things?' asked Gareth. 'Liz said Sarah's been struggling a bit lately.'

'Yeah, she's still really angry about her diagnosis. I'm not sure what she can do about it, though.'

Gareth sighed and nodded in agreement. 'Yeah, Liz is exactly the same. She's like a dog with a bone. She just won't leave it alone.'

'It's the mood swings that get me.' George's face took on a haunted appearance as he described Sarah's moods. 'One minute she's fine and the next it is as if I've started world war three. I'm not sure what to do.'

'I wouldn't beat yourself up about that. That's just women, mate. Liz has always been on her high horse about something or other.'

George frowned, lost in thought, then tapped his fingers on his pint. 'No, this is different. Sarah's really changed lately. She's more argumentative. It's odd.'

'Sorry to hear that, mate. It can be really tough.'

George waved his arm across his abdomen. 'It seems like a never-ending process which just gets progressively worse. To be honest, I'm struggling with knowing how to deal with the continual bad news.'

'Tell me about it,' said Gareth with a forlorn look on his face. 'I can't believe Charlton lost 3-0.'

'No,' George continued, 'Sarah's always so tired all the time. If I go near her, she's swatting me away saying she is exhausted or in pain. She won't let me see her without her wig on. When her hair started falling out, she was hysterical. Did your Liz lose all her hair?'

'Yeah, the lot. I'd wake up in the morning and there'd be a clump of hair on the pillow. She'd pick it up and look at me and ask me if she looked dreadful. I'd always say no,' Gareth waved his hand dismissively in front of him, 'you look a picture, hun.'

'What? And she believed you?'

Gareth leaned in. 'Women love compliments, George. She'd smile and say "really?" I'd say of course, hun. I didn't have the heart to tell her she looked like Beetlejuice. I mean, she was losing so much of her hair you could stuff a pillow and I had to stop myself from jumping with fright some mornings. I told her it was my bad knee giving me jip'. Gareth laughed and shook his head as he took another sip of his pint.

George felt quite affronted by Gareth's joviality regarding the situation.

'I don't understand how you can make such light of something so dark. I mean our wives are going to die of this.'

Gareth sat back into the sofa and stared at his pint for a few seconds. 'Listen, mate,' he said, as his voice took on a serious tone, 'there's not a day goes by when I don't think about that. You live with the reality of cancer every single day. You worry about the future, seeing the person you love suffering and deteriorating in front of your eyes, knowing that you can't protect them from what lies ahead because it's so far out of your control. You can be there for them, though, holding them up and supporting them. Don't let my joviality fool you. It is my coping mechanism. You have to be strong for them, you have to believe that the treatment's going to help because you don't want to face the fact that it might not. You have to convince yourself to carry on as normal and hope that life will get back to normal... that this is just a passing phase. I can't focus on a negative result because to me that would mean I was giving up on Liz, on us. I love her too much.'

There was silence as Gareth and George absorbed the enormity of what Gareth had just said.

'Sorry, mate,' George patted Gareth on the arm. 'I was out of line. I shouldn't have said that.'

Gareth shrugged. 'That's okay. It's understandable.'

'It's definitely a dreadful disease. What I can't understand is why they couldn't find it earlier. I mean Sarah was seeing this specialist guy for months and he kept telling her she was fine.'

Gareth drained his pint placing it on the table, then wiped his mouth with the back of his hand. 'Listen, mate, if you want your pipe work fixing you'd stand a better chance phoning up Pimlico Plumbers than that lot. That's my impression, anyway. No one listened to my Liz and I'll beat myself up about that for the rest of my days. She told me no one was listening to her and I thought she was hormonal.'

Gareth stood up tipping his hand as if drinking from an imaginary pint glass. 'Another pint?'

'I'll get this one.' George went to stand up. 'You've already got a round in.'

'Nah, that's okay.'

'Thanks,' said George. 'Actually, could I have a craft beer? Any one will do.'

'Yeah, no worries.'

Gareth walked over to the bar and waited to be served. After a few minutes the barman came to take his order.

'Could I have two pints of your finest craft ale please, barman?'

The barman pointed to the pumps. 'Any preference? If you're looking for something warming I recommend Winter Porter or Adnams Broadside.'

'Two pints of Winter Porter, I think.'

As the barman hand pumped the ales, Gareth busied himself getting his card out ready to pay. He was nudged to his right as a slightly inebriated man slumped forward onto the bar.

'Oi, steady mate.' Gareth put his hand on the man's shoulder to steady him.

'Champagne, barman. Your best champagne, my good fellow,' said the man as he clicked his fingers.

The barman placed Gareth's drinks on the bar as he looked towards the man and then indicated towards Gareth. 'I'm just finishing serving this man, sir.' As the barman took Gareth's payment the man huffed and shuffled impatiently from foot to foot knocking into Gareth again. He gave the man a sideways glance then went to pick up his drinks. As he lifted the drinks from the counter the man lurched unsteadily sideways knocking into him again. Some of the ale spilt onto the counter and splashed onto the man's tie.

'Watch what you're doing! You've spilt drink all over me,' said the man shaking his tie angrily.

Gareth raised an eyebrow at him. 'You did it mate, but as I'm in a good mood I'm not going to charge you for it.'

He returned to the sofa and handed George the drink. He beckoned towards the bar where the man was being served.

'There's a right arrogant knobhead at the bar.'

George peered across. 'I think I know him. Yes, that's the head of corporate strategy. What's his name now? I can't think of it. You're right, though. He is a bit of an arse. They say he shags anything that moves.'

Gareth took a sip of his ale and smiled knowingly. 'He's what we call seagull management. They fly in, squawk bullshit, crap everywhere, make a mess, and then fly off leaving everyone else to clean up their shit.'

George laughed. 'You've got that right.'

'Oi, Oi. Here they come. Old Teds United.' Gareth beckoned towards the door as a group of five men came into the pub and walked over to them.

Gareth stood up to greet the men then turned to George.

'Everyone, meet George.'

———

As George travelled home on the train, he smiled to himself. Gareth was a good bloke and he'd enjoyed himself for what seemed like the first time in ages. He'd found someone he could talk to. The other lads were quite a laugh and for once he had forgotten, even if only for a short period, about Sarah's illness. It felt good.

Hugh stumbled out of the black London cab and up the front steps of Penelope's flat. He wasn't going home to Alice in this state. Penelope opened the front door dressed in her cream silk negligee. Hugh had phoned half an hour before and she was only too willing to accommodate him. She had her eye on a pair of red Jimmy Choos and the latest edition Louis Vuitton handbag.

'To what do I owe the honour?' she asked.

Hugh smiled, kissed her on the cheek and stumbled into the lounge sinking into the sofa. He loosened his tie. 'We made a shit load of money today, my dear, and I was out celebrating. It was all going well until some arrogant bastard threw drink all over me.'

He shook his tie at Penelope. She took it and wrapped it back around his neck grabbing both ends and pulling him towards her as she placed her knees on the sofa sitting astride Hugh on his lap.

'My poor baby,' she cooed, 'what can I do to make you happy?'

43

REGINALD FUKER HOWARD

THE LAW OF ERRANT BALLS.

'*I*s this him?' asked Liz, wearing an incredulous expression.

'Yes, that's him,' replied Alice.

Liz pointed at the image on the iPad. 'I know this guy.'

'You went to see him too?'

'No, but I know someone who did, and he's an absolute idiot.'

'Oh great,' said Alice. 'Trust me to get sent to the village idiot.'

'I think we were all sent to village idiots by the sounds,' said Sarah.

'No,' said Liz, pointing repeatedly to the image on the iPad screen. 'This guy's off the wall. My friend Stacey was having heavy periods and they thought she had fibroids. He was looking after her jointly with a gastroenterologist as they weren't sure if it was her bowels or her bits that were the issue. She was waiting for him to explain to her what had been found in the surgery the night before. He strutted into the ward in the middle of the afternoon.

'He went into the room, pulled up a chair and sat down. "Well now," he said, "this is Sister," as he waved behind him towards the nurse, indicating her presence in the room.

"Would you like a cup of tea?" he asked. She said she was fine, so he turned to the nurse and said, "I'm very thirsty and have been running around all morning seeing patients. Sister, get me a cup of tea, would you?"'

'Noooo,' said Vicky in horror. 'I hope she told him where to go.'

'She did. Apparently she said, "Sorry?" He raised his eyebrows at her and repeated "A cup of tea, now there's a good girl." He turned back to Stacey and winked as he said, "The measure of a good nurse is in the quality of the cup of tea they can make."'

'How rude!' exclaimed Sarah. 'What did the nurse say to that?'

'She asked him what year it was. He said 2006 and asked why. She thanked him for clarifying that for her as she thought she had recently stepped back in time to 1945. He didn't get it. So she walked over to the call bell and pushed it. He asked her what she was doing. She said she was calling for a cup of tea for him as she was here to accompany him on a patient consultation. She also said she was happy to make tea for a patient but drew the line at consultants. Then she welcomed him to 2006.'

The women all giggled.

'Good on her,' said Alice.

'It was like water off a duck's back,' said Liz. 'He turned back to Stacey and went on to say he wasn't sure what had happened in the surgery the night before because he had been at a pop-up theatre. Stacey was becoming slightly concerned by this point and said, "I'm sorry, are you saying you weren't there at all?"

'He said, "No, not at all! It's rather a funny story, I tell you. You see, I was at this pop-up theatre and I have to say I rather enjoyed it. I had never been to one before. Have you ever been? No?"

'Stacey said she was shaking by this stage and said she could tell what was running through the nurse's head by the look on her face. Stacey looked back to him and repeated, "Are you saying you weren't in the surgery at all last night?" He chuckled and said, "No, not at all, I told Rajesh that we could arrange to do the surgery jointly but he's dreadful at communicating. I mean, he has that phone permanently stuck to his ear, but do you think he had time to let me know? No. Not at all. So, the thing is my dear, he phoned me in the middle of the pop-up theatre, I'll have you know. Right in the middle! Well, I was rather annoyed I can tell you... We were already on the second act and it was so wonderful. You really must go some time. I said Rajesh, my dear fellow, this is really inconvenient and I can't possibly come now. I'm in the middle of a Midsummer Night's Dream!'"

Liz waited to gauge the women's reaction. They all gasped.

Then she continued. 'He pointed and shook one of his short fat chubby fingers at her. He said to her, "You were already on the table opened up so I told Rajesh to just check your insides and see what he could find. Don't worry, my dear, Rajesh is very capable. He thinks you have a fibroid so we can give you some medication for your period pains to help adjust your hormones. I can have a quick check now and feel inside." Then he looked at the nurse again and said, "Now Sister, where's that tea?" as he tried to wave her out of the room. Stacey asked him to leave immediately and never return. She made an official complaint.'

'Oh my God!' screamed Alice. 'That's definitely him, alright. How is this guy still allowed to practise?'

'He even had the audacity to charge her a surgical fee.'

'The snake has reared his ugly head again. At least this time we can chop it off, though.' Alice smiled. 'I was thinking about a nice round of golf, girls. A great deal of accidents happen on a golf course… I read that there was a study in *Golfers Digest* that reported each year an estimated 40,000 golfers seek emergency treatment due to injuries caused by errant golf balls and flying club heads. Sports injuries statistics suggest golf is more dangerous than rugby.'

'Ohhh, lets google it,' said Vicky, tapping away at her phone. 'Hey look, it says here that golf carts can reach up to twenty-five miles per hour. Forty per cent of golf cart accidents involve a person falling out of a cart and 10 per cent involve rollovers. Ohhh and this is interesting… If you google further it says you shouldn't be sued for manslaughter as the golf course would be sued for wrongful death for not taking precautions to prevent such an accident occurring. That's why some golf courses have those huge nets up, right? To prevent the balls from travelling outside the course? It says that President Ford hit several people with golf balls. He even knocked one person completely unconscious and was never sued. Alice, I think this is perfect for your guy,' said Vicky.

'I think we need to find out if he plays golf first,' suggested Sarah.

'Don't be stupid. All posh blokes play golf,' scoffed Vicky.

Alice smiled. 'That will be easier than you think. I know for a fact that he does play golf and the club he plays at.'

Liz frowned at Alice. 'How do you know that?'

'Because my husband plays golf with him.'

Liz, Sarah and Vicky all turned to Alice and screeched in unison, 'What?'

'That's decided then,' said Liz laughing and throwing her arms up in the air.

They all looked at Alice waiting for her to elaborate.

'I found out they've recently started playing golf together so it won't be hard to find out when he plays. It also won't be that hard to get us all in for a round of golf. Hugh and I are both members of the local club. We're sorted, darlings,' purred Alice.

'But what are we going to do? Hit him in the head with a golf ball? We'd have to be pretty good at aiming and, frankly, I played golf once at school and struggled to actually hit the ball,' said Liz.

'Considering where I come from, the chances of me knowing what to do on a golf course are slim,' said Vicky.

Liz laughed. 'I don't know about that, Vicks. You certainly came in handy on the slopes.'

They turned to look at Sarah who shrunk into the large cushions on the sofa.

She looked back at them. 'What? Don't look at me. I've played golf on occasion but there's no way I can guarantee I'm going to be able to hit him in the head. Besides, from those statistics it doesn't sound like golf balls actually kill that many people.'

'It doesn't need to be a golf ball, my dear,' said Alice.

———

The very next morning Alice phoned the golf club and asked to book her friends in for a round of golf. She knew Reginald Fuker Howard played every Thursday morning which gave them exactly five days to get things sorted. There was no point waiting an extra week. Strike while the iron's hot, thought Alice.

44

LATE MARCH 2019

*A*lice was sitting at the bar when Reginald walked in. She waved to him as he entered the room. He glanced over and when he realised who it was, he tried to pretend he hadn't seen her. This was to no avail, as she was determined he come over and speak to her. People were staring so he cleared his throat and scuttled across to Alice.

'Hello, Reggie. How are you? I must say I haven't seen you in some time.' Alice smiled and patted the stool next to her.

'Well, err, yes, umm, I have been rather busy,' stuttered Reginald.

'Hugh tells me you're working hard. You remember my husband… Hugh Bledisloe?'

'Oh yes, yes I do. Damn fine chap he is.'

He glanced around the room looking for Hugh. Alice's husband was not a bad old stick and seemed friendly enough. When Reginald had discovered Hugh was her husband, he'd asked him to the nineteenth hole for a drink and a chat. Just to try and find out how she was doing. He wanted damage control and needed to find out if he might be pursued down the legal route. Some women did try but fortunately it was very hard to prove as the cancer would have occurred anyway. The only grounds they might have is if they could prove it could have been diagnosed much sooner but as there was no effective screening tool for ovarian cancer it was easy to get away with this. So, he had arranged to meet Hugh today for a round of golf. He didn't expect to see Alice here.

'Is Hugh here with you now?' enquired Reginald.

'No, no, probably at work I expect,' sighed Alice.

Reginald was feeling a bit on edge. He wasn't sure if he should tell Alice that he was about to play a round of golf with Hugh. It might not go down very well as it was obvious to Reginald that the poor dear was not expecting her husband to turn up. If she found out she might guess what he was up to, but he wanted to ensure damage limitation. She was a fierce woman.

His mind drifted back to the last time he'd seen her. Alice had been to see him initially and then had the audacity to complain to Percival that she didn't like his tone. When she was diagnosed with stage four ovarian cancer she then came back to visit him saying she felt he was to blame for her delayed diagnosis. She was wearing bright red lipstick that day… she was wearing bright red lipstick today. He remembered it as though it was yesterday. He shuddered as his mind momentarily wandered back to their last meeting…

'Now now, my dear, I really do think you're overreacting. How could I cause your cancer? Surely, you can see that has nothing to do with me?'

'I'm not talking about the cause of my cancer, my dear fellow,' Alice had replied. 'I'm talking about the fact that you're the expert, and after me paying hundreds of pounds for your expert advice all I got was a discussion about how I needed to lose weight. You were more interested in where I went to dinner. I mean you call yourself a gynaecologist, but I honestly think a rat might have done a better job.'

'I think you're rather cross. It might be best if you go

home and lie down. I'm afraid I'm rather busy today and can't really give you any more time.'

'Excuse me?' Alice had shrieked. 'Are you serious? You haven't heard the last of me you know, you feral little man.' With that, Alice had stood up and leant over the consulting desk. She reached over to a vase of freshly cut pink and white roses, took the roses out of the vase, and before Reginald had time to extricate his rotund derrière from his chair, Alice had proceeded to pour the water over his head. She then took the bunch of roses and threw them at him as she stormed out of the room.

Reginald had sat there for several minutes, completely stunned, with water dripping from his forehead into his rose covered lap. 'Damn women. Why are they always so tetchy?' he'd muttered to himself, as he began to mop his brow with a tissue.

———

Alice had moved towards Reginald causing him to jump nervously, jolting his mind back to the current conversation.

'Oh, my dear Mr Fuker Howard, I must apologise for the roses incident. You won't hold that against me, will you? You know us women. We can be a bit irrational at times. I want to apologise for my behaviour. If I'd known you were a golfing buddy of Hugh's then maybe I might have restrained myself a bit more.' She sniggered. 'Have a drink on me.'

'I'm not really ready for a drink,' he said. 'I'm just about to play a round of golf, you see. I only came in to grab a bottle of mineral water and to collect my packed lunch. Perhaps another time.' Reginald nervously looked towards the door, hoping for a quick exit.

Alice leant towards him and placed her hand on his. 'Now, Reginald, please. I insist. To put the past behind us, my dear fellow.'

Alice waved to Stuart the barman. 'Excuse me, Stuart. Two scotch on the rocks please. And make them doubles,' she said as she winked at Reginald.

———

He was so nervous he ended up having several drinks. Alice was rather insistent, and he didn't want a repeat of the roses incident in front of some of his chums. It was one thing to have water poured over your head in the safety of your consulting room, but it was an entirely different matter when your golf buddies and relatives of potential clients might be watching. He wasn't sure how she might react. He was feeling a bit tipsy after the four scotch on the rocks.

'Well, I must be off.' Alice made to stand up. 'It's been lovely to see you again, Reggie dear, and I do hope there's no bad feeling between us.' She offered her hand and left.

Reginald realised he was sweating. He fished in his pocket for his handkerchief and mopped his brow. I think that went okay, he thought. He stood up and went to the bathroom to relieve himself, humming a tune as he stood and admired his reflection in the mirror. He couldn't help thinking how good he looked in his smart check plus fours, his white golf neck shirt with his pink and grey argyle sweater and white golf shoes. Yes, they did make him look rather dapper. He waltzed out of the club house and placed his golf clubs on the back of the golf cart and waited for Hugh. He was standing by his cart soaking up the morning sun, humming away to himself when he realised Alice was standing next to him with a group of women who were attempting to get into two golf carts next to his. His heart sank.

'Hello again, Reggie,' said Alice. 'May I introduce you to my dear friends? Ladies,' she said with a flourish of her hand, 'this is my ex-gynaecologist, Reginald. They know all about our little disagreement, Reggie.' Alice held her hand up to her mouth and giggled. She slapped him playfully on the arm. 'They found the flower incident especially funny. Didn't you, ladies?'

'Yeah, I'd have loved to have seen that!'

Reginald turned to see a rather common sounding plump blonde woman in track pants, trainers and a hoodie edging towards him. He couldn't help thinking she looked like she'd been dragged through a hedge backwards. What on earth was Alice doing socialising with someone like that?

Alice began the introductions. To Reginald they looked rather an odd bunch. There was the overweight woman, a thin mousy haired plain looking woman and then a rather pretty blonde woman. He couldn't help but admire her. She was wearing a bright pink golfing visor on her head and was dressed in a bright pink close fitting golf shirt and tight fitting navy blue Capri trousers with a bright yellow and white sweater draped over her shoulders. She smiled nervously back at him.

'Reggie! Alice?'

The group turned in the direction of the voice travelling across the car park. Hugh Bledisloe was striding towards them with his golf clubs slung over his arm.

He was wearing a confused expression on his face. 'Reggie,' he said in greeting as they shook hands.

Hugh turned to Alice and gave her a kiss on the cheek. 'Alice dear, now what on earth are you doing here? You should be at home resting.'

Alice threw Hugh a warning glance which stopped him in his tracks.

'My dear, I'm fine. I'm taking my friends here for a round of golf.' Alice waved her hand in front of the group and began introducing the women to Hugh.

Reginald coughed nervously as he shuffled his feet on the spot, anxious to get away.

Hugh turned to Alice. 'I'm playing a round of golf with

Reggie today.' He glanced at his watch. 'We must go, our tee slot's booked for eleven.'

Hugh turned to Reginald. 'Are you ready, old chap?'

'How funny,' exclaimed Alice. 'We're booked for ten past. We'll be right behind you.'

45

*A*lice smiled, waving to Reginald, watching him drive off to the first hole. She was seated in the passenger seat of the golf cart and turned to Liz who was at the wheel. 'Did you manage to make the switch?'

'All done,' said Liz quietly. 'I switched the three wood and the driver as you instructed while you were chatting. He didn't notice a thing.' She paused staring straight ahead. 'Alice, is this going to be okay? You know, with your husband being here. We can call it off.'

'Of course not, my dear. This is all turning out rather well.'

Liz glanced across at Alice with a look of confusion.

Sarah and Vicky were in the second golf cart which was to the left of Alice and Liz's. Sarah was at the wheel.

'Right, ladies,' called Alice as she lowered her sunglasses onto her nose. 'Just relax and look like you're having a fun day out learning to play golf, but keep your ears and eyes peeled. We don't want to raise suspicion.'

Liz started up the cart and reversed out. Sarah sighed then followed them. Vicky pulled out a Twix from her hoodie pocket and smiled at Sarah. 'This is going to be fun.

How are we going to make sure we don't hit the wrong one?'

———

Reginald could not stop glancing at the women slightly behind him. Alice and the pretty blonde woman appeared to be the only ones who knew what they were doing. He felt uneasy. There was something not quite right about them, but he was unsure exactly what. Maybe it was the scotch. He really shouldn't have had anything to drink before playing, but he'd felt rather bad about the poor dear, and anything to stop another complaint from a patient. He definitely couldn't afford any more. He'd had a few complaints laid against him over the years for unprofessional comments. People just couldn't take a joke anymore, could they. Everything had become so PC. Reginald wished for the good old days when doctors were viewed as gods. No one had ever dared question their practice back then. Medical practice was becoming rather complicated these days...

Reginald and Hugh continued around the course discussing the intricacies of politics and the stock market. Hugh was waiting for Reginald to tee off when he heard a squeal, and a golf club came flying past. Reginald ducked and stumbled backwards. The club narrowly missed him. The men looked in the direction the club had come from. Alice and her friends were looking rather bashful. Reginald walked over and picked up the club. The tall mousy haired woman walked over to retrieve it.

'I'm so sorry,' she said. 'Vicks hasn't played before and she obviously has quite a strong swing.' The short plump blonde woman waved at Reginald shouting, 'Sorry!'

He shook one of his chubby fingers at her. 'Now look here, my dear girl. You need to tell her to be careful. She can't go round playing golf like that. You're not meant to be following so closely behind us. If she can't play she shouldn't be here. There are rules to be observed, you know.'

'Alright, alright,' smirked the mousy haired woman, as she held her arms up. 'Keep your trousers on, mate. We're just trying to have fun.'

'Humph,' said Reginald as the woman walked off. He turned to walk away.

'Fat little fart,' said the woman under her breath.

'I beg your pardon,' said Reginald, turning back to face her.

'Fore,' said the woman. 'I said "fore". You said we had to observe the rules. I'm saying "fore" to warn you about the flying stick.'

'But you've already thrown it! It's too late to say "fore",' said Reginald in an exasperated tone.

The mousy haired woman made to walk away. She turned her head back towards Reginald smiled and waved at him.

Reginald was sure she had just flipped him the bird.

Hugh glowered in Alice's direction. He shouted out to her. 'Move back to where you're meant to be, woman.' She smiled back at him waving. He couldn't understand why she was here playing golf with these women. They clearly didn't know how ill she was. Surely they must find her behaviour odd.

Reginald couldn't pinpoint what was worrying him. He and Hugh were now at the nineth hole. The women's golf carts were sitting on the eighth, but they kept edging nearer to the men. The women were once again attempting to hit the ball, which appeared to be proving somewhat troublesome. There was a great deal of chattering and giggling going on. At least the poor old dear was having some fun. She didn't look like she had long left. He picked up his grandfather's old wooden driver and got ready to tee off. Everyone joked about him using it. He thought it was beautiful. The shaft was fashioned from hickory and the head from persimmon.

Hugh saw Reginald pick up the driver. 'Oh no, looks like I'm in trouble now. Grandpa Howard's lucky driver's making an appearance.'

'My lucky charm,' he said, waddling over into position, then stared down the fairway, preparing to tee off.

Reginald could not shake the unsettled feeling. He began to perspire. He pulled his handkerchief out of his pocket and began to mop his brow.

'Come on, old boy,' egged Hugh, 'we haven't got all day.' Reginald took a breath and prepared for the shot.

As he swung through, the driver contacted with the ground instead of the ball. A fat shot. Several things then happened.

One. A clump of turf flew into the air and hit Hugh squarely in the face, obscuring his view of events.

Two. The ball shuddered on top of the tee, fell sideways onto the grass and rolled a few centimetres away.

Three. Reginald's driver snapped in two with the lower half flying across the green.

'Ouch,' said Reginald, registering the pain, as he stumbled forward. He looked down, and as the realisation dawned on him that the driver had broken, he stared at the remaining part in his hand. Hmm, odd. This doesn't look like Grandpa's driver, he thought. Why hadn't he noticed earlier? And what was that God-awful pain?

———

Everything appeared to be happening in slow motion. Reginald's brain started to piece together what was happening. A splinter from the driver had torn through his trousers and lodged itself in his groin. What he didn't realise was that it was firmly lodged into his femoral artery causing him to haemorrhage. He was in shock. Not sure if he'd gone deaf. He could see Hugh moving towards him and Hugh's mouth was opening and closing, but he could only make out a muffled sound. He turned in the direction of the women. They just seemed to be staring at him from a distance. Then as if someone had pushed fast forward, events seemed to rapidly speed up. Hugh had managed to tie Reginald's argyle jumper around his leg to try and act as a tourniquet. He was bleeding quite a bit by now and beginning to feel rather faint. He stumbled backwards. Hugh had moved the golf cart closer and assisted Reginald into the cart. His hearing had returned; Hugh was muttering beside him.

'Damn it. I can't find my phone. Reggie, Reggie, do you have your phone? Christ. Come on old fellow. I'm going to get you back to the club house. Alice, Alice! I need your phone… anybody… what the *hell* are those women *doing?*'

The next thing Reginald felt was the tourniquet loosening around his leg.

His instinct told him something wasn't right with this whole situation. He wasn't sure what was going on but he didn't like it. He could make out Hugh and Alice arguing by the side of the cart.

'For God's sake, what are you doing, woman? You can't loosen that. He'll bleed to death,' shouted Hugh.

'I think it's too tight,' came Alice's reply.

Reginald edged over on the seat of the cart, pushed his foot on the accelerator and sped off.

'Quick he's getting away,' he heard Alice shout.

'Oh dear, dear,' Reginald muttered, as the realisation of his situation sank in. He was trying to stay awake. His mouth was dry, and everything was fading in and out. He was falling over the steering wheel of his golf cart, swerving erratically at pace across the fairway and could hear voices behind him.

He tried to head towards the club house, struggling to get his bearings. When he looked up, he could make out a golf cart directly in his path. He was about to slow down and shout for help but then realised it was the mousy haired companion of Alice's. She was standing by the cart holding a golf club as if ready to swing and take his head off. Instinct made him push his foot back on the accelerator as hard as his sapping energy could allow, veering sharply to the right to avoid her. Reginald didn't see it coming. The left-hand wheel of the golf cart got caught on a raised edge of the green. The steering suddenly turned to the right, changing the direction. Reginald and his golf cart were propelled forward flying though a small gap in the bushes. His fat chubby fingers sliding all over the place trying to grip the steering wheel. The cart rolled down the twenty-foot embankment straight into the pond below. It was too late. The cart ended up on its roof and poor Reginald never knew what happened. His last thought was, Oh dear, perhaps I should have been kinder to the old bitch.

———

As Reginald sped off in the golf cart. Hugh had a sinking feeling this was not going to end well.

'You stupid woman,' Hugh shouted at Alice. 'Now look what you've done! We need to go after him.'

'I'm on it,' shouted Liz, as she sped past the rest of the group in her golf cart.

Sarah pulled up in the third cart alongside Hugh and Alice. Vicky was seated in the passenger side.

'Right, you two idiots, get out,' Hugh barked at Sarah and Vicky.

Sarah jumped out.

'Who are you calling an idiot?' replied Vicky as Hugh pulled her from the passenger seat.

He then turned to Alice. '*Get* in the cart,' he shouted. Hugh and Alice sped after Reginald and Liz leaving a disgruntled Vicky and Sarah standing on the fairway.

'Typical bloody toff,' cursed Vicky as she watched them

disappearing across the fairway. 'Now we'll have to walk. And my Twixes are in that cart.'

Hugh could make out Liz with her golf cart positioned across Reginald's path. She was standing on the fairway with her golf club raised mid-air as if to strike him.

'What the hell is she doing?' asked Hugh. 'It looks like she's about to hit him.'

'Oh, just making sure she stops him, I guess,' said Alice.

Reginald's cart then swerved to avoid Liz, spinning out of control. Seconds later the cart had disappeared through a small gap in the hedge.

'Where the hell has he gone now?' asked Hugh.

Alice smiled. 'I think he might have gone for a swim, my dear.'

———

The group arrived back at the clubhouse to find quite a commotion going on.

'We're not sure. Some sort of accident.'

'They say it's that poor devil Reggie Fuker Howard. Drove through the bushes. Crashed into the pond.'

'Oh dear. Apparently he's dead. Has just been found drowned. I never liked the chap, to tell you the truth.'

'Weren't you just drinking with him at the bar. Alice?'

Hugh turned to stare at Alice. He was trying to register what had happened. He glanced round at the women. They all returned his gaze and shrugged at him. Alice had tried to take the tourniquet off. The mousy haired woman. What was her name? Lou or something, looked like she had been deliberately going to hit Reggie. Or maybe she knew there was a pond on the other side of the hedge. And then there were all the missing phones. Hugh decided he might have been overdoing things. Surely there was an explanation. If not, he had just witnessed a murder. Visibly shaken, he walked up to the bar and ordered a drink. He put his hand in his pocket and frowned. He pulled his mobile phone out of his pocket. How the hell did that get back in there? He glanced at the women to see the two blonde ones on their mobiles.

Alice explained to the other club members that she had had a few drinks with Reggie before his round of golf with Hugh.

Hugh listened with disbelief. She glanced towards him then announced she suddenly didn't feel well. Her friends fussed over her saying it must be the shock of it all and the effects of her treatment. Water was brought and she was made to lie down and put her feet up.

'The poor dear, she's been through so much,' someone was heard to say.

'Don't worry,' Liz said, 'we'll make sure she gets home. She's just in shock.'

Hugh went back to the bar and ordered another drink.

46

*H*ugh was pouring himself a drink from the drinks cabinet. Alice lay on the couch resting with a throw laid over her and a glass of gin and tonic perched in one hand.

'Dreadful business with old Reggie,' said Hugh nervously. 'The boys at the club are saying his death was a freak accident. They say that his blood alcohol level was twice the limit. Silly man, drinking before playing a round. Didn't he tell you he was playing golf? All rather unfortunate if you ask me. Why he was still using that old driver, with the number of fat shots he always plays, is beyond me. It was bound to snap in two sooner or later.'

'Yes,' said Alice, peering cautiously at Hugh to judge his reaction. 'All rather unfortunate. He seemed such a cheerful chap earlier in the day when I met him.'

'About that,' said Hugh.

'Hmmm,' said Alice.

'Why did you meet him?'

'Just a chance meeting at the bar. I was making amends for the roses incident.'

Hugh tipped the glass back, emptying the contents down

his throat. He turned to the decanter, removed the stopper and poured himself another drink.

————

Alice felt deliriously happy. She spent the evening soaking in a hot bath with a few drops of lavender essential oil. She lay there reliving the day's events. It hadn't taken her long to weaken the shaft of the wooden driver her father had left her. It was virtually identical to Reggie's. All she had to do was place it in water over several days. Liz made the switch while Alice had distracted Reggie. He wasn't the best golfer, so they only needed to unnerve him enough to play a fat shot.

It couldn't have played out more perfectly.

Alice lifted her glass of gin and tonic from the side of the bath and took a sip. I must remember to take Reggie's driver back to Middlemoor and dispose of the evidence, she thought.

She went to bed that night and for the first time in a very long time she slept soundly without the addition of any painkillers or sleeping tablets.

————

Hugh sidled up to the bar at the club. He had arranged to meet Stuart for a chat and waited for him to finish serving a customer.

'What will it be, Sir Hugh?'

'Scotch on the rocks please, Stuart.'

Stuart smiled wistfully. 'That's what your wife ordered for poor old Reggie before he died. They had quite a few, you know.'

'Now listen, Stuart. You see, that's what I needed to speak to you about.'

'I thought it might be.'

'Between me and you, my wife hasn't been herself lately. What with her illness and everything.'

'So I've heard. From what I hear she blamed old Reggie.'

Hugh choked on his drink. 'Now, now, my dear fellow. I'm not sure where you heard that, but I wouldn't go round repeating it.'

'Well now, Sir Hugh, I'm sure you're right, but something like that might come at a price.'

'I thought it might,' muttered Hugh.

Hugh took out his wallet and slid a wad of notes across the counter.

Stuart quickly took the wad and placed it out of view under the bar and counted it.

'Five hundred for your silence,' said Hugh, nodding towards the wad of notes.

'Fifteen.'

'What?'

'Fifteen,' repeated Stuart. 'Five hundred for keeping silent about her blaming Reggie for her diagnosis. Another thousand for saying to anyone who asks that it was Reggie and not your wife who paid for the drinks, and for not telling your wife about that woman I found you with out in the car park a few weeks ago.'

Hugh stared at Stuart in disbelief. He could feel beads of sweat forming on his forehead. He took a handkerchief out of his pocket to mop his brow.

'Ball breaker,' Hugh muttered, handing over another wad of cash.

'Always a pleasure, Sir Hugh,' said Stuart as he took the money and began to count it under the bar again. He paused for a moment then looked up at Hugh.

'How are things at home?'

'I beg your pardon?'

'At home. I mean you obviously don't talk much to each

other do you? Your wife came back in the other day and told me all about you and your marriage.'

Hugh could feel his heart start to race. 'What was she doing here?'

Stuart smiled. 'She came in to pay for my silence. Just like you.'

'You little shit,' muttered Hugh.

47

'What the fuck! Yo man, you gurls are plain evil!' Dwayne was in the lounge of Alice's country estate, Middlemoor Manor. He'd been sitting in one of the oversized armchairs listening to the women relay the story of Reginald's fate, but was now pacing the room and waving his arms about as if trying to round up sheep. 'You need to be careful, man, or you bitches could get locked up.'

Alice sighed. 'It was a rather unfortunate accident, my dear. I also would refrain from addressing us as bitches. You don't want to upset us, dear boy. I think you'll find we're all in this together.'

'What are you talking about, man?' asked Jusu in a rather worried tone, as he leaned forward in his seat.

Jordan was on the sofa staring into space. He put his head in his hands and started laughing.

Dwayne waved his hand at Jordan. 'What's so funny, man? This is well bad. These chicks are messed up!'

Alice's face clouded over as she slammed her fist down on the arm rest of her chair. 'Might I remind you young gentleman that you stayed in my chalet and were happy to share my hospitality. This was a very unfortunate accident and if you do or say anything...' Alice paused and wagged her finger at the three men. 'Anything at all… the Meribel incident may be linked to this and you might find yourselves linked to a crime.'

'Listen here, I ain't going down for someting I ain't had nothing to do with, man,' said Dwayne. 'And anyways, I thought you said the police have decided it was an accident.'

'I think we all might need to calm down. Have a drink, gentleman, please,' said Alice indicating towards the walnut drinks cabinet on the far wall. 'I'm sure we can sort this out. Liz dear, pour them some drinks to calm their nerves.'

Liz put on her 'why me?' face and sighed as she dragged herself up from the sofa. 'What will it be, guys?'

There was a commotion at the door. Harold the butler could be heard muttering in a slightly annoyed tone, 'Well really, this is most unusual. I don't know what's got into madam since she became ill.'

'Yap yap yap,' said Mocha and Snowy as they came scuttling into the house with Olivia trailing behind. She burst in to the lounge in a long flowery maxi dress. Her face was obscured from view by a large-brimmed cream fabric hat. Olivia pulled the hat off, kissed Alice on the cheek and collapsed into the chair next to her.

'Alice, darling,' she exclaimed as she surveyed the room, 'this is a fucking mansion. You really are loaded!'

Olivia paused registering the atmosphere in the room. 'Cheer up, guys, anyone would think someone's died.'

Dwayne, Jordan and Jusu all shot Olivia an icy stare.

'What? What did I say?'

———

'What the fuck, babes. You're fucking mental, aren't you?' Olivia's eyes were aghast for a brief moment before she bent forwards, laughing. 'What a pack of gangsta bitches! Are you sure no one will link you to this?'

'My dear girl,' said Alice as she waved her hands

dismissively in the air, 'I really don't care. He was a dreadful little man and he was terribly rude. When Elizabeth told me that story about that poor young woman I lost all sense of compassion I'm afraid… and what is this fixation with bitches with you lot!'

Alice turned to stare at the boys. 'I'm surprised that you young men are so mortified. We didn't actually touch him. He drove through that hedge himself, you know. We think the club broke and he got a splinter or something. He appeared to be bleeding and tried to use his jumper as a tourniquet for his leg. He thought we were after him so we diverted him from the clubhouse, that's all.'

Dwayne stared at Alice incredulously. 'Oh my dayz. You gurls need to be working the scene down in Brixton, man. You're well bad. You look like butter wouldn't melt in your mouths, man, but no wayz.'

'He sounded like a right twat anyway,' said Jordan. 'What did your husband tink?'

'He won't be a problem. He thinks it was a freak accident,' said Alice.

'So promise us you ain't gonna do no more of this sort of shit ladyz?'

Alice smiled. 'Dwayne, my dear fellow, on the contrary, we've asked you here to help us.'

'Ohh man,' said Dwayne.

Jordan and Jusu exchanged worried glances.

'I'll help you whatever way I can,' said Olivia. 'These guys deserve it. You'd all be facing a brighter future instead of death sentences because of them.'

'That's true,' said Jordan. 'I mean what if it was our mum or sister, you know. What would we do?'

'Kill the fuckers,' said Dwayne.

'Too right man,' said Jordan. 'So are we in or out?'

'I really hope we don't regret this, bro,' said Jusu as they each made a fist and reached out laying their fists one on top of the other. 'We're in, man,' they said in unison.

Alice sat back in her chair with a wry smile on her lips and sipped her gin and tonic. She was wearing her bright red lipstick. She never used to wear bright red lipstick, but lately she found it quite empowering.

Liz was seated on one of the floral chintz sofas with Sarah and Vicky. She leant over to them and said quietly, 'Is it my imagination, or does Alice seem to be enjoying this just a bit too much?'

'I think she's enjoying it,' said Vicky. 'Right guys, I'm going to have to go. Kurt's out of jail and picking up Alfie from school. I promised we'd all go out for pizza tonight. My chemo starts again tomorrow, so we'll have to continue this conversation later.'

'Okay,' said Liz, as she grabbed her bag.

'I'd better get going as well,' said Sarah.

As they walked outside to their cars Liz studied Sarah.

'Sarah, you're looking good. I love your dress.'

'Thank you!' She spun round showing off a cotton aquamarine v-necked shift dress with cap sleeves and matching aquamarine ballet pumps on her feet. 'I made it myself.'

'Really? Wow, it looks lovely on you, doesn't it, Vicks?'

Vicky looked Sarah up and down appraisingly. 'Yeah, it suits you.'

As Sarah got into her car and disappeared down the drive, Liz's gaze continued to follow the car.

'Come on then,' said Vicky as she hopped into the passenger seat. 'We need to get moving. What are you doing?'

'Vicks, did you notice anything different about Sarah?'

'Like what?'

'Not sure. There was just something different about her.'

48

KNIGHTSBRIDGE

*H*ugh walked into the spare room looking for his old editions of *The Economist*. There was a particular article he wanted to read. As he walked over to the bookcase, Alice's set of golf clubs standing in the far corner of the room caught his eye. Something made him cross the room to pause and study them for a moment. He pulled out Alice's old wooden driver and held it up in his hands. It looked just like Reggie's. Could it be? No…

'What are you up to, my dear?'

Hugh gave a start and turned to see Alice standing in the doorway.

'Nothing really. Just, ummh, well, just thinking about Reggie, the poor devil.'

Alice grabbed the driver from Hugh and placed it back in the golf bag.

'I wouldn't touch that if I were you, darling. It might bring bad luck.' She winked mischievously, escorting him from the room. 'Now what about a drink?'

Hugh was having a terrible time breathing. He had severe pains in his chest, travelling down his left arm. He'd not long ago had his morning coffee and put it down to the caffeine. He was starting to sweat profusely, but he couldn't find his angina tablets, which puzzled him as he'd seen them only a few hours ago on the side table. He was sure of it and couldn't remember moving them.

'Darling, are you okay?' asked Alice.

'Yes dear. Just feeling a little bit out of sorts,' grimaced Hugh, as he clutched his chest. He picked up the phone and dialled 999.

'Hello… Yes, ambulance please. I think I may be having a heart attack.'

———

'Mr Bledisloe,' said the young emergency doctor. 'You appear to have had a coronary event. You have had angina in the past?'

'Yes,' said Hugh.

'How much of your medication did you take today?'

'None.'

'Hmm.' The young doctor flicked through Hugh's notes again and frowned.

'Just spit it out my good man,' demanded Hugh.

'It is just that we've found elevated levels of nitroglycerin in your blood stream.' The doctor paused. 'Are you absolutely sure you haven't taken more than your normal dose today?'

———

Alice was lying on the couch of her Knightsbridge flat, sobbing.

'I don't know what I'd do without Hugh. I know he can be a bastard at times, but he's not a bad old egg.'

'Do you know what happened?' asked Olivia.

'No, not really. He just said he felt unwell and then the ambulance arrived.'

'Gosh,' said Sarah, looking aghast.

At that moment Alice's daughter, Sophie, walked into the room carrying a tray with a bone china cup and saucer and a tea pot. She came to an abrupt halt and frowned as she caught sight of the women.

'Oh, hello. I didn't realise we had company.'

'Sophie, my dear,' said Alice waving her arm in a flourish round the room. 'These are my dear friends. I asked them to come. I needed comforting. Perhaps you could get them all some tea.'

Sophie forced a smile at the women and then threw Alice a steely stare. 'Mother, we need to talk.'

Alice's face crumpled. 'Is it Hugh? Oh dear, is he okay?'

'In private please, Mother,' commanded Sophie.

'No. Whatever you have to say it can be said in front of my dear friends.'

Sophie hesitated for a few seconds, studying the women seated around Alice. They all looked back at her.

What an odd bunch, she thought.

Liz nodded at Sophie and then reached over and squeezed Alice's hand. Alice nodded at Sophie to continue.

She sighed in exasperation. The tea tray shuddered in her arms. Sophie could not help but think there was something not quite right about this situation. 'Right, well then,' she said, as she slammed the tea tray down on the side table and ironed the front of her dress with the palms of her hands. She took a deep breath and exhaled. 'It's just… well… it is just that Daddy appears to have taken a rather large amount of angina tablets this morning. That's why he was so ill. Do you have any idea how that could have happened?'

Alice gasped, then put her hand over her mouth, as she

broke into a fit of giggles. 'Oh dear,' she exclaimed. 'I have been a naughty girl, haven't I?'

———

'*Brain mets,*' screamed Liz. 'She never mentioned that! Sophie says she's had brain mets for some time! We've been chasing after doctors and dishing out punishments under the guidance of someone who has brain mets.'

'Look, babes,' said Olivia, 'she didn't want you guys to know. She wanted to have some fun in the time she had left. She thought it might upset you all.'

'What?' asked Liz.

'Well, you know, she thought you might worry the same thing could happen to you,' explained Olivia.

'*I beg your pardon,*' replied Liz.

'What, babes?' Olivia couldn't understand what the fuss was about.

Sarah could be heard muttering something about not wanting to go to prison.

Liz held up her hand with her palm facing outwards towards Olivia, as if directing traffic to a halt. 'Just repeat what you said.'

Olivia looked back at Liz blankly. 'What part?'

Liz spoke very slowly enunciating every word, 'The… part… about… you… knowing… she had… brain… mets,' as she stabbed a finger repeatedly in the air at Olivia.

'Oh yeah, she told me when we were in France. She showed me all the drugs she was on and told me what they were for. We had a good laugh about it. I told her she was on more drugs than Ozzy Osbourne. She swore me to secrecy, babes. You know me. I always keep my word.'

Liz thought she was going to pass out.

———

The late morning sun was shining in through the bay window in Liz's lounge.

'I phoned Vicks,' said Jordan. 'She's struggling a bit with her chemo. It's made her really tired and constipated.'

'Do you think we should tell her what we're planning?' Liz asked Olivia and the boys, as she sipped her oat milk latte.

'No. She has enough to deal with at the moment,' replied Olivia. 'The boys have agreed to help out on this one.'

'We could get her husband to help. I mean he's already a felon.'

'He'd be the first person they'd look to, though,' suggested Olivia. 'Then Vicky might also be under suspicion. We can't have that.'

'How's Alice getting on?' asked Jusu.

'She's at Middlemoor, resting,' said Liz. 'They've increased her steroids as the cancer's growing and causing some agitation and confusion. They're also trying to sedate her a bit.'

Dwayne shifted in his seat. 'This sucks, man. We need to fix those other bastards. Right, so here's the plan…'

49

KURT AND ERNIE

'Kurt, how would you kill someone in a car and make it look like an accident?'

Vicky was lying on the sofa recuperating from her last cycle of chemotherapy. She was surfing the net on her phone. Kurt had been sitting at the dining table reading *The Sun*.

He leaned back in his chair and studied the ceiling. 'Well love, I'd probably loosen the steering wheel.'

'What if it was a newish car?'

'Hmmm, these modern cars are difficult to tamper with.' Kurt turned in his chair raising a questioning eyebrow. 'Why?'

Vicky sat up and stared directly at Kurt. 'Well, you know how my GP missed all my symptoms. I could have been caught a lot sooner, so I've decided he needs to be taught a lesson.'

Kurt shifted his position in his chair. 'Interesting, but that don't sound like no lesson, hun. Sounds more like a punishment to me. I'm guessing you need my help?'

'Yeah, sorry to ask, but I need the help, and I don't want to ask the others now Alice is ill.'

'Sure. I never liked the geezer,' replied Kurt. 'This could be fun.'

———

Ernie was laying on the sofa watching television. He leant down and peered at his mobile phone buzzing on the floor. Kurt's name flashed across the screen. He picked up the phone and answered it.

'Kurt. How are ya, mate? So good to hear from ya. When did ya get out?…

Yeah, yeah, sure… No problem… Anything at all. I owe you, mate… Tomorrow. Sure… Okay. See you then.'

———

Kurt had met Ernie in prison when they'd shared a cell together. Ernie was a nice lad. He was a few years younger than Kurt, and when he arrived he had the appearance of a lost puppy that needed taking care of. Kurt was ideal in his role as Ernie's minder; rough around the edges but he had a good heart. He'd just wanted to keep his nose clean but he soon realised Ernie needed some protection. The poor kid didn't have a clue about how to survive in prison. Kurt on the other hand had done several stints. He knew the ropes, and although he kept to himself, he had proved out of bounds to the other inmates after a few initial altercations. In one of these altercations, another inmate called Billy the Boss Man lost an ear for taunting Kurt. Billy was shouting at him in the toilet block. Kurt tried to ignore him, but Billy asked if he was deaf so Kurt decided to teach him a lesson. The lesson involved the sharp edge of a section of broken mirror which had met the full force of Billy's head as Kurt slammed it into the wall.

Wherever Kurt went you would find Ernie. If they ever became separated and someone picked on Ernie, you could guarantee Kurt would find out who the culprit was and they would be swiftly dealt with. They quickly became known as the Sesame Street Duo. Kurt and Ernie. Ernie felt he owed Kurt for this protection and had made a pact with him that if he ever needed anything when they got out, he could call on him.

Ernie was a trained mechanic who had fallen on some rough times. The problem was he had narcolepsy. Narcolepsy is a long-term neurological disorder which meant he has periods of excessive sleepiness and can fall asleep in an instant. He tried to get regular sleep at night to minimise this happening, but what with the clubbing with his mates, it never really became a regular habit. He fell asleep one too many times at work and was fired from his job, and although he managed to get several other jobs each time the same thing would happen. He was once found asleep under a car, which was jacked up as he worked on it. On another occasion he was found fast asleep leaning over an engine, under an open bonnet, when he was meant to be fixing the radiator. On another occasion he was talking to a customer and just fell asleep standing up mid-conversation. The customer went to get the manager, who promptly chucked a bucket of cold water over Ernie.

Word soon got round, and Ernie would be turned down for job applications without even getting an interview. When money became short he ended up helping a mate out with some night time burglaries to get some cash. He managed one successful attempt. On the second attempt, he broke in and gathered up some cash and jewellery. He came back downstairs and as he went to leave through the kitchen he saw a loaf of homemade bread on the counter. It smelt delicious and must have only been made that evening. He found a bread knife and went to cut a slice.

The homeowner heard a sound downstairs. They phoned the police to say they thought they were being burgled and then came downstairs to investigate. Ernie was found standing in front of the loaf of bread with the knife raised ready to cut the loaf. His stash of takings was beside him. The homeowner screamed, not realising that Ernie was asleep. The scream woke him and he lunged forward still holding the knife. The homeowner was knocked sideways and fell, hitting their head on the kitchen counter. The homeowner was out cold. Ernie bent down to check they were still breathing. His heart was racing. Still breathing... Phew! Then he heard the faint sound in the distance of police sirens approaching. He opened the back door and ran out onto the lawn. A police officer on foot rounded the corner as Ernie came running down the path with the bread knife still in one hand and his bag of stolen goods in the other.

Ernie's lawyer managed to get his sentence reduced as he only had a history of one drink driving charge from his teenage years. In that incident he had been out drinking and fell asleep at the wheel. He'd driven off the road into a hedge. No one else was involved. Then there was one shoplifting offence as a minor. Ernie got four months.

He was fortunate in the fact that Kurt's previous cell mate had recently hanged himself. The only other spare cell was with someone they called Big Daddy. No one wanted to share a cell with Big Daddy. The last man who did went out in a box. Big Daddy had the knack of just appearing out of nowhere, creeping up on you, literally scaring the shit out of you. At six foot six, he was built like a machine, towering above the other inmates. He had a large spider's web tattooed across his face and scalp which was rather a frightening image for people meeting him. So frightening in fact that he could scare toothpaste back in the tube. Big Daddy's real name was Bogdan Domlijanovic. Most of the inmates had trouble pronouncing his name correctly so he was known affectionately as Big Daddy (in reference to his tattoo and his creeping up abilities). He was doing life for murder. Rumour had it he was some king pin in an Eastern

European drug trafficking ring. No one liked to enquire in too much detail. They just knew he was bad. It didn't take long for him to become king pin in the prison.

Kurt fortunately managed to get on with Big Daddy, by what ended up being a stroke of luck. He got wind that Billy the Boss Man was going to attempt to get Kurt back for the ear incident, so he managed to convince Big Daddy that Billy was trying to take over Big Daddy's position as king pin. He also managed to convince him that Billy's plot involved murdering him in his sleep. Big Daddy wasn't having any of that. He would have done away with Billy completely but decided to make an example of him, to remind the other inmates of what messing with the current pecking order might achieve. One night, Billy the Boss Man was attacked in his sleep and brought in front of Big Daddy to confess, which he did. Straight away. This quite surprised Kurt, considering he thought he had made it all up. Billy ended up in such a bad way that he was never right in the head again and lost the use of one arm. They had to transfer him out into a psychiatric unit. Big Daddy said he owed Kurt big time for informing, so if he ever needed a favour Big Daddy was the man to come to. He grabbed Kurt's face in a vice-like grip between his meaty oversized hands. He pressed his tattooed face against Kurt's, and said in his thick Eastern European accent, 'A man's word is a man's word. Anything you need. Anything. Just ask.'

———

Ernie glanced at his phone. Kurt would be here any minute. He ordered two Bishops Fingers and took a seat at a table by the window. A few minutes later Kurt arrived.

'Yeah, alright. How are ya, Ernie son?' said Kurt, as he shook Ernie's hand.

'Not too bad. Not too bad. You're looking good,' beamed Ernie.

'I'm good. I'm good.'

Kurt sat down and took a sip of his beer. He wiped his mouth with the back of his hand. 'Listen, mate, I need a rather large fayva.'

'Sure. No problem. Anything, mate.'

'It's me missus. She's no good. Dying of cancer.' Kurt pointed to his groin. 'Women's trouble an' all that, ya know.'

Ernie looked slightly embarrassed and shifted in his seat. 'Sorry mate. I had no idea.'

'Well, can't be helped, son. The thing is her GP missed it. He's a right tosser an' all. They could've caught it earlier.' Kurt leant in across the table towards Ernie. 'So here's the fayva, son…'

50

*P*reeti was busying herself looking through the
racks of clothes. She had just had coffee with
friends and felt like a bit of retail therapy. It would be such
fun to see Jagpal's face when the credit card bill came in.
She chose a new pair of skinny jeans, several tunic tops and
a yellow and pink floaty chiffon top with cerise satin edging.
She left the shop laden with her shopping bags. As she
walked out into the main shopping mall she stopped and
adjusted her sunglasses on her head. She did not notice the
woman in the shop watching her through the store front
window. Nor did she notice the woman on her phone seated
outside the coffee shop next door as she passed by.

She walked to the car park, pushed the key fob, then
placed her purchases in the boot. As she walked back round
to the front of the car, she felt someone behind her and
turned to look. The door was being held open by a tall
young black man with dreadlocks. It only took a few seconds
for her to realise he was not alone. Preeti froze. She wanted
to scream but nothing came out. The young man smiled at
her and held his arm out as if offering her a seat.

He leant in close to her ear and spoke in a low voice.

'Now we don't want no trouble, so don't do nothin' stupid. Take a seat nice and quiet.'

Preeti got into the driver's seat.

Dwayne went round the other side of the car and sat in the passenger seat. Then two young black men sat in the back and leaned forward. The man in the passenger seat with the dreadlocks leant back then turned to Preeti. He pulled out a photo of her husband.

'Is this the prick you're married to?'

'Yes.' She stared at the image of her husband.

The young man then pulled out photos of her daughter, Jashan. 'Mmm nice,' he said.

She gasped. 'What do you want?'

Preeti listened to him. When he had finished she turned sideways in her seat to face all three men.

'You could have saved yourselves a lot of bother. I know you're not going to harm me or my daughter. You have no weapons or you would have guarded my door. I could have quite easily run and raised the alarm. To be honest, you'd be doing me a favour. I hate the fat little bastard. What do you need from me?' Preeti smiled expectantly at the young men.

Dwayne, Jusu and Jordan looked at each other.

———

Liz and Olivia had been watching from a distance, in Olivia's car. They saw the boys get out of Preeti's car and then moments later she drove off. The boys walked over and hopped in the back seat looking at each other with bemused expressions on their faces.

'So, what happened?' asked Olivia and Liz.

Dwayne leant forward into the space between the front seats, towards Liz and Olivia. 'Well, we told her we wanted to rough him up and why. She said she already knew what he'd done and wants to hire us to kill him.'

51

JAGPAL DHILLON

APRIL 2019

*I*t was late at night and the road was very icy out in the country lanes near Eynsford. Jagpal started his morning clinics at the practice at about seven thirty, so he would need to leave home at seven at the latest, maybe a little before, to make his way along the country lanes and onto the A20 to his practice on the Sidcup estate. Jagpal finished his scotch as he read the latest edition of the *British Medical Journal*, then switched the lamp off in his study and went upstairs to bed.

As the lights went out and Jagpal turned over to settle for the night he was completely oblivious to the activity about to occur outside his house.

———

The alarm went off at three a.m. Kurt shook Ernie to wake him. He drove Ernie close to the house, but they didn't notice the black Range Rover parked several metres down the road. Ernie got out of the car and Kurt drove off. He crossed the road and ran up the drive making sure to stay in the shadows and walked into the garage, admiring the sleek silver grey BMW. He stretched and yawned. Ernie decided that as the alarm was off he would take a peek inside the house. He went into the large modern kitchen and then into the lounge running off the side of the kitchen. 'Now this is nice,' he muttered to himself. He walked back into the kitchen and opened the fridge. There was a left-over curry in a bowl and some naan bread. Wouldn't hurt, he thought, so he began heating up the curry. He found a beer in the fridge and then sat down in the lounge and turned the television on with the volume down low. He polished off the curry, wiping the remnants up with the rest of the naan bread. That was the best, spiciest curry I've ever had, he thought, as he burped contentedly and sipped on his beer. Ernie woke up a couple of hours later. He got up off the sofa placing his dishes in the sink, before moving into the garage.

———

Jagpal pressed the snooze button on the alarm and sighed. Another day of the same thing. One patient after another. They would be lining up all over the waiting area by the time he got to his desk. There were so many patients that it was difficult to get an appointment these days. To cope with the demand they'd had to offer drop in clinics in the mornings. He rolled out of bed, had a shower and got dressed. He went downstairs and made a cup of tea. Preeti was still in bed. She's become rather fat and lazy, he thought. A good wife would be up and making him breakfast. He tutted as he saw the dirty dishes in the sink. She couldn't even put them in the dishwasher. He was the breadwinner in the family. Like all woman of a certain age, she had become very irrational and very rude. If he was in India he could find another wife...

He finished his cereal and brushed away the crumbs from his tie then picked up his briefcase and wandered through to the garage where his BMW was parked. He flicked the garage light switch. Nothing. Hmm. He flicked it again. Dear dear. How annoying. The bulb must have gone, so he left the door from the kitchen open and navigated his way across to the car as he pressed the key fob and tried the door. Locked. Maybe I pressed it twice. He pressed the key fob again. Yes. He hopped in, placed his briefcase on the passenger seat and opened the garage doors with the remote. He turned on the engine and listened to it purr, adjusted his seat belt and turned the radio on. The car rolled out onto the driveway with the familiar sound of gravel crunching under the tyres. He smiled to himself. As a boy he had always dreamed of having a house with a gravel driveway. When Jagpal and Preeti had started their practice, they'd bought a semi in Sidcup but had moved to a larger detached home in the country as soon as they could afford it.

Due to Jagpal's diminutive size, his head did not reach far over the steering wheel, which made quite a comical sight, and gave the appearance of the car being rather oversized.

He turned left onto the country lane and started his journey to work. It was an icy cold morning with a hoar frost covering the fences and fields. The lane wound backwards and forwards across an undulating plain of fields with a scattering of trees. Jagpal could make out the shapes of the trees in the fields as the morning light threw them into shadow. He loved this part of the day. It was his time. A time when he could listen to the radio and think about things that he found particularly bothersome.

That woman Vicky Wallis had been bothering him a lot lately. Now her husband was out of prison he was making things worse. They'd banned him from the practice, saying that if he kept coming in and abusing Jagpal they would have to phone the police. The first time he'd managed to make an appointment. When he got into the consulting room he started asking Jagpal why he had ignored his wife when she came in asking for help.

'Mr Wallis, Mr Wallis,' he had stuttered, waving his arms about. 'I think you need to leave.' Jagpal had pushed the emergency buzzer and one of the receptionists came running.

'Hello, is there a problem?'

'Mr Wallis is just leaving,' Jagpal had said.

Kurt had stood up from the chair and bent forward towards Jagpal. 'Are you kidding me? You wanker. Had to go crying to your receptionist, did ya? Too afraid to answer my questions, are ya? You fuckin' coward. Yeah, that's what you are, mate.' Kurt picked up some papers from Jagpal's desk and threw them across the floor. Then he turned to the secretary. 'And you can watch yourself an' all love.' Kurt had wagged a finger at her. 'I hope you're not one of his patients, you won't last long here if you are, love.'

Then he had stormed out but not before telling Jagpal once again that he thought he was a wanker.

The next day Vicky had come in to the practice and sat herself down.

'I want to discuss what happened.'

'Yes. Most definitely,' Jagpal had replied.

'What?' Vicky had looked slightly confused.

'Yes, you can discuss what happened. And I hope there will be an apology,' Jagpal had said.

'Oh, right. Well, go on then.'

'Go on, what?' he had asked.

'Apologise, then.'

'Me? For what?'

'For leaving me to die. What the hell are you referring to?'

'Your husband's behaviour.'

'There's nothing wrong with my husband's behaviour.'

'He came in here and verbally abused me,' Jagpal explained.

'That's because you deserved it.'

Jagpal had tutted and shook his finger at Vicky.

'Don't you shake your finger at me,' she'd growled. 'I was in here week after week asking you to help me. I kept telling you about the same signs and symptoms and you just kept giving me tablets for chest infections and urinary tract infections. You know there's a blood test called a Ca125 that you could've done. You could've examined my bloated stomach or you could have referred me to a specialist. Instead, you just left me.'

Jagpal shifted nervously in his seat. 'Well now, Vicky.'

'It's Mrs Wallis to you, sunshine.'

She was angry so he'd tried to placate her. 'Mrs Wallis, I know you're very angry right now and this is understandably very upsetting for you, but I can assure you I did everything I could.'

'Well, I don't think so. How would you feel if it was your mother or sister or wife or daughter, yeah? Exactly. You'd be as angry as me. As angry as me because you put your faith in some fat ignorant little twat who sits behind his desk all day writing prescriptions and looking at his computer screen instead of looking at the person sitting in front of him.'

He was not going to get anywhere with her, and she was going to make him run behind with his clinic. 'Mrs Wallis, we are very busy and have a great deal of patients coming through our doors. Our practice is under extreme pressure and I can't be responsible for you developing cancer.'

'Oh, but you can be responsible for ignoring my symptoms and not picking it up sooner, you little git,' she had said through gritted teeth. 'I now only have a less than a 30 per cent chance of surviving the next three to five years because of you, and don't think you're going to get away with it, you little bastard.'

Jagpal shuddered as he recalled that conversation. It was too awful to even think about. Women could be so demanding. His wife was even worse.

Jagpal started humming along to the radio. He still couldn't work out what was wrong with Preeti. She had become so rude. When he first started seeing Kiran, Preeti was very angry. It was her fault for becoming so fat after having the children. She still had a pretty face and dressed superbly but… it just didn't compare to Kiran with her long slender limbed body and those gorgeous breasts. All Kiran had to do was smile and show just a glimpse of cleavage and Jagpal was hers. Kiran had started at the GP practice four years ago. They had consummated their relationship at a GP conference in Exeter. Preeti guessed straight away. That damn woman was sharp. They would try and sneak in a few sessions in the practice after work until one night Preeti had turned up and walked right in on them. By the time Jagpal returned home his entire collection of suits had the sleeves slashed off them and all his ties had been cut in half. Preeti was screaming at the top of her voice, 'You little bastard.' Of course she knew she was better off staying with him than leaving him, so she decided to make him pay. Their credit card was being maxed out every week with morning coffee sessions, shopping sprees and holidays with friends to faraway locations. He could not get her to stop spending. Jagpal shuddered with this image still in his head as he rounded a tight bend in the road. There was a low hill with trees to his right and a few trees in a field to his left.

52

*E*rnie had taken the car key fob from the shelf behind the pot in the garage as instructed and headed towards the car to examine the steering wheel. He yawned and looked at his watch. This wouldn't take long. Without realising, he'd fallen asleep again.

A noise had woken him with a start. He was still standing in the garage with the car fob in his hand. Someone was moving around in the house. Ernie went into a panic. He opened the rear car door looking for somewhere to hide. There was a cushion and a blanket on the back seat so he jumped into the rear floor well and quickly pulled the blanket over, trying to hide himself from view. Several minutes later he heard the garage side door from the kitchen open, and then after a few seconds the driver's door of the car opened, and he felt someone moving around in the front. The door slammed shut. The car started up and crawled out onto the gravel driveway. Ernie was not sure what to do. He decided it might be best to wait until Dr Dhillon parked at the surgery and then make a getaway. Meatloaf's *Two out of Three Ain't Bad* was coming out of the car radio. It was then that his bowels started to react to the best curry he had ever tasted. The build-up was excruciating. The spasms made poor Ernie break out in a sweat. He just couldn't contain them, alongside the additional burning pain, as they made their way along his colon towards his rectum. His colon then contracted so suddenly and violently that Ernie could do no more. The immense pressure that had been building up in his bowels was suddenly released into the car with such force that, as the resultant sound resonated around the interior of the car, Ernie could have sworn he heard the fabric being ripped from the seats. *Phwhhhhhhhhhhhhhhhhhhhh.* As the noise reached a crescendo and began to fade, there followed what could only be described as an intensely hot and sulphurous aroma. Ernie recoiled at the smell. He decided the game was up. There was no way this curry was staying in. He would have to follow through.

———

Phwhhhhhhhhhhhhh.

Jagpal had forgotten his worries and was in the moment, singing along to the radio so when he heard the sound it took him completely by surprise. How could he possibly have produced a fart that loud without feeling it? Preeti's curries were good; it must have been the result of last night's one. She always used freshly chopped red chillies. When the aroma hit Jagpal's nostrils it made him recoil. He thought he was going to be sick. Yes, it definitely smelt like last night's curry.

Oh my goodness, thought Jagpal, I've shat myself. It's that damn woman's fault. She must have put too much chilli in that damn curry. He retched. He looked up into the rear vision mirror. He was going to have to pull over. It was then that he saw the man in the back seat of his car. His eyes locked for a second with Ernie's. It took Jagpal a few seconds to register. The distress at the possibility of shitting himself and the shock of someone suddenly appearing in his rear vision mirror was too much for his heart. He grabbed his chest as he felt a weight bear down upon him, crushing him like a vice. He instinctively tried to pump the brakes and veered to the left as fast and as hard as he could, trying to pull over to the side of the road. He hadn't realised he'd hit the accelerator instead. The last thing he remembered was the screech of the tyres on the road and then the impact of the car hitting the fence, bumping along into the field. He was still pumping hard on the accelerator. It was only then that he saw the tree.

The last chords of *Two out of Three Ain't Bad* could be heard lifting skywards through the cold morning air as the car came to a standstill, a mess of cold hard metal, steam hissing from the remains of the bonnet. There were skid marks everywhere, along the road, through the field and in the back of Jagpal's and Ernie's pants.

———

Ernie could see what was about to happen, so he rolled into the foot section of the back seat. He was battered and bruised by all the bumping to and fro as the car went through the fence and navigated across the field towards the tree. He groaned. As the car impacted with the tree, he hit his head. Fortunately, the cushion and the blanket had protected him. He managed to open the rear door when the car finally came to a standstill, climbed out and ran straight into a set of bushes nearby to try and clean himself up, throwing his boxers into the undergrowth. He looked around hoping to make a quick getaway then went back to the car and briefly looked into the driver's seat to see what was left of Dr Dhillon.

'Ouch! That must have hurt,' said Ernie to himself.

He felt for his phone in his back pocket. He would need to ring Kurt. He heard a car approaching on the road, looked up and couldn't contain a smile. What a stroke of luck. Kurt slowed down, waving at him. He waved back and ran over.

Ernie hopped in the car still smiling, feeling very pleased with himself.

'Where've ya been, mate? What happened? I've been looking for your ugly mug everywhere. I've been right propa worried 'bout ya,' Kurt said, appearing rather annoyed.

Kurt turned to Ernie, screwing up his nose. 'What the hell's that smell? It's propa nasty. Did you just do a jam tart in my car, you filthy bastard?'

Ernie shrugged. 'Sorry, mate. I couldn't help it. It just slipped out. And I've ruined me boxers.'

Kurt recoiled, shooting Ernie a look of disgust. 'You filthy bastard,' he said again as he waved his hand in front of his face trying to fan the aroma away. 'What happened?'

'Well, he's brown bread, that's for sure,' said Ernie.

'Are ya really sure about that?'

'Yeah, the tree branch came through the windscreen and took his loaf clean off.'

Kurt raised his eyebrows at Ernie.

'It's a long story, and it involves the best Ruby Murray I've ever had.'

'I bet it does. Ohh mate, did you just do another one? Get outta me bloody car.'

———

PC Harper and PC Jones had had a busy night, but things had just started to quieten down and they were looking forward to going home. They'd stopped at Burger King and were sitting in the squad car devouring their breakfast. PC Harper received the call from HQ. Accident reported by a driver about a mile from Eynsford. One fatality.

'Roger that. On our way.'

PC Harper turned to PC Jones. 'This'll be your first fatality, Jones. I'd put that burger down if I were you.'

PC Jones gulped the mouthful of burger as he hastily put the rest of it back in its wrapping.

As they approached the accident scene, they could see the car resting in the field. It was facing them on the opposite side of the road with the bonnet up against a lone tree. A light blue saloon was parked at the side of the road and a gentleman was waving frantically at them. PC Harper slowed down, performed a U turn and pulled the patrol car to a stop.

'Ready?' he asked.

PC Jones climbed out and approached the distressed looking man on the side of the road.

'I just saw the car and pulled over… I went to have a look… dead… oh my God, it's awful!'

He told the man to wait by the squad car. PC Jones and PC Harper entered the field via the gaping hole in the fence that Jagpal had made. As they approached the vehicle from the driver's side, they could hear the radio still playing. The branches of the tree had shattered the windscreen and obscured their immediate view of the driver. Through the branches they could make out a body slumped over the steering wheel. There was a lot of blood and a dreadful stench. PC Harper frowned. There was something not quite right about the body. He walked around to the passenger side of the vehicle and realised what the issue was. He nodded at Jones beckoning him to have a look.

'Take a look at this, Jones.'

He walked over, stood next to PC Harper and looked into the vehicle. Jagpal's lifeless eyes were staring back up at them from the passenger seat. PC Jones reeled backwards and started retching into the grass.

'Head has come clean off,' said Harper. 'And the poor devil's shat himself. See, Jones, I bet you are glad you didn't finish that burger now.'

53

*V*icky was waiting for Kurt.

Liz had made breakfast and had the kids up, attempting to get them ready for school.

'Alfie, turn that music down please, and go and get dressed,' said Liz, shooing him off the sofa.

Kurt arrived at the front door, nodding at Liz as he entered. She smiled back at him as she tidied up the sofa which Alfie had just left in disarray. He's been up to something, she thought.

Liz walked over to the kitchen and started to wash the dishes which were piled up in the sink. She stared out through the kitchen window which looked over the estate, watching the morning flurry of people heading out for work. Vicky had phoned Liz to ask her to stay the night as Kurt was meeting up with some mates. He was definitely up to no good. She placed the last plate on the draining board, switched the kettle on and made two mugs of tea and carried them through on a tray to Vicky.

'Vicks, it's me,' she called through the bedroom door which was ajar.

'Come in,' said Vicky.

Liz pushed the door open with her shoulder. Kurt was

sitting on the end of the bed holding Vicky's hand. Liz put the tray down and handed him a mug of tea.

'Ta, luv,' he said.

Liz bent forward, leaning over Vicky to help her to sit forward. She began plumping up the pillows behind her as Vicky groaned with the effort of sitting forward.

'Here you go, a nice cup of tea.' Vicky grabbed hold of the tea and rested it in her lap.

'Thanks, Liz,' she said as she smiled weakly.

The last round of chemo was taking its toll on her.

'Alfie's in the shower, and I've set the breakfast table, so the kids will be out soon. Kurt, will you be able to stay until Janice gets here later? I'll need to get home by lunch time.'

'Sure. Thanks, Liz, for taking care of them.'

'That's okay.'

Liz gave Vicky a kiss on the cheek and turned and left the room.

Kurt leant towards Vicky and lowered his voice.

'I don't know how you managed it, luv, but thanks. It made the job a lot easier, I can tell you.'

'Thanks for what?'

'For disabling the alarm and unlocking the garage door.'

Vicky looked blankly back at Kurt. 'What are you talking about?'

'You sent me a text.'

'No, I didn't.'

'Yeah, you did.'

'You lost your phone so I gave you mine. How could I send you a text?'

Kurt scratched his head. 'I dunno, but I got a text at eleven saying the alarms were disabled, the garage door would be open and the car fob was on the shelf in the pot. It said he will leave in the morning at five to seven. I sent one back saying thanks babes, and you sent another text with a thumbs up and a smiley face emoji. Here.'

Kurt passed the phone to Vicky showing her the text and the phone number.

'Well, I thought it was you,' he continued slowly. 'I thought you must have another phone.'

Vicky stared at the screen and then looked back at Kurt. 'I didn't send you this. I don't know who this number belongs to.'

Kurt frowned and scratched his head again.

'Where's Ernie?' asked Vicky.

'That's a long story. I think we might've been set up here.'

Kurt leaned back in his chair and stretched his arms above his head. He rubbed his brow with the palm of his hand and breathed out a large puff of air.

'I think we're going to have to lie low for a while.'

'What? Why?' Vicky asked as she peered anxiously up at Kurt.

'Well, Ernie fell asleep in the garage. He never tampered with the steering wheel. Anyways, your man's dead that's for sure. Good and propa.'

Vicky grabbed Kurt's hand. 'How do you know?'

'Well, either he's brown bread or he's running around without a loaf.'

Vicky rested her head back on the pillows. 'Are you sure?'

'Yeah, Ernie said it was sitting on the passenger seat next to his body.'

She stared at Kurt then shrugged. 'At least the bastard's dead.'

54

PREETI

*P*reeti was lounging in bed watching BBC *Breakfast* with a nice hot cup of tea. Nothing had happened. She frowned and stared at her mobile phone screen. *I sent the message and they replied… so why didn't they turn up?* She sighed and threw the phone on the bed in exasperation. She should have known they wouldn't go through with it. They'd only wanted to rough him up. Men. *If you want something done properly you should just do it yourself,* she thought.

There was a crunch of tyres on the gravel driveway. She slid out of bed and padded over to peer out of the window and saw the police car.

A few minutes later there was a knock at the front door. Preeti grabbed her dressing gown while pushing her feet into her silk embroidered slippers. She padded downstairs and opened the front door to find two police officers standing there.

The male officer cleared his throat and then started to speak.

'Mrs Dhillon?'

'Yes.'

'I'm PC Carter.'

He looked to the female officer who continued. 'And I'm PC Arthur. We're from the family liaison team. May we come inside?'

'Yes, of course officers. Do come in.'

Preeti sat on the couch as the officers informed her of her husband's demise.

'I'm afraid there has been an accident… nothing we could do… could you come with us to the station… identify the body…'

She went upstairs to get changed, smiling to herself. My, my. What had they done?

———

'My gorgeous boys! What have you done?' she said with a gleeful tone.

'Who is this?' replied a woman's voice on the other end.

Preeti pulled the phone away from her ear and checked the number on the screen.

'Sorry, wrong number,' she said as she quickly rang off. She checked her diary notes and gasped as the realisation sank in. She had sent the message to Vicky.

Preeti dialled Dwayne's number.

'Yo.'

'Dwayne. This is Preeti.'

The line was silent.

'Dwayne?'

'Mmmh?'

'He's dead.'

'Who?'

'My husband. Who do you think?'

'What? We wouldn't know about that, would we? Must be the other bloke.'

'What other bloke?'

'The other bloke we saw go into your house.'

Preeti's heart started to beat a little bit faster.

'Dwayne, I don't know what you're talking about. There was no one at our house last night.'

'I think you'll find there was. We parked up and waited, but you never phoned. A car pulled up and some bloke got out. He ran up to your house and went inside through the garage. So we took off. We thought you'd set us up.'

Preeti spoke very slowly. 'Dwayne, this is really important. What did he look like?'

Dwayne gave a description of Ernie. 'A tall slim gangly guy, short hair.'

That was no one she recognised. What was going on?

———

Dwayne dialled Liz's number. 'Yo, Liz.'

'Hi, Dwayne.'

'Dhillon's dead.'

'What?'

'Nothing to do with us. Some other dude went in and did the job for us, apparently.'

———

'Vicky, what did you do?'

Liz was sitting on one side of Vicky's bed. Kurt was sitting on the other side.

Kurt sighed and looked at Liz. 'Listen darlin', we didn't do nothin'. We only intended to rough the geezer up a bit, that's all.'

She looked from Kurt to Vicky.

Vicky shrugged and sighed. 'Apparently, the tree took his head clean off.'

———

The next day Preeti collected a large bouquet of flowers from the local florist and drove to Vicky's house. She knocked on the door and waited. There was the sound of footsteps and then the front door opened. Kurt was standing in the doorway.

'Mr Wallis?'

'Yes.'

'I'm looking for Mrs Wallis.'

'She's not well. Who are you?'

'But she is in?'

'Yes.'

With that she pushed past Kurt and bustled in.

'Hey, you can't just barge in here…'

Vicky was lying on the sofa with a duvet wrapped over her. Preeti walked in and introduced herself to Kurt over her shoulder. He was hovering by the lounge room door, and when he heard who she was he started to pace up and down, running his fingers nervously across his scalp.

The chemo Vicky had had three days prior was wreaking havoc on her body. The constant nausea and retching had taken two days to get under control. The aching joints and metallic taste on her tongue reminded her that her chemotherapy infusion, which had been drip fed into her body, was a concerted effort to slowly poison her in an attempt to keep her cancer under control. It took all her energy to glance up at Preeti.

'What do you want?'

'I've come to give you this and say thank you.' Preeti presented the bouquet to Vicky.

She weakly held up her hand and took the bouquet, sniffing the flowers and then sat them in her lap. 'I'm not sure what I did to deserve these.'

'It was me,' said Preeti. 'I sent you that text.'

Vicky just stared at her blankly.

Preeti turned to face Kurt and fluttered her bejewelled wrist in front of her dismissively. 'My husband told me you'd come into the surgery and that he'd banned you. He told me about you, Vicky.' She pulled up a chair next to the sofa. 'I went in one night and read your file and got your contact details and mobile numbers. That husband of mine was cheating on me and making me look a fool. I'm a GP by trade but left it behind to raise my family. I would have been good, you know. Much better than that idiot I married,' she said as she spat the words out. 'I'm a partner in the practice and still do the occasional shift to help out. You're the second woman he's missed with ovarian cancer. Wouldn't you know it? Most GPs see one in a lifetime; he gets two and misses them both. I tried to make him do his online training regarding ovarian cancer, but he's so arrogant and refused to do it. I was sick of him, sick of him dragging down the reputation of the practice I'd struggled to set up. When those men spoke to me about you, I thought I'd give you a hand.'

'Are you accusing us of having something to do with your husband's death?' asked Kurt defensively. 'Hang on. You said those men. What men?'

'Your friends. They wanted to mess him up for you. I turned the alarm off for them. They were going to make it look like a burglary. To be honest I wanted them to kill him, but they said they didn't do that kind of thing. They were going to scare him a bit but I sent the text to you by mistake. They said they saw a man go into the house, so they left. I'm not sure what he did but it was just an unfortunate accident from what I understand. The coroner said Jagpal had had a heart attack while driving. He had a bad heart. I wanted to thank the man, but I guess you can do that for me.'

They all just sat in silence for several minutes. Kurt and Vicky were not sure what to say.

Preeti examined her perfectly manicured fingernails waiting for Kurt or Vicky to reply. There was nothing but silence.

Vicky and Kurt were clearly not in a chatty mood. Preeti

sighed. 'Right, well all's well that ends well. I'll leave you to rest, my dear,' she said, patting Vicky's hand.

———

Preeti was relieved when the funeral was over. Jashan, Sunny and Tej were devastated. They adored their father. They never knew about his affair and Preeti wanted them to have good memories of him. A tragic accident. Nothing more.

Kiran was there sobbing the whole way through the funeral.

'I am so sorry, Preeti,' she sobbed.

'Hmm. I'm sure you are.'

She drove home and sat in her large empty house and cried. She wasn't sure if they were tears of sadness for all the years she had missed, or tears of joy.

———

Preeti stopped by to check on Vicky several weeks later.

'By the way, I've set up an account in your name, Vicky. It was from the proceeds of the silly man's life insurance. I know it won't go any way near to making amends for what my husband has done, but it will mean your children might have some quality time with their mother now. Here are the details,' Preeti said as she handed Kurt a piece of paper. 'The money is to help pay for some of your medical bills and the children's education. I'll be around to make sure it's spent on what you need for your care,' she said as she threw a warning glance over to Kurt.

'Oh, and another thing. I hope you don't mind but I'm returning to the GP practice full time and have taken the liberty of becoming your named GP, Vicky. You take care of yourself. I'll see you at the practice.' Preeti moved towards the door and left with a wave.

Kurt and Vicky stared after her as she left.

After a few moments of silence Vicky shifted position, wincing with the discomfort. She looked at Kurt who was studying the piece of paper Preeti had handed him. 'Kurt, how much is in the account... Kurt?'

Kurt could not hear Vicky. He was too busy looking down at the figure at the bottom of the page on the account details.

55

ALICE

EARLY JUNE 2019

*L*iz drove up the sweeping driveway of Middlemoor Manor. Harold the butler came out to attend to her as soon as he heard the crunch of the tyres on the gravel driveway.

'Hello, Harold. How is she?'

'She's been demanding to see you all, so hopefully she'll calm down now you're here.'

Liz began giving out commands to the other women. 'Sarah, could you get the flowers out of the back please? Olivia, can you give me a hand to help Vicky out?'

'Yes, sure.'

Dwayne's large 4 x 4 black Range Rover appeared on the driveway with rap music blaring. She looked up, waving as the boys parked up and began tumbling out of the car.

'Here Liz, we can help Vicky.' Dwayne reached into Liz's car lifting Vicky out and carrying her to the front door.

'M'lady,' said Dwayne, as he deposited Vicky on the threshold with a bow and a flutter of his hand. Vicky beamed up at Dwayne.

'You're such a gentleman.'

Liz nudged Olivia as they followed Sarah up the stairs

and through the main entrance. 'See, what do you think?' she whispered.

Olivia studied Sarah's outfit. She was wearing a close fitting knee length cross over halter neck dress with a pattern of large black bordered bright crimson, yellow and cream squares. She was wearing matching crimson ballet pumps.

'Nothing wrong with that, babes. I think she looks quite smart.'

Harold led the group through the large oak panelled foyer with its wide sweeping staircase and flagstone floor, towards the rear of the house, into a large oak panelled sunny south facing room. The room had large mullioned bay windows and French doors overlooking a long flagstone terrace. The terrace appeared to spread the length of the house, overlooking a large sweeping manicured lawn and formal garden. There was a large stone hearth in the middle of the back wall which was tall and long enough to fit about four or five people standing side by side.

The room had the appearance of having been transformed from a large hall into a temporary bedroom.

Alice was sitting in the middle of an enormous bed in the centre of the room at the far end propped up in the bed with a cacophony of various sized lace edged pillows. She was wearing a white cotton nightdress with embroidered lace edging and a tie dyed multicoloured head scarf wrapped precariously around her head.

Liz gasped at Alice's appearance. Her face was swollen from the steroids. She had lost a large amount of weight and due to her fragile emaciated state she appeared incredibly small amongst the covers.

Alice appeared to be studying something intently on her lap and was muttering to an elderly lady who was sitting at the bedside. She looked up as she heard the visitors enter the room.

'Ahh, here they are!' she exclaimed. 'And about time too.

Where have you been? Now come here all of you and give me a hug. I want to hear what you've been up to.'

Alice turned to the elderly lady. 'Marjorie, if you attend to the lunch menu… and if we could have some tea for everyone.'

'Yes, certainly,' said the woman as she then disappeared from the room.

'Now don't worry,' said Alice, as she looked towards Liz and winked. 'I have vegan options, my dear.'

She patted the bed. 'Climb on board, everyone.'

Dwayne and Jordan were holding onto Vicky and assisted her onto the bed positioning her next to Alice. Alice hugged her and gave her a kiss. Then Liz, Sarah, Olivia and the boys all climbed on as well. They sat and had tea and scones and chatted. Vicky updated them on what had happened with Dr Dhillon and the strange events with Preeti. They all laughed and said how they would all love to meet Ernie and Kurt.

'You had us so confused,' said Olivia. 'It all got a bit messy. Isn't it hilarious? We were all trying to rough him up! We thought we were doing you a favour. You should've told us. Remember we're all in this together. I can't believe his wife, though. I'm telling you, babes, Hell hath no fury like a woman scorned. If you get women banding together you get a formidable force.'

Marjorie returned announcing lunch was ready. Trays laden with various dishes were brought in.

In the middle of everyone eating, Alice suddenly turned and said to Sarah, 'My dear child, could you PLEASE tell that girl to stop it.'

'Stop what?' asked Sarah.

'Stop chewing so loudly,' exclaimed Alice.

'Which one?' asked Sarah, looking blankly at the others.

'That one there.' Alice pointed to Liz, with an annoyed expression on her face.

Liz looked up mid-mouthful and stopped. She quickly

swallowed, looking slightly guilty. 'I'm sorry, Alice. I'll try and be quieter.'

'Hmmph. I should hope so.' Alice looked down at her plate and began to pick at her food.

Liz threw a confused look at the others. They all continued eating. Liz sat silently, opting to sip her water instead, although she knew she'd been quiet in her chewing and felt she had been unfairly singled out.

'There. There she goes again,' said Alice, pointing at Liz. 'Oh dear, dear, dear. It's so loud.'

'Alice, darling, I'm not eating at the moment.' Liz looked at the others, wearing a frown that said, 'She's not right.'

'But it's so loud,' exclaimed Alice, as she threw her head back dramatically on the pillow, cradled her head in her hands and sighed.

Liz got up and left the room saying she was summoning the nurse.

As they all left, Sarah and Liz asked Harold to phone them if Alice deteriorated. They knew Hugh wouldn't notify them.

Alice woke at half two in the morning and called for the nurse.

'My dear, I need the bathroom.'

'Okay, Alice darling,' said the nurse. 'Up we get.'

She struggled to her feet and managed to walk several yards across the flagstone floor. Her vision was not right and her headache was blinding. Alice screamed as a hot sharp burst of pain radiated across her skull. She collapsed to the floor grabbing hold of the velvet floor length curtains as she fell. The nurse went to grab her and gently lowered her to the floor with the curtains falling down around her.

'Alice, Alice, can you hear me?'

Her breathing was shallow. The nurse ran back to the bedside table and phoned for the GP and then phoned Hugh.

A few minutes later the room was a flurry of activity as

Hugh and Harold arrived, followed by the GP. Alice was carried back to bed.

She never woke up. Half an hour later she was gone.

'Shall we phone the children?' asked Harold.

'No, not until the morning,' said Hugh.

Harold went into the kitchen and phoned Liz and Sarah.

'Elizabeth? This is Harold. They say it was a bleed in her brain. It happened very fast and she never recovered.'

56

MR ASHREN

*D*inesh Ashren was standing in front of the bathroom mirror admiring his reflection. He was good looking, and he knew it.

The image staring back at him was of a tall, olive-skinned man with a muscular physique. The result of a combination of carefully watching his diet, daily work outs in the gym and running in Regent's Park.

No woman could resist him. He had proof. He'd had to get restraining orders out on several of his patients who had become rather attached to him. One even had a wedding venue booked. 'The perils of the trade and of being so good looking,' he said to his colleagues as he laughed it off. It was his dark brown 'come to bed eyes', he was sure of it. His wife, Mona, did not find it so funny.

He ran a hand through his thick black wavy hair, smoothing down his fringe as he pulled it over to one side with some scented hair gel. He slapped aftershave onto the designer stubble which lay across his top lip, chin and jawline. He flashed one of his wicked smiles back at the mirror revealing a perfect set of dazzling white teeth.

'The word irresistible just doesn't do you justice,' he said to the reflection in the mirror.

Dinesh waltzed into his Harley Street practice, humming.

'Morning, Gloria,' he said to his secretary as he walked into her office. 'What do we have today?'

'A full clinic today, Mr Ashren.'

'We always like to be busy, don't we?'

'Umm, we also have a couple of emails. One is from the lady you saw several months ago. The one I phoned you about yesterday. She doesn't sound very happy.'

'Oh? What's the matter now? Honestly. It was just a mistake. A little mix up. These women do get so het up about things.'

'Perhaps you should read the email,' she suggested.

'Right, well, I'll be in my room. Coffee for me when you're ready, Gloria.'

Mr Ashren closed his consulting room door and switched on his computer. The computer blinked slowly to life, and he opened his inbox.

Gloria had forwarded the message.

Mr Ashren,

I assume you will remember me. I saw you for a consultation in February for lower abdominal pain. You sent me for a scan which you informed me was clear. I returned to see you at the beginning of April saying I was still having abdominal discomfort. You took a swab and I have not heard anything since. I phoned your secretary yesterday to ask what was happening. She informs me that the swab results showed I have a pelvic infection which requires antibiotics. She informed me yesterday that she searched your desk and there must have been an error as she found the prescription from four weeks ago still sitting under some paperwork!

I would like to know where these antibiotics are and why you haven't written to me or requested I come back to see you. I have instructed your secretary to fax the prescription to my GP immediately.

I will not be returning to see you again and would like to express my dissatisfaction in the terrible standard of care you appear to deliver to your patients.

Hilary Noble

Dinesh sighed and closed the email. He couldn't please everyone. Why was his secretary so stupid? Of all the things to tell a patient. She could have blamed it on the lab at the very least.

He picked up the phone. 'Gloria, could you come in, please?'

———

Gloria was fed up. Fed up with working for an idiot. Fed up with being undervalued and underpaid. And now he was blaming her for upsetting that woman. She had only apologised and told the truth.

He had really shouted at her this time and then thrown his pen at her. How rude. Fortunately she'd seen it coming and ducked at just the right time so the pen narrowly missed her.

'How could you be so fucking stupid, Gloria?' he had shouted.

———

She typed up the next day's clinic list. 'Sarah Postlewaite,' she muttered under her breath as she got up and went to the filing cabinet to retrieve the patients notes. 'There they are. Postlewaite.' She opened the notes and checked that the last clinic letters were included and the last set of scans were on the system.

That poor woman, she thought. It doesn't sound like she'll be around for long. I don't know how he can sit there without a conscience. She was under his care for so long, over six months, and he doesn't think it's anything to do with him.

Gloria had read up on ovarian cancer and she knew that it was often missed but she had also read how women were dying needlessly from a disease that should be picked up much earlier. What could she do? She sighed as she closed the notes and put the file in the pile of notes ready for the next day's clinic.

———

Sarah arrived with Liz at Mr Ashren's rooms fifteen minutes early in order to complete the regulatory paperwork. She had been up late last night finishing her new outfit. It was a tie back halter neck maxi dress with a layered waterfall skirt which fell from the knee. She had chosen a cotton fabric with a bright floral pattern on a black background and she matched the outfit with a pair of red kitten heels.

'I didn't realise it was such an occasion,' said Liz, feeling rather drab in her olive green shift dress and FitFlops. 'If I'd known, I would've baked a cake.'

'What are you on about?'

Liz waved her hand at Sarah's outfit. 'The dress.'

'Do you like it? It's another one of my creations.'

'It's lovely but I have to ask, what is it with the outfits? All of a sudden you look like you're on a catwalk.'

Sarah shrugged. 'I don't know. Maybe the clothes make me feel good. I feel feminine and in control again. Just as I did when I was at fashion school. This is my art. My way of expressing myself. Who I am.'

'Ahh, so that's it. Well, good on you.' Liz squeezed Sarah's arm affectionately.

The two women entered the waiting room and walked up to the large mahogany reception desk. A young dark-haired woman was seated behind the desk peering at her phone screen. She didn't even look up as they approached.

'Hmm hmmm,' said Sarah, as she cleared her throat attempting to draw attention to their presence.

The receptionist glanced up in their direction. 'Good morning. Who have you come to see?'

'Mr Ashren.'

'And your name please?'

'Sarah Postlewaite.'

The receptionist proceeded to check the list in front of her. She picked up a pen and made a mark next to an entry. 'Take a seat, please,' she said, as she fluttered her arm in front of her indicating the waiting area behind them. 'And if you could complete this form and return it to me,' she said tapping a clipboard on the desk in front of them.

Sarah picked up the clipboard and the two women sat down on a large modern black leather sofa positioned up against one wall of the waiting area.

She completed the form and handed it back to the receptionist.

After a few minutes Liz stood up and walked over to the water fountain to get a glass of water. She returned and sat down.

'Now, Sarah, remember what we're going to say.'

'Yes,' said Sarah. 'I'm going to remain calm but ask him for all copies of my notes and scans, and then I'm going to ask him to explain why he has never apologised for not detecting my cancer earlier.'

Sarah's eyes narrowed as she looked at Liz and whispered through gritted teeth. 'I don't understand why you seem hell bent on me having to have this conversation, though, you never spoke with your consultant.'

'Because I tried to sue my guy from the start,' said Liz. 'I doubt he would've been amenable to discussion after I'd sought legal advice.'

'Okay,' said Sarah sighing hopelessly 'I doubt it's going to do any good, though.'

'We have to go through the motions,' said Liz. 'If he doesn't come to the party then we'll make him see sense.'

'Is this really necessary?'

'Yes. Now grow a spine, Sarah, and stick up for yourself. Look at you. You look amazing. You are a strong brave woman and you need to make this guy know you mean business.'

She didn't exactly feel like a strong brave woman and really would have preferred not to make such a fuss, but Liz was quite a force to be reckoned with. Sarah wished she was more like Liz, but she would have preferred to be at home on the sofa with Patrice in her lap. In saying that, she also enjoyed spending time with Liz, Alice and Vicky, to the extent that she couldn't remember what life was like before them. And she did look good in this dress…

———

'Mrs Postlewaite. You can go up to the first floor now.' The receptionist rose from her chair and pointed in the direction of the hallway, before disappearing back into her seat.

Sarah and Liz went back out into the hallway and ascended the flight of heavily carpeted stairs to the first floor. At the top of the first-floor landing they found Gloria waiting for them.

'Hello, Mrs Postlewaite. Mr Ashren is ready for you now.' Gloria took a moment to admire Sarah's dress. 'Ohh I do love your dress. Where did you get it?'

'I made it,' gushed Sarah, twirling around to allow Gloria a 360-degree view.

'Wow, it's amazing.'

Bzzz, bzzzzz. Mr Ashren was becoming impatient and wanted her to know he was waiting. Gloria glanced irritably towards the intercom buzzing on her desk. She stepped aside and waved her hand towards the open door behind her. 'Sorry, he's letting me know he's waiting for you.'

Sarah took a deep breath and walked through the doorway. Liz turned to Gloria as she walked past, smiled and said, 'Thank you.'

Gloria smiled back at the woman accompanying Mrs Postlewaite. The woman looked rather intimidating. She also got the impression that Mrs Postlewaite appeared a little apprehensive. Like she had something to unburden. Gloria wished she could be a fly on the wall for this consultation. She could tell it was going to be very interesting.

———

'Ah, Mrs Postlewaite. Take a seat, my dear,' said Dinesh, as he studied her carefully. Somehow she looked different.

The smile he had worn quickly disappeared as he saw the mousy haired woman appear next to her. She had brought company. This looked rather ominous.

He shook Sarah's hand and then turned towards Liz. 'Hello, I'm Mr Ashren,' he said as he offered his hand.

'Elizabeth,' she said as she sat down, ignoring his gesture.

Mr Ashren hurriedly dropped his hand and moved back round to his side of the consulting desk, taking a seat.

He forced a nervous smile at the two women as he squared the notes in front of him with his hands. He had an odd feeling that his charm and good looks were not going to help him today.

'Well now, what can I do for you today, Mrs Postlewaite?' he asked.

Sarah coughed nervously clearing her throat.

'I wanted to come in and just go through some things with you about my original diagnosis.'

'Is there something specific you wished to discuss?' enquired Dinesh, with an air of caution.

'Yes, there is actually,' replied Sarah. 'I wanted to know why I was under your care for over six months, repeatedly coming in to see you, yet you never once considered that I might possibly have ovarian cancer. I now know there's a

305

Ca125 blood test which I should have had taken, and yet you never took it.'

Dinesh could see where this conversation was heading…

Sarah continued. 'When I came in and told you I'd been diagnosed with ovarian cancer you seemed genuinely surprised.'

'It was a shock,' he replied as he leant forward opening his hands on the desk as if opening a book. 'Now, you know you presented with classic urinary tract infections and I treated you accordingly with courses of antibiotics—'

'Yes,' interrupted Sarah, 'but I informed you I had lower abdominal pain, bloating, urinary frequency and urgency and I felt full after eating. You should have tracked my symptoms. You should have taken a Ca125 blood test and further scans. You didn't do any of these things.'

Dinesh shifted in his seat. 'I can assure you, Mrs Postlewaite, that I did everything appropriate.'

'Sarah, my name is Sarah. I'm a person and I'm sitting in front of you right now as one of your patients and I would like *you* to answer my questions.'

Dinesh raised his arms up defensively as if pushing the two women away. 'Well now, I can assure you, as I have just explained, that there's nothing more I could have done.'

Liz had been sitting silently so far, wearing a stony expression.

'This is absolute bullshit,' she said.

'Excuse me?' questioned Dinesh, as he looked over to her, appearing rather startled.

'You are absolutely unbelievable,' Liz exclaimed. 'You sit there behind that desk of yours as if you are so high and mighty. But you're not. You are so full of shit.'

Liz pointed at Sarah. 'This woman is your patient and she deserves answers to her questions. You're trying to fob her off. Why didn't you take any further scans? Why didn't you take a Ca125 blood test? And don't give me that nonsense about there being no screening test for ovarian cancer. You're a gynaecologist for God's sake. This,' said Liz as she waved her hand at her and Sarah, 'is your bread and butter. What hope do we have if you can't even perform the basic functions of your specialist role?'

'I'm not sure who you are, but I'm beginning to find your tone offensive,' bristled Dinesh.

'She's my friend and she's able to speak on my behalf,' said Sarah, glancing over at Liz in admiration.

Dinesh knew he would have to try and wrap this up. He took a deep breath... if all else fails there is always the counselling option he thought. 'Now, now, ladies. I think it might be best if you both calm down. I can assure you I have done nothing wrong and not missed anything. There's nothing more I can tell you. You're obviously upset and it must be a difficult time coming to terms with your diagnosis. Have you considered counselling?' He threw Sarah a look of mock concern. 'It might be helpful.'

Liz and Sarah both rolled their eyes.

'Have you?' asked Liz.

'Excuse me?' he replied.

Liz jabbed a finger in the air at Dinesh. 'Have *YOU* considered counselling? Simple question, isn't it? You're quite clearly displaying the behaviour of a narcissistic little twat and are in need of it.'

'Now hold on a minute,' Dinesh spluttered. This hadn't quite been the reaction he expected.

Liz jabbed a finger at Dinesh again as she leant over the edge of the desk. You... have... no... idea...,' she said, emphasising each word.

She turned in her chair and swiped her hand upwards towards Sarah in a windscreen wiper style movement. 'Right, Sarah. Tell him.'

Sarah was looking ahead at Dinesh as if in a daze. Dinesh was staring down at his knuckles which were gripping the edge of the consultation desk. He could hear the swish of the blood in his veins getting louder and louder. He suddenly felt very hot.

Liz nudged Sarah.

Sarah turned to look at her. 'What?' she hissed.

'Go on, then.' Liz nodded towards Dinesh.

'What?' Sarah repeated.

'Ask him about your vagina.'

'My vagina?'

Liz pointed to Sarah's groin sighing in frustration. 'Yes. Your vagina.'

Sarah gave Liz a 'what the hell are you on about' look.

'Oh, for goodness' sake.' Liz turned in her chair back towards Dinesh. 'I'll ask him, then.'

Liz pointed at Dinesh several times as she emphasised the next sentence.

'What… did you… do…' Liz then pointed at Sarah, 'to *her* vagina?'

Dinesh was not quite sure what this woman was asking and felt it was quite clear that neither did his patient. 'Excuse me? What are you talking about?'

'You shortened her vagina and never bothered to tell her,' Liz announced.

'Oh my God,' said Sarah, as she shook her head and waved at Liz as if fanning the flames of a fire. 'Leave this to me, Liz.'

Sarah leant towards Dinesh. 'I've come here today to tell you that I've now changed gynaecologists. My lovely new female gynaecologist has informed me that the reason sex is so painful for me is because you shortened my vagina considerably during my hysterectomy. Don't you think you should have informed me?'

'Well, ummm, err. It was a necessary part of the procedure.'

'Is that all you have to say?'

Sarah now felt herself becoming rather incensed. She was beginning to realise that this man was a genuine idiot and he was looking increasingly flustered. With the support of Liz by her side any previous concerns she had had about expressing herself were melting away. 'You also left me post op with no discussion about the menopause. When I asked you to go through this, you said if I had any issues that you could prescribe some HRT.'

'Umm, yes.'

'My cancer is hormone linked, so why did you offer me HRT?'

'It can be helpful... and it's not as hormonally linked as breast cancer. The evidence states...'

'The evidence states.' Sarah's tone took on a childish mimicking tone. 'I don't give a monkey's what the evidence states. If you knew that, why didn't you discuss it with me first? Oh, I get it. Because you think I didn't need to know. I should have just taken my medicine without any questions. Is that it?'

'Now look here. I really don't think you can come in here and question me in this manner.'

'Why not?'

'It's really not appropriate.'

'Appropriate,' yelled Sarah. 'And what bit of your care was considered appropriate, you arrogant man. You treated me for months on end completely missing the underlying cause of my symptoms. You then ripped my ovaries out and didn't think it appropriate to sit down with me and discuss the effect a surgically induced menopause would cause, or the fact you needed to shorten my vagina. Did you think because my ovaries were gone that I wouldn't want to have sex again? You probably hoped that I would disappear and die. A woman without ovaries. What use is she to society? That's what you think, isn't it? You pathetic conceited piece of shit.'

'Now look here,' said Dinesh, as he began to rise up from behind his desk. 'You cannot come in here and speak to me like that.'

'No? It's okay for you to misdiagnose me and then pretend that it's nothing to do with you, but you think it's not okay for me to be allowed the opportunity to question you.'

'You are being verbally abusive.' Dinesh was shaking and finding it hard to hold his tongue.

'This is not verbally abusive. I'll show you verbally abusive...' Sarah began to rise in her seat raising her fist.

'Right Sarah, that's enough,' said Liz as she rose from her chair grabbing Sarah's hand to restrain her. 'Come on, we're leaving now. There's no point even talking to this idiot.'

Liz beckoned to Sarah to follow her.

Sarah let out a long, frustrated sigh. 'Arrrrrgh, okay, we'll go. But you haven't heard the last of me.'

Dinesh was still gripping the edge of his desk. He was apoplectic with rage and could not move. He stared straight ahead at the two women as they made to leave.

Sarah turned back towards him, 'Oh, and I wish to have all copies of my notes today before I leave the premises. I will also be instructing a letter from my lawyers asking for all copies of my notes to be forwarded to them.'

'Well now, I don't think that's necessary.'

'We're really not interested in what you think, though, are we?' said Liz. 'Clearly it counts for nothing. If she had taken your advice as the complete and utter nonsense it is then she might not be in the predicament she's in now.'

Sarah opened the door to leave. 'I trusted you,' she said. With that, both women turned and left, slamming the door behind them.

57

$\mathcal{D}$inesh sat down and realised he was shaking.

'Oh no, fuck, fuck, fuck.' She was getting a lawyer. He didn't want to lose his no claims bonus. He took a gulp of water and tried to take a deep breath. His heart was racing. Who *was* that woman who was with her? She was fierce.

He picked up the phone.

'Gloria, could you come in here please? Right at once.'

'Err yes, but I'm with someone at the moment.'

'Right now!'

'In a moment, Mr Ashren. I'm with your last patient. She's requesting copies of her notes.'

'Tell her to take a seat downstairs and get in here now!'

'Okay.'

Gloria put the phone down and looked up at the two women with a forced smile.

'Would you like to take a seat downstairs and I'll be back in a moment.'

'No, thank you, we'll wait right here,' said the tall mousy haired woman.

'Umm... well, it would be more comfortable downstairs.'

'As well that maybe, but we would prefer to wait here,' said Sarah.

There was a moment's awkward silence.

'I can't leave my office unattended. If you would like to step outside into the hall while I go and speak to the consultant…'

Sarah sighed in frustration. 'Fine. We'll go downstairs, but we'll be back up in five minutes if you haven't come to see us,' she said giving Gloria a steely look.

Once they had left, Gloria went into the consulting room.

Dinesh was glowering over his desk. He was dabbing at beads of perspiration appearing on his forehead.

'Those women,' he uttered. 'We need to get them out of the building as soon as possible.'

'But she wants copies of her notes.'

Dinesh put his hand up to stop Gloria speaking. 'Well, I don't care what you do but you need to stall them. I need to make sure everything is in order before I hand over anything to them.'

Gloria sighed and looked up at the ceiling then back at Dinesh.

'They're waiting downstairs and refusing to leave.'

'Oh for fuck's sake, Gloria, just do it,' said Dinesh, as he threw a pile of patient notes at her. The files fell to the floor, with a few stray pieces of paper fluttering out across the room.

Gloria bent down to pick up the pile of notes where they had settled. She arranged them into a neat pile, then stood up and placed them back on the consulting desk, handing Dinesh a set of notes she had kept tucked under her arm.

'These are your next set of patient notes,' she said coolly. 'I suggest you read them while I make you a herbal tea and use the time to calm down. I'll then call the next patient up and tell the two women to go and have a cup of coffee or some lunch while I scan all the notes. This will give you time to see your next two patients. You can then go through the notes during your lunch break.'

'Yes, that's a good idea. Right, let's do that.'

Gloria left the room without Dinesh noticing that she had taken Sarah's notes with her. He had placed them to one side on his desk ready to read later on.

———

'Gloria?'

'Yes, Mr Ashren,' Gloria said, as she answered the phone a few seconds later.

'Chamomile tea. I don't want any of that peppermint shit you keep feeding me. And remember to get my suit from the dry cleaners. Ohh, and I've changed my mind about lunch. I'll have a Pret crab sandwich after all.'

'Yes, Mr Ashren.'

———

Gloria phoned downstairs to reception.

'Listen Jules, could you do the lunch run and pick up some dry cleaning for Mr Ashren? Please? It's a big ask I know, but I have a crisis here.'

'Okay,' said Jules, 'but you owe me.'

'Thanks.'

Gloria made Dinesh his chamomile tea. When she appeared in the doorway of the consulting room he seemed to have calmed down a bit. He was busy reading the next patient's set of notes.

'Mr Ashren, shall I send Mrs Barratt up now?'

'Yes, that's fine,' he said, as he waved her away without even an upwards glance.

Once the next patient was in the consulting room, Gloria busied herself with photocopying Sarah's notes. Jules informed Sarah that Gloria was scanning her notes.

By the time Gloria had the second patient in the consulting room with Dinesh, she had all the notes scanned. She went downstairs and asked Sarah and Liz to follow her up to her room. She closed the door behind them and handed Sarah the files.

'Everything should be here. He doesn't know I've scanned them yet, so I'd appreciate it if you didn't say anything.'

'Thank you,' said Sarah.

'Just out of interest,' said Liz. 'You seem a nice enough person, so why do you work for such a rude arrogant man?'

'I'm not for much longer. I'm looking for another job.'

'Good for you,' said Liz. 'I don't suppose we could ask you for another favour, then?'

———

Dinesh called Gloria in.

'Have you seen Mrs Postlewaite's notes?' he demanded.

'Yes, I took them out along with the afternoon's clinic notes. When you threw them at me some of the loose paperwork fell out.'

'Why was there loose paperwork?' he bellowed. He started to point a finger at her accusingly. 'That is your job. To ensure the notes are all contained securely in one file, Gloria.'

'Apologies, Mr Ashren, but they're all secure now,' she said, as she handed the file to him. 'Let me know when you need everything copied, I'll need to allocate extra time to do this.' As she turned and left the room she couldn't help but smile. It would be nice to get a few hours off.

Dinesh stared after Gloria as she disappeared into the corridor. God she was infuriating, he thought. I really am going to have to replace her.

———

Gloria had been only too eager to hand over the details of Mr Ashren's schedule to Liz. It was time someone gave this guy a taste of his own medicine.

'Right guys,' said Liz to Jordan, Jusu and Dwayne. 'He'll be running in Regent's Park tomorrow night. You just need to frighten him. You know… unsettle him a bit. Olivia, every Friday night he goes to The Marylebone Hotel for a drink at the bar with his friends. Do you think you can pull this one off?'

Olivia fluttered her eyes, pursed her lips and pushed back her shoulders to enhance her pert bust. 'It'll be hard for any man to resist these babies,' she said.

'Yeah, I think this'll be easy enough. We'll need to know exactly what time to be there and the route he takes,' said Dwayne.

'Great,' said Liz as she spread out a map of Regent's Park on the dining room table. She had a route outlined in yellow highlighter pen. 'Gather round, guys. This is the plan…'

58

*D*inesh got into his running gear and trainers and put his headphones on. Music always relaxed him, and he had a lot on his mind with that recent incident with the Postlewaite woman and her friend. Perhaps he shouldn't have had those two glasses of scotch earlier but the whole incident was playing on his mind. He crossed the busy Marylebone Road and jogged through Chester Gate into Regent's Park, making a right turn along the gravel path and then a left onto Avenue Gardens. He ran steadily along the central gravel path. There was a small strip of grass in front of a low hedgerow to his left and a single tree in front of the hedgerow every few yards. In his peripheral vision, he thought he saw someone following him quite closely. He stopped and turned... no one there. Maybe he was imagining it.

Several minutes later he had the same sensation again. This time when he stopped and turned, a figure ran out of view behind one of the single trees in front of the low hedgerow to his left. When it happened the third time, he went over to the hedgerow to investigate and peered around the tree. A young black man wearing a hoodie was standing there smoking a joint. He turned and stared back at Dinesh.

'Yo, bro, what's up, man?' said the guy.

'Uhh, nothing. I just thought someone was following me. Apologies. My mistake.'

'Might not be a mistake, bro.'

'Excuse me?'

'I'm just saying. You know?' replied the man.

'You know what?'

'All the "you being followed", stuff, man,' said the man as he made inverted commas in the air. 'It might be for real. So, this is your ends, bro? Very nice.' The man looked around nodding his head approvingly. 'Must be nice living round here.'

The man smiled pointing to his joint and offered it to Dinesh. 'You want some, bro?' He reached into his pocket and pulled out a bag of weed, lifting the bag up, offering it to Dinesh.

'No. Thank you,' said Dinesh as he shook his head and went to run off. As he turned he realised there was another young man with shoulder length dreadlocks blocking his path. He did not have time to stop himself bumping into him.

'Yo man, you leaving? You only just got here,' said the second man, grinning at him. The late afternoon sun glinted off a gold tooth in the top right-hand corner of his smile.

Dinesh took a nervous step back. 'Ummm, yes I have to be off now. I have to be somewhere.'

'Well, that's a shame,' said the first man. 'We haven't really got to know you yet.'

'Yeah, man,' said a third young man who suddenly appeared from the bushes. Dinesh saw a flicker of metal as the third man flicked open a pocket knife. Dinesh took a sharp gulp of air and then breathed out in relief as he saw an apple come out of the man's other pocket and he proceeded to peel it with the pocket knife.

'Whoah, is that a Rolex?' said the second man. 'I always

317

wanted one of those, man. They're way cool. Can I have a look?'

Dinesh had a feeling this was not going to go well unless he was quick on his feet. He took the watch off and said, 'Here, you can take a look at it if you want.' He handed it over. The three men huddled round admiring the watch together. Dinesh seeing the men visibly distracted saw his chance. He was off like a robber's dog.

Jordan looked up. 'Hey, man, where did he go? The dude's left without his watch.'

Dwayne began to run after him.

'Yo, bro, come back.'

Dinesh turned to check he was not being pursued. He could see the young man gaining on him, shouting and waving. Was that his watch he was waving at him? Dinesh did not wait to find out. He was a strong runner; he knew if he ran as fast as he could he might possibly outrun him. So Dinesh ran like his life depended on it, and after several minutes he turned to realise he had managed to lose the man. He didn't stop running until he reached Marylebone police station.

———

Dwayne had given chase but Mr Ashren had been too fast. He was obviously quite fit. Dwayne sighed, looking at the watch. He put it in his pocket and turned back to rejoin Jordan and Jusu.

'Well, we certainly gave him a fright,' said Dwayne. 'Looks like we got a watch out of it though.'

'How much do you think it's worth?' asked Jordan.

'Not sure,' said Jusu, 'but we'll have to figure out a way of getting it back to him.'

'You're going to give it back?' asked Jordan.

'We were only meant to be scaring him, not actually mugging him, bro.'

Jordan shrugged. 'I'm just saying, man. It is a pretty cool watch an all.'

———

'So, are you saying your watch was stolen?' asked the police clerk.

'Yes.'

The clerk began to read back the statement Dinesh had provided. 'You were running in Regent's Park and you thought you were being followed. So you checked behind a bush and found a young black man smoking weed.'

'That's correct. I thought I saw him following me.'

'Then this man and his friends noticed your watch and asked to look at it. You then voluntarily gave them the watch and ran away.'

'Well, yes, but I thought they were going to mug me. I mean they had a knife.'

'A knife?' questioned the clerk. 'You didn't mention that. Did they threaten you with the knife?'

'Kind of.'

'What do you mean *kind of*?'

'One of them pulled a knife and started to peel an apple, but I knew they were trying to intimidate me.'

'They were trying to intimidate you by peeling an apple with a knife?' said the clerk incredulously. 'How big was the knife?'

'Umm, like a pocket knife.' Dinesh started to become agitated. 'Look, it doesn't matter what *size* the knife was. They were trying to mug me.'

'They clearly didn't need to. You were quite freely giving your items away.'

'Well, I ran and then one of them came after me,' Dinesh replied.

'Came after you?'

'Yes, he was chasing me, shouting at me, and I thought he was wielding the knife.'

'Was he?'

'I'm not sure,' mumbled Dinesh. 'It might have been my watch.'

'Perhaps he was trying to give you your watch back?' suggested the clerk as he put his pen down and leant over the desk narrowing his eyes at Dinesh. 'Can I ask, have you been drinking, sir?'

'Why do you ask?'

'I can smell alcohol on your breath,' said the clerk. 'I don't think this really warrants any extra paperwork, do you?'

'No I guess not, officer. I apologise for wasting your time.'

Dinesh stormed out of the station.

Damn it, he fumed. That was my favourite watch!

59

*O*livia adjusted her lipstick, then puckered her lips at the mirror. She adjusted her hair, admiring her fresh set of clip-in hair extensions, as she flicked them over her left shoulder.

'Let's see you try and resist this baby,' she said to herself, as she admired the reflection staring back at her. She was in a low-cut chiffon apple green dress which had a crossed over bodice and a floaty empire line ruched belt tie which Olivia had tied at the back. The shade of apple green highlighted her perfect tan. She was wearing a simple silver chain with a single tear drop diamond and a pair of matching diamond stud earrings. The outfit was completed with a pair of silver strappy shoes. She smiled admiringly at her reflection, then turned and waltzed out the door into the foyer, making her way to the bar. Her phone lit up. One message. She tapped the screen several times. An image of the bar lit up on her phone. In the image a group of men in suits were seated in a circle of comfortable looking chairs by the window of the hotel foyer.

Which one, babes? she texted back.

The young good looking one with the black wavy hair, came back the message. *He's wearing a red patterned tie.*

Right. On it.

She sat down at the bar and ordered a cocktail. After about ten minutes, Olivia and Ricardo the barman were best of friends.

'So, Ricardo, what are you doing in a place like this? I mean, seriously, babes, you seem super intelligent and you're working behind a bar.'

'Actually, I'm funding my way through law school.'

'Oooh, I do like a nice lawyer,' gushed Olivia, as she fluttered her eyelids and pushed her cleavage up just a little bit higher. 'Do you have to wear them white wigs in the court room?'

'Yes. But I'm not quite there yet.'

'Well look me up when you do, babes.'

'I don't think your friend's showing up,' said Ricardo.

Olivia peered around the bar with a look of mock disappointment and sighed. 'No, I think you're right. What a waste of an evening.'

Dinesh appeared at the bar. 'Excuse me,' he said to Ricardo in an officious tone, as he pointed back towards his group of friends gathered around the table by the window, 'we have been trying to get your attention over there. What does it take to get some service around here? We would like to order some more drinks.'

Olivia leant over and placed her hand on Dinesh's arm. 'I'm so sorry, darlin'. It's my fault. I've been distracting him. You see, I was waiting for my friend and she hasn't showed, so I've been chewing his poor little ear off. Haven't I, Ricardo?'

Ricardo smiled back at Olivia then glanced over at Dinesh. 'I'm sorry, sir,' he said. 'What can I get you?'

'Listen,' said Olivia, stopping Dinesh from placing his drinks order. 'How about I get this round? I'm guessing you're a consultant of some sort?'

'Why would you think that?' said Dinesh with an indignant air.

'Well, you dress very smartly, and you certainly know how to look after yourself,' purred Olivia. 'I can see those gorgeous manicured nails.' She leant over and picked up one of Dinesh's hands and stroked his fingers. 'There's nothing more attractive than a man who looks after himself.'

Dinesh had had a hard day. The last straw was this incompetent barman ignoring him... but this woman, this woman... now she was quite interesting. Just what he needed to take his mind off recent events.

———

'Now, come on. Here we go. Oops, not far now. Is this it?'

'Yes,' slurred Dinesh. He could barely stand. Olivia was holding him by the waist and his arms were draped around her shoulders.

'Let's get you upstairs and lie you down. Have you got your keys, darlin'?'

Dinesh smiled a cheesy grin and hiccupped. He pulled out the keys from his pocket, dangling them from his fingers suggestively.

She smiled back, winking at Dinesh as she took the keys from him. She opened the front door and he began to fumble with the alarm, managing to turn it off.

Olivia got him up the flight of stairs and into his consulting room.

As Dinesh stumbled across the threshold, she lost her hold of him.

'Did I tell you I was mugged? At knifepoint,' he slurred, as he stumbled about the room waving his arms drunkenly in the air.

Olivia followed him around the room making sure he didn't fall. 'No, that's terrible.'

'Yes. I was running in the park and they jumped me from the bushes. I run, you know.' Dinesh patted his chest proudly. 'That is why I'm so fit looking. They took my watch. A bloody Rolex. I reported it to the police in Marylebone and you know what they did?' Dinesh's voice began to shriek in annoyance.

'No. What did they do?'

'They bloody well thought I was drunk! Me. Drunk. Can you imagine it?' Dinesh said with outrage. He was pointing to himself repeatedly, as he tried to hold himself upright. He waved a drunken hand in the air. 'They did a report and then did nothing. The idiots. They said the men were probably chasing me trying to give me my watch back. Unbelievable, unbeliebable,' he slurred as he muttered to himself, falling back onto the examination couch and burping. 'Oops, pardon.'

Olivia adopted an expression of mock horror. 'No way, that's dreadful. Now let's get you up here.' She helped Dinesh to lie down on the examination couch. 'Here's a blanket. Now let's get those trousers off of you,' she said, as she placed her phone on the side table.

———

Gloria came into the office and started making coffee. Gathering up some notes for the morning's clinic, she opened the consulting room door, humming as she went, and walked over to place the pile of notes for the day's clinic on Dinesh's desk. She turned to leave the room and gasped at the sight awaiting her. She couldn't believe her eyes. Dinesh was lying on the examination couch completely naked from the waist down with large red lipstick smudges all over the lower half of his body.

Gloria screamed and ran from the room.

Dinesh groaned, rolled to his side and held his head. 'What the hell's going on?' he said as he fell off the side of the couch into a heap on the floor.

———

Olivia had the images on her phone.

'Ugghh,' screamed Sarah. 'No, I can't look. I'm going to be sick.'

'Gosh, it's not that big is it?' said Vicky.

'No,' replied Olivia. 'It wasn't much fun, I can tell you. I couldn't do much with it.'

'Olivia, you're dreadful,' squealed Sarah.

The boys were killing themselves laughing. 'He's such a wanker, man,' said Dwayne as he sat admiring his newly acquired Rolex watch.

'So, babes, what do we do next?' asked Olivia, turning to Liz.

———

Dinesh was not sure what had happened but he needed to act fast. He had a clinic starting in fifteen minutes and he could barely put one foot in front of the other. He remembered going out last night… the bar… a woman…

He dialled Joshua's number.

'Hey.'

'Hey you,' Joshua said. 'I guess you're updating us on last night's activities? I know you didn't make it home, you dog. Mona phoned asking where you were.'

'She did? What did you say?'

'I said you'd been stressed lately with work and had had a bit much to drink. I told her I'd put you up in my flat above my rooms.'

Relief washed through his alcohol filled body. 'Oh great. Thanks for that.'

Dinesh's phone lit up with an image of the woman from last night.

Hey, big boy, it said. *Thanks for last night. You were amazing.*

Dinesh smiled. Maybe things were looking up.

60

*L*iz prepared the speech. Vicky and Sarah pored over it. Vicky chuckled to herself.

'Very good,' she said.

———

Olivia met Dinesh at Regent's Park.

'Hello there,' she said looking him up and down in an approving manner. He was dressed in a chocolate brown long sleeved turtle neck jersey which was close fitting enough to show off his muscular chest. He was wearing black chinos and chocolate brown suede loafers.

Dinesh smiled like a Cheshire Cat. What could he say? The women loved him.

He looked Olivia's perfectly gym toned and fake tanned body up and down appraisingly. Not bad, not bad at all, he thought. She was dressed in a pink halter neck top and a pair of cut off denim shorts which revealed an ample portion of her perfectly toned buttocks at the base of the shorts. She was also wearing flip flops, a big floppy sun hat and a pair of large sun glasses.

'What is that?' he asked pointing at the pram she was pushing.

'Oh, that's me dogs. I'm taking them for a walk.'

Dinesh peered into the tiny stroller and saw two sets of dark beady eyes amidst a mass of fur looking back at him.

'Mocha can't walk too far because of her little legs so I have to push her. Don't I, love?'

Olivia patted one of the dogs on its head.

'Yap,' it replied.

'Yap yap,' said the other dog.

Dinesh's eyes narrowed. 'That one's got pink ears.' he exclaimed pointing to the light coloured mass of fur.

'That's Snowy. He's me boy. We're off to the pond to see the ducks. They love the ducks don't you my babies?' Olivia cooed, as she leaned into the pram blowing kisses at the dogs.

'Yap!' said Mocha.

'Yap yap yap,' said Snowy impatiently.

He stared at her in disbelief. Olivia turned round to face him, pushing her sunglasses down her nose, enabling her to peer at him over the top of them.

'So anyway, the reason I wanted to see you is this…'

Moments later, once Olivia had delivered the bombshell, Dinesh stared at the images he held in his hands in disbelief. He looked up at her.

'You're blackmailing me.'

'Yap yap yap,' said Snowy again, as he peered over the edge of the pram, becoming more impatient.

'If you want to call it that, then yeah, I'm blackmailing you,' replied Olivia.

'How much do you want?'

'Oh, I don't want money. I want you to change your presentation next week at the gynae conference.'

'Yap yap yap yap!' said Mocha and Snowy in unison. How long was this going to take? The ducks were waiting.

'I'm not going to do it... and you can you tell your silly little dogs to shut up,' he said as he shook his finger towards the direction of the pram. Snowy and Mocha both had their heads peering over the edge of the pram. They both let out a low growl. They were not sure what was happening, but they didn't like the tone this man was taking with their mum.

Dinesh's head was spinning. Things were going from bad to worse. He had been set up. How could he have been so stupid? He closed his eyes hoping it would all go away. This woman was infuriating, and her dogs were really starting to get on his wick. He was feeling rather queasy.

Olivia stood there, with her arms crossed, waiting.

'The way I see it you don't have any choice,' said Olivia. 'And no, I won't tell my babies to shut up.'

'This,' he said shaking the images at Olivia, 'would be professional suicide.'

He knew Mona would not tolerate another infidelity. She'd warned him last time that she would take him to the cleaners if he did it again.

'Look, you either read the statement out at the conference or we publish the images. I have a mate at *The Sun* ready to run the story either way.'

'I'm not going to do it,' he said matter-of-factly.

Olivia shrugged and turned towards the pram making to leave.

'Suit yourself, babes. I'll be outside the ExCeL centre next week at nine in the morning with the images to give you. If you don't make the speech then the images will be sent straight to my mate at *The Sun*. We have a copy ready to give to your wife as well.'

'HOW do you KNOW how to contact MY wife?'

———

328

Dinesh was shaking as Olivia strolled off with her pram. He followed her for about fifteen minutes as he wasn't sure what else to do. He needed time to think.

She really was taking the dogs to see the ducks! He watched her pushing the ridiculous little pram with the damned silly dogs in it, facing forward so they could see through the black mesh at the front. This woman was pushing the pram up to the duck pond and actually talking and cooing at the dogs, showing them the ducks, as if they were children. How had he fallen for this?

He stuffed the statement into his briefcase and made his way back through Regent's Park. It had been a set up. It was something to do with that Postlewaite woman. He was sure of it. Bloody Gloria! That must be how they found out he would be at the bar that evening. He sat down at an empty park bench in the rose garden to gather his thoughts and read the statement in closer detail. They were asking him to call for an immediate national reporting system for all ovarian cancer patients. They wanted all stage three ovarian cancers that had been presenting for more than six to nine months prior to diagnosis to be treated as a serious incident and stage fours to be reported to the Care Quality Commission. This would end his career. He would be a laughing stock. They would think he had gone soft in the head. No colleague of his would support this. It would be admitting that they were a part of, and supported, a system which failed thousands of women every year. The statistics were clear in the statement. Either way he was ruined. Or perhaps not. Maybe his colleagues would back him and say it was entrapment if the pictures were released. He might not be able to practise for a while but surely they would let him back in. Once everything settled down. His wife would divorce him and take him to the cleaners. That was a given. He might just have to cut his losses. Dinesh leant over into the edge of a nearby flower bed and promptly threw up.

'Sophia?'

'Yes, Mr Ashren.'

'Could you cancel my clinics for the next week?'

'The next week?' questioned the temp.

'Yes. I'm afraid I've just had some rather bad news and I'm going to need to take a few days off.'

61

*D*inesh was at the ExCeL centre waiting for Olivia. It was a slightly cool morning, with a leaden sky, strong gusty winds and the forecast predicted some light showers. He stood under the shelter at the entrance to the pedestrianised area, searching for her amongst the crowd that was slowly arriving.

'You alright?' Olivia asked, as she approached.

Dinesh looked her up and down. She was wearing tight denim jeans with a white T-shirt, a black leather jacket, a pink and white scarf round her neck with a pair of navy blue rope wedge shoes. She might be a right bitch but she was definitely an attractive one.

'Here,' he said as he passed an envelope to her.

She opened it up and saw a handwritten cheque for £120,000.

'What's this?' she asked as she looked up at him, waving the cheque in front of her.

'Money to shut her up,' he replied, grinding the words through his teeth.

Olivia looked at him blankly. 'Money for who?'

Dinesh's voice took on an edge of irritation. 'For that bloody Postlewaite woman. I know it's her behind this. She thinks I'm responsible for her illness. I didn't give her the bloody cancer. She did that herself.'

'Well fuck me, babes, but I think you've got an overinflated opinion of yourself. Aren't you the fucker who she saw for over six months and told her she had urinary tract infections? You're meant to be a gynae specialist. People trust you. God knows why, though, you're going round killing the poor girls. Do you have no conscience whatsoever? A blood test. You didn't even take a bloody blood test. You told her GP there was nothing wrong, so she took your advice, seeing as you were the expert. This money is not going to make it right,' Olivia said as she shook the cheque at him. 'You need to get in there,' she pointed towards the entrance, 'and make the statement. And you can shove this up your arse,' she said as she pushed the cheque down the front of Dinesh's trousers.

His instinctive reaction was to pull away. He grabbed her hand and pulled the cheque out and glanced around quickly to make sure no one he knew was around.

'Jesus Christ, you silly bitch. What do you think you're playing at?' he said through gritted teeth. 'What do you want from me?'

'Considering Sarah's lost her ovaries, and more, I thought I could ask for your balls on a plate.' She held out her hands to resemble a plate. 'No?'

Dinesh stared at her, lost for words.

Olivia crossed her arms and tapped her feet impatiently. She then flicked her chin up and beckoned to her right.

It was then that he saw Sarah purposefully walking towards him with a steely glare of determination.

She looked ready for action dressed in navy blue Capri trousers, a navy blue and white striped jersey knit boat neck top with blue and white sneakers.

She came and stood next to Olivia.

'He won't play ball.'

'Huh,' replied Sarah, looking Dinesh up and down

distastefully. 'Right, you spineless arrogant little twat,' she said as she leaned towards Dinesh, 'we haven't got all day. So listen up. If you aren't going to do as we ask then my friends here,' Sarah gave a wave of her hands to the left and the right, 'will have to rough you up.' Dinesh's eyes followed the direction Sarah had indicated, first to the left. He recognised one of the young black men he had seen in Regent's Park. His mind was trying to piece it together, but things happened so fast. His instinct was to run. He wanted to run back to the safety of the ExCeL centre but the young man was in front of him. He turned to his right, behind him, to see if he could get round him. He turned further behind him to find another of the young black men sitting on a low wall. The second man started to get up while locking eyes with Dinesh. Dinesh glanced backwards to find that other mousy haired woman, who had accompanied Sarah to his consulting room, walking down the steps towards them. She appeared to be talking to someone on her mobile phone while fixing her gaze upon him.

'Oh shit, shit, fuck,' he muttered under his breath, as he ran his hand through his hair. Dinesh pushed Olivia forward. She stumbled, trying to stop herself from falling but had overbalanced in her wedge shoes and hit the concrete, letting out a squeal as she fell.

Sarah grabbed hold of Dinesh by the shoulders and brought her right knee up impacting with his groin. He doubled forward grabbing his crotch then grabbed hold of Sarah's arm and tried to push her backward, but she was too quick and darted out of his way.

'Oi!' shouted a stocky looking man with a closely shaven head and beard. The man quickly moved over, lunging at him. Dinesh tried to move away but as he was still recovering from the blow to his groin he was too slow. The man grabbed Dinesh's suit jacket sleeve. There was the sound of ripping fabric as he struggled to get away.

'What the fuck do you think you're playin' at?' he heard

the man say, as he broke free from his grasp.

Dinesh knew he did not have time to wait around. He decided to make a run for it while he still had the chance. The stocky man was in close pursuit. He quickly glanced down at his damaged suit sleeve as he ran towards the Emirates cable car office straight ahead of him.

He turned to look behind him again to find the stocky man had been joined by the two young men.

Dinesh ran for his life. He glanced across the road and saw a tall gangly shifty looking young man suddenly turn and run towards him. Dinesh was now not sure where he was actually heading. He just knew he had to get away, so he continued running down the road. The cable cars were to his left in front of him. Suddenly in his line of vision he saw the young man who had taken his watch in Regent's Park. He must have been waiting ahead knowing Dinesh would run this way. There was no time to think. All he knew was he needed to cross the road or risk getting cornered by the cordoned off area serving the Emirates cable car. He turned to his right to attempt to run across the road.

He was completely unaware that a bald-headed woman was running along in the distance behind him, chasing her wig, which had blown off her head. He didn't notice several people running along trying to assist her in chasing it. He didn't see the stocky man stop to assist the bald woman or hear him berating her. 'For fuck's sake, babe. You're having a laugh. What a time to lose your fuckin' barnet.'

As he approached the kerb he saw a black cab moving in his direction. Maybe there is a God, he thought. He put out his arm to hail the cab. It didn't appear to see him. He took a step out into the road frantically waving his arm at the cab and tripped. He fell forward. He was still falling when he heard the screech of the brakes. Then everything went black.

———

'Did you get him?' Liz was panting as she came to a stop in front of Dwayne.

'Not quite.'

'What do you mean?'

'We stopped him if that's what you mean.'

'So, where is he? Is he going to do the statement or not?'

'No.'

'No? If the answer's no, then how have you stopped him?'

Jordan stepped forward and pointed at the road ahead. There was a black cab in the middle of the road. Liz could see Jusu standing by the cab with several people milling around.

'We didn't stop him. A black cab did.'

At that point Olivia appeared hobbling along in her wedge shoes. She threw her arms up in the air.

'What's going on, babes? Why's Vicky crying? And what's happened to her wig?'

———

'Officer, it was so strange. I saw this bloke… right… and I recognised him from the other week. Me and my mates we were in Regent's Park… right… and he found us smoking weed. We thought he wanted some, but then realised he'd been drinking, so we was just chatting, you know. Then he gave us his watch to look at. This one here.'

Dwayne dangled a Rolex watch in front of the officer.

'Then he just ran off like he was crazy or summ'ink, you know. So I's ran after him trying to give him his watch back, but he was running like he was crazy, man. Then today I was here with my mates. We recognised him and went to shout after him, to tell him about his watch, and he just started running away like he was crazy. He was mad, officer.'

'Yes,' said the clerk at the Marylebone police station. 'We did have a Mr Ashren come in reporting he had been mugged last week. A Rolex watch. Yes. He'd been drinking and we think the young man was trying to give the man the watch back. Have you tested his blood alcohol level? It sounds like the poor bloke's having a hard time. Counselling might help. Yes, we have the report here. A time waster I am afraid.'

'He'll need more than counselling,' said the PC. 'He's just thrown himself under a black cab.'

'Oh dear,' said the police clerk.

———

Olivia couldn't stop laughing.

'It's not funny, Olivia,' said Liz. 'We didn't get our statement out, and now he's probably brain damaged, so he's not going to be much help.'

'But, babes, they think he was losing his mind. I mean the watch scenario, you have to agree, is hilarious.'

'Hilarious for you maybe. I have to buy a new wig,' moaned Vicky. 'This one's ruined.'

'Alright, alright, luv. Just keep your hair on,' said Kurt as he winked at Vicky. She gave him a playful punch on his arm.

'It just blew off my head while I was talking on the phone. I must have moved the edge of the wig when I was scratching my head. It is so damned itchy. Then it just blew off into the road so fast I couldn't catch it.'

'I don't know how you managed that,' said Sarah. 'Of all the things to happen at that precise point in time. You completely distracted the cab driver.'

62

'Mrs Ashren?'
    'Yes?'
'I am afraid we have some bad news…'

Mona arrived in the intensive care unit to find her husband ventilated.

It had taken an hour just to get herself ready. Any opportunity to show off her wardrobe. Mona had styled her long dark wavy hair and applied her make-up. She was wearing a bronze coloured high neck sleeveless top with a pair of skin tight tan and black animal print trousers. She wanted to show off her perfectly toned body. She loved to see men's reactions as she swept into a room. Mona had completed the look with large oversized bronze filigree earrings, a chunky ochre coloured choker and bracelet and bronze coloured embroidered satin kitten heel sling back shoes.

She listened to the intensivist describing Dinesh's injuries.

'He appears to have thrown himself under a cab. Has he been under a lot of stress lately?'

'Well, yes as a matter of fact he has,' she replied. 'One of his colleagues phoned me only last week to say he had been stressed of late. I didn't realise it was this serious.' She sobbed.

'He's in an induced coma at the moment to keep the intracranial pressure down. We won't know the damage for some time.'

The intensivist left. The nurse began adjusting settings on several machines connected to Dinesh. Once she had finished she turned to Mona and handed her a briefcase and a carrier bag with his clothes in. 'These are his belongings.'

Mona opened the briefcase. Just notes from the conference. Maybe that was it. He'd been working so hard on his conference presentation. She phoned the office and spoke to a strange sounding woman.

'Gloria?'

'No, I'm Sophia, the temp.'

'Where's Gloria?'

'She left.'

'Left?'

'Yes, last week.'

'Umm, this is Mrs Ashren.'

'Hello.'

'I'm afraid I have some rather bad news. Mr Ashren has been involved in an accident and won't be in for some time.'

'Oh dear, I hope he's going to be okay.'

'You'll have to cancel his clinics.'

'I've already cancelled the next week's clinics as he instructed,' said Sophia.

'What?' said Mona.

———

Mona unlocked the front door and walked into the lounge, placed the briefcase on the coffee table and sat down. She sat for several moments staring at it, drumming her perfectly manicured nails on the coffee table. Dinesh had been up to something.

She opened the briefcase and studied the contents: Dinesh's wallet, iPad, keys and a set of presentation notes on A4 paper with a USB port. She picked up the presentation he had been due to give and glanced at the front page. She looked back at the briefcase to see a plain brown envelope, which had been lying hidden under the presentation. Inside the envelope she found a cheque, in Dinesh's handwriting, for the amount of £120,000. It was not made out to anyone.

Why would he be writing a cheque for that amount? Who was it for? Was he being blackmailed? A cloud of anger passed across her face. That bloody man. He was always up to something. It was probably some woman he'd got pregnant. Mona was in a rage. Yet again he'd lied to her. He had promised it wouldn't happen again.

'The lying bastard!' she yelled as she tore the cheque and presentation up and threw them in the bin. In her rage she didn't see the statement which had been attached to the back of the presentation. She went into the kitchen and grabbed a bottle of chilled white wine and a wine glass. She went back into the lounge and switched on some music, then collapsed back onto the sofa and poured herself a large glass of wine.

'Fuck you, Dinesh,' she muttered to herself.

―――

Mona was at the gym at her bi weekly yoga session.

'These poses are so difficult,' said the long dark-haired woman next to her.

'Yes, they are,' replied Mona.

'I'd better not bend too far forward, I've only just had me Botox injected in this morning,' the woman exclaimed.

'Oh, where do you go to get yours done?' enquired Mona.

'I own a couple of hairdressing salons, so I have someone come in once a week to inject my clients. They're very good. Would you like a card? I'll give you one after the class.'

'Yes please,' said Mona.

Olivia and Mona chatted after class. This chat somehow extended to coffee. Mona welcomed any form of distraction at the moment and Olivia seemed so friendly and approachable. Mona felt she needed to offload to someone about the terrible time she had had recently. Olivia seemed the perfect person. I mean they say people tell their hairdressers everything.

'My goodness! A coma you say. That's awful. Do you know if he'll make a full recovery?'

'If he wakes up, he'll need intensive therapy,' sighed Mona.

'Oh dear,' said Olivia. 'Do you think he'll remember anything?'

'The doctors aren't sure. They doubt it. He might remain in a vegetative state.'

'Well, if you need anything, anything at all, let me know,' said Olivia.

What a kind person. This must be karma. This is just the sort of person I need coming into my life right now. Mona felt she could do with the support. Her family said Dinesh could rot in hospital. They couldn't believe she put up with him but she knew what side her bread was buttered and she wasn't exactly the innocent party herself any more.

'Actually there is,' said Mona, tapping her fingers on the table and frowning in concentration. 'I'm not sure if I'm overreacting, but I think my husband was involved in something,' she said, as she leant across the table towards Olivia.

Olivia's eyes widened. 'Really? What kind of something?' she whispered.

'I think he had another woman on the side. I found a cheque for £120,000 in his briefcase. It wasn't made out to anyone.'

'Ohh, anything else in the briefcase?'

'There was his iPad and a USB port but there was nothing of interest on them. Then there was his presentation, for his gynae conference. I tore up the cheque and the presentation and threw them in the bin. I was so angry.'

'I bet you were.' Olivia leant over and patted Mona's arm soothingly.

———

As Olivia left the café, she phoned Liz.

'It's me. I think we're in the clear. She tore up the presentation and the cheque and said there was nothing else in the briefcase of interest, so she must have torn up the statement as well. She thinks he had a woman on the side. I've told her I'll help her find the woman for her. In a few weeks I'll tell her I found the woman and show her the images. That should put the nail in his coffin.

'Listen, babes, any date on Alice's funeral yet? Did they manage to find Tarquin?'

63

---

*T*he boys managed to locate Tarquin. They had promised Alice they would find him for the funeral. It didn't take long. Where there were drugs Tarquin would pop up. Alice knew the area he moved around in. He was so high when they found him that he didn't register that his mother was dead. They managed to get him cleaned up enough for the funeral and hired him a suit which looked about two sizes too big. When he realised Alice had gone Tarquin was inconsolable for several days.

Hugh and Sophie had made no attempt to contact him or inform him of his mother's death. They planned to go ahead with the funeral without him. It was Harold and Alice's lawyer who kept Liz updated on the funeral arrangements.

Alice's funeral, late June 2019

Alice's funeral was held on a warm sunny June day in the church on the edge of her family estate. At her request, the church was filled with white roses, the rose to symbolise ovarian cancer. The coffin had lain inside the church overnight.

The tiny church was filled to capacity. All the mourners were dressed completely in black, bar Sarah who decided to add her own finishing touches to her homemade close fitting black one shouldered cocktail dress. She had finished it off with an oversized purple organza bow on the shoulder which trailed behind her.

'Loving the dress,' said Olivia. 'Alice would have loved it.'

Alice had requested that the boys and Tarquin be pall bearers. Hugh and Sophie had been mortified when she had suggested this. She knew they would ignore her wishes when the time came, as sure as she knew snow would fall on the Alps in winter, so she left specific instructions with her lawyer regarding her funeral arrangements.

At the sight of Tarquin arriving in the church, Hugh and Sophie were visibly shocked.

Tarquin walked up to them and made to shake his father's hand. Hugh just pulled his hand away out of reach and gave a firm polite nod of his head in Tarquin's direction. Sophie drew back behind her father not even making eye contact with her brother. Tarquin took his place in the pew, behind his father and sister, which Alice had specifically requested be reserved for Tarquin, Liz, Sarah, Vicky, Olivia, Jusu, Jordan and Dwayne.

Once everyone was seated the vicar rose and began the service.

'We are gathered here today to celebrate the life of Alice…' The vicar began to recount her life.

As the service came to an end the vicar asked the congregation to follow the coffin out to the churchyard to say their final goodbyes. As the first few bars of Alice's favourite song *Stand by Me* began to filter up through the air, the boys and Tarquin walked over to the coffin. Swiftly, six well-dressed men in mourning gear cut past them, surrounding the coffin, making ready to lift it into position.

Dwayne moved and stood in front of the coffin, with

343

Jordan and Jusu behind him, blocking the pallbearers' exit. Tarquin stood helplessly behind them nervously shuffling from one foot to the other. The boys looked a formidable sight in their dark mourning suits and black sunglasses. Dwayne straightened his shoulders, shaking his shoulder length dreadlocks. He stood legs apart with his hands clasped in front of him and his chin jutted out at an angle.

'Oi, vicar,' Jordan shouted as he indicated for the music to stop with a slicing motion across his neck. The vicar 'ummmed' and 'ahhhed' and eventually waved to the woman controlling the music indicating for her to stop. The congregation was suddenly enveloped in muffled silence. The atmosphere within the church hung heavy as if on a knife edge.

'So guys,' Dwayne said in a low voice as he leant in towards the pallbearers, 'it's up to you how you want to play this.' He opened his right palm out to face them sweeping his hand from his midline outwards. 'After all, this is your ends an' all, but I suggest you make room for us four. I'm not sure which of you are going to be the bigger men and step down, but I would make up your minds nice and quick. We don't want to make a scene now do we?' Dwayne smiled a wide smile, flashing his gold tooth.

The six suited men all looked nervously at each other, and then towards Hugh, who was glaring across at Dwayne from the front row. Dwayne followed the path of the pallbearers' gaze back towards Hugh, realising they took their orders from him, so he took a few steps back and walked over. He leant over and whispered in Hugh's ear, placing his hand very firmly on his shoulder.

'Listen man, I'm sorry about your loss an' all… but if those fuckers don't move I'm gonna have to mess them up. You know what I'm sayin'?'

Hugh winced as he felt the grip on his shoulder tighten.

Dwayne stared down at Hugh for a few seconds,

released his grip, and then shrugged. 'Your call, bro. I'm just acting on your wife's wishes.'

Hugh looked sideways at Dwayne distastefully as he grasped his shoulder and rubbed it. Sophie was sitting next to Hugh. Dwayne looked her up and down and smiled. She gasped in disgust and grabbed onto her father's arm for protection.

Without saying a word Hugh waved his hand resignedly to the pallbearers. Four of the men rapidly stepped aside making way for the boys. As Dwayne walked back towards the coffin he gave a challenging stare to the remaining two pallbearers.

'Now try not to fuck this up,' he uttered quietly to them. 'Follow my lead.'

Dwayne nodded towards the vicar and with a thumbs up said, 'Alright, vics, we're good to go.' The bars of *Stand by Me* began to filter once again through the air to the accompaniment of the astonished gasps of the mourners.

Dwayne, Jordan, Jusu and Tarquin took their places. They raised Alice's coffin onto their shoulders and carried her out into the churchyard for her final journey.

———

Back at the Manor House for the reception, Hugh and Sophie smiled politely and greeted the women and the boys as if the situation in the church had never occurred. Once the pleasantries were over, the group were then ignored. Tarquin followed them around like a lost puppy. None of the congregation spoke to him.

'No wonder you turned to drugs, man,' said Jusu. 'What happened to family, bruv?'

'Excuse me,' said a middle-aged bespectacled man as he approached the group. 'Might I borrow you for a moment, Tarquin?' he asked as he placed an arm around Tarquin's shoulder and guided him over to a corner. He spoke for several minutes, then he returned and asked which one was Elizabeth.

'That would be me,' said Liz.

He held out his hand to her. 'My name's James Colchester Evans. I'm Alice's lawyer.'

'Pleased to meet you,' said Liz.

'It's probably not the best time, but could I give you my card and set up a meeting?'

'A meeting?' enquired Liz. 'What for?'

'Yes, a meeting. It appears Alice has left a trust for your campaign.'

'A trust? What campaign?'

'A meeting about the trust she set up for you regarding the campaign she wants you to run. You will get all the details at the meeting,' replied James.

'But is it legal? I mean she had brain mets,' queried Sarah.

'It's all legal and above board,' replied James. 'She informed me of this sometime ago. We got a medical examination and it was deemed she had capacity at the time of setting up the trust.'

'But what about her husband… he might contest it,' suggested Liz.

'Oh no, I think you'll find he will not raise any issue with it,' smiled James with what appeared to Liz to be a very wry smile. 'She did have specific instructions on what the money was to be spent on, though,' said James. He tapped the business card and smiled at Liz. 'Please ring my office at your earliest convenience to arrange a meeting.'

———

Liz and Sarah walked down the stairs of the lawyer's' office in Lincoln Inn Fields. Liz held her face up to the warmth of the late afternoon sun and closed her eyes. This was going to make things so much easier. She opened her eyes and turned to Sarah. They grabbed each other's hand and smiled.

———

Everyone gathered around the TV screen to watch. Alice's smiling face appeared.

'My dear, dear friends… if you are watching this it means I am no longer around. Hmm… odd thought. *Que sera sera.* Please don't mourn me for too long, my dears. Meeting all of you has been the most pleasant part of my life to date. I know that sounds sad, but it's so true. I don't think I have ever laughed so much. You all gave me a purpose.

'Liz, you lit a fire in me with your cause for justice. Please keep going and do all you can to raise awareness of our plight. James will have made touch with you regarding the trust, so there's no excuse. I'm counting on you,' she said as she pointed a finger to the screen. 'Sarah and Vicky… keep Liz on track. You know how she can go off on a tangent.'

The group all laughed affectionately at Alice's remark.

'To my gorgeous boys, carry on living life to the full and remember to always show respect to the women in your life. And Olivia. My dear Olivia. Just carry on being you because there will never be another you.

'I have spent my whole life trying to please everyone else. Being the perfect mother, wife and daughter. I married out of duty, not love, and I gave away all my hopes and dreams along with it. Look where it got me,' she said as she held her hands out hopelessly. 'You have all allowed me, for a brief time, to finally be my true self, to laugh and to live. Ironic that it took my facing death to enable me to finally live. As we girls know all too well, this disease really batters the shit out of you. It's been a short ride with you all, but an amazing one. To all the wicked women in the world and the men who support them.'

Alice raised a full glass of what appeared to be scotch to the screen.

'Take care my darlings and God bless.'

Alice's image faded from the screen. The room was in silence for a few moments while the group absorbed her words and wiped tears from their eyes.

'Another life over,' said Liz, as she turned to the others, breaking the silence. 'How many more will it take before anything changes? We've done nothing to change medical practice apart from try and prevent four of the culprits from practising. There are loads more out there still misdiagnosing or delaying women's diagnosis of ovarian cancer. Where do we go from here?'

'Go from here?' questioned Sarah. 'I thought our initial intentions were to frighten these guys. We've done more than that. I think we've done enough.'

'Sarah, we've started something and we have to finish it… for Alice's sake if nothing else.'

'Listen Liz, I love you and you're a very dear friend, but we really need to stop and think about what we're doing. We can't single-handedly change years of medical practice just by killing or maiming several doctors and surgeons. We're making more of a problem as there'll be less doctors to go around by the time we've finished,' said Sarah.

'Well, conventional methods won't work,' said Liz. 'We really need our own Joan of Arc like Alice said.'

Dwayne sat up. 'Who?'

'Joan of Arc,' Liz replied. 'She was a saint in France. She led the French troops into battle against the English in the 1400s.'

'What happened to her?' asked Dwayne.

'She was burnt at the stake for being a witch. They declared her a saint posthumously,' explained Sarah.

'Post what?' said Dwayne.

'Hang on a minute,' said Liz, sitting up in her seat. 'I think Alice was right, and I think I know how we can get Joan to make an appearance.'

'What now?' asked Jordan as he wiped his eyes. He hadn't been able to stop crying after seeing Alice's video. 'I am still cryin', man!'

Sarah rolled her eyes.

Liz leant forward and began to discuss her plan. When she'd finished, Olivia breathed out a long sigh and sat back in her chair. She stretched her arms above her head and then rested them in her lap. 'If that doesn't make an impact, I don't know what will. You really think we can pull it off?'

Dwayne, Jusu and Jordan looked at each other.

Dwayne said, 'You girls are brilliant. We can help pull everyone together. Liz, you concentrate on the show.'

Vicky smiled. 'I think it's a brilliant idea. How long do you think it'll take to organise?'

Liz frowned and mouthed silently as she appeared to be counting up with her fingers. 'A month or so I guess. Why?'

Vicky was very weak. She'd been told that she had exhausted all lines of chemo and there were no more treatment options.

'Guys, I've something to tell you and I'm afraid it's not good news.'

64

VICKY

FIRST WEEK OF AUGUST 2019

*V*icky was tired. She slept that night dreaming she was well again. She was standing on the edge of a field. It was a warm summers day and she could feel the warmth of the sun on her face. She looked across at the field ahead of her, put her face up to the sun and smiled and stretched her arms. She started walking across the field. For the first time in what seemed like ages she felt no pain and at peace with the world. Alfie and the girls were standing at the opposite edge of the field waiting for her. As she got closer she could see them smiling and waving. She ran towards them but didn't seem to quite be able to reach them.

'Mum, Mum,' sobbed Bronagh. Alfie just sat staring at his mum looking absolutely petrified. Her breathing was ragged and she was sweating profusely. Vicky hadn't eaten since yesterday and she had become unresponsive that evening.

She'd gone into the GP surgery two weeks ago and sat alongside Kurt while Preeti explained Vicky's management plan.

'As you are aware from your last oncology appointment, there are no further treatments available for you. We'll be referring you to palliative care services.'

Vicky had smiled at Preeti. She turned in her chair and grabbed Kurt by the hand.

'Take me home, hun. I need to be with my children.'

Preeti walked them to the door. She grabbed Vicky's hand as they went to leave.

'Please call me, any time night or day. I'll pop in every few days to check on you.'

'Thanks,' said Vicky as she patted Preeti's hand and let go.

Preeti placed her arm around Kurt's back. His shoulders were slumped, weighted down with sadness and hopelessness. He lowered his head in disbelief, rubbing his forehead with his hand. He took a minute before being able to compose himself and look back up at her.

'Thanks, doc. For everything. You know.'

'I know, Kurt.'

When the surgery door closed behind them Preeti went back to her chair and cried.

———

Once Vicky deteriorated Preeti had stayed until she had become more comfortable. The community hospice at home nurses had come in and settled her and replaced her syringe driver with pain relief as well as something to dry up her chest secretions.

'Just call me, Liz. I'll come straight back,' Preeti said.

'Okay,' said Liz, as she saw her to the door.

Liz had sat with Vicky before she fell into a coma and they'd relived the short time they'd shared.

Vicky looked up at Liz from the bed. 'You know, Liz. I have no regrets. None whatsoever… about anything we've done. Meeting you and the girls has made me come alive. I've lived more in the last short while than in my entire life.'

Liz could not help but smile. 'It has been an adventure hasn't it?'

'I'm going to miss my children.' Tears began to form in Vicky's eyes. 'Life can be cruel. I'll never see what they'll achieve. Never see my grandchildren.'

'I know.' Liz grabbed Vicky's hand. 'I'll keep an eye on them while I can and Preeti has ensured they'll receive the financial help they need.'

'That's a relief off my mind. Mum's not sure how we got the money but she trusts that it's in their best interests. The kids will go and live with her when I'm gone, and Kurt's happy with that as long as he sees them every week.' Vicky laughed though her tears. 'I'm the typical mother hen worrying about her babies.'

Liz had tried to hold back her emotions but couldn't control them any longer. Tears began to roll down her cheeks. Vicky patted her hand and reached up to hug her close. 'Oh, come here. Don't cry, Liz. I'm okay with it. I've come to accept it now. I can't go on like this anymore. It'll be a release for me. I just wish I could be around for your grand plan. You promise me you'll carry on with it. I'll be there in spirit looking down on you, with Alice. We'll have a drink for you when we meet. The two of us will cause havoc up in heaven.'

'I don't even want to think about it.' Liz laughed.

Liz snuggled up next to Vicky on the bed. They sat in silence, holding each other for what must have been half an hour. Vicky suddenly winced with pain and shifted her position in the bed. She coughed and grabbed her chest to brace herself. Her breathing had become increasingly laboured.

'Liz, could you… bring… Alfie… and the girls… in here. I want to… say goodbye.'

Liz's heart skipped a beat as she took in the change in Vicky's appearance, the ashen colour of her skin, the change in her breathing. She grabbed Vicky's hand. 'No, no, Please, Vicky. You're not going anywhere. Not yet.'

'I am. I want to… say goodbye to the kids… while I still

have the strength. So please… wipe those tears away… and be strong for me and the kids.'

Vicky tugged at Liz's hand and looked up at her earnestly. She fondly tucked a loose strand of Liz's hair away from her eyes. 'Please, for me?'

Liz held Vicky's hand to her cheek. She half laughed, half choked on her tears as she nodded, wiped her eyes, then leant over and kissed Vicky on the forehead. 'I love you so much, Vicks. I'm not leaving you. I'm going to be here with you until the end.'

'Thanks. I wouldn't… have expected… *cough cough*… any less from you.'

Liz went out and called the children in. She closed the door behind them leaving Vicky to say her goodbyes and went to the kitchen table and sat with Janice and Kurt. After a few minutes Kurt got up and went into sit with Vicky.

Janice and Liz sat in silence for some time, then Janice looked up.

'I think it has to be the hardest thing for a mother to lose her child. You think the one thing you can do in life is protect your own, but how can you protect anyone from this? She should be enjoying life not lying there fighting for her breath. God forgive me, but I'm glad that man's dead. It only seems fair. I remember the day she was born. Me and Arthur were so excited.'

Janice laughed fondly at the memory.

'I was in labour for hours. Vicks eventually arrived kicking and screaming. My bundle of joy I called her. It was the happiest day of my life. I brought her into this world and now I have to watch her leave.'

Tears were rolling down Janice's cheeks. Liz leaned across and grabbed Janice's hands in hers.

'You poor girls,' sobbed Janice. 'None of you ever stood a bloody chance.'

About an hour later Bronagh came out to Liz.

'Mum's sleeping,' she announced.

Liz went into check on Vicky and noticed her breathing had slowed. Vicky was strong and determined to stay for as long as she could, for the sake of her children, but she could no longer resist the tiredness that wracked her body.

'Hi Preeti, could you come over?' Liz said into the phone.

At quarter to four on a Thursday morning Vicky took her final breath. Kurt, Janice and the children were all around her bed holding each other's hands. Alfie and Briana sat either side of their mother each holding one of her hands to make a complete interconnected family circle around her.

Liz leaned over and kissed Vicky on the forehead for the last time. She bent over Kurt's sobbing form and gently touched him on the shoulder.

'She's gone. Kurt,' she whispered softly.

He just sat there shaking, in shock, tears streaming down his face, struggling to digest the realisation that the love of his life had gone forever. Alfie clung to his dad, sobbing. The girls ran to their grandmother throwing themselves at Janice, wailing inconsolably. Liz stepped back, taking in the scene of immeasurable grief and walked out into the living room leaving them to grieve in private.

Ernie was asleep on the couch and stirred when he heard the cries. He sat up and rubbed his eyes.

'Liz?' he asked expectantly.

She stood in front of him staring blankly into the distance above his head. 'She's gone, Ernie.'

Liz walked out onto the small balcony off the lounge. She took a deep breath inhaling the warm summer night air. Several moments later she took her phone out of her pocket and sent a text to the others.

A few minutes later, Preeti's car pulled up. She turned and walked back into the lounge and headed towards the door to allow Preeti to come in and certify the death.

That day was a flurry of visitors for Kurt and Janice. Liz stayed on to help make funeral arrangements with the help of Olivia, Sarah, Ernie and the boys.

The period between Vicky's passing and her funeral felt like a blur to the group of friends. They had no words of comfort for Kurt, or the children, and struggled to deal with the irreparable loss they were experiencing themselves. Sarah and Liz found it particularly hard as it only emphasised what the future held for them and their loved ones.

They all went back to their homes and families, trying to make sense of what had happened, struggling to work through their own grief at losing a dear friend.

Dwayne, Jordan and Jusu went home that evening and asked their family how their days had been.

'Hmph. What is going on with you, my boy?' asked Jordan's aunt. 'What've you been up to?'

'Nothing, Auntie.'

'Are you sure? Coming in here and saying you love your old auntie? You must have me mistaken, boy. I know when s'mething's up. What kinda trouble have you got yourself into now?'

'None, Auntie, honest. I just never tell you how much I love you, man.'

Jordan kissed his aunt and hugged her tightly. She sighed and snuggled into the hug.

'Hey, Mum,' said Dwayne as he leaned over and kissed her. He sat down in the chair next to her as she sat watching television, reached over and grabbed her hand and kissed it. She shot him a glance and frowned quizzically. She then turned back to face the screen, wobbled her head and shoulders moving her position in her chair. Dwayne looked at her and smiled. She smiled back and patted his hand. She wasn't sure what it was, but her son seemed to care just a little bit more about his poor old mother. She was old enough and wise enough to enjoy the moment and not ask too many questions.

Jusu had supper waiting for his mum, his dad and sister.

'What's this?' said his mother to Jusu as she glanced suspiciously at her husband. Her husband smiled and shook his head as he picked up a wooden spoon to taste the food, then did a thumbs up to show his approval.

'Just cooked you dinner. I like to show my family how much I appreciate them an' all.'

'Are you feeling okay, my boy?' asked his mother as she placed the back of her hand across Jusu's forehead. 'You must be coming down with something. I ain't never seen you lift a pan before.' She shook a finger knowingly at him. 'Something definitely ain't right.' She looked out of the kitchen window.

'What?' asked Jusu. 'What are you looking for, Mum?'

'The police, boy.'

'Mum… Come on, man. I ain't dun nothing wrong. I just want ta show you how much I luv you guys. That's all.'

Jusu's mother was confused.

———

The funeral was a small sedate affair held at the local crematorium. Liz, Olivia, the boys and Sarah were there. Sarah arrived in yet another homemade creation. This time it was a tightly ruched close fitting knee length dress with a boat neck and bishop sleeves. It was made of pink floral chiffon and she wore matching pink Jimmy Choos.

'Vicks designed it. She asked me to make something extra special and very pink. So this is it.'

'It's beautiful, Sarah,' said Liz wiping away her tears.

'Yeah, bloody beautiful. Just like Vicks,' replied Olivia.

The service was short and sweet. Kurt and the children all spoke. There was not a dry eye in the chapel when Alfie spoke about his mum. The children then placed red and white roses on the coffin.

As the curtains opened to draw the coffin away, Vicky's favourite song *The Rose* by Bette Midler began playing.

As the curtains began to close, the mourners led by Kurt filtered out into the car park, where the air was heavy with the scent of rain.

'She'll be up there,' Sarah indicated skywards, 'having a drink with Alice now.'

'Heaven won't know what's struck it.' Liz laughed.

A loud crack of thunder came bursting through the gathering clouds, taking the small crowd by surprise. They all stopped for a moment and looked up.

'See. They've started the party already,' said Jordan.

Preeti had organised the wake at Kurt and Vicky's house after the funeral. Towards the end as everyone began to leave, Liz pulled Kurt and Preeti aside.

'Could I have a word?' she asked.

65

LIZ

MID-AUGUST 2019

*L*iz sighed as she clutched her phone in her hand. She stared at the screen and then pressed dial.

'Hello Kurt,' she said. 'Are you ready?'

'As ready as I'll ever be, love. How's my boy?'

'He's fine. He's right here.' Liz placed her arm around Alfie. 'Alfie, your dad's on the phone.'

Alfie grabbed the phone from Liz.

'Hiya, Dad.'

'You alright, son?' Kurt asked. 'I hope you're behaving for Aunty Liz.'

'Of course, Dad.'

'Now you be a brave lad today and make your mother proud.'

'I will.'

'Alfie, Alfie,' shouted his sisters as they came into view on the screen waving at him and giggling. 'Hiya, Liz,' they shouted.

Liz peered at the phone, smiled and waved back at them. 'Are you ready, girls?'

The girls stopped smiling and stared at Liz with sombre looks on their faces. 'Yes, we are.'

Liz nodded and smiled nervously. 'Take care, girls. We

have to go now. It's nearly time. Good luck. We're thinking of you.'

Kurt appeared back in view peering at the screen. 'Right luv. Ready when you are.' He nodded his head and winked at Liz. With that Kurt rang off.

Liz squeezed Alfie's hand and turned to Olivia.

Olivia placed a hand gently on Liz's shoulder. 'You alright, babes?'

'I'm fine.'

'Of course you are, darlin'. You're going to make those fuckers stand up and listen.'

'That's the plan,' said Liz as she straightened her shoulders and looked down at her phone again. 4.57 p.m. She tapped the screen several times and flicked right until she arrived at the contact group she had been looking for. She pressed send, then turned to the small group of people behind her. 'It's time, guys,' she shouted, as she waved an arm in the air.

Olivia and Alfie came and stood either side of Liz. They both grabbed her hand and stepped out onto the road. Sarah, Jusu, Jordan and Dwayne came and stood beside them.

'Here comes our Joan of Arc,' said Olivia.

———

At exactly five p.m. ten black hearses, which had been waiting parked up in Selfridges' car park, rounded the corner of Orchard Street, turning left into Oxford Street. A lone piper in full highland dress led the way piping *Maid of Orleans* in 6/8th time. The piper was accompanied by two drummers. Behind them was a man dressed in full morning dress paging away. Liz, Sarah, Olivia, Alfie and the boys followed directly behind, with George and Gareth behind them. They formed a line across the road, with their arms linked, walking slowly in time to the beat of the drums.

A black hearse followed them containing a casket of carved mahogany with elaborate gold handles. The casket was covered head to toe in white roses. The remaining nine hearses followed behind, each containing a casket identical to the first hearse. The second hearse had thousands of white roses inside, which young women began to hand out to the crowds on the street, from the open windows of the hearse.

Placards with images of women who had recently died from ovarian cancer were held by their loved ones as they walked alongside the procession. Traffic immediately came to a standstill in the warm late afternoon heat. Horns could be heard blaring in the distance, disgruntled at the delay. The cars within view of the procession just stopped; their passengers not quite sure what was going on. The procession drew attention from the crowds moving up and down Oxford Street busy with their late afternoon shopping. They weren't sure if it was a protest or an actual funeral procession. Slowly, crowds started filling out into the street with phones aloft sensing this was something that needed to be recorded. Every few yards, among the crowds of shoppers, people began to leave the pavement to join the procession... members of a flash mob strategically placed along the route from Oxford Street to Westminster. At the end of every block another drummer and piper would start up as if calling a welcoming cry to the approaching procession. When it came their turn they would fall in behind the main piper like soldiers on parade.

Images began to be taken by the crowds stopping to watch. It did not take long for the images to be quickly relayed via social media.

A similar situation was occurring at the exact same time in several main cities across the UK. There was also a procession on the M25 and the M1 for maximum impact, causing traffic chaos.

'I think Alice and Vicky will be up there laughing with us,' said Olivia.

'Oh, I have no doubt about that,' said Liz.

The procession wound its way along Oxford Street towards Oxford Circus and then turned right onto Regent Street.

It hadn't taken long for traffic control centres across the UK to start receiving reports of several large funeral processions. Police had been alerted to investigate. Sergeant Connor had been dispatched to Regent Street to deal with what he was told was a silent protest causing local traffic chaos. He wasn't quite expecting a funeral procession. He had stationed his men across the lower end of Regent Street blocking off the southerly lane of traffic. As the procession approached the police line, he walked towards them.

The band had been instructed to continue piping and drumming no matter what.

Sergeant Connor stopped in front of the main piper who stood staring straight ahead marching in perfect time on the spot.

'Hello. I'm Sergeant Connor.'

He got no response.

He gave a throat clearing cough. 'Who's in charge?'

No response. He sighed, looking behind the band.

There were a number of people directly behind the person paging away so he walked up to them. Some members of the crowd had started booing the police and he could hear voices calling out 'shame on you.'

Sergeant Connor counted, 'One, two, three, four.'

PIG, PIG, PIG came the chants.

'There it is,' he said. 'I knew it was coming.' Every day the same abuse. He was sick of it.

At the head of the procession were three women, a young boy and three rather intimidating looking young black men. They were all dressed in black bar a slim blonde woman who was dressed in a tight knee length teal satin

1950's style dress with a cross over neckline. It was finished off with a large diamante brooch. He approached her immediately assuming she was in charge.

She smiled at him shaking her head and indicated towards a woman of medium build with short cropped brown hair, who stepped forward.

'Can we help you, officer?'

'I'm sorry but you're causing a public disturbance. We'll have to ask you to move on.'

'Excuse me?' replied the woman with a hint of annoyance. 'We're a funeral procession. Are you denying us access to the streets of London?'

'Well, err, now it appears to be a protest, from what I can see.' He shifted nervously from one foot to the other.

The young red haired boy who had been standing next to the woman stepped forward grabbing the woman's hand while looking imploringly up at Sergeant Connor.

'Please officer. It's for my mum.' The boy held up a photo of himself with a woman with short blonde hair. 'She's dead,' he said as he beckoned to the coffin.

Sergeant Connor raised an eyebrow and pointed towards the hearse. 'Are you saying there's actually a dead body in there?'

'Yeah, it's me mum.'

He thought he saw a quick glance exchanged between the young boy and the woman. The boy shrugged.

'Ma'am? Is there a body in that coffin?'

The woman looked down at the young boy, then back at Sergeant Connor. She narrowed her eyes at him and pointed back to the boy. 'Are you accusing him of lying about something so serious?'

'No. I'm merely asking…' he shrugged and sighed. 'And these people are?' He waved his hand to indicate the crowd, walking alongside the procession, holding placards of various different women.

'People saying goodbye to their loved ones,' replied the woman.

'I'm sorry, ma'am, but I can't allow you to go any further. What's the reason behind this protest?'

'It's not a protest. It's a funeral procession. A funeral procession for all the women who have died and are dying of ovarian cancer. Women who have been diagnosed too late due to a system that has let them down and continues to fail them. A system that allows this practice to go unchecked.'

She had tears in her eyes.

Another woman stepped forward and took her hand. She was dressed in a rather tight black dress, a black wide brimmed hat with oversized sunglasses and she was wearing a pair of very high black stilettos. A pair of overinflated red lips produced the words, 'Liz darling,' in a low soothing voice.

She then addressed Sergeant Connor. 'Officer, she's not well. She has ovarian cancer and she needs to do this. Please.'

'Liz?' He peered at the woman, recognition on his face. 'Liz it's me, Doug. Gareth's mate.'

He removed his sunglasses and hat to reveal the happy smiling face of Gareth's old school mate and drinking buddy, Doug.

Liz smiled. 'This could be our lucky day,' she said to Olivia and Sarah.

'Doug. How are you?'

'I'm okay. How are you more to the point? Looks like you are keeping yourself busy,' he said as he indicated to the procession. 'Is Gareth here?' Doug peered behind Liz into the crowd.

'Doug mate!' Gareth came bounding forward with George in tow. 'Mate, what are you doing here? I didn't recognise you in your fancy dress.' Gareth slapped Doug affectionately on the back. 'You remember George from the pub?'

'Yeah, hello again, mate. Yeah well, I didn't realise you were planning a big bash. My invitation must have got lost in the post.'

'It wasn't lost. It was never sent in the first place,' replied Gareth in jest.

Doug laughed. 'So, what's she up to this time, mate? Hang on. The radio. I have to get that.'

'Yes, sir. This is Sergeant Connor… The protest appears to be a funeral procession… unsure if they are actual bodies, sir… no… no, I will not take a look… can you speak up… bagpipes… I can't hear you over the *bagpipes!*' The radio fell silent.

There was a crackle and then a voice at the other end. 'You have to stop them… what… hang on… 40! The M1, the M25… Jesus Christ.'

Sergeant Connor's eyes widened as he heard the report coming back to him.

'It appears you're making quite an impression up and down the country,' he announced as he turned back to Liz a few minutes later.

'You're one brave and determined lady. Where are you headed?'

Liz, Sarah and Olivia looked nervously at each other and then down at Alfie. Alfie returned their gaze, with tears in his eyes. 'Please, we promised Mum,' he said.

Liz turned to Doug Connor with a renewed look of determination.

'We're heading to Downing Street to deliver a petition to parliament.'

'I wouldn't have expected anything less from you, Liz,' he replied, trying to contain a smile.

Doug scratched his receding hairline and looked at the ground as he shuffled his feet. He then looked around him taking in the scene. The piped band, the cortège and the large swelling crowd around the procession, which continued to grow. He shook his head in disbelief as he chewed his lower lip contemplating the consequences of what he was about to do.

'Guys,' he shouted behind him, 'listen up.' He moved back to the police line. 'I want a police escort for these people,' he said as he waved his arm in the direction of the procession. 'On foot, and bikes ahead to clear the way. Someone radio the prime minister and tell him to put the kettle on. He's expecting visitors.'

'I'm sorry, sir... breaking up... can't hear,' Doug said into his radio. He then approached the women, winked and said, 'Let's get this show on the road, shall we?'

Gareth gave Doug a thumbs up. 'Thanks, mate.'

Doug smiled. 'No worries, mate. I handed my resignation in last week.'

———

Police had been diverted to deal with the congestion in all the major cities. They were holding the processions waiting for further instructions. Flash mobs walking alongside the processions waited patiently and quietly with no intention of moving.

Suddenly people in the crowds began looking at their phones and shouting 'look!' They lifted up their phones. 'Look!' it was BBC news live. In Manchester, Kurt looked down at his phone. There was Alfie looking very smart in his suit. He was holding Liz's hand as he walked at the head of the procession. There were police bikes clearing the way and police forming a guard around the procession, escorting them to Downing Street. Crowds were following in droves to see how and where this would end.

'That's my boy,' said Kurt.

In Cardiff, Rhodri, Liz's step son, smiled as he stood in the procession looking at the images coming through from

London. Ernie was in Leeds and Preeti was in Edinburgh, all taking part.

The police who were holding the processions back in the other cities and towns suddenly heard their radios crackle into action and then into overdrive. Police were running back and forth. Finally ranks were broken and the processions were all escorted across the cities to their destinations.

―――――

'This is the BBC evening news. We are receiving reports of a number of flash mob funeral processions taking place across the UK. They're causing travel chaos across the UK road network. It appears to be a protest on behalf of ovarian cancer patients aiming to highlight the high rates of delayed diagnosis. We have Lucy in Oxford Street. Lucy, can you tell us what's going on there?'

'Hi, Suzanna. Yes, well, I'm here in Oxford Street, in what can only be described as organised chaos. Traffic routes in and out of central London are jammed due to this protest. As you can see behind me there are thousands of people on foot walking as part of a funeral procession. It started right at the peak of the evening rush hour at exactly five p.m. outside Selfridges on Oxford Street. There appear to be several hearses with coffins in. We're unsure if there are actual bodies in them. These coffins are covered in white roses and members of the funeral procession have been handing out white roses to the crowds on the streets.

'The funeral processions are being led by highland piped bands piping *Maid of Orleans*. This is apparently in reference to Joan of Arc, with people indicating that the woman leading the procession, who is a late-stage ovarian cancer patient herself, is their Joan of Arc. They are apparently attempting to make their way to Downing Street to deliver a petition to improve ovarian cancer survival rates and press for a compulsory national audit of all late-stage ovarian cancer patients. A police blockade was set up at the bottom of Regent Street near Piccadilly Circus, but it appears, in what can only be described as extraordinary scenes, that the police have broken rank and allowed the protestors to carry on to Downing Street. Instead of stopping them the police are now escorting the procession via police motorcade to Number 10! Back to you, Suzanna.'

'Thank you, Lucy,' said Suzanna. 'Absolutely extraordinary scenes there. We will try and speak with the woman leading the protest at some stage. As we mentioned, and you can probably already see on your screens, this is also happening in other areas of the UK. We have similar reports from Edinburgh, Glasgow, Cardiff, Manchester, Birmingham, Leeds, Oxford, Cambridge, Norwich, the M25 in both northerly and southerly directions and the M1.

'If you are wishing to travel on the roads tonight we suggest you check before you travel. We will keep you updated on the situation.'

———

Iain was about to leave his office. A BBC news alert came up on his phone screen. His eyes widened when he saw her face at the front of the funeral procession. It appeared to be making headline news. Her friends seemed somehow familiar. Iain frowned. This woman was not going to go away. Hang on. He frowned again. That look as she stared straight at the screen. Why did that look feel so familiar? Oh no, that blinding headache was coming on again.

———

Dinesh stared at the television screen as he sat in his chair in the neuro rehab ward.

'Ohh look,' said Mona, 'there's my friend Olivia from yoga.'

'Urrgh,' Dinesh said, as he became agitated.

'Are you okay, dear?' she asked, patting his hand. 'Do you recognise someone on the screen? Yes dear, I bet you probably do. You're looking a bit hot and agitated. I'll get the nurse.'

As Mona left the room, she smiled to herself. Life was much more pleasant now. She no longer had to worry about her husband's affairs. She knew exactly where he was, and the insurance payout from his accident was going to keep her quite comfortable. She wouldn't have to sneak around hiding her own affair with his friend Joshua, any more. People would understand. She was a woman with needs. Dinesh's family were a wealthy Mumbai family from Malibar Hill. They had several properties around the world. They had arrived in England to oversee their son's care but were staying in their own apartment in Mayfair, so Mona wouldn't have to worry about them interfering in her new lifestyle too much. Her new friend Olivia was lovely. She would order a bouquet of flowers congratulating her and saying how glam she looked on the television. Yes, that would be a good idea. She pulled out her phone and ordered the flowers. Then she phoned Joshua.

'Darling, I think we deserve a night out to celebrate tonight don't you think?… No… He's fine… I wouldn't… No, not yet… Yes I know, but you never know, Joshua. He might put two and two together.'

———

Hugh had just poured himself a scotch. He'd just had a rather annoying phone call from Paddington Green police station. Tarquin had been making a nuisance of himself again and was being held in the cells. They wondered if

Hugh would be posting bail seeing as Tarquin had provided his details.

'No, I bloody well will not! Let him rot,' Hugh had replied as he slammed down the phone. He was still seething when he heard his phone buzz across the surface of the drinks cabinet next to him. He ignored it until he realised it was Sophie's name flashing across the screen.

'Hello?'

'Daddy?'

'Ah Sophie, my darling. How are you? Now, if you're phoning about that damned brother of yours, I've already told the police I'm leaving him there to rot.'

'What? No. No, Daddy are you watching the news?'

'I was about to switch it on. Why darling? Don't tell me he made the news?'

Hugh walked over to the sofa and switched on the television. The image that greeted him was an image of Alice's face on a placard being waved at the screen. The camera then panned to show that woman... what was her name Lou or something... with her group of motley friends. Hugh could feel his blood pressure start to rise. He massaged his left arm as he felt a pain travel down his arm from his chest. The glass in his hand crashed to the floor.

'Damn that woman!' he said.

'Daddy... Daddy... are you okay?'

'No, of course I'm not okay,' Hugh replied.

———

Liz was on the BBC *Breakfast* couch.

'So Elizabeth, welcome. You have made quite a few headlines in the last twenty-four hours. Tell us your story.'

66

The prime minister called an emergency meeting of the cabinet.

'Who is responsible?' he bellowed.

'Well, errr,' spluttered the secretary of state. He was cut mid-sentence by a rather irate prime minister.

'I don't want any excuses. Why is it, that time and time again, I have to put up with incompetence and ineptitude? You're nothing but a bunch of bumbling idiots.' The prime minister was looking a dreadful shade of purple. The members of the cabinet sat round the table staring blankly at him.

'I mean we have Brexit to deal with and now this! Who allowed this to happen?' he continued, thumping his chubby fists, on the table.

'Umm, excuse me, prime minister,' said a nervous looking minister for health and social care. 'I think this has been in the press a great deal lately… and there was a House of Commons debate on this matter.'

The prime minister's beady eyes narrowed as they locked sights with the minister. 'Well, who attended this debate?' He looked around the table. 'Any of you?'

'Umm,' replied a few ministers accompanied by the sudden erratic shuffling of papers in front of each of them.

'What does umm mean? Fifteen, twenty MPs? Or nobody? Absolutely nobody is that what you are saying?' He thumped his chubby fists back on the table in frustration and threw his hands up in the air. 'Oh, this is great. Bloody marvellous. *They*,' he shouted as he pointed to the windows indicating the public, 'are carrying placards of all the MPs who did not attend. The feminist lobby groups are loving this. They have the support of all the equal rights campaigners and now we have the eyes of the world on us yet again, showing us to be a government of the unsympathetic elite.'

'Prime minister,' interrupted Lucas Faversham-Todd, the minister of the Foreign Office. 'I don't recall you being concerned about it in the past. In fact, when we had the House of Commons debate you were asked to attend by your constituents. You laughed and said "I have no time to be bothering with such trivial affairs. If it ain't the big five they can take a running dive," is I think, what you said, if I recall correctly. Besides, they are women just blowing hot air. It will soon blow over.'

'What?' bellowed the prime minister. 'You think you are so fucking righteous all of a sudden. I know what I said. I don't need some sanctimonious twat to remind me. The difference is that now it *is* in the public interest, so that changes everything. I mean, why was this not flagged up before? They're saying we're ranked forty-fourth in the world for ovarian cancer survival rates. They're comparing our survival rates to Europe which is all we need right now. This woman is on every single channel saying she has written to me and that my reply was brief, only briefly mentioning our cancer strategy in the broader sense of the word. Where is her letter and my reply? Well? Anybody?'

He threw his hands up in the air. 'No. Not a soul.

Hardly surprising is it. I could find more enthusiasm in a dead body.'

The prime minister had gone from a shade of purple to a bright scarlet. He felt as if his tie was strangling him. Beads of sweat were forming on his brow. He loosened his tie and took a gulp of water, then slammed the glass down, showering the remnants all over the table.

'Right,' he said decisively, as he jabbed his finger repeatedly in the air at his MPs sitting round the table. 'I suggest you all work something out. You're going to have to find some money from somewhere to channel into ovarian cancer.'

'Prime minister,' began Felicity Burrows, the minister for women. 'We don't have any spare pots of money.'

'I know *that*, you stupid woman. You'll have to take it from somewhere else, without anyone knowing. Hide it in a cost cutting exercise or whatever. Think, think,' he said as he slammed his finger into the side of his head repeatedly. 'Use your bloody noggin. I don't care how you do it, as long as you come up with a figure for me to make at my press statement at six this evening. And get someone onto that damned audit she's banging on about.'

Everyone froze waiting for him to continue.

'Don't sit there. Bloody move.' He slammed his fists into the table. 'And get me Fillerup-Standing. He'll have to hang for this one. They have phone video footage of him saying he couldn't help them back in October last year. Someone will have to take the fallout.'

———

Fillerup-Standing was summoned to No. 10.

'Hello, prime minister.'

'Now look here, Fillerup. Why did you tell those women last year that you couldn't help them? That was bloody stupid of you. You know the rules regarding the public. You talk to them like they have dementia. You tell them that they have raised some interesting and valid points. You nod and smile and say, "oh yes, very interesting" and then they leave. Easy peasey, lemon squeazy. But no, oh no, you had to go and fuck it up didn't you. They have video footage of you on their phones. How did you let that happen? You're going to have to go I'm afraid, Fillerup.'

'What? Now prime minister, I really don't think that's going to solve the problem,' he spluttered.

The prime minister leant forward over his desk, narrowing his gaze, looking him up and down as if he was examining something rather distasteful. 'You don't, do you? Well, I really don't give a monkey's what you think. The public are baying for blood and someone has to be the sacrificial lamb.' He leant back in his chair and brushed the top of the folder in front of him. 'It's going to have to be you, Fillerup, I'm afraid.'

'But prime minister.'

'Oh, Fillerup, stop being so damned bothersome. Be a man and grow a pair, old chap. Now out.'

The prime minister pointed dismissively towards the door. 'You need to give your resignation speech tonight. You had better get cracking.'

———

The health secretary was going to be busy.

'Right,' he said to Felicity and the minster for health and social care. 'We need to get a focus group together and get a few ideas kicking about. We're going to have to move some numbers around with regards to our health budget.'

67

What is crucial to understand is that to keep records is to insist on significance: by doing so, you place something on record, and assert that it is of note [...] women have not historically kept records. They have quilted and stitched. They have scrapbooked, pasted in remnants, sewn fables, passed stories down through generations, while men have filed official documents. And through these documents, men have dictated the past and determined who we see as winners and losers [...] Historically archives have excluded the stories of women, of people of colour, of those inhabiting peripheries. The records of their lives have been discarded or lost, while those of small groups of powerful men have been carefully polished [...] now the rest of us need to insist our stories matter.

— JULIA BAIRD, PHOSPHORESCENCE

*L*iz sat in the chair looking at her reflection in the mirror. Not bad. Not bad at all, she thought to herself approvingly. She was dressed in a pair of black linen/cotton mix wide leg trousers with a sleeveless emerald green crepe de chine shirt with a pussycat bow collar. Her mousy short brown hair was now a mass of layers with a large fringe flicked across her brow from a parting on the right. She was perfectly made up with neutral shades of eye shadow, her lips were painted perfectly with a red berry lipstick. She fastened her bracelet on her wrist.

Sarah sat beside her in a matching pair of black linen trousers and matching top but in cerise pink.

'Ms Fitzpatrick? Mrs Postlewaite? We are ready for you on set.' The young assistant gestured to them to follow her.

Sarah grabbed Liz's hand. 'Are you ready?'

'Yes, I'm ready.'

Sarah nodded. 'Right, let's do this. For Alice and Vicky.'

'For Alice and Vicky,' repeated Liz. She squeezed Sarah's hand tightly and they both followed the assistant out onto the set.

They took their places beside Cynthia Moore, the host of the show. Felicity, the minister for women, then arrived and sat to Cynthia's left. Liz and Sarah studied the woman. She was very slim and of slight build with blonde hair cut into a bob. She had a grey pencil skirt and jacket and looked rather nervous, but with a hint of annoyance. Probably annoyed at being dragged in here at the last minute, thought Liz. Suddenly there was a hum of activity. Cynthia leant over to Liz and patted her hand reassuringly.

'Don't worry, dear. You'll be fine. Just take a deep breath and enjoy the experience.'

Liz smiled back at Cynthia. She doesn't know how much I'm going to enjoy this.

'Lights, camera, action!'

Sarah and Liz grabbed each other's hand under the desk, each taking a deep breath and squeezed tightly.

Cynthia smiled into the camera. 'Good morning viewers. Today we have Felicity Burrows, the minister for women, Liz Fitzpatrick and Sarah Postlewaite. Most of you will have seen Liz and Sarah protesting in Oxford Street recently. So today is a discussion on women's health and ovarian cancer diagnosis. Ovarian cancer is the most deadly of the gynaecological cancers due to it being mistaken for other conditions such as IBS. This results in many women only being diagnosed in the later stages, and therefore, the survival rate is very low.'

She turned to Liz. 'Liz, we know you were presenting to the medical profession for over nine months and yet your cancer was not detected. You feel let down by the consultant who saw you and by the medical profession as a whole. But this runs deeper doesn't it?'

Liz listened to Cynthia then turned to face the camera and smiled. 'Yes Cynthia. It does. We know that only 18 per cent of GPs have done the online training for detecting ovarian cancer and 44 per cent of GPs still believe that ovarian cancer can only be detected in the later stages of the disease. We also know that some consultants and GPs are not following the national guidelines for the pathway for detecting ovarian cancer. Women are being dismissed and left struggling for months on end, being labelled hypochondriacs. Months later they find out that they have ovarian cancer and are ultimately being given, what is effectively at that stage, a death sentence. We need to change policy and we need to address the dire situation with regards to women's health in this country. This is not the dark ages. It's the twenty-first century. The recent Every Woman study revealed that the UK is ranked forty-fourth in the world for ovarian cancer survival rates. We're a first world nation. How can that be? It's shocking and unacceptable. Women in the UK have almost universal access to specialists but the lowest proportion of women diagnosed within a month of seeing a doctor. That's very worrying. Women are also not getting the information they need and when they do it's mostly verbal. Why aren't we signposted to ovarian cancer specific support groups? Also one in five women have been given less than five minutes to be told their diagnosis. It's appalling.'

Cynthia flicked her hair at the cameras, as she tapped the end of her biro on the table in front of her, then sneered across the table at Felicity. 'Felicity, you are the minister for women. How do you propose to address the issues raised by Liz today?'

Felicity was feeling rather nervous. She hadn't planned on being called into the television studio this morning. 'Well now, Cynthia, let me first start by saying that our government is very sensitive to the service needs for women's health and are doing all we can to provide a world class service when it comes to women's health.'

'Well then how do you explain—'

'Please let me finish,' said Felicity as she put her palm up to stop Cynthia. 'We have a cancer strategy which we announced last October. This includes a package of measures to be rolled out across the country as part of the NHS long-term plan, with the aim of seeing three-quarters of all cancers detected at an early stage by 2028. This plan will be underpinned by additional funding to guarantee the future of the NHS for the long term. Our new five-year budget will see funding grow on average by 3.4 per cent in real terms each year to 2023. This means the NHS budget will increase by over £20 billion in real terms compared with today. This increase in funding will be reflected in extra staff, better infrastructure, technology and facilities. We aim to ring fence the NHS budget and the tax revenues that pay for it—'

Cynthia interrupted. 'So Felicity, you are admitting that you currently fall short of the mark. And in doing so, that countless women are being failed by a broken health care system which clearly does not meet their needs. I mean, I'm flabbergasted by what Liz and her fellow patients have had to endure.'

'No, not at all,' replied Felicity. 'We are definitely not failing these women.'

'So, you're saying that Liz has got it wrong then?' questioned Cynthia.

'I think, Cynthia, that you are putting words in my

mouth. What I am trying to say is that we as a government have been looking at systemic problems within the system, and as a result, have identified areas which require a higher level of focus. Yes, one of these areas is oncology services. We have reacted by developing a robust strategy to cope with this forecast of an increased demand for oncology services.'

Liz leant forward across the table. 'Could you repeat what you just said, because I can't quite believe my ears. Were you just speaking English?'

'Excuse me,' said Felicity sounding rather affronted.

'You heard me,' said Liz. 'We're fed up with all this wordology the politicians keep vomiting forth. What does it mean to the people on the street?'

'Well now, I really don't think...'

Liz would not let Felicity finish. Liz tapped her finger repeatedly on the desk. 'How many of you were in the focus group that sat up all night trying to prepare that wordy little statement, which, by the way, means absolutely nothing to the women currently living in the UK with ovarian cancer? Four thousand of these women will die this year alone. That's eleven women in the UK dying of ovarian cancer every day.'

'If you would let me finish,' said Felicity, 'I'll tell you what it means. As I was saying we have developed a robust, cancer strategy which will meet the service users' health needs. This means looking at the right numbers and skill mix of staff.'

'Yes, but you aren't, are you?' said Liz.

'You haven't let me explain,' began Felicity.

Liz's voice began to rise an octave. 'You have spent the last few minutes providing us with long wordy sentences which actually are not telling us anything. You couldn't explain your way out of a box. I am asking you now. How much of this money are you putting into women's health? How much of this will be for gynaecological cancers and how much of that is dedicated to treatment, and how much to prevention?'

'Well, I don't have those figures to hand.' Felicity glared at Liz and shuffled her notes. This woman was really starting to annoy her.

Cynthia sat looking from one to the other as if sitting courtside at a tennis match. She was rather enjoying the experience and felt pleased with herself as she knew the viewing figures would be good.

'I think that we need to be a bit level headed on our approach here,' said Felicity. 'We need to consider that the number of women affected by ovarian cancer is small in comparison to other cancers, therefore the service needs are much less than other areas. This is reflected in the amount of funding it receives.'

'There it is. So, you're saying we are worth less?'

'No, I'm just saying that we need to be aware that the service needs are quite varied and it can be difficult to quantify. I understand that emotionally you feel very strongly about this due to personal experience, but I think you will find that other service users have similar health needs. Ovarian cancer is difficult to detect remember; it's a silent killer.'

Liz shrank back in her chair aghast at what she had just heard, throwing her hands back in resignation. She turned to Sarah giving her her cue.

Sarah leant forward towards Felicity, sensing Liz's loss of momentum. 'Did you say what I think you said? You just admitted that women with ovarian cancer are not justified in receiving extra funding because there are not enough of us? Breast cancer, prostate cancer and bowel cancer might affect a greater number of people but they have 80 per cent success rates. They have effective screening tools. We have no screening tool for ovarian cancer and seven out of ten women who are diagnosed in the late stages have been presenting for over six to nine months, as Liz has just mentioned, with their symptoms being confused with IBS or dismissed as hormonal. GPs and consultants do not always adhere to national guidelines in relation to diagnostic pathways because they are just that… guidelines. They are not law. This is resulting in women being diagnosed too late, with instances like mine and Liz's. When we question our care we're treated as difficult patients and told it's all in our head. The excuse of it being a silent killer is… *completely… unacceptable.* The fact there's no screening tool does not make poor practice acceptable practice, and I for one, cannot believe that you as the minister for women would come on here completely ignorant of the fact that ovarian cancer is *NOT* a silent killer. You really need to get your facts right before coming on national television.' Sarah turned to stare directly into the camera, pausing a moment… to add effect and gauge the audience's reaction. The audience started clapping and cheering.

Sarah knew she had the audience on her side.

Liz leant forward. '*And* for decades women have put up with a healthcare system which is institutionally elitist and supports a culture of denial. If the policy makers and regulators do not hold anyone to account nothing will ever change. The regulatory agencies just keep on recycling doctors.' Liz twirled her index finger round and round.

'Well, well,' said Cynthia smiling gleefully. 'Felicity, how would you like to answer that?'

'I, umm, err,' Felicity stuttered.

Sarah was raging. 'An apology might be in order. It's quite clear that you don't care, and frankly I think it's an insult to every single woman with ovarian cancer that you are representing us if you can't even do your research.'

Felicity just sat and stared at Liz and Sarah. This really was not going well.

A voice in Cynthia's earpiece told her to wrap things up.

'Right, ladies, we're running out of time. Felicity, I think it's clear that your government have quite a bit of work to do in convincing the women of the UK that you have our health interests at heart.

'Thankfully we have women like Liz and Sarah who are not afraid to challenge the medical profession and politicians, and by raising these issues they are bringing them into the public domain.

'Thank you, Liz, and thank you, Sarah, for coming in today and sharing your story with us. It has been a harrowing road for you both and I can only say thank you for all you are doing to try and raise awareness of the difficulties facing women in accessing women's health services. If you have one thing you would like women to take away from today what would it be?'

Sarah gestured to Liz to speak.

'Thank you, Cynthia.' replied Liz. 'I would like women to be more aware of their rights, empowering them to question the medical profession if they feel something's not right. We should not be dismissed as hormonal women without having the appropriate tests or investigations undertaken. We need to start the conversation about women's health. This can only start with women talking to other women. If all women banded together with regards to women's health we would be such a powerful force. It's not a taboo subject. We need to be more open when talking about our sexual health… what's normal and not normal. We need to talk about the menopause more openly. The menopause does not mean you are no longer of use to society. Menopausal women are an integral part of society. The time of women sitting down and being told their sexual health issues "are just part of being a woman" and that "you just have to grin and bear it" are over,' Liz said drawing emphatic quote marks in the air. 'The medical profession and the way they view women's health must change. I would like to see government and the regulatory agencies hold the medical profession to account, enforcing adherence to national guidelines and making online training mandatory for all GPs *and* gynaecologists. The current system is failing us. We demand greater transparency with regards to delayed diagnosis. We would like to see an annual national audit as well as investigations for all women who have presented and been dismissed more than once by their GP or consultant with any gynae issues and then gone on to receive a diagnosis of late-stage ovarian cancer. We need good data on ovarian cancer so we can track, audit and improve outcomes. There needs to be a central database where this data is held *and* it needs to include retrospective data. The medical profession and the politicians should be embarrassed at their world ranking with regards to ovarian cancer survival rates. I need to highlight at this point that the issues with women's health are a global issue not just a UK issue but we trail in the rankings. Women will no longer accept a poor level of service. We demand a health service that adequately meets our needs. A women's health service must be led by women, for women.'

Liz turned once again to the audience. The audience clapped and cheered.

Cynthia smiled. 'Well, thank you Liz, Sarah… and thank you, Felicity.'

Felicity could barely manage a smile.

———

'You imbecile. What kind of car crash interview was that?' asked the prime minister. 'I'm surrounded by buffoons. My dog could have done a better job. I want your resignation on my desk in one hour.'

Felicity decided it might be best not to argue.

68

TRISTAN

SEPTEMBER 2019

'*H*ello?… Ahh, Iain. How are you?… What?… Are you sure? I really don't think she would be capable of that! I can't imagine her as the murdering kind… Alright… Okay. Okay, I'll see what I can find out.'

Tristan ended the call. He had never heard Iain Kuntz-Finger so irate. He sounded like he was losing it. Tristan didn't want to rock the boat too much as he was seeing the benefits of Liz's campaign already. He had recently been informed that his research grant was being expanded to push more research on ovarian cancer detection and treatment. He picked up the phone and waited for his secretary to pick up.

'Maria? Hi. Tristan here. Could you schedule an appointment for me with Elizabeth Fitzpatrick? Yes. Just tell her it's a routine check-up.'

Liz, September 2019

'Hello.' Tristan walked round the edge of the desk and shook Liz's hand.

'So how have you been?' he enquired, walking back to his seat.

'I've been fine,' said Liz. 'Very busy.'

'Yes, I saw on the news… and I saw your interview. I guess congratulations are in order on all fronts. Well done.'

'Thank you.'

'Your recent blood tests are fine,' said Tristan as he looked at the computer screen in front of him. 'Have you been having any problems?'

'No, none at all.'

'No headaches?'

'None.'

'You're doing extremely well, so I'd recommend just carrying on doing whatever it is that you're doing. Perhaps we should do an MRI scan of your brain just to be sure.'

'I don't think so,' said Liz.

'Sorry?'

'No,' said Liz. 'I don't want one. If you find anything, what would you do?'

'Whole brain radiotherapy probably,' said Tristan.

'Exactly,' said Liz. 'I don't want whole brain radiotherapy. I'd probably end up with dementia and the side effects of the steroids would be horrific. I'd rather not know.'

'I don't think it would be that bad,' said Tristan.

'That's easy for you to say,' replied Liz. 'I feel fine, and you're measuring my Ca125 blood marker. I think that's enough.'

She really wondered if all these scans were necessary. They refused them at the beginning and were now ordering them left right and centre when it was too late. Liz and Gareth had begun to fondly refer to Tristan as Scan Man.

'Okay, well it's good you're channelling your energy into something positive.'

'It is, isn't it?' said Liz. 'I do feel like I have a purpose in life.'

384

'I guess you've forgotten about your anger with Mr Kuntz-Finger, then?' Tristan queried.

'Oh yes, I really don't want to think about him anymore,' smiled Liz. 'He's in the past. A rather unfortunate interlude in my life's rich tapestry.'

'That is good to hear,' said Tristan. 'Well, you take care and I'll see you in three months.'

Tristan got up and walked Liz to the door and shook her hand.

'Bye, Tristan.'

Liz closed the door behind her.

He smiled and shook his head. She still had that fire in her and she was doing very well. No, Iain must be losing his marbles.

———

'Iain? Hi. It's Tristan. Listen, I saw Elizabeth Fitzpatrick today. She seems fine. In fact she appears so busy with her campaigning that I think she's forgotten about you. I really don't think you have anything to worry about.'

Iain put the phone down. The bitch! She had them all fooled. He would have to do something about that.

69

OXLEAS WOOD

LATE OCTOBER 2019

*L*iz and Sarah were seated on a park bench overlooking Oxleas Wood at the top of the meadow. The sun was shining brightly on a crisp October morning. They sat clasping their warm mugs of herbal tea, warming their hands. The café was busy with groups of walkers and locals leisurely strolling across the meadow taking their dogs for their morning walks.

'We certainly have left a path of destruction behind us, haven't we?' said Sarah as she stared straight ahead of her admiring the view.

'You could say that,' said Liz.

'Do you think it was worth it?'

Liz turned to Sarah and smiled. 'I wouldn't change one minute.'

Sarah smiled back at Liz patting Liz's hand. 'Me neither. We've raised the profile of ovarian cancer and that's what we set out to do. We have memories that no one can take away from us. How are Olivia and the boys?'

Liz smiled. 'Oh, Olivia's new best friends with Mona, and it looks like Mona's loving life with her man Joshua. There are no signs that Mr Ashren will be practising again. They say he's a vegetable. Unfortunate… but convenient.

The boys are doing well. The women love them. They help at ovarian cancer charity events and are hits on Instagram and Twitter.'

Liz slapped her hand against her forehead. 'Oh, I forgot to tell you. Jusu has got engaged.'

Sarah beamed. 'Really? That is nice. What's she like?'

Liz filled Sarah in on Jusu's fiancée, Monique.

They finished their drinks. Liz took the mugs back into the café and returned taking a seat back next to Sarah. Patrice had taken the opportunity to jump up onto Sarah's lap as soon as Liz took the mugs in. Sarah was stroking Patrice's back.

'Have you told Gareth anything?' Sarah asked Liz.

Liz wrinkled her nose up to the sun. 'No, and I think it's better that way. Some things are best left unsaid, don't you think?'

'I guess you're right. Liz… I know I was a bit worried when we set out on this adventure.'

'Just a bit, Sarah!' Liz chuckled. 'Who would have thought we'd have been marching down Oxford Street and appearing on television and upsetting the prime minister?'

'I know! Well, I just wanted to say that I don't think I've ever felt more alive since meeting you all. I think when I die I'll see all of you in front of me.'

'Steady on,' said Liz. 'We aren't going anywhere just yet. You can't get rid of us that easily. We're like weeds, remember. Besides, we have too much work to do.'

'About that,' said Sarah. 'Listen, I know I said I've had fun, but I think this whole episode has taught me to cherish what we have… and I'm tired, Liz. It's been such a fight to get ourselves heard. Don't get me wrong, it's been worth it, but it's taken me away from my husband and my children and I hope now I can spend the time I have left with them.'

Liz frowned and peered at Sarah. 'What are you talking about? Is there something you're not telling me?'

Sarah paused. 'It's back. I got my results about two

months ago but didn't want to say anything with everything that was going on. They've started me back on chemo again and then I might need to be on PARP inhibitors. I had a scan before the chemo and it's spread into my bowel and lungs and bladder. They'll scan me again after the third chemo session and I may need some more surgery as well.'

Liz stared at Sarah with tears in her eyes, clasping her hand so tightly.

'Oh no, Sarah, you can't give up, please. You need to fight this. I can't lose you as well. We're a team. I need you to help me campaign.'

'I know, but I need to rest and decide what to do. I need to be still for a while and gather my thoughts. I have to do what's best for me and my family now. I'll see how the chemo goes but I'm not sure I can cope with much more. It's too hard. If I choose to have more treatment I may reduce my quality of life. I'd rather have two weeks in the sunshine than five weeks in the rain.'

Liz patted Sarah's hand and sniffed. 'This horrible disease. It's taking too many beautiful lives.'

For some reason Liz thought she detected an aura of calmness she'd never seen in Sarah before.

Sarah smiled back at Liz. 'You know, I thought I'd be so afraid of the moment when I had to face up to dying but I'm not. I think you and Alice and Vicks have given me so much courage. You allowed me to believe in myself for once, and I'll always be grateful for that. They say you either meet people for a season or a reason and I definitely met all of you for both. I love you Liz and the friendship we have is so special. You're so strong and you'll do so much good in raising awareness of this dreadful disease. Just never forget the reason behind your mission. Promise me it will now stop.'

'What will stop?'

'Chasing your guy. You'll never change their practise

unless you change the system. As you said you also have to go for the policy makers and the regulators.'

'I know that more than ever now, Sarah.'

'Here.' Sarah passed Liz an envelope.

'What's this?'

'My memoirs. I want you to keep it safe in case you ever need it once I'm gone.'

'I don't understand.'

Sarah waved a hand at Liz. 'You will when you read it.'

They sat in silence for some time embracing the final rays of the warmth of the late morning sun with Patrice's snores and the distant chatter of people enjoying their morning coffee being the only sounds breaking the silence.

———

Liz had read the letter Sarah had given her. It took a while for it to sink in. It contained letters from Vicky and Alice as well. Each one admitting the misfortune of their gynaecologists were accidental incidents in the pursuit of seeking admissions of misdiagnosis. She had been given strict instructions to only use the letters if absolutely necessary and to burn them in her last days. Liz walked upstairs to the study and placed them in the shredder.

70

NOVEMBER 2019

*L*iz sat at home in her dining room sorting through the post. She had so much post these days. Offers to speak at cancer charities, functions, nursing conferences, offers to appear on TV programmes and feature articles in magazines. She had been offered a large sum of money to write a book on the women's journey, but she had turned it down. Sarah and Liz agreed that they didn't want to draw any more attention to themselves than they already had.

There had been no disease recurrence so far for Liz. She had come to terms with her disease and life was so much better now than before she was diagnosed. She'd lost two very dear friends but life was much richer for meeting them all. She still had Sarah and hoped she would for some time to come.

Liz was humming away lost in thought. There was a knock at the door. A young lady was standing half hidden behind a large bouquet of white and pink roses.

'Someone's a lucky lady,' said the young woman. 'These are gorgeous.'

Liz went inside and placed the bouquet on the dining room table and stood back to admire it. She opened the small envelope attached to the bouquet. A plain white card was inside. She pulled it out and read the message.

Dearest Liz,

I always knew it was you.

Love Always,

Iain.

She stared at the card for a few seconds and then placed it next to the enormous bouquet of flowers, drumming her fingers on the table as she tried to think what to do. He was obviously trying to rile her.

'Sorry Sarah. I know I promised, but I need to sort this guy out once and for all,' Liz said out loud. She smiled to herself and then dialled Olivia's number.

When Liz arrived back home, it was dark and the air was chilly. The house was in darkness. She reached for the light switch in the hallway. Gareth wasn't home. She went into the lounge and stared at the bouquet of flowers. The card was missing. Liz then noticed Gareth's work bag on the floor.

———

Gareth had come home early and hoped to surprise Liz. When he walked in to the lounge and saw the flowers, he assumed they were from her family. He called out but there was no reply so he picked the card up and read it. As he put the card down he noticed a mobile number on the back and *'call me'* written next to it.

He couldn't believe it. Iain Kuntz-Finger and Liz. It couldn't be right. Maybe he was reading too much into it. But the flowers?

Gareth dialled Mr Kuntz-Finger's number.

71

*I*ain was waiting for him and indicated to Gareth to take a seat, Gareth noticed he was limping.

Iain gestured once again to the chair.

'Please take a seat, Mr Fitzpatrick.'

'No. I'd rather stand. And it's Mr Evans *not* Fitzpatrick.'

'Oh, I'm sorry. I do apologise, Mr Evans.'

'What's going on between you and my wife?'

'I don't know what you mean,' said Iain calmly, as he sat with his elbows resting on the desk, steepling his fingers.

Gareth started to pace back and forth in front of Iain's desk. 'You sent flowers to my wife. I read the note. Are you shagging her? You *sick* bastard.'

Iain looked up at Gareth with an amused expression. 'Perhaps you should ask your wife.'

'I'm asking you,' said Gareth as he slammed his fists down on Iain's desk.

Iain shrank back. 'I can assure you there's nothing improper on my part.'

'So why the hell are you sending her flowers and asking her to call you, then?'

'That was to get your attention.'

Gareth wore an incredulous expression. 'What? The

flowers were for *me*? I'm not gay, so you're wasting your time, mate.'

Iain held up his hands. 'You're not listening. Do you know what your wife has been up to?'

'What do you mean?'

'I think she's trying to kill me.'

'You're bloody nuts, mate,' said Gareth, as he repeatedly tapped his temple with his index finger. 'You're the one who stuffed up, not her. Trying to discredit a dying cancer patient so she doesn't show you up. Is that it?'

'How do you think I got this limp then?' said Iain, as he pointed to his leg. 'Did you know I had a serious skiing accident earlier this year?'

'Yeah, probably because you're such a bloody shit skier. That's why.'

'We were both in Meribel in January.'

'What are you implying? Isn't it just a coincidence that you were both there at the same time? I know the friends she went with,' said Gareth.

Iain rested his elbows on the desk and placed his chin in his hands. 'It was no accident. Your lovely little wife and her group of friends seem intent on revenge. They're not as sweet and innocent as they look. They tried to kill me on a chairlift and when that attempt failed they forced me off the side of the mountain.'

'Don't be daft,' Gareth laughed disbelievingly. 'That is ridiculous. *My* wife?'

'Possibly, but then a colleague of mine has also met a much worse fate than me. Hit by a taxi and now he's brain damaged. Turns out he was your wife's friend's gynaecologist. Isn't that a bit too much of a coincidence?'

'You've lost your marbles.' Gareth's head was spinning and his stomach sank. He suddenly thought it might be true. He needed time to think.

'I understand this must be shocking for you. You'll need some time to process it.' Iain leant back in his chair, noting the sudden change in Gareth. He knew he had the upper hand.

'You're wrong,' said Gareth. 'I'm going home to speak to her.'

Iain raised an eyebrow. 'Well good luck. Give her my regards, won't you?'

Gareth turned and left, slamming the door behind him.

'That went well,' Iain muttered, feeling rather pleased with himself.

———

When Gareth got home, Liz was waiting for him.

'Hun, where have you been?'

'Where the hell do you think I've been?' Gareth pointed at the bouquet of flowers. 'I went to confront Iain Kuntz-Finger. I thought you were having an affair.'

'What?' Liz paled and grabbed hold of the wall.

'I phoned and arranged to meet him. It wasn't until I got there that I realised it was a ploy to see me.'

'What do you mean?' Liz's legs were like jelly. She pulled out a chair from the dining room table and sat down.

'You're unbelievable,' raged Gareth. 'You lied to me. You told me you were going skiing.'

'We did go skiing,' she insisted.

'You knew he was there and you tried to kill him.' Gareth held up two fingers. '*Twice*! Are you crazy? You could go to prison. He knows it was you.'

Liz shook her head. 'No, he doesn't. He *thinks* it was us. He can't pin anything on us. He had concussion. He skied off the cliff right in front of us.'

'In *front* of you? You're unbelievable. You did go there to try and kill him, then?'

'Not to *kill* him,' replied Liz. 'Just to shake him up a bit.'

'Shake him up? He fell off the side of a mountain.'

Liz grabbed Gareth by both his hands and made him sit

down next to her, attempting to reassure him. 'Look, it was an accident. He skied down the run we were on, and Olivia's bindings were loose so she sat down. He came over a lip and swerved to avoid her. Then Vicky, who was on the run above, was out of control and ended up cutting down onto our run, so he had to make a quick turn to avoid her and he skied off the edge.'

'Have you *completely* lost your mind?' yelled Gareth.

'It was an accident. We waited until the helicopter came and Alice went to find out if he was still alive.'

'What about the other guy then?' demanded Gareth.

'What other guy?'

'His colleague, a Mr Ashren?'

Liz's heart started to race. 'Mr Ashren?'

'Yes, run over by a taxi apparently outside the ExCeL centre. Coincidence?'

Liz sighed. 'Oh, for goodness' sake. Olivia tried to get him to make a speech at the gynae conference, but he wouldn't do it. He said it was professional suicide and tried to buy us off. He pushed Olivia over so we chased him. He ran in front of the cab. He's still alive. Brain damaged and in a vegetative state, but still alive. The police were involved. They say he threw himself in front of the cab.'

'Oh Jesus Christ.' Gareth smacked his forehead with his hand.

Liz put her hands on Gareth's knees. 'Listen, it's not that bad.'

'*Not that bad?* You're a bunch of mad women. I can't believe you involved Olivia in all of this.'

'Excuse me?' said Liz. 'They all deserved it and Olivia's a grown woman. She can make her own mind up.'

'*ALL? ALL?* You mean there are more?'

Liz looked slightly sheepish.

'Ummm.'

'Oh Jesus, Liz, what the hell have you done? Does George know?'

'No, of course not. Now calm down. We'll be fine. Kuntz-Finger's just trying to call our bluff.'

'How could you be so stupid?'

'Stupid?'

'Yes, stupid. After all we've gone through and you want to throw it all away for a chance at revenge. That's pretty stupid if you ask me. It's not just about you, you know. I've been there for you every step of the way because I love you. I'd do anything for you, but this… this is too much.'

'What did you say to him?'

'Say? Nothing. I told him he was mad and that you would never do such a thing.'

'What are you going to do?' Liz peered anxiously at Gareth.

'Nothing. You're my wife. What would you have me do?'

'I love you, Gareth.'

He got up and went and got his coat and car keys.

'Where are you going?' Liz followed him out into the hallway.

'Out.' The door slammed behind him.

Liz stood in the hallway. Things were worse than she imagined.

———

'Olivia, darling, how are you?… Great. Hun, I have a big favour to ask. Can we meet? No, it's just we have some unfinished business to attend to. Tomorrow?… Eleven o'clock's fine. Great… No, Sarah's a bit unwell with her treatment but she's doing okay… Thanks Olivia… 'You too. Bye.'

'You'll wish you never sent that bouquet, Iain,' Liz said to herself.

———

'So what did Gareth say?' asked Olivia.

'Not much. He stormed out after a few minutes,' said Liz.

'Did you tell him about the other two?'

'Oh no,' said Liz. 'You know Gareth, he'd have freaked. He kind of guessed there were more. Anyway it's best he's kept in the dark about that, don't you think?'

'Definitely,' said Olivia.

72

*I*ain looked at his watch. She would be here any minute. He got up from his chair and peered out of the floor length sash windows into the cold darkness. The evening shadows from the lamplights were dancing in the street below. He saw a familiar figure walking along. The figure stopped outside his door and looked up towards his window. The front door buzzed. He limped out into the corridor and into his secretary's office to buzz Liz in then limped back to his room and glanced out of the window again onto the street below. A group of three or four people were arriving across the other side of the street and standing under one of the street lamps. He thought for a minute that they stared directly up at him. He shook his head. No, he must have imagined it.

———

Liz ascended the steps out of the tube station. It was an early November evening and there was a distinct chill in the air. She shivered and pulled the collar of her coat up round her ears. The main road was busy with early evening traffic. She walked along with her head down dodging commuters racing in the opposite direction for the underground, pushing her hands deeper into her pockets trying to keep warm. She turned left and walked along until she found herself in front of Iain Kuntz-Finger's building and looked up at the old red brick building in front of her. Hesitating for a moment, she looked up and down the street. No sign of the others. She checked her watch and decided not to wait. She took a slow deep breath, then walked up the steps and pressed the buzzer next to the brass name plate at the side of the heavy double wooden doors. She was buzzed through into the hallway. Liz slowly made her way up the flight of stairs. Iain's door was ajar so she walked up to it and peered in. He was limping around the side of the desk and moving towards her.

'I understand you wanted to see me,' said Liz, as she held up the card from the flowers.

———

Iain offered Liz a seat. She sat down and stared directly at him.

'I know it was you. What are you playing at?'

'I'm not sure I know what you're talking about,' replied Liz innocently.

'You were in Meribel when I had my accident. I know it was you. I saw you there.'

Liz feigned a look of bewilderment. 'When was this?'

'January,' said Iain, with a hint of annoyance in his voice.

'What? You saw me in a popular ski resort on a skiing holiday?'

'I know what you did, and I also know what you did to Mr Ashren,' said Iain tapping his finger on his desk at each accusation. 'You might as well admit it.'

'I'm not sure what you want me to admit to. I've done nothing wrong,' replied Liz calmly as she appeared to scrutinise her fingers, slowly turning her palms over and then back again. She paused then stared back up at Iain, smiling.

'You,' Iain said as he pointed at Liz, 'tried to kill me.'

She leant forward, raising an eyebrow. 'Excuse me? That's a bit rich coming from you, don't you think? How about we discuss what you did wrong with my care? You never did answer my questions about my delayed diagnosis. I've recently lost two of my friends to this disease. They would still be alive today if it wasn't for men like you ignoring their symptoms.'

Iain sighed and sat back into his chair. 'I never ruled out ovarian cancer because I never considered it. Just the same as I never did a Ca125 blood test because I didn't consider it. There. Are you happy? You think you're going to take on the medical profession, do you? Good luck with that.'

Liz sat in the chair, shell shocked. 'Are you serious?'

Iain glared at her. 'About what?'

'You never considered ovarian cancer even with all my signs and symptoms.'

'No, I didn't. What are you going to do about that?' he snarled.

Liz's face paled as she absorbed Iain's admission. 'So, I never stood a chance.'

Iain fluttered his hand in front of him dismissively. 'You would have had cancer anyway. That's nothing to do with me.'

'But… you could have found it earlier. Are you saying you don't place any importance on finding it earlier?' Liz could feel her shock and anger rising inside her. She would need to concentrate on remaining calm. She needed to ensure she had the upper hand.

'We might have found it earlier if we'd done the CT or laparoscope,' Iain continued. 'Yes. But you still would have had cancer.'

'But at an earlier stage… Oh my God. I can't believe this.'

Liz was holding her head in her hands in disbelief. She'd never expected Iain to admit his oversights in her care. Now that he had she wasn't sure what to do with the information. She felt her jaw tighten with tension and was hanging onto her cool with her fingertips.

'Umm. I think I need a minute…' She reached into her pocket checking her phone was still recording the conversation.

———

Iain was watching Liz, hoping to see just a flicker of fear in her eyes. He could tell she was getting anxious as she was starting to shift in her chair. He saw her hand move into her pocket. She appeared to be trying to desperately grab onto something.

He thought she was reaching for a weapon. He wouldn't put it past her. He quickly stood up. As he did so he opened the drawer in his desk, grabbing the pistol he had hidden away. He pointed the weapon at her. Within seconds he'd moved around to the side of the desk still pointing the gun at her. Liz looked up at Iain, his hands visibly shaking.

'You wouldn't dare,' she hissed as her hand came up and knocked the gun flying onto the floor. Iain gasped in surprise, his head spinning around to follow the path of the gun. Before he realised what he was doing he'd lifted his hands, pressing them into her neck, pushing her backwards in the chair. The chair toppled over with Liz in it. As she fell, the force of the impact with the floor caused Liz's chin to snap downwards. She bit her lip as she fell. Everything went black. She was out cold.

73

*I*ain leant over Liz's body. She was bleeding from her lip. He put his hand in her coat pocket to pull out the weapon. Rather than the feel of cold hard steel, his hand wrapped around something soft and spongy. He withdrew his hand to find he was holding on to the soft toy Stick Man she had been holding during her hospital stay.

'Oh shit,' he muttered. He threw the Stick Man to the floor and put his hand back into her pocket. A mobile phone. He checked her other pockets. No weapon. Nothing that even resembled one. He picked the mobile up and tried to open it. No use, it was locked with a PIN. He slipped it into his trouser pocket.

She was breathing. He checked her pulse and then dragged her body across the floor to the examination couch. He was about to lift her up when he realised the curtains were open.

What the hell was he going to do now? He ran to the window and glanced out onto the street. The group of people were still on the pavement under the street lamp across the road. One of them happened to look up at him as he looked across at them. Iain quickly pulled the curtains.

He didn't notice the man standing at the window on his mobile phone in the building on the opposite side of the street. Iain went over to the gun and quickly placed it back in the drawer of his desk.

———

Frederick was tidying up his paperwork. It had been a long day and he was about to go home. He was sipping the last of his cup of tea. He stretched in his chair and then stood up and walked over to the floor length sash windows overlooking the street. The light from the room in the building directly opposite attracted his gaze. The man was there working late again. Frederick could see him sitting at his desk talking to a woman. He was tired so thought he'd imagined things at first. The man stood up pointing what Frederick thought was a gun at the woman. What followed appeared to be a struggle when the gun must have been lost. The man knocked the woman backward and then appeared to be trying to strangle her.

'Yes hello, emergency services? Police and ambulance please. I think I may have just witnessed a murder... no, a murder... a gun... yes... he's strangled her in her chair. He's now dragging the body across the floor.'

———

The boys and Olivia saw the curtains close. They looked at each other.

Olivia said, 'Oh my God. That doesn't look good. Why didn't she wait for us? What's that fucker up to?'

They raced across the street and started banging on the large wooden door and pressing all the buzzers.

A man suddenly appeared behind them, breathing hard as if he'd been running.

'Did you see it as well?' he gasped.

'See what?' asked Jusu.

'The man strangling that woman. He had a gun. Up there,' Frederick said as he pointed to Iain Kuntz-Finger's window. 'I was across the street up at my desk. I saw it all from my window.'

'What?' screamed Olivia. 'We have to get in there now. Break the door down.'

'I've phoned the police and the ambulance; they're on their way,' said Frederick.

At that moment they heard the scream of police sirens rapidly approaching and then the flashing of blue lights. A police squad car drew up and two uniformed police officers jumped out.

They pressed the door buzzers. There was no reply. They banged on the door. No reply.

'It is no use, babes. The fucker won't open up. He's murdered my friend,' Olivia screamed.

'Calm down, please,' said the young officer. 'Stand back.'

After a few seconds one of the police officers took a few steps back on the pavement looking up at the window above and shouted out, 'This is the police. Open up now or we will break the door down.'

At that moment they saw Iain's head appear out of one of the sash windows.

'I'm coming down now. She's okay. She just collapsed.'

The door was buzzed open and they all rushed in to the foyer. Iain appeared at the top of the stairs. 'This way,' he said. They raced up to find Liz lying on the floor beside the examination couch looking very groggy.

A paramedic arrived as if out of nowhere. He leant over Liz and started to check her over.

Olivia flew at Iain. 'You bastard. What did you do to her?'

The young police officer managed to grab hold of her and pull her back. 'Madam, you need to calm down. Please go outside until we call you back in.' Jordan took Olivia by the arm and steered her outside.

The policeman sat Iain down. 'What happened here?'

Iain tried to explain that he thought the woman had tried to kill him.

'But someone saw *YOU* run around the desk with a gun and attack *HER,*' said the policeman.

'What?' asked Iain, suddenly seeing visions of himself in handcuffs.

The policeman pointed to the sash windows and then to the window directly across the street. 'They called the police and said you pointed a gun at her and then appeared to be strangling her.'

'No, you've got it all wrong. She tried to kill me. I don't have a gun,' said Iain waving his hands at the officer, dismissively.

'Well now, we have statements from the man across the street *and* her friends who were waiting outside for her,' said the officer.

The older officer was on his radio. He beckoned the younger one over and whispered something to him. The younger officer nodded and then walked back over to Iain.

'We've also just had an interesting phone conversation with her husband. It appears you lured her here with the intention of harming her.'

'No! I thought she had a gun and was reaching for it,' insisted Iain.

'A gun?'

'Yes, in her pocket.'

The young police officer beckoned to the other officer.

'Does she have a weapon?'

'Yeah, she does,' he replied.

'Really?'

'Really,' said the other officer, 'and it's a serious piece of kit,' he said as he waved Stick Man at him.

The young officer turned to Iain and said, 'This doesn't appear to be going too well for you, sir. It might be best if we escort you down to the station.'

Iain sighed and put his head in his hands. 'I'll need to phone my wife first.'

He picked up his phone from the desk. At that moment the familiar Coldplay *Viva La Vida* ring tone of Liz's phone rang in Iain's pocket. Everyone turned.

'That's my phone,' said Liz, wearing a confused expression. 'Where is it?'

The young police officer walked over to Iain with his hand out, indicating to Iain to hand over the phone. 'Sir?'

Iain sighed, pulled the phone out of his pocket, and dropped it into the young officer's hand.

He read Iain his rights. He was being arrested for theft of a mobile phone, assault and attempted murder. Iain was handcuffed and about to be escorted out of the room when Liz stood up and walked over to him, cupping her swollen and bloodied lip.

'Come on then. Hand over the gun.'

The police officer gave an exasperated sigh. 'What gun are you *now* referring to?'

'The gun he had in his desk drawer,' said Liz.

'Now wait a minute, officer,' said Iain. 'I wouldn't believe everything she says. She's crazy. She's been trying to kill me.'

The officer opened the top drawer. He pulled on a pair of gloves and pulled out the pistol dangling it from his index finger and thumb.

Iain sighed in resignation. 'Alright officer. That is my gun, but I only bought it for protection.'

'Protection?'

'Yes. From the likes of her,' Iain said as he pointed at Liz. 'I wasn't going to use it. Check. It's never been used.'

Liz peered up at both officers innocently. 'He lied to you about having a gun.'

The two officers looked at each other and then back to Iain.

'Bag it,' said the older officer, 'and pass it to forensics. Get the lab to dust it for finger prints.'

Iain had a sinking feeling in his stomach.

'At least now you might finally get charged with trying to kill me,' said Liz.

'You bitch.'

Iain was ushered out to the squad car. There were several more squad cars that had arrived at the scene, a paramedics car and an ambulance. A small crowd had appeared to see what was going on. Iain was lowered into the car and it sped off into the night leaving the small crowd staring after it.

———

While Iain was being interrogated the police began checking the pistol for prints.

They couldn't believe their luck. Interestingly, the gun had been fired fairly recently. It was the weapon they'd been searching for in relation to a recent Eastern European drug trafficking gang murder.

Unfortunately for Iain, what he had thought of as a timely encounter with a young man outside his office one evening, was not by chance at all. The young man loitering, offering protection against the rising surge in gun and knife crime on the streets (he had been worried when his colleague Dinesh had been held up at knifepoint during an evening run in the park), was not Tudor Studebaker as his business card suggested. The mobile phone number on the card was a burner phone so the police couldn't trace it. The CCTV footage of the encounter unfortunately was only of the back of the young man's baseball hat covering his head, so no one was able to identify Ernie, especially as he'd padded out his shell suit to enlarge his frame. The drop of the weapon was held in Regent's Park away from the ever-present CCTV cameras covering almost all of London.

Kurt had used his favour Big Daddy owed him. Big Daddy used his contacts and made sure they got hold of a *real dirty* weapon for Kurt. It was the least he could do for his mate. 'A man's word is his word,' Big Daddy had said. And he meant it.

———

The paramedics allowed Liz to go home. Olivia and the boys escorted her back outside.

'Oh, babes, are you okay?'

'Yes, Olivia. Don't fuss,' insisted Liz. 'I'm okay.'

'Right let's get you home. We phoned Gareth. He's sick with worry. I told him not to come. We'll get a cab home, all of us together.'

'Olivia?'

'Yes dear?'

Liz grabbed Olivia by the arm. 'I think we might need to make sure we all have our stories straight.'

'Don't worry about that now,' said Olivia patting Liz's arm reassuringly. 'We'll be fine. I've already spoken to the press and they're onto it.'

'What?' Liz somehow found that announcement a bit unsettling.

'Gynaecologist trying to murder his patient as he doesn't want anyone to find out she was misdiagnosed. He tries to discredit her when she puts ovarian cancer misdiagnosis into the public domain, by accusing her of trying to murder him. It's going to be frontline news. You might not have killed him but I certainly think you may have killed his career.' Olivia grabbed Liz's shoulders reassuringly. 'All taken care of, babes.'

Dwayne turned around in the passenger seat. Liz rolled her eyes at him. He smiled back at Liz, his gold tooth catching the light.

'You'll need a good night's sleep tonight,' said Olivia. 'You'll need to look your best for the press tomorrow.'

'What press? *Olivia*. No press. No, no way…'

'All sorted, babes. Don't worry. I have it all under control.'

Liz sighed. How was she going to explain this to Sarah? As if on cue her phone beeped. There was a message from Sarah.

Gareth phoned George and updated him. Hope you nailed the bastard. Love you. Will speak tomorrow. XXX

Olivia and Liz sat in the back of the cab for the remainder of the journey with Jordan and Jusu seated either side. Liz closed her eyes and rested her head on Jusus' shoulder.

'I know it was you, Liz,' he said softly.

Liz opened her eyes and looked up.

'The woman in Clapham… when I had my accident.'

'How long have you known?'

'Ever since Meribel.'

'Do the others…'

Jusu gave a slight nod of his head. 'Yeah. They know. You saved my life that day. So… thanks for rescuing me.' He punched her gently on her arm.

'Well, thanks for rescuing me tonight,' Liz replied as she gently punched him back. 'Do you think you could rescue me from Olivia and the press tomorrow?'

Jusu laughed. 'That's a tall order.'

He grabbed his jacket, rolled it up into a pillow for her, placed it under her head then put his arm around her.

She smiled up at him as she put her hand into her coat pocket and wrapped her fingers around the comforting familiar shape of Stick Man. She was so tired. Yes, a good night's sleep was what she needed… safe in the arms of Gareth.

Liz smiled a contented, rather wicked smile, and closed her eyes.

The End

ACKNOWLEDGMENTS

To my Whanau (family),
Without you I am nothing

This book has been a difficult journey. A long and sometimes tumultuous road where I have had to relive some of the most difficult and darkest times of my life. Without the incredible love and support from my family and friends I believe I might not be here now. They have picked me up and carried me when things were too much to bear. So, for that I thank them from the bottom of my heart.

This book was initially written as an outlet for my anger. My anger at not being listened to, my anger at being dismissed and then my anger at being shut down every time I questioned my care. I felt utterly devastated and broken at that point not knowing who to trust or where to turn.

My sister Vivi and my dear friend Jenny Rollo encouraged me to write down my thoughts as a way of processing my anger. My frustration and anger soon turned into a novel. Jenny read it and encouraged me to publish it.

The rest is history.

I have so many people to thank but it goes without saying that there are some no longer with us who have inspired me... to the amazing brave ovarian cancer patients who have gone before me. Too many taken too soon. Lives needlessly lost. Your stories are the true inspiration for this book. I pray this novel starts a conversation and is a catalyst for change so we can look forward to a future where women's gynaecological cancer services have equal footing with other cancer services regarding funding, research, screening tools, audits/data collection and greatly improved survival outcomes. This book is based in London, but this story could be anywhere in the world. The issues regarding women's health which are addressed in this book are a global issue. Our stories and voices do matter. No woman should ever have to be in a position where they are left literally begging for their life. The impact of a delayed diagnosis has massive implications for not only the women affected but also their husbands, partners, families, and friends. I hope that this novel in some way has portrayed the frustration and despair of the families and loved ones left behind.

To Dr Jenny Rollo, my fellow writer and friend. Thank you for the endless late-night conversations and your unending belief in me to tell my story. Without your encouragement and setting up a writer's group to encourage me to keep going I doubt I would have even started this book. Thank you for the imprint design, the website design and construction, the proof reading, the daily words of encouragement... the list is endless... when I have barely been able to put one foot in front of the other you were there encouraging me. You are a true friend and kindred spirit.

Thank you Vivi, my 'little sis', for just believing in me. You have the uncanny ability to make me laugh at myself and find humour in my situation. You were also my sounding board when life had truly p***d me off.

Thank you, Jacqui Rota, my 'big sis' for dropping everything to fly from one side of the world to the other to be with me when I needed you. There are no words... you were there for me from day one, whenever I needed to talk, offering practical advice, and kept me constantly motivated with images and videos of our dear little Nikayla, an inspiration all on her own.

Thank you to Phredi (Alison McDonald) for all your support and encouragement. You have amazed me with your emails, gifts and endless support. You are a true friend in every sense of the word.

Thank you also to my dear friends Tanja, Emer, Tim, Christelle, Sarah, Christine, Luisa, Joanne, Suzanne, Elise, Claire, Roz and Renata. Your unending support has been invaluable. David Roche, thank you for being a sounding board in my angry phase!

Lynette Walker, I will never forget what you did for me... staying behind to recover me from surgery so that the first words I would hear would be a 'kiwi' voice. That gesture meant the world to me.

To my stepson Mark Richards... You have been an absolute rock to your dad and me. You have been there whenever we have needed you, just sat and listened when I have needed someone to talk to and given me so much encouragement and support.

Thank you to all the rest of my whanau for your constant love and support. You know who you are... Clare, Merilyn, Stephen, Tim and Brendon, Roger, Bira, William, Danny, Sam, Charlie, Hamish and Archie, dear old aunts and uncles, all the cousins.

Thank you to my lifelong friend Miriam Verhoef for dropping what you were doing to sketch me an image for my book cover. I knew you could pull it off! I wish I had half your talent. Your constant support has been amazing.

Thank you to my editor Deborah Blake for the endless hours of editing transforming my story into a much more refined version through your expert editing experience. Thank you to my formatter Robin and Jen at Author Help and Catherine Clarke for your book cover design.

Thank you to my lawyer Nadia Tymkiw at RPC for your expert legal advice and guidance.

A special thank you to all my beta readers and to my brother-in-law Gary Richards for your in-depth critiques.

Finally, to my husband Lawrence Richards. You have defined true love beyond all measure. I am truly blessed to have you by my side and none of this could ever have been achieved without you. You have put up with the tears, the tantrums, just sat and held my hand when I thought all was lost. I love you more than the sun, the moon and the stars and so much more.

Aroha Nui,
Sharon Dobbs-Richards April 2021

GLOSSARY

Avastin – A drug which prevents the growth of blood vessels which feed tumours.

Ca125 blood test– Ca125 is a protein that is found in greater concentration in ovarian cancer cells than in other cells in the body. The normal value is between 0 and 35 units/ml.

Differential diagnosis – A doctor will ask a patient questions and based on the answers makes a list of possible disorders that could be causing the symptoms. The doctor would then order any tests and dependent on the results rule out conditions and/or determine if more testing is required. Most differential diagnoses include a physical exam and a health history.

Endometriosis – A condition where tissue similar to the lining of the womb starts to grow in other places, such as the ovaries and fallopian tubes.

Every Woman Study™ – The first global study undertaken on women with ovarian cancer. It highlighted the obstacles many women face in gaining a diagnosis of ovarian cancer.

Gastroscopy – A procedure which uses a narrow flexible

tube to look inside your oesophagus, stomach and first part of your small intestine.

Hormone Replacement Therapy (HRT) – This is a treatment which supplements hormones (oestrogen and progesterone) that are at a reduced level as you approach the menopause. Ways of taking HRT include tablets, skin patches, gels and vaginal creams, pessaries or rings.

Laparoscope – A long thin tube (laparoscope) is inserted through an incision in the abdominal wall. This is used to examine the organs inside the abdomen.

Late-stage ovarian cancer – Stage three/four ovarian cancer. *Stage three* involves one or both ovaries and fallopian tubes with spread to the peritoneum (tissue that lines your abdominal wall and covers most of the organs in your abdomen) outside the pelvis and/ metastasis to the lymph nodes in the back of the abdomen. *Stage four* involves the above as well as cancer spread to organs outside the abdominal cavity and further spread into the organs functional tissue i.e. impacting on the organ's ability to continue to work. In both stages, if not detected earlier, the patient will present with any or all of the following symptoms: pelvic or abdominal pain, constipation, feeling bloated/uncomfortable, vomiting, nausea, kidney pain/back pain, frequent urination, weight loss, ascites (build-up of fluid in the abdomen), fatigue and breathlessness.

Leptomeningeal disease – Cancer cells which have spread from their original site to the thin layers of tissue that cover the brain and spinal cord (the leptomeninges).

Metastases/metastasis/Mets – These words are all used to describe the spread of a tumour from its primary source to other areas of the body by way of the blood / lymphatic vessels / organ surfaces.

Metastatic burden – The number of cancer cells/size of a tumour which has spread.

National guidelines – Guidelines produced in the UK for the National Institute for Health and Clinical Excellence

(NICE). These guidelines make recommendations on how health professionals should care for people with particular conditions ranging from information and advice, prevention, diagnosis, treatment and longer-term management.

PARP inhibitors – Olaparib (Lynparza), Rucaparib (Rubraca), and Niraparib (Zejula). These drugs stop the repair work in cancer cells causing the cell to die.

Pelvic mesh scandal – Pelvic mesh is a mesh which has been used to treat urinary stress incontinence and vaginal prolapse since 1998. It is known to have serious side effects leaving women in severe pain. The surgical profession was found to have failed to register patients getting mesh implants, despite warnings from NICE and others dating back to 2003. Please refer to the report 'First Do No Harm', which was published in 2020.

Portacath – A portacath is a small chamber or reservoir that sits under the skin at the end of a tube inserted into a vein in your chest. When treatment is required, a needle is inserted into the chamber via the skin and injections can be given/a drip can be attached/or blood samples taken.

Radical hysterectomy – Women with late-stage ovarian cancer undergo a radical hysterectomy at the same time as their surgery. This is different from a 'simple' hysterectomy because not only are the cervix, uterus and fallopian tubes removed, but also the top 2–3 cm of the vagina and the tissues around the cervix. The pelvic lymph nodes will also be removed at this time because the cancer can spread to these nodes first.

Retroverted uterus – A retroverted uterus is a uterus that curves in a backward position at the cervix instead of a forward position. It is a standard variation of pelvic anatomy that many women are either born with or acquire as they mature.

Secondaries – Sometimes cells break away from the primary cancer and are carried in the bloodstream/ lymphatic system to another part of the body.

The cancer cells may settle in that part of the body and form a new tumour.

Speculum (Vaginal) – A metallic/plastic instrument shaped like a duck bill used to widen the opening of the vagina so that the cervix is more easily visible. These are used in smear testing.

Transvaginal ultrasound – A type of pelvic ultrasound used to examine female reproductive organs. It is an internal examination 'through the vagina'. The thin probe is covered with what looks like a large condom and is inserted 2 to 3 inches into the vagina.

Ultrasound – A test using high frequency sound waves (not able to hear these waves with the human ear) to create images of your internal organs. A cold conducting gel is placed on your skin and the ultrasound wand/probe is then pressed against the skin.

SUPPORT LINKS UK

http://www.targetovariancancer.org.uk
http://www.ovacome.org.uk
http://www.ovarian.org.uk
http://www.eveappeal.org.uk
https://www.cancerresearch.uk.org
https://www.macmillan.org.uk

For other countries you can google the words ovarian cancer followed by the relevant country and you should be taken to your local ovarian cancer charity web page.

The most common symptoms of ovarian cancer are listed below. There are additional ones such as migraine, shoulder pain, low energy levels to also consider.

Please contact your GP if you have any of these symptoms persistently for two weeks or more. Please ask for a pelvic examination, a Ca125 blood test and do not rest until you have answers. You know your body best! If you are not satisfied with the outcome, please ask for a second opinion. Your life is too important to be dismissed.

Ovarian cancer symptoms

B – bloating that's persistent and doesn't come and go
E – eating difficulty and feeling full more quickly. Low energy levels
A – abdominal and pelvic pain you feel most days
T – toilet changes in urination/bowel habits
(Source: Ovacome)

ABOUT THE AUTHOR

Sharon is a clinical nurse specialist in Tissue Viability (Wound care) & Plastic surgery. She holds post graduate qualifications in Burns & Plastic surgery, a BSc (Hons) in Tissue Viability from the University of Hertfordshire, an MSc in Advanced Nursing practice from Kings University London as well as a prescribing qualification. She is a dedicated outdoor sportswoman and keen sewer who enjoys travelling extensively. As a survivor of late-stage ovarian cancer Sharon has become a passionate campaigner for improving women's health services. Her first novel is drawn from her lived experience of a delayed diagnosis of late-stage ovarian cancer. Sharon is located in London where she resides with her husband. To stay in touch you can email her at sharon@sharondobbs-richards.com, visit her website www.sharondobbs-richards.com

 twitter.com/DobbsRichards

linkedin.com/in/sharon-dobbs-richards-189168b7

Printed in Great Britain
by Amazon